The Black Rain Chronicles
Book One

# SPIRIT OF SHADOW

By D. A. Holley

# Contents

# ALONG CAME A SPIDER

# A Door at the End of the World

Lothor seethed.

For all of his long years of life, he had never known such troubling times as these. The old ways were forgotten. It seemed he was doomed to live out the rest of eternity in a persistent state of agony. Were it that he could, he would sequester himself in a dark, dank forest and deny mortals his presence, the power that came with it, but Hanzo—*that bastard*—had taken the right to solitude away from him. The scum who took his place was no better. Eight even less palatable men and women, each with their own agenda, their own desires, and each had left the world an uglier place in their wake. This last one had known something they did not, and even he had proven an incompetent ruler.

A door opened somewhere in the west, almost at the end

of the world. A sonorous scream tore past his mandibles, echoed through the shadows. Agony ripped across his thorax. He squeezed his abdomen against it as pressure built in his joints. It was like someone was squeezing his bristly legs, splaying them apart. At any moment, they would be divorced from his body. Pulp and fluid would leak from the craters they left behind. His carapace would be prized apart by firm but delicate hands. The one who called him relished his pain, drinking in his cries like song as he twisted him to his whims, compelled him to do what was needed.

The door opened in the shape of a man. Through it, he glimpsed the world outside. Torchlight and smooth, gray stone filled the man-shaped cavity. The light played off a pallid form, his hair black as ink and falling almost to his waist, his ears tapering sleekly to points just behind his head.

He saw the man falling into shadow, the world outside, through eyes sheeted with water. He hated him. Hated what he represented.

*"I'll kill you one day."* He promised. *"I'll kill you all."*

The figure twisted at the last moment, landed soundly on his feet. There was a grace to his movements, a feline reflex, a soft adjustment that spoke of long practice.

Shadow flooded into the door, and it was shut. A lesser ache leaked into Lothor's body to replace the sharp pain he had felt for those moments while the Wraith fell from a world of light and warmth into shadow. He quieted, and the ambient whispers of countless men and women filled his ears, whispers inspired by dark thoughts, the dark hearts of mortals. He invited them, for there was relief in the familiar, and he knew they were no friend to the intruder.

The Wraith walked freely, confidently, through the endless gloom, ignoring the whispers of the shadows. He denied them as he crossed his tiny corner of Lothor's domain, navigated toward his destination by some sixth sense the poor creature knew would come with pain for another, less experienced traveler.

A fresh wave of pain wracked his body as a new door opened in the long shadow of a dirt-floored cell. The Wraith rose into the cell to his sternum, stole something—a pewter tray, a cup and a bowl—and sank back into the shadows once more.

The pain faded. It resurged as the Wraith rose through a final door—a battered, old table, a water trough along a stone wall, the harsher light of a bulb powered by electricity filling the amorphous space around him—and left him, finally, alone.

# A Path

Lance awoke with a start. A wave of visceral panic stole rationality from him for several moments as the dregs of a nightmare leaked out of him. Calm was not swift in coming. His heart pounded, and his lungs seized around short, choppy inhales as he stuffed the details of that cursed dream into the back of his mind. Cold sweat covered his body, and the sheets under him were uncomfortably damp.

He lay back, rolled onto his side, his bunk creaking under his weight as his eyes darted from shadow to shadow, looking for signs of intruders. Finding none.

Somewhere further up the wide corridor of the Servants' Quarters—a barracks populated by narrow bunk beds and illuminated by moonlight through arrow slit windows—two others were fucking. From where he should be sleeping, he heard their bed creaking, followed the sounds to see a young man's bare back painted in sweat and silver light, the edge of the upper bunk's rail keeping his partner well concealed. Soft gasps and moans issued from both of them, but if the sex was good, he could not tell.

# SPIRIT OF SHADOW

It hardly mattered, anyway. A momentary distraction, enough to draw his attention away from the storm of crazed thoughts caroming through his head. He was beginning to calm down.

He knew he had nothing to fear from the barracks—he had lived in them most of his life. In none of those years, on none of those nights, had he ever been attacked. The most substantial thing that had ever come out of the shadows was a deep cart overflowing with fresh laundry—uniforms, linens, wash rags and bath towels, and if it were the end of the week, a duvet cover to replace the old one.

But he only half believed it—that he was safe here, with terrors in the night gripping onto his mind, pawing at old insecurities, squeezing out irrational conspiracies to haunt every blackened corner in this hall bathed in moonlight.

He turned his back on the nearest shadow. A frock of wavy, auburn hair peaked over a coverlet draped over the next bunk, where Laramy slept. Above and behind him, in a window thick with fog, was an intricate web. A spider labored diligently to repair it, awaited a meal to sustain it until death came for it at sunrise...when a servant dashed its home into ruin. He closed his eyes, and as fast as he had, fresh flashes of the old nightmare resurfaced to chase him away from sleep.

*I'm losing this fight.* He thought sourly. *It would be tonight, too.*

In the nightmare, he was a child. It was dark as pitch, and whatever space he occupied reeked of feces. He sat on coarse gravel, which dug into his bottom and the soles of his feet. He hugged his knees to his chest, a thick layer of oil pressed unpleasantly between his belly and his thighs. He could not recall the last time he had a bath, and in a child's mind the words *weeks, months* played over and over. His scalp and genitals itched, and his hair was a messy, dirt infested tangle.

And he was alone. Always alone. In every variation of this

nightmare, even the worst ones, there was just the absolute darkness, and him.

*At least it wasn't the bad one.* He smiled at the ridiculousness of it. This version of it had been bad enough. What sense was there in inviting a worse variation. He watched the moon from his bed, a vague orb behind the fogged glass, and tried to find some sense of inner peace— that doorway into sound sleep and pleasant dreams.

He lay awake for hours, lay there as the bed across the aisle creaked, the boy groaned and the girl gasped. One theatrical moan, and the pitch and keel ceased. The couple drifted off to sleep, leaving him alone to stare at the beams above him, and wonder what had gone so wrong that he couldn't be like them. That he couldn't just be normal.

He gave up on sleep with the darkest hour of the night upon him. Dawn would be coming soon. He might be able to convince the palace guard stationed on this floor to let him out early, so that he could prepare for the coming day.

He kicked his legs over the side of the bed, slid the drawer under his mattress open and removed shirt, briefs, pants and a towel. He tiptoed across poured stone floors, and approached a door made of plank boards bound together with bronze straps. He opened it, and peaked into the hall.

A Wraith stood sentry just outside. He was elven—his ears long, sleek and pointed, his features soft and round, dark eyes framed in thick lashes, and hollow cheeks drawn down into a firm chin. A curtain of ink black hair fell over his shoulders and down his bare back, and bands of black script stood in relief against his torso. Bands of writing in the language of Shadovane coiled around his midriff and bicep, paying honor to the Shadow Queen. The image of an elf who might have been close kin—a brother or a cousin—was branded over his heart, encircled by more of that writing.

The Wraith turned a stern gaze on him. "Go to bed, boy."

"I can't sleep." Lance whispered. "It's almost time, isn't it?

# SPIRIT OF SHADOW

So...can you take me to the showers. I promise I won't disturb anyone."

The wraith grumbled something under his breath. His lip curled into the hint of a grimace. "This once, but you've had your last favor from me."

"T-thank you." Lance tried on a modest smile. It felt wrong.

After seventeen years living in the palace, he should be used to the Wraiths, but in all of that time, he had only managed to hide his anxiety around them a little better. More than anything else about the palace, they were an unsettling reminder of the relative distrust between the crown and the noble houses, between the noble houses and each other, and in all of them, a unique distrust of the servants who kept them all comfortable. His fear of them was as sourceless as his complex about shadows and as raw as any of his nightmares. On occasion, he dreamed about them, too. Confusing dreams full of fire and chaos, and broad patches of unrelieved darkness. Those were comparatively rare, and less visceral besides.

*It's okay to be afraid of soldiers.* He told himself. He was far from the only one who gave them a wide berth.

The Wraith Core was perhaps the most well natured sect of the military. It was the one most populated by the lower classes, and though the ones who came from outside the palace seldom spoke of their former lives, they were as prone to laugh and banter as any of the servants.

Still, some itch at the back of his mind told him not to trust them.

"Come now. Let's not waste time." The guard took him by the shoulder and shoved him lightly forward. They marched by the cold light of glow bulbs, which worked by channeling electricity and were almost exclusively used for lighting where the nobles refused to roam. The candles they used in

## A Path

their own chambers were nearly always perfumed with lavender or bees wax, and the light they gave off was softer and warmer. These glow bulbs washed the color out of flesh, making all but the few kitunes scattered across the various departments the servants took ownership over look deathly ill.

The Wraith pulled a door matching the one in the barracks they had just left open, and gestured him down the spiral staircase it looked in on. They descended four floors out of the tower proper and into its first basement, where the Wraith drew up short of another door, which was fitted with a small, glass window set high into its face.

Beyond the fogged out lens, he could see blurred silhouettes moving about, though he could make out no more detail than that. Men and women of nearly every race across empire were present in that room, but there were no elves among them.

A caste system was enforced, with the nobility in their high towers, behind their impassible walls, and commoners in the city which expanded into the box canyon beyond its gates, rising higher toward the First Turn and then flatlands where farms were rumored to be abundant. All of those that were free were elven, and the rest...they were servants, taken into the castle and bound never to leave except by explicit order, and he had never heard of any such order being given.

"Well, go." The Wraith said. "Unless you would rather I took you back to your barracks?"

Lance lingered for a moment. He hated this place, the way the Shadovani elves insisted on making bathing a group activity. At least this way, this early, there would be few chances for him to embarrass himself, and ample room to stare at blank walls and flooring.

He pulled the door open.

Hot, vaporous clouds billowed around him as he entered. The Wraith was already marching back up the stairs when he took a last look over his shoulder. He took the plunge, stepped beyond the cloud of rapidly cooling fog, and nearly smacked his shin against a knee high block of poured stone, avoiding a painful scrape and the days spent dealing with it by some uncommon luck.

The block was one of perhaps ten like it which spanned the distance from one wall to the other, framing a narrow aisle between the entrance and the shower pit. Bundles of discarded clothing sat atop them.

A laundry worker, dressed in a snow white shirt—sleeves rolled up to the elbow—and trousers, scooped them up and threw them in a large cart parked near the door. Some of those bore brands of grim the like of which seemed beyond repair—grease and black dust, and all manner of other substances which stained as surely as water was wet.

She favored him with a tender smile that didn't quite touch her eyes. "The work never ends, does it?"

He returned the gesture. "I'm sorry for adding more."

A mechanical chuckle. Her gaze slid from his face and all the artifice that was there to hide her discontent faded away. She moved up the row, back about her business.

*She's not very pleasant.*

He stripped off his clothes and set them atop the block, then crossed over to another series of blocks deeper in. These were framed on three sides by shelving units like those that might be found In a nobleman's study, except that these were not covered in books but clean towels and fresh changes of clothes brought in by servants from the night crews. Lance's own bundle went into an empty space with the rest, and then he turned, and the awkward and mortifying game of getting through this part of the morning began.

Night workers toweled off amid shelves and blocks, gabbed and laughed, their hair limp and sopping wet, and falling into their eyes. A kitune boy twisted his damp towel

## A Path

and snapped it across another boy's rump. The other boy yelped, glowered indignantly at the first, who roared with laughter.

Several others joined in.

"It's not funny!" the boy sulked.

"Oh, grow a pair, James." Another boy, tall and dark-haired with thick lashes framing deep, brown eyes—said, and snapped his towel across the complainer's thigh.

The complainer screwed up his face into a wrathful scowl.

Lance deposited his clean clothes on one of the shelves, and left them to their business. He tried very hard to avoid looking at them, but despite his best efforts, his eyes drifted from one to another, among the blocks and beneath the showers.

Fluted spigots poked out of the ceiling in concentric rings throughout the central portion of the room. They resembled flowers hanging from tree branches in a way. Their spouts were designed by a queen long passed to look like the blooming buds of tulips, and the pipes were hidden inside intricately worked tubing, which was made to look knobbly and organic, though the whole contrivance was cast in a silvery metal of a kind he had never identified.

Against his better judgment, he snatched a look at a Jua boy—coal dark with dense curls that hugged his scalp and taller than nearly all of the other boys in the showers.

His gaze lingered too long and the boy noticed, shed a withering look on him. Fire climbed into his cheeks.

*Dead things.* He thought, as he hurried away. *Old people. Lady Jain.*

He summoned the image of a wizened, old hag. Lady Jain was among the most powerful nobles in Shadovane, and kept the Royal Office of Operations, which oversaw all of the coordination efforts behind the palace's grandest parties, as well as its more mundane services. Age had melted her in the way of a large candle left to burn for several hours. If all else

# SPIRIT OF SHADOW

failed, he could count on her image to banish the embarrassing results of his minds more perverted forays.

He approached an unoccupied spout in a sparsely populated section of the room, and depressed a blackened, stone pedal in the floor in front of it with his heel. Water fell from the spout. He tested it with his fingers, depressed a gray pedal next to it and released it when the water had reached a bearable temperature.

He kept the image of Lady Jain's pug-like face hard in his mind as he bent to a dish on the floor and pulled out a bar of soap, and swiftly rushed through the work—lather, rinse and done. The whole affair was over in record time. He had no desire to linger here longer than was strictly necessary, and so backpedaled until his feet depressed both pedals, cutting the stream of water off.

*Lady Jain.* He thought as he returned to the blocks and the shelves, snatching harried looks at a number of other boys as he passed them—among them, a kitune with a thick mat of black curls covering his chest, and a lanky human a little older than him with smooth cheeks and piercing, ice-blue eyes.

He pulled his effects off the shelf, set his clothes on the nearest block, ruffled a towel through his hair, and patted his face dry. It was then that he noticed him.

A boy who shared some features in common with the Giida people—loose, chestnut curls and eggshell skin, a beak of a nose thrust out from between eyes framed by dark circles. He was clean shaven, his eyes a warm, mud brown, lips somewhat thin and quirked upward at the corners. There was a natural, rosy flush to his cheeks, a feature that made Lance weak in the knees and sent his heart racing. He struck a slender figure, was not particularly muscled, and as he toweled himself off, he stood slightly duck footed, making him appear somewhat awkward without meaning to.

## A Path

Lance didn't realize he was staring, that his towel had dropped from his fist and was now a rumpled mass soaking up dew on the tiles. The other boy bent to towel off his calves, turned at that moment and met his gaze, and froze.

His eyebrow twitched, and something that might have been curiosity, anxiety or frustration stole over him. His lips firmed, his gaze jerked away from the voyeur servant Lance had become, and he snapped his towel to his crotch.

Lance shifted his attention pointedly away, a knee jerk response as the awkwardness of the situation caught up to him, that he had been watching this stranger, breaking the one unspoken rule regarding conduct in these compromising times.

He snatched his clothes from their place and hustled to get them on. Underwear flew up his legs. His arms snapped into shirt sleeves, fingers worked frantically over the buttons. He needed to get out of here while there was still time to salvage—

*Shit! He's coming over here. Why is he coming over here. What do I do? What do I do?*

He thought about running. Grabbing his pants off the block and bolting out of the showers in his briefs, but he would be out of the frying pan then, open to more trouble than he had any business entertaining. At best, he would be sent to Lady Tamalsen for a caning, then. The Mistress of Servants would carry the insult in her bones.

He whipped his pants straight and nearly jumped into them, hiked them up as fast as he could.

"Hey!" the other boy called. "Hey wait!"

He broke into a jog as Lance buttoned his fly.

Lance didn't give him time to get any further. He bolted out of the showers, missed a step on the way down the stairs and caught the rail just short of a tooth cracking fall; and then hurried down the flight barefoot, with his shoes hugged to his chest.

# SPIRIT OF SHADOW

When he reached the bottom, the towering doors into the canteen just ahead, he bent to catch his breath. And cussed.

*"FUCK!"* he said through clenched teeth. "What were you thinking!"

He stood there, bent double, his lungs on fire, trying to gather the thread of what had just happened. It had all gone off the rails so quickly. Before it had a chance to get anywhere good.

"You fucking coward! You absolute weirdo!"

He noticed the stitching on the hem of his shirt, and realized he was wearing it inside out. One last reminder to tell him just how badly he had messed up. How easily he had let his one shot with that boy slide through his fingers.

*Oh god. What if I see him again? What if he approaches me.* He thought. *I need to talk to Sami. She always knows what to do.*

The canteen reminded Lance of the temples he had seen in picture books when he was young. Towering, stone walls rose to shadowed heights where thick timbers obscured most of the ceiling, and at the heart of the expanse was a massive clock with four faces. Each of them was oriented to face a cardinal point. A long pendulum hung from it, and swung back and forth a man height over the tallest servants heads, carving a channel down the center of the long hall. Narrow aisles ran between long benches throughout the space, and a window precluded a bronze counter behind which Janice, one of a few elder servants who still worked in the kitchens, served up plates of food to the various youth trickling in for an early breakfast before their shifts began. She had been with the palace staff so long the youth joked she must have started her career as a stone mason.

The canteen was filled with the excited chatter of servants coming off the night crews when he arrived. Most of the

**A Path**

gossip was about a coming state visit from the Sun Emperor, who would be in the city for the first time in a decade. A visit which was to happen at the beginning of the following month. With his visit so close, rumors swirled about his retinue of Mirrhvalians, about the ruler himself, and some of those verged on the hysterical. The older servants spoke of his last visit with an air of self-importance, while the younger—whom had not been old enough to remember it—absorbed as much as they could take in of their tales.

The emperor was one of nine creatures with near limitless power, a body of legendary figures called Immortals. The most mundane rumor about him was that he had lived for two millennia. For a boy of seventeen, or a man of forty-three, such a long life was nearly impossible to imagine. He would have seen everything from almost the time of the Sealing—when the one true god was imprisoned by his offspring—to the present day, having lived to witness nearly all of recorded history.

The wilder rumors painted him like a character from the stories—like Boreas the Hero, or the Pirate Queen Anastasia. They told of an impossibly tall elf with eyes like fire or pure light, whose very voice called whatever room he entered to silence by some magic that went beyond ordinary reckoning, and who wore golden light as a shroud. He was a mysterious figure even to those who had been old enough to remember his last visit, was loved, perhaps, because he was mysterious.

In the grand tradition of the Sun Empire, the Shadow Queen was his betrothed. In the modern era, that was Queen Meredith, the latest in a long line of politically necessary arranged marriages that saw Shadovane the crowned jewel of the empire's thirteen wards. The tradition dated back almost to the city's founding, to the first queen to hold the title, Alice the Reborn.

Fingers lightly brushed Lance's shoulder, bringing him out of his funk as he picked at his eggs. He had found on sitting at one of the long benches which filled most of the hall that he had very little appetite. He turned to find two familiar faces looking back at him, and smiled, his mood brightening at the sight of Sami and Ariana, two of his closest friends.

"Long time no see, squirt." Sami said.

They set their trays down, blocking him in to either side as they took their seats.

Sami was almost a decade older than he was, with sand-colored hair that she wore in a single tail down her back, a long face and hooded eyes that she sometimes shadowed with coal ash to draw attention away from the heavy bags under them.

The other woman, Ariana, was just nineteen, and already a sous in the kitchens under Mistress Dina. She had the tilted eyes and caramel skin tone common to *Harua* people, of the unincorporated territories known collectively as the Free Lands.

Many of the servants traced their lineages back to foreign places—to Juakali or Haru or Ozos, or the Imperial Borderlands around Aranor or Ash Island, or Morgrotten, the lake city the *merenern* were supposed to have originated from. It was anyone's guess how they had ended up here.

"I've been working a lot more, lately." Lance said. "I think Lady Talmalsen intends to work me to death before my birthday."

"She does that to everyone when their time comes up." Ariana said. "But it'll be over soon, and then you'll have your path and you won't have to worry about it anymore."

"Yeah." Sami agreed over a mouthful of potatoes. She swallowed them down. "Everything's easier once you've made your decision.

"Were you nervous before you chose your path?" Lance asked, extending a searching look to both of them.

Ariana took his hand in hers. "Of course, I was. I wasn't

fucking sure I'd made the right decision until about a month after I started. Peter was a big help, but you can't really be sure you chose right until you get into the rhythm of things."

"Really?" Sami cocked an eyebrow. "You weren't sure about your path? You? The queen of the carpaccio?"

"Fuck off." Ariana grumbled. "Being good at a thing doesn't mean you want to spend your whole life doing it."

"Well, hopefully, I make the right decision, then." Lance said.

"Sky Lord's mercy, they didn't fuck the food up that bad, did they?" Ariana glanced pointedly at Lance's plate. Most of his food was still untouched.

"No." Lance said. "I'm just not very hungry."

Sami snorted. "The only time you refuse to eat is when you're dwelling on something. Out with it."

Ariana eyed him like a hawk might a rabbit. "It is sort of shitty timing, isn't it? Your choosing a path on the heels of the emperor's arrival. I suppose it is your first time."

"First time." Lance mused sardonically. "It's my first time for something anyway."

Ariana's expression turned quizzical. She exchanged a look with Sami.

"This isn't about the emperor or your path, is it?" Sami said knowingly.

"It's about a boy, actually." Lance said. "He kind of...well, anyway, it doesn't matter. I messed it all up."

"Is he cute?" Sami asked.

"Does it matter?" Lance replied, meeting her eye.

"That's a yes." Ariana said to Sami. "Look. He's even blushing!"

"No, I'm not." Lance protested, though he could feel the burn in his cheeks and across his forehead.

"Well, did you ask the fucker out or not?" Ariana said.

"No." Lance said. "But I don't know if I'm ready for all of that and—"

# SPIRIT OF SHADOW

Lance." Sami cut in. "Hear me out. He's probably just as inexperienced as you are, and I doubt he's trying to get in your pants. If he was trying to do that, it would have been much easier to invite you up to the Teacher's Tower or to ask you to meet him in a supply closet off the tunnels. Not as many opportunities to be interrupted that way, you know?"

Ariana looked at Sami like a new animal. "You have some experience with this, don't you?"

Sami waved her off. "A little."

"Maybe just don't think about it."

"But—"

Sami raised an eyebrow at Ariana.

Lance took a bite of his toast.

"Worst case, you just imagine Lord Bran's pock-ridden five-head if you see him again. And take the fucking shot next time, loser. He might even say yes." Ariana said.

Lance choked. "Lord Bran's five-head?"

"That's what Peter told me he thinks about when he needs a boner to go away." Ariana shrugged.

"Your boyfriend's a masochist." Sami said. "Lord Bran's forehead is quite the canvas. Where is Peter, anyway?"

"Working." Ariana replied. "He drew the short straw, so Mistress Dina made him open the kitchen. He'll be done in a couple hours."

Lance looked at the clock face on his side of the boxy chandelier in the middle of the canteen.

Ariana eyed him suspiciously. "You're gonna try to pull the late card so you can ditch us before we get back to talking about this boy, aren't you?"

She forked some eggs into her mouth, and spit them out as soon as she had.

"What was that for?" Sami asked.

"Too much salt." Ariana growled. "The damned things taste like a sweaty ballsack!"

# A Path

She slid off the bench, took two steps in the direction of the kitchen window where Janice was still passing out trays of food, turned around.

"You'll get another chance." Ariana said. "Just take it next time, okay?"

"That's not your decision." Sami pointed out.

"The Pits if it isn't." She said, glancing at Sami before turning her full attention on Lance. "If I have to drag you all the way from your barracks to the Core by your earlobes, you're gonna do it. Do we understand each other?"

"Sure." Lance said.

Ariana had that look in her eye. She wasn't going to let it go, and he knew it. The last thing he wanted was a shouting match in the middle of the canteen, which is exactly what he would get if he didn't go along with her thinking.

"I'll try." He said.

"Good." She stalked off toward the serving window. A few moments talk with Janice produced a boy about the same age as Ariana, and a kitune dressed in a black chef's coat. Some choice words and chopping gestures from Ariana saw the poor boy reduced almost to tears. The kitune, her boyfriend, patted his back, exchanged a few more words with Ariana, and led him back into the kitchen.

"Don't mind her." Sami said.

"We should plan on a game of stones soon. Peter and Ariana might even be able to get Mistress Dina to give them some wine."

"Sure. That sounds nice."

"I've got to go, though. The armory's been swamped with orders for repairs and polishing all week."

"Has it now?"

"It has." She slid off the bench with her empty tray in both hands. "You'd be amazed at how many soldiers think they're going to be allowed within viewing distance of the emperor."

"They won't be?"

# SPIRIT OF SHADOW

"If it goes anything like last time, the only ones that will see him are the Bloodless and the Council of Liam.  See you, Lance."

"See you." Lance waved her off, feeling much better than he had on entering the canteen, more sure of himself by far.

He looked to the window, wondering how Peter had ever let something so bad hit the pass.

Lance stood in front of a cedar door in one of the palace's upper halls. The door was embellished with a silver knocker in the shape of a raven's head, a thick ring held in its mouth. All of the nerves he had lost in his talk with Sami and Ariana were back with him, fresh and raw, as he stood there twiddling his thumbs. After several moments of standing there, with servants and the occasional noble passing behind him on their way up the hall, he summoned up the courage to lift it.

He stood there with the ring in his hand for another several moments, breathing shallowly and casting glances this way and that. The halls of the palace proper were lit with mirrored lamps and chandeliers, all of worked gold, and the walls and floor were white-glazed tile, kept in pristine condition and free of dust. He had toiled away on those walls on too many days, and now the opportunity to escape the humdrum drudgery of making the palace look well was upon him, he wasn't sure he was ready to let it all go. Porcelain daises sat between cedar doors all down its length, each topped with a vase glazed with cobalt patterns of flowers and vines, and each of those contained a bushel of well-tended snapdragons, the queen's favorite flowers. Friezes ran the length of the walls at level with Lance's shoulder, displaying ravens flying over bushes of blackthorn, and smaller creatures—songbirds and rabbits—hiding within them.

## A Path

He tapped the knocker against the door three times, and waited.

"Come," a woman said from the other side, her voice slightly muffled.

He turned the knob and pulled the door open.

Lady Tamalsen sat at her desk—a simple affair, though heavy and made of oak—which was flanked by a pair of mirrored lamps which were her office's only source of light. Three piles of papers sat to one side on its surface, each arranged just so. An inkwell sat next to them, and she held a thick pen styled after the calligraphy brushes which the nobles had used commonly ten years previous, but with a nib inserted to replace the brush head. She tapped its handle against her lip as she observed a paper half-covered in her cramped, linear hand, ignoring him for the moment as he took the unoccupied chair across from her.

The office was really more of a cupboard, the walls covered in ancient portraits and landscapes that rose almost to the ceiling's height. All of those were fine pieces, worthy of a high price at auction, and half of them had been commissioned by the previous lords and ladies of her house. They were a comfort to the lady, nothing more. To another noble, they would be seen as a show of the long-lived wealth of House Tamalsen, the peculiar choice on the part of the lady to take up work, as Mistress of Servants no less.

Lady Tamalsen was a woman concerned with modesty and tradition above all. Her hair was done in a voluminous coil atop her head—a style that had long gone out of fashion, and her dress was cut high with a closed collar. Her cheeks had begun to sag, and wrinkles creased the corners of her ocean-blue eyes. She had a motherly build, but a stern disposition, which made her seem colder than she was.

The color of her eyes was a rarity in Shadovane, where most were so deeply brown they appeared black until the sun touched them. It had led to rumors that her family had some of the Mirrhvalian blood in them, which might work to her advantage in a society obsessed with posturing. It was said that Lord Haman Bran, who was descended from one of the most powerful women ever to hold the title of Shadow Queen, had been so confused by her appearance he assumed for three years she outranked him. His own family, though certainly not his branch of it, was of a similar disposition, with many lending credence to the rumors that they, too, were descended of Mirrvhale. Unlike Lady Tamalsen, Lord Bran had cultivated some of those rumors himself.

She looked to Lance, and he held her gaze, wondering what to expect from this meeting, and how many more like it he could anticipate in the near future.

"It's almost your time." She said, stating the thing which had been bothering him without naming it outright.

Lance tried on a smile. His stomach did cartwheels inside him, slapping his lungs and making them flutter.

He had seldom been so nervous around her, as she had always treated him with kindness, but the coming choice changed things. Soon, he would choose a path, and then she would be his master and guide no longer. He would fall under someone else's care then, and perhaps his new master would be meaner. Most of them were.

"There are several departments I see as a good fit for you. You have the people skills to be a courier, and your math skills would make you a fine fit for keeping records in the palace treasury. Lady Ethelia would be glad to have you.

"I understand you have friends there, but I do feel I must warn you against the kitchens. You might like it initially, but you would eventually grow tired of the bating, the flaring tempers...you may even begin to resent the friends you keep down there. I rather feel you might benefit from shadowing Mistress Dina for a shift before you decide to commit."

"I...can do that?" he asked, though he had never

considered cooking to be the right fit for him.

"With my approval." Lady Tamalsen said.

"Is that the case with other departments?" he asked.

"It is. Again, with my approval." She replied, favoring him with a level gaze that suggested he not press his luck too far.

She set her pen aside, folded her hands together. "You will have to perform a trial in any department you wish to enter before you settle on any one path. It's called a stage, and you'll find it provides you with an opportunity to see how you fit into a department without need to commit. These stages also give the heads of department an opportunity to see how well you fit into their teams. They will judge your fitness for the work on the basis of how you perform, and make their decision on whether to extend employment to you on that basis. You will need to be on your best behavior, you understand. You will only have the one shift to prove yourself.

When you decide on a path, we will discuss the specific trials you must undergo to get there. As an example, a furnace worker must learn to command and extinguish flames or summon and dispel wind, a bookkeeper must pass an aptitude test, and a courier must run a gauntlet designed to test his time management skills, as well as his attention to detail."

"I have thought about the furnaces." Lance rubbed the back of his neck, tried to break eye contact.

Lady Tamalsen made it very difficult to. "Most young men do, but you would have to be stone dumb to take that duty on. Unless you were a kitune, and I don't see fur growing out of your ears."

"It sounds like—"

"Like a great opportunity to learn a very limited bit of magic that, while useful, will eventually lose its novelty. When it does, you'll come to realize it is sweaty, backbreaking labor in a sweltering pit in the palace's bowels. It stinks, it's loud, and your fellows would be most politely described as coarse."

"Can I..."

"I will approve a shift. A night shift, as that is where Master Gregor is most likely to start you." Lady Tamalsen said. "If learning to do magic is important to you, however minimal your knowledge of the craft is permitted to be, I might suggest you shadow with the couriers. They do make use of a rite in their day to day activities, but their duties require more of an intellect than what you would get in the furnaces."

"I would like that."

"I have just the one in mind." She smiled warmly, putting on display a file of small, pearly teeth behind her rouged lips. "He is green, but he is a good role model, and the head of his department quite likes him."

He smiled back.

"Is there anywhere else you may like to shadow?" she asked.

"No. I think that will do." *This isn't so bad.*

He had feared he would face a sharper reprimand for his interest in the furnaces, that Lady Tamalsen would not permit him to take up a job there. It was not so much his first choice as it was a choice he had considered in more detail than most others.

"I'll schedule you for a shift in Lady Ethelia's offices as well. We'll make that one first."

"Okay. But I don't think I'll like that very much."

"You might well be surprised, boy. Many servants come to me with fantasies about one path or another, but they are simply that. Fantasies. You might find you quite like running numbers."

"Maybe, but I think sitting in one place all day would bore me. I'd much rather be in a more active position."

## A Path

"You say that now, but time and new experiences will, I think, warm you to some ideas you never thought were for you."

"We'll see, I suppose." Lance said amenably, though he thought she didn't know him well if she genuinely believed he would change his mind.

"I think we are done here for today." She said, turning back to her letter. "Now go to your other duties. The palace will not clean itself."

He rose, and bowed to her, but she did not raise her head to see. He let himself out, and went on with his day with a little more pep in his step.

# A Servant's Place

The thick sponge in his hand was a tool without use. Sopping wet and oozing thick suds down an already pristine wall, it provided a simple comfort to him in that this work was familiar. After the morning's events, his head was spinning. He could almost swear he caught movement from the looming shadows which pooled together in a nearby intersection, eyes peering out to monitor the servants in their work, but what need there was for such surveillance escaped him.

He worked alongside several other servants, all close in age to him. Some of them whispered with their heads together about the choices they had been presented in their own meetings with the Mistress of Servants. Thin prospects for the dark-complected kitune a few feet off, who was lackadaisically dusting a vase with a dingy rag, a bottle of vinegar held in his off hand.

"She said I can work in the furnaces or the boilers. But I'm smarter than that. I can do other things." He groused.

"They give those options to all the kitunes." His friend, a runt of a boy with a mop of shaggy, brown hair falling into his eyes, said.

"What did she tell you?"

"Operations with Lady Jain, but she's a bitch. I asked for laundry. She said I would be wasting my talents, but at least Mistress Rosaline is nice." He grimaced. "Well, nicer anyway."

Lance leaned into his scrubbing, trying to put distance between himself and their conversation. Several almost identical exchanges were occurring down the hall, and he tried his best to ignore those, too. They infected him with intrusive thoughts anyway.

*The couriers might be okay. They move around a lot. But Lady Therien...I don't know if I want to work for her. Lady Ethelia is as bad as Lady Jain. I'd rather not work for a nobleman. Sami likes her job. Maybe they're not all bad. Who was the head of her department again?*

He couldn't remember. A retired soldier. A shadow elf who had made Bloodless before he stepped away. He wasn't particularly old, either. Had managed the elite corps before he turned thirty, served another ten years in that position. He couldn't be more than forty.

He dunked the sponge into a scrub bucket, dragged it a little way down, started up again.

*God, this sucks. The kitchens, the couriers, the treasury or the furnaces. All bad options. Why didn't I push for something better?*

A dull thunk roused him from his thoughts. Down the hall, near the intersection on that side, a servant had overturned his scrub bucket. Soapy water spilled over the tiled floor, marring it with grime.

# SPIRIT OF SHADOW

At the same time, a nobleman came around the corner. Lord Haman Bran, the worst of them. Acne scars from a misspent youth dimpled his cheeks and forehead, which provided ample real estate beneath a receding hair line he tried valiantly to cover with what wispy hair remained. His shoes and the hem of his pants were spattered with wash water, and seeing this, the servants' whispered conversations all died.

Everyone was looking at Lord Bran now. Everyone was pointedly ignoring the servant. No one, Lance not least of them, wanted to be caught in the crossfire of this exchange.

Haman Bran stomped over to the servant, snatched him up by his hair and pulled, forward and down. A snarl painted across his lips wriggled, worm-like, around a stream of curses for the unfortunate youth. He dragged him head first into the floor, smashed his face against the tiles in the midst of all of that soap.

"Drink!" he roared.

"I'm sorry, Lord Bran. I didn't mean to it was an accident." The servant pleaded.

"My pants need drying, *boy!*" he raved. "Your inattentiveness has made me late. I can't be *seen* like this!"

"I'll take them to the laundry. I'll...I'll tell Lady Tamalsen what happened. I'll take the punishment, just please let me go!"

The servant was sobbing. His cheek pressed into the pool expanding over the floor. Lord Bran pressed the heel of his shoe against the poor boy's temple, and for a moment, Lance thought he might kill him. An irrational thought. He had never seen a nobleman do it before. Had never seen one take it that far. But Haman Bran wasn't like other nobles. He was far crueler than most of them. If anyone would take it there, it would be him.

He bared down on the servant with his heel, snarling,

manic glee lighting his eyes as he tortured that poor soul, and though Lance's insides writhed, he couldn't look away.

Another man came around the corner. An older man with salt and pepper hair running down the length of his back. He was dressed in military reliefs unadorned by patches or medals, but none of those embellishments were necessary. Everyone knew who he was.

Lord Tarkenta of the Council of Liam approached Lord Bran, took him by the back of his overcoat and yanked. Lord Bran stumbled back, released the boy's hair and spun round to face his new assailant.

"Enough." Lord Tarkenta said.

Lord Bran blanched. "Lord...Lord Tarkenta. This insolent..." he gestured curtly behind him. "...*fool* has made me late for my affairs."

"And how has he done that?"

"Look at me!" he snapped, arms thrusting down to address the state of his pants and shoes."

Lord Tarkenta glanced at the hem of his pants. "A little water?" he met his gaze. "I will escort this servant to Lady Tamalsen. You will go back to your chambers. In the meantime, I will send word to your peers that you will be late for their gathering. I am sure they will understand.

"Who is it that you are meeting?"

"Lady Bethel. Some others."

"Drinks?"

"It hardly matters what we are to be doing. The point is—"

"The point is you have misstepped by jumping over Lady Tamalsen in her official capacity as Mistress of Servants. I will leave that out of my report when I see her, if you leave the matter alone."

"I..." Lord Bran's shoulders slumped. "Okay. *Okay.*"

He marched off, and Lord Tarkenta removed the servant from the hall in short order.

*Maybe the furnaces, then. At least I'll be out of his way.*

# SPIRIT OF SHADOW

Lance thought. His heart was beating a furious rhythm in his chest. He picked up his sponge, and scrubbed, and the hall was silent.

# The Treasury

The halls in this part of the palace were almost devoid of activity. A security checkpoint manned by two Wraiths looked much the same to Lance's eyes as the guarded entrance to the tunnel four floors removed that provided access to the Military Compound, but then the heightened security made sense given what lay here.

A Wraith stepped forward and patted him down. Every contact between the elf's wide hands and his body sent tremors through him. His heart fluttered in his chest, and thoughts for what they might find on him—what might be wrong with the way he presented himself, what he might have done in the preamble to this search—rippled through his mind. He had nothing but a small notepad in his pocket, which had been issued to him by Lady Tamalsen for this day's stage, which he would return to her when he told her this department was not for him.

The Wraith asked him to remove the contents of his pockets, and he set the notepad on a low table one side of the checkpoint. The other riffled through its pages while those wide hands assailed his body, beat a rhythm against his chest and flanks, slithered up the inside planes of his legs and arms, coming far too close to too many sensitive areas.

He backed off, leaving Lance disabused of any notion he could have hidden something away if he had been so inclined. He had never intended to. He was, if nothing else, loyal to the crown. Was obedient in the execution of his duties. He would not have come to this reach at all if he wasn't.

The other returned his notepad to him, and they let him through.

A peculiar feature of this network of halls, like the dungeons well below, there were no cedar doors. Instead, heavy, bronze doors were inlaid with intricate, combination locks and pull bars, and those locks were inlaid with a silver metal which must have some function in enchanting. He suspected those vaults possessed other security measures, nasty sorceries for the would be robber, should any such person make it past those doors. Enchanters were not known to be merciful, and the elves of Shadovane were no strangers to cruelty. He doubted whatever traps lay in waiting would kill a thief outright. There was nothing to be gained from a corpse.

One door in this expanse was lacking a lock, and lay slightly ajar. A slice of dim light carved a path across the floor at angle with it, and he stood to one side of it, listening in the quiet to the sound of pens scratching against paper, the clatter of something else, and sporadic, mumbled conversation.

He pushed it open, and found what he had expected. The Office of Legers, the beating heart of the Royal Treasury.

The office was outfitted with rows of writing desks set behind a long counter where several couriers waited, and those all held small lock boxes at their hips. An old woman poured over papers, and another, somewhat younger hefted small, burlap sacks onto a scale, ran weights by her senior who performed calculations.

"Account of Lord Bertram." The bespectacled elder said into the quiet.

A courier approached. He noted that none of these were new recruits. All of them were at least ten years his senior.

He set his silver-chased box on the counter, and the woman produced a key. Bright green gems encircled the lock, and the key was outfitted with a piece of topaz the size of his thumbnail. She slid the key into the lock, and the gems all glowed momentarily as the mechanism was disengaged. The lid swung open of its own accord, and she deposited a hefty sack into it, then closed it back up and locked it once more.

The junior accountant drafted out a receipt, and handed it to the courier, who marched away with the box cradled in both hands, the receipt tucked away safely in his pocket.

A woman a handful of years older than Lance hustled around the counter then. She thrust out her hand. "I'm Lexis. You must be the stage."

"Lance." He shook her hand.

She smiled warmly. "You'll be with me today."

A flush in her cheeks seemed less a byproduct of physical exertion and more a natural feature. Hair the color of straw fell lank against her cheeks, was cut shy of her shoulders by a few inches. Bottle-thick lenses magnified her eyes, which together with her hunched posture and long arms reminded him of some bugs he had seen.

"How's your math?"

"Decent, I guess."

She led him around the counter, down a wide aisle and to a writing desk near the back, which was outfitted with an extra chair for him. Cushions rested on both seats, and it did not take long for him to understand why. Each time he leaned back, his spine was sandwiched between two bars, and the rest pressed painfully against a series of knots in his back. The cushion provided small comfort in that it saved his tail bone, but just barely. It was no plush thing; merely a stop gap to alleviate some of the ache of long sitting, which after hours in this chair would come as a ghost to haunt him anyway.

"Before we get started, you need to take an aptitude test." She passed a sheet with several math problems over to him. "You'll be judged based on the answers and how you came to them. Don't worry, though. Most of what we use on a daily basis is simple arithmetic. Addition and subtraction, multiplication and division. You don't need much more than that to count money."

A manic glint entered her eyes at the word money.

He nodded, took the pen she offered to him, and set about solving the equations written out there. She waited until he was done, waved the paper dry and then stowed it away in a drawer.

"That was fast." She said without inflection. "You must be in a hurry to get to the real stuff."

"No hurry." He assured her.

"Anyway. Our job here is to process the taxes our people collect from the Shadovani citizenry. We also handle requests for credit, but that won't be your department. Not right away, anyway. When you get some tenure, they'll start letting you handle real money, but as a new entry, you'll just be handling ledgers, which is what we'll be doing today."

She pulled a stack of notes to her. "Lady Tamalsen gave you a scratch pad, right?"

"Yes." He took it from his pocket and opened to a blank page.

"Good. I'll need you to calculate out the balances of these accounts against the withdrawals that have been made against them over the last month. That's the standard turnover period, but we do have some clients who have weekly, or even daily checks. You can think of those as high risk accounts. We even have a blacklist for withdrawal requests.

"The names on that list are only there until any delinquent balances are paid, but you'd be surprised at how many people are chronically on it."

"Like who?"

"Lady Bethel for one." She screwed up her nose. "A friend in the Palace Commissary told me its all wine. She's a lush and it shows in her funds. Her brother won't let her access the house coffers, either."

He chuckled.

"Lord Bran would be right up there with her if he didn't have a controlling interest in the iron mining trade."

"Isn't that illegal?" he asked.

"It's certainly immoral."

The rest of his day was spent pouring over ledgers and balance sheets, running numbers until his eyes ached and he was wishing for death. The work was boring. He was permitted to leave only to use the bathroom, and the nearest lavatory was outside the perimeter of the Treasury, which forced him to make the uncomfortable decision between holding it in until his shift ended, or getting frisked by the Wraiths again. He chose the former.

At the end of the day, he was dismissed with the rest of them. He did not see Lady Ethelia once in the entire time he was present, was left to wonder why that was. She would pass final judgment on his performance, after all. It seemed only right that she should want a first hand account of how he measured up.

He stood in line with Lexis and the rest of the accountants and waited as the Wraiths patted down the servants in pairs, turning out their pockets, patting them down, even turning their shoes over. When his turn arrived, he closed his eyes and kept them closed until it was over. On the other side,

Lexis approached him.

"Don't worry about that. You'll get used to it in no time." She said.

"Why is it necessary, though?"

"Well, we're working with hard coin." She explained. "No one really expects an accountant to steal any, but why take the chance?

"Anyway, I've got an appointment to get to."

*What does that mean?*

She hurried off, waving behind her. "See you in a few weeks."

"Yeah, no. I don't think so." He mumbled.

He took an adjoining hall away, headed for the stairs and then the kitchens. Ariana or Peter, one of them would be getting off their shift soon. He needed to unwind.

An intricate network of pipes and ducts populated the ceilings of the servants' tunnels. Poured stone walls were marred in numerous places with hairline cracks, only some of which had been mortared closed. There was a sense of instability in these reaches, as if the whole subterranean floor could come down at any moment, taking much of the palace above with it, yet he had grown so accustomed to this advancing neglect he barely noticed, even as fresh water trickled down the wall just next to the open entrance to the kitchens, a sure sign a pipe somewhere nearby had sprung a leak. Or several. A weakened pipe was prone to them, and the problem rarely registered as in need of mending until a nobleman was left with a trickle of hot water to fill his basin.

The kitchens were silent except for the dry whispers of copper wool grinding against metal, the occasional clank of a new pot being dropped into an empty sink. The relative calm became a chilling omen when set against the usual banter and laughter he was accustomed to witnessing when he arrived in this reach. What professionalism the other, more elite departments were bound by did not exist here, where the rejected goods of the palace came to play.

He peaked his head through a second door, which led from what passed for a break room into the kitchens proper, and found several men and women entirely too focused on their work, and pointedly avoiding each others' eyes. Mistress Dina loomed heavy near the back, and just visible behind a metal shelf elevated over a matching counter by thumb-thick posts, he saw that Peter was arms deep in the sink, scrubbing at dishes profusely as a string of soft cusses issued from his mouth.

He ducked back out again, but too late.

"Don't be a coward, kid." Mistress Dina shouted. "Come on with ya."

Slowly, he passed the threshold, and traveled down a narrow lane which was populated on one side with refrigerated drawers, on the other with a variety of ranges and grills. He halted a few feet from the Mistress of the Kitchens, and bowed.

The Mistress was a stout woman and uncommonly tall. Hard silver eyes, set into a pie plate face, danced with fire. A barely contained fury pulled plump cheeks apart around thin lips pressed tight together, and her nose—hooked and beak-like—was thrust upward, compressing the thick waddle at the base of her chin against her wide neck.

"Well?" she said.

"I just wanted to pop in and say hi." He said, avoiding that blistering gaze. He glanced in Peter's direction, then shifted his gaze to the floor tiles.

"He'll be a while." She said.

"O-okay."

"I look forward to seeing you for your stage tomorrow. Show up fifteen minutes to the hour. You are to be on the floor at six sharp. Any later and I won't consider your interest in my department to be serious."

*It isn't.* "Thank you for the opportunity." He said. "Is it alright if I wait for him outside."

"Again, he will be a while."

"I take your point." He said. "Sorry for inconveniencing you."

She sniffed at that. "It's these assholes who've done that tonight. If you're half as good as my sous, you'll be better than all of them together."

Several heads ducked lower. The scrubbing picked up intensity.

"You can go." She said.

He bowed again, and hurried away from her.


Peter found him in the hall an hour later. He eased up next to him, slid down the wall and sat. The scowl he'd been wearing earlier was gone now. He looked tired, a little downtrodden, though generally okay.

A scattering of dark moles and lighter freckles peppered his face and neck, and the cast of his eyes was a dark, deep green. His skin was the color of blood, a common feature among kitunes, and his nose was large and bulbous. Full lips were set wide and slightly upturned at the corners, so that when he was angered he looked quite as if he might kill someone and take joy in it.

But now...now he had deflated, he was that disarmingly soft spoken boy Ariana had taken such a shine to some two years back now. His chef coat was a sopping wet nonobjective painting, a scattering of smudges and smears of various sauces and powders, and he smelled like mingled sweat and raw fish.

"You want to talk about what happened there?" Lance asked.

He hugged his knees to his chest, and buried his face

between them. "Not really."

"How bad was it?"

He hissed. "It started off okay. We were training someone new on the grill. Had him making steaks. Of course, you can't prick them. Too much juice will leak out, so we test them with our fingers. Pretty simple stuff once you get the hang of it, and he was doing fine. But then we got busy, and he grabbed the wrong tray. Sent six well done orders to Mistress Dina. A courier took one of the plates when she wasn't looking. I guess he was in a rush.

"Well, it went to Lord Cree."

"Ouch." Lance said.

"He sent the courier back with a black eye and a few bruised ribs. Said he'd never tasted something so foul. The courier got an earful from Mistress Dina. So did the cook. Then midway through service, another cook burned the shit out of a demiglace we were supposed to be serving tomorrow. It was just black foam cemented to the bottom of the pot. That's what set Mistress Dina off.

"I cut the poor guy."

"You *cut* him?"

He lifted his head, set an impatient look on Lance. "What was I supposed to do? He fucked up."

"So you stabbed him?" Lance said flatly.

Peter guffawed. "Oh, no." He made a warding gesture in front of him. "No, no. Nothing like that. I sent him back to the...do you really think I'd take a knife to someone over something like that?"

"I'd hope not."

"Hell, I don't have the balls to stab someone over much of anything. I'm useless in a fight."

He was smiling now, gaze distant as he pondered the absurdity of it. "No, if I did that I'd have half a dozen knives pointed at me before I got the tip in." He laughed, a rich, warm sound.

# SPIRIT OF SHADOW

"Is she always like that?"

"Just when someone fucks up. Even then, it takes a lot with her. Ariana is way more aggressive."

"Really now. I never would have guessed."

"So what about you?" Peter said, changing the subject. "You didn't come all the way down here for nothing."

"I had my first stage today. In the Treasury. Got frisked by a Wraith twice."

"Yeah, they do that up there."

"You know some of those noblemen aren't as wealthy as you'd think. Some of them aren't wealthy at all."

"Oh?"

"Lady Bethel's currently delinquent on her account. Lady Jain's got her shit together, but she isn't pulling in much new revenue. And don't get me started on Lady Therien."

"What's Lady Therien got going on?"

"Well, she'd be flat broke if not for her husband. He has a secret account that's pretty flush. At least, if she knew about it, I suspect she would have drained it a long time ago."

"She's cheating on him, anyway."

"How did you find that out?"

Peter rolled his eyes. "You think the couriers don't talk? We get a lot of them down here. They gossip worse than anyone."

Lance nodded. "She's the head of their department. Of course."

"Yep." He agreed. "So you liked it up there?"

"Nope."

"They liked you?"

"Not sure. I think so."

"Then you're not going to take the offer even if they do make one."

"Nope."

Peter clapped him hard on the back. "I knew you weren't a

sellout. But hey! We've always got a place for you down here."

"Maybe." Lance said. "We'll see."

"What you've got your heart set on something else?"

"Not exactly." He said. "To be honest, I'm not sure any of the departments I'm supposed to stage in are a good fit for me. Accounting wasn't, but who knows. Maybe its the kitchens. Maybe it's the furnaces."

"Maybe the couriers?" he furrowed his brow.

Lance chuckled. "What if it is?"

Peter shrugged. "You know they run interference, right? When she wants some strange. She makes them."

Lance snorted. "Really?"

"Really."

"Like...they distract her husband?"

"That's the rumor."

"You feeling any better?"

Peter nodded. "Thanks for that. Now do you want to get out of this shit hole?"

Lance rose, and helped him to his feet. "Where to?"

"Well, I'm meeting up with Ariana soon. But if you want to come?"

"No, you two have fun doing whatever you're doing. I think I'm going to call it for today."

"Alright. Fair enough."

He walked him to the stairs, said his goodbyes.

Lance watched him head off in the other direction. It didn't take much figuring to conclude he was on his way to the Teacher's Tower. Once the center for noble education, the tower had been abandoned with the end of Queen Tania's reign, and was now primarily used for storage. But the servants had taken to using it for all kinds of other shenanigans over the intervening years. Before curfew, it was most often populated with couples who wanted a private moment. At night, when the nobility slept and the Wraiths were on the prowl, it was said there were lecherous parties up there. That the servants who could shadow walk came together with pilfered spoils from their various departments, and rebelled.

He wondered how they managed to pull it off. If they did. The Wraiths commanded the shadows. They did not need to reveal themselves to see what transpired in any room in the palace. Everyone was under constant surveillance, so it followed that they knew about these alleged parties. They might even condone them.

He marched up the stairs, made his way to the third floor of the Servant's Tower and his bunk. It was time to unwind in truth, do some light reading perhaps. He was allowed few books, and none of them anything consequential. No histories, no grimoires, nothing a servant might use to learn anything worthwhile. But there were those books they were given for the study of literacy, so that they could read well enough to execute their duties, and those could be stimulating.

The Legends of the Five was his favorite, and it was this tome that called to him now. He could think of nothing he wanted more than to spend his evening immersed in it.

# Chance Encounter

orning came on the heals of another sleepless night. He wasn't sure if it was the knowledge that he would have to impress Mistress Dina or make his friends in the kitchens look bad for their proximity to him, or if it was the usual fare. He had not awoken to the old nightmare. Had not experienced the worst one, either, but sleep had been slow in coming, and when it arrived it had lasted no longer than a scant few hours, enough to leave him worn out and groggy. The interplay of shadows and the occasional disruption of Fat John's sawtooth snoring might have complicated sleep by themselves, and as he lay awake he found himself staring at a spiderweb which was a precise copy of the one which had been there two nights prior, when the nightmare had come on. The spider was the same in its dimensions. Lit by moonlight from behind and cast in silhouette, it might have been a trick of the eye, but he felt certain it was the very same spider, which had escaped destruction with its web even as he had not seen it the night prior.

There had been whispers in the dark to accompany him, talk just on the edge of hearing, and he had not been able to make out the words.

With morning's arrival, and the first blush of sunlight creeping over the high cliffs behind the palace, he was awoken by the call of the Wraith stationed on this floor.

"First Bell!" he roared, and Lance hurried to gather up his uniform and a fresh towel.

He made quick work of washing, avoiding eye contact with the various others in the showers as he scoured his slender body clean, washed excess oil out of his cold, blonde hair and, with the washing concluded, put himself together in a corner removed from most others. Even with the work done quickly, he was nonetheless unable to obtain breakfast before his stage began, was forced to work it on an empty stomach.

Ariana was in the kitchens when he arrived, and swept him up as soon as he was through the door. He was assigned an apron and a cap, and a small pile of clean towels, and then ushered to a refrigerated cabinet she referred to as Garmo.

She pulled back its lid, revealing a vacant compartment with a series of bars inside that she helped him assemble into a uniform grid.

"We'll fill this with pans and then get our mise, okay." She said. "You'll be in charge of cold appetizers and salads for the military brass. Most of them will be leading training exercises about now. They won't be done for a while. It'll get busy later, but that gives us some time to run you through the pickups before it does."

"Alright."

"Great." She grinned. "Follow me."

## Chance Encounter

She led him into the dish pit, where a series of racks were arranged in close proximity to the various sinks, all filled already with cook pots and long serving pans. "We'll need three third pans, another nine sixth pans, and some nine pans for garnishes."

They gathered the needed items, and returned with them to his station. She ran him through the setup, which required several trips to the various pantries, root cellars and a refrigerated closet she referred to as the walk-in, before they were done. Then it was to the real work.

She took a knife from a magnetic strip mounted on the wall near the fryers, tested its edge and then presented it handle first to him.

"Keep that down and by your side when you're walking with it. If you trip, you won't stab yourself that way. It'll keep you from fucking someone else up, too." She explained as they walked the short distance back to the garmo station.

"So, knife work. You won't be doing anything with heat today, but you should at least know the basics of how to handle yourself with a knife. So do it like this."

She curled up the fingers on her left hand, tucked her thumb behind them and set the flat of the knife against her knuckles. "As long as you keep your off hand like this, you won't cut yourself, okay?"

"Okay."

"Alright. So, see how I'm rocking the knife as I cut. It'll feel awkward at first, but as you get better it'll be a lot faster and easier on your wrist to do it this way than to try to use that thing as a fucking hammer. And if Mistress Dina sees you flailing around like that, she'll make you wish you were dead."

"Why are you smiling?"

She shrugged. "It's just nice training in someone I like for once. The last guy was such a bitch."

"Yeah?"

# SPIRIT OF SHADOW

"So, tomatoes. A serrated knife works better for those, but I had the guys sharpen all the house knives yesterday. This'll work just fine. Just slice them into crescents."

She went through several exercises with him, saved the more tedious tasks for herself. As she promised, the first orders came in sporadically, leaving little for him to do in the intervals. She kept him busy with simple cleaning tasks, which were familiar in that they resembled the same duties he had been tasked with for much of his life. Couriers flitted in and out of the kitchen, taking plates from him after she had inspected them to make sure they were within her standards.

"You're doing good." She said. "I knew you would."

"I'm just glad Mistress Dina isn't—"

"Isn't what?"

"Mad." He said. "Didn't Peter tell you what happened last night."

"We, uh...we had other things on our mind."

"So, I'll leave that right there." He finished the last few touch ups on the plate in front of him. A Courier came to retrieve the plate, and he domed it. He looked up at the newly arrived Courier, smiled.

His stomach did a back flip.

Looking at him from barely two feet off was the boy he'd seen in the showers. A boy he had hoped never to see again, even as he wished each morning he might. So that he could talk to him, diffuse the awkwardness, make amends for the way he had left things that morning.

Now he was faced with him, in view of a startled expression which undoubtedly matched his own, he couldn't quite find the words.

"Hi, Ben." Ariana said. "How's it going?"

"Um...I guess I don't know. No one's been...complaining...about me. Yet."

Chance Encounter

"That's good." She said. "This is Lance. He's staging today."

*Oh please, dear lord, get me out of here. Or at least let me get through this without putting my foot in my mouth. At least give me that win.*

"I...we've met. Kind of." Ben said.

"Y-yes." Lance said. "We have. Kind of."

"Anyway, if that's all ready."

"Of course."

"I can't really *stay* but I'll catch up with you later, okay."

"I understand. You just get your shit handled. I'll be here."

He picked up the lidded tray, carried it off a short distance. As he stepped away, a dull ache formed in Lance's head. He massaged his forehead as the sensation quickened from a dull ache to sharp pain. Almost at the edge of hearing, whispers broke across the kitchen, in his ears but distant, as if the other cooks were all talking at once, but when he looked around it was to find a few shouting out calls and the rest silent.

No one was whispering.

Ben took another step forward. His shadow darkened from a deep gray to matte black. It stayed in place, the feet divorced from his, and he stepped into it, and then through. He slid into the shadow to the hips, and then shoulders, and all at once he was gone. The shadow collapsed behind him, was absorbed by the floor tiles, and the portal he had entered fell into dissolution.

The headache remained. A vicious pain like white fire thrashing through his skull. For several seconds, he could not see for the sheer volume of tears leaking from his eyes.

Ariana's hand found his shoulder, squeezed, drew him around to face her. "Are you okay?"

"Just a headache."

"It looks like a little more than that. Do you need to go to the infirmary?"

# SPIRIT OF SHADOW

"I don't know. Maybe we should just...wait a minute. Let it pass."

"I can take you there if you need to—"

"No. It's fine." He gripped the edge of the cabinet, planted his feet and bit down on his cheek.

The pain began to leak out of him. White fire became clamping jaws, which ebbed to a dull throbbing which was not really pain but the memory of it.

"I think I'm good." He said. "I don't know what happened, but it seems like it's going away."

"O-okay." She said. "Are you sure you don't want to—"

"No, I'm fine. Let's just get back into it."

# Walking in Shadow

fter two shadow shifts, Lance felt drained and dejected. A newfound pessimism about his future in the palace had crept in and settled in the back of his mind. The Treasury had been a mind numbingly boring experience, and the kitchens were not at all what he wanted for himself. Peter and Ariana may love them, but he saw there an environment of extremes in which little respect was paid to an individual's well being, emotionally or otherwise, and everyone seemed hellbent on being better than their peers.

He had begun to dread his stage in Lady Therien's offices. If Peter was right about the way she operated, working for her would inevitably mean covering up her misdeeds and placing himself in her husband's warpath should he find out about her extramarital activities. And there was the other problem, as well, which he tried very hard not to think about. There was the elephant in the room, and it had a name now.

*Maybe I'll get lucky. Maybe I won't see him.*

# SPIRIT OF SHADOW

Entering Lady Therien's spacious office was a hardship by itself. His experiences thus far did not bode well for his future.

He passed an hourglass that reached as high as his chest. It was made of gold and glass, and a red, silk sash was tied tight around its bottleneck. The table under it was an ornate piece hewn of chestnut with gold foil depressed into the floral shapes around its feet. Lady Therien's desk was its match, with a high-backed chair stationed behind it that the woman herself sat in.

She wore a powder blue dress today, cut low and sheer in the *Mirrhvalian* fashion. Many nobles had taken to the fashions of their cousins in the Bone Sands ahead of the emperor's arrival. Silver chains glittered in her hair and around her neck, and she had penciled in a mole on her upper lip that, to Lance's eye, looked ridiculous.

He bowed low, his hands clasped together behind his back, and said: "The shadow preserve you, Lady Therien."

She looked up from the papers she had been reading and set a gilded fountain pen aside.

"Lady Tamalsen said you chose to shadow here of your own will." She said, surveying him. "You may rise, now, boy. But keep that etiquette with you today. You will need it if you are going to make it through without embarrassing your mentor.

"Come, Benjamin." She barked.

He stood upright.

Ben came hustling out of a cupboard holding a thick stack of papers in the crook of his arm.

"You can set those down." She said.

He twisted and dropped the bundle on another table, this one unadorned and loaded down with so many other parcels it was hard to fathom how it didn't crack in two.

The stack thudded against the tabletop.

Lady Therien winced. "A bit more care in the future."

"My apologies, Lady Therien." He bowed in her direction, then turned his gaze on Lance, and froze.

"You'll be showing this boy how we do things here." Lady Therien said. "His name is Lance. He comes with high regard from Lady Tamalsen, but do not let that cloud your judgment. I am counting on you to make an unbiased decision as to his fitness to join us."

# Walking in Shadow

"I'll do my best." Ben said. "Thank you for the opportunity."

He favored Lady Therien with a mechanical smile.

Had he the choice, Lance would have asked Lady Therien for a different mentor on the spot. It did not do to further antagonize Ben. He had made his discomfort clear enough. It didn't make sense to keep nudging him when he so clearly didn't want anything to do with him. But what option did he have? He couldn't exactly demand a high lady suffer more inconvenience than was strictly necessary. She'd throw him out of her department as soon as he did.

*Maybe that's a good thing.*

Lady Therien selected a paper from the smallest stack on her table and held it for him to take. He plucked it from her grasp and scanned it.

"Lance will be with you throughout the day. There is a window for your lunch in the itinerary. You will remain with him during that time as well." She explained. "You are dismissed."

Another bow. Lance mirrored him.

"The shadow preserve you." He murmured.

Ben crossed to the door, opened it and gestured Lance through. Grinning, he closed it lightly behind them. "You know I'm not gonna go easy on you, right?"

"I didn't expect you to."

He scanned the list.

"First errand is…for Haman Bran. He'll be intolerable, like he always is."

He led Lance away from Lady Therien's office, into a servant's staircase that spiraled downward toward the lower levels. "He's in his study drinkin' hard liquor with Lady Bethel and Elrin Stormbreaker if I know him at all. They like to get on early. We'll have to hurry or we'll catch him when he's good and sauced. You don't want to see that."

Lance opened his mouth to say something. Shut it again.

*Why hasn't he mentioned the other morning? He's acting like nothing happened.*

He decided that if Ben was willing to let it go, he should to. At the very least, it would get them both through this day without things becoming more awkward than they already were. When it was over, he could swear off the Office of the Couriers forever, and then it would be down to the kitchens or the furnaces for him. Lady Tamalsen wouldn't take it well, but the decision was his at the end of the day, and he could not fathom how he would get through the intervening years between his decision day and the moment of his death with the tension being ratcheted up again and again every time he saw him.

Ben stepped forward, and as he did, a dull ache formed in Lance's head, pushing uncomfortably against his temples. He grit his teeth as Ben stepped forward again, and again, his shadow deepening from its organic shade to matte black.

Ben looked over his shoulder. "Are you comin'?"

"Where are we going?"

"Into the shadows. How else do you expect us to get anywhere?"

"By walking?"

Ben chuckled. "Not so much, no. We'd never get anything done if we did it that way. Here, just step into my shadow. I'll be right behind you."

He moved forward, that ache filling him up like so much hot tea in a clay cup. His leading foot touched the shadow, and he plunged face first into it. He hit hard ground on his hands and knees.

Darkness swirled around him, an unrelieved black blocking all sight. On the edge of hearing, voices whispered, crooned to him in tens and twenties, all talking over each other so that he couldn't quite make out what any one of them was saying. The air was cool against his skin in a way it never was in the palace halls, cold and humid, as if they'd stepped into some kind of cave, or maybe a far flung corner of the dungeons.

Ben thudded aground behind him, and helped him to his feet.

"Do you hear that?" he asked.

"Just ignore it. As long as I'm here, you have nothin' to worry about from them."

"Who are they?"

"No one and nothin'. What you're hearin' is the voices of the Dark Heart. People's insecurities mostly. This place exists within shadow, and a lot of shadows are attached to people. Their negative feelings come with them, and they act kinda like ghosts. They can hurt you, but only if you can't resist them. If you came here alone somehow, you'd be swallowed up right away, but since you're with someone who knows how to resist them, you don't need to worry."

"This is how the Wraiths travel."

"Well, they're better at it than I am. They can move in four

## Walking in Shadow

dimensions here. Couriers are only trained to move in three." He explained. "Come on. Follow me."

He took Lance under the arm and led him off. They traveled a few steps, turned corner and traveled a few more. Ben reached overhead and yanked at something Lance couldn't see. A veil parted, and blinding light stabbed into the dark, a rounded hole through which an expanse of corridor, the edge of a dais and a cobalt-glazed vase housing snapdragons, was made visible.

Ben, illuminated in that shaft of light, reached up and touched the image, and they rose rapidly. Rose through it.

The shadow underfoot eased off from that peculiar, dead black to a more natural shade, and he found the footing under him was quite firm. They stood outside a cedar door with a knocker in the shape of a raven's head. The raven held a thick ring in its beak, which Ben swung thrice.

"Enter." Came Lord Haman Bran's voice.

Ben swung the door inward, and ushered Lance through.

"Ah. You're late."

"I'm terribly sorry, Lord Bran. I have someone shadowin' me today. This is Lance." He gestured at him. "

"No excuses. Just take all of *that* to the armory." He gestured airily at a rack outfitted with a full suit of armor Lance doubted very much he had earned the right to wear.

The pauldrons were treated to appear as if smoke was trapped in the metal, a design feature only given to the Bloodless. Those pauldrons were crafted masterfully to look like raven heads, and the heavy plate that accompanied them was embellished with a wide, purple sash around the midriff.

"They did a piss poor job of polishing it the last time. Just look at the thing!" he grumbled. "How am I to judge it worthy of me when there are so clearly fingerprints all over it!"

Lance looked the armor over. There were no fingerprints that he could see anywhere on it, but he bit his tongue. It would only worsen Lord Bran's temper if he commented. He did not want to become his next victim.

"I'm sorry on their behalf, Lord Bran."

"Well tell them to put someone competent on the job this time! The Emperor's arrival is coming swiftly, and I will not be caught looking like a common Maul in his presence!"

# SPIRIT OF SHADOW

"Help me with it?" Ben said.

Lord Bran marched over to a small table near the windows at the back of his rooms. He snatched up a clay jug and poured its deep, red contents into a crystal glass until the wine was nearly flush with the rim.

Lance helped Ben dismantle the armor, took the breastplate and greaves in his arms when he handed them to him. Ben took the rest. They hustled out of Lord Bran's chambers, and once clear, Ben opened his shadow.

As the shadow went from its usual color to stark black, that headache returned, and more intensely than it had been the last time. It persisted throughout all the time they ventured through that dark other world, and did not fade until they were well within sight of the armory.

The hall the armory occupied was wider and better lit than most other reaches of the palace, and the walls were unfinished poured stone like any of the servants' tunnels. The poured stone here was in better repair. What cracks may have been present were mortared closed, and the pipes in this reach did not drip. The military handled its own affairs, allocating its discretionary funds without need for approval by the nobility, for the queen saw fit to ensure they were well cared for. If the servants were disposable cogs in this grand machine, the soldiery could never be that.

Men clad in gray reliefs marched up and down the long hall, their backs straight and their chins held high. They ignored Lance and Ben for the most part, though an occasional peon soldier spared a grin and a curt hello for the courier.

"Do you come here a lot?"

"Not really. Some of the Mauls were born peasants. Most of the Wraiths were, too. We get along fine, I guess. They're more like us than they are like the nobility, anyway."

"The Wraiths kinda scare me."

Ben nodded.

He approached a security checkpoint which was manned by two Mauls, infantry in the ranks of the Shadovani armed forces, and the same ritual as had taken place in the Treasury was repeated. They set Lord Bran's armor on a table, and he was glad to have the burden relieved from him, even if it was only temporary. They then proceeded with a thorough pat down before allowing the servants to retrieve  the

## Walking in Shadow

armor set and pass them by.

"What happens if you shadow walk into the military compound itself?"

"Without permission?"

Lance nodded. "Yeah."

"What do you think? They'd kill you."

"Noted."

They hauled their burdens halfway up the hall. A wide gap in the wall housed the open entrance to the armory, and they dipped into it. The armory was an unfussy carve out with rooms behind vault doors in the back, and all of those doors lay open. Halberds, swords and maces looked back at him from within the nearest one, and several suits of armor decorated the walls in the main chamber, where servants in white uniforms fussed over them with strange tools, or soft cloths and brushes.

They approached a tall elf whose muscled arms pressed tight against the sleeves of his military reliefs, who was otherwise whip slender. Thin lines spun out from the corners of his eyes, and his hair was cropped short, a departure from the more traditional, flowing cuts most other elves wore.

Ben deposited his share of the armor pieces on the floor at the elf's feet, and backed up a step. Lance followed his example, adding the greaves and breastplate to the pile.

The elf glanced at the pile, at Ben. "Lord Bran again?"

Ben nodded. "Yep."

"How does an early lunch sound?" he said. "I'll give you permission to eat in our canteen. The food is better there anyway."

"Sounds good."

"Is Sami here?" Lance asked.

The elf chuckled. "You a friend of hers? She's here." He twisted around, shouted to the back. "Hey Sami! Your lover boy is here!"

"You know I don't like boys!" she shouted back, emerging from one of the vaults. She saw Lance then. "Oh shit!" she rushed over and launched herself at Lance, took him in a tight hug. "What are you doing here?" she said after she released him.

"I'm on a stage."

She glanced in Ben's direction. "With the couriers today. They set you up good. Ben's good people."

Ben furrowed his brow. "You're friends?"

# SPIRIT OF SHADOW

"Of course. Lance is the best. He hasn't been giving you trouble, has he?"

"Not yet."

"So…how long will it take?" Lance asked.

The three of them exchanged a look.

"Sami snickered. "Fuck off, Duriel! You're gonna make me lose it."

That's Lord Halan to you, miss." He chided, but he spoiled it by smiling.

"What's uh…what's going on here? I feel like I'm missing something."

"Oh, we're not going to touch it." He said. Haman does this twice a week. You're going to give us an hour to look pensively at it and pretend we care, and then you're going to take it back and tell him Lord Halan polished it himself—

"And he's going to gasp like a girl who just had her first orgasm." Sami said.

"Something like that." Lord Halan flushed. "But you two enjoy your lunch. Maybe I'll let Sami off early today since you'll have so much to talk about."

"That won't be necessary." Ben said. "We have orders for Lord Aren today, too."

"What's that old cunt want?"

"Is that any way to talk about—

"Relax. He's an old friend." Lord Halan said, cutting Sami off. "In any case, if you say so, I suppose I can use Sami a little longer. We can knock out that order for Lord Elise."

"UGH!"

"Why the melodrama? He just wants a sword sharpened. And *you* don't have to deliver it."

"Who drew the short straw on that one?" Ben asked.

"I did, actually. I wouldn't send a servant up to his office under any circumstances. He's too volatile."

"And yet he's sitting on the Council of Liam." Sami grumbled.

"A seat he has more than earned." He said, his grin falling away. He produced a scratch pad and a pen from his shirt pocket, wrote out a note for them and signed it. "You two better get going. He'll be drunk as a fish by the time you get back to him anyway, but at least he'll be awake."

"We'll be back in an hour, then." Ben said. He led Lance out into the hall, turned west. They marched up the way, deeper into the military complex.

Lunch was a quiet affair. The food was far better than what they served in the servant's canteen, and the cooks were all military men, as best Lance could tell. Most of them were of an age with him, were likely assigned these duties to keep them humble, and they treated him kindly as he took his plate from them, and brought it back to the table in the corner Ben had chosen.

"It's not bad, you know." Ben said as he tucked into his meal. "Being a courier. You could do worse."

"I guess." Lance said.

"I mean, it comes with its drawbacks. Lady Therien isn't easy to work for, but she's not as bad as some of the others. I've seen Lady Jain throttle a servant for asking a simple question before. Mistress Dina threw a plate at someone once, too."

Lance grimaced.

"Does she really make you guys cover for her affairs?"

Ben shrugged. "Sometimes. It's a fun game I like to play sometimes, though. Who's she fucking? Where is she fucking them? If she's being a bitch to us, sometimes one of us will leave a clue about where she is with her husband. But I wouldn't do that with the current guy."

"Why not?"

"He's military. Imagine what would happen if Lord Therien got a hold of him. Best case, they walk away after a shouting match. Worst case, her side piece beats him half to death and gets demoted."

"Hmm."

They spent the rest of their lunch in silence, returned their empty plates to the disposal window and then made their way back to the armory, where Lord Halan returned the disarticulated armor to them and sent them on their way.

When they arrived at Lord Bran's rooms again, he was indeed so drunk he could barely stand up, and Lady Bethel and Elrin Stormbreaker—a man who's father had purchased a seat as captain in the military for him, who hadn't so much as held a sword since—were seated in a pair of cozy, wing backed chairs near a burning hearth with him.

# SPIRIT OF SHADOW

He was snatching up a jug of wine when they entered, and two more were arranged behind it. Both, he assumed, were empty.

"Oh, you've finally arrived!" Haman slurred.

"Yes, Lord Bran. Lord Halan tells us to let you know he took on this task himself. He did not trust his charges to perform the job to your high standard." Ben said.

Together, they arranged the various pieces on Lord Bran's armor stand.

Just as Sami and Lord Halan predicted, he was all glowing praise. He gushed over every detail of the armor plating, and encouraged Lady Bethel and Elrin Stormbreaker to join in. They bowed when he dismissed them, and returned to the hall outside. Ben did not open his shadow this time, but set off down the corridor with Lance trailing him.

"Are we not going to take use that shadow place?" Lance asked him.

"I need a break. Traveling that way starts to wear on you after a while. We'll have to eventually. I just need a few minutes."

"Alright."

They followed the hall almost to its end, then turned corner and traveled down another which followed the western side of the palace. Down two staircases, they went, and then followed yet one more back the way they had come.

Ben froze.

Lance followed his gaze to an ornate gate. Bars of a silvery metal, the same as was on all the vault doors he had seen in the last days, were framed by a thick border bearing designs that imitated honeysuckle and hyacinth, the remains of another queen's sensibilities. Beyond was a wide stair that descended into impenetrable darkness, beyond which lay something that drove fear like a sword deep into Lance's heart.

On impulse, he reached out and snatched up Ben's hand.

Ben's gaze snapped onto him. What are you doing?"

Lance pulled away. He couldn't bring himself to look at the other man. To see him risked redoubling his embarrassment. "I'm sorry, I didn't mean to…I just…I usually avoid this place. It gives me the creeps."

Ben nodded, but something in his gaze was off when Lance finally found the courage to look at him. Something he couldn't quite put his finger on.

## Walking in Shadow

Ben took him by the shoulders and kissed him. He retreated, leaving Lance with a vibrating sensation on his lips, which was quickly spreading to encompass the rest of him. His cheeks burned, and though he tried to say something the words wouldn't pass his throat.

"I thought that might be it." Ben said. "Do you want to get out of here."

"I'd…I'd like that."

"Good. Me, too." Ben opened his shadow.

Matte darkness loomed under his feet and he took Lance's hand in his. They plunged in together, and though pain blossomed in his head as the magic stole away his sight, he would not let go. He could not let go.

The Mauls at the checkpoint called for a Wraith when they arrived, and they were taken into the shadows by him. Lance's headache intensified, and vibrant auras marred the darkness at the edges of his vision. The pain thrashed through him, a cold sweat breaking over his body as he followed the Wraith with Ben holding onto him. They emerged in a far removed hall in the military complex, outside the open door into a cramped office.

A silver-haired elf with crystal blue eyes sat behind a writing desk at its heart. A wardrobe stood against the right hand wall, and a lock had been fitted around its handles. Above and behind the desk was hung a staff like a shepherd's hook with a snowflake pendant attached by a fine chain to the tip of the hook at its head. A pair of younger elves dressed in black tunics that hugged their necks, and slacks entirely free of wrinkles stood at attention next to the desk, and Lord Aren passed orders to them before dismissing them. The Wraith took his leave after them, and as soon as they were gone, Lance collapsed.

Lord Aren rounded his desk, ducked low over Lance's prone form. He laid hands on him, searching for some injury he would not find, and Ben knelt with him.

"What's wrong with him?"

"Some people are more sensitive to the Dark Heart than others." Lord Aren said. "Give me a moment."

Ben backed off a short way.

Lord Aren's wide palm settled on Lance's forehead. He whispered words in a language Lance could not understand. As he looked into the general's wizened face, watched as words spilled from his lips, the pain began to fade.

Lord Aren uttered a word he could not hear. His lips framed the syllables in a way he could not quite read, and he was left with the impression of something missing, something that in its absence held true power. The pain faded at last, leaving him feeling mollified.

"He should be fine now."

He climbed to his feet, and helped Lance to sit up.

"I'd recommend you not join the couriers if this continues. It will be dangerous for you." He turned to Ben. "Don't speak to anyone of what happened here. The healing has been done, but it will do your friend no favors to alert anyone of what afflicted him. Especially the nobility."

"I understand." Ben said, though it was clear he was shaken by what had just transpired. "I won't say a word."

"Good." He said. "Now, while I have mended him, he will not tolerate shadow walking better than he has. I have only given him temporary relief. You should go about the remainder of your shift by more conventional avenues. You may count yourself lucky that my needs of you are not demanding."

"What can we do for you, my lord." Ben asked.

Lord Aren rounded his desk. He took up an envelope, heated a daub of bright blue wax and dropped it onto the fold. He impressed it with his seal, a circlet of blackthorn, and waited for the wax to set, then handed it to Ben.

"Take this to Lord Tarkenta, then return to Lady Therien. I assume I am your last errand for the day."

"You are."

"Then may you both have a bright evening." He said. "And sir?"

"Lance." Ben supplied.

"Yes, Lance. I assume you have not chosen a path."

"I haven't."

"Then let me be clear. This is not the right one for you, but there is a department which takes on people like you, where you will not encounter much interference from the Dark Heart. If you have not been granted the opportunity, I will ask that Lady Tamalsen schedule you for a stage in the furnaces."

"That is my last stage, Lord Aren."

Lord Aren nodded. "Choose that path, then. Tell Master Gregor I have given you my recommendation."

He offered the letter to Ben.

Ben took it, and placed it in his pocket. "May the shadow preserve you, Lord Aren." He said, his gaze fixed on Lance.

He bowed, and helped Lance out of the office.

"Are you okay?" he asked.

"I'm fine now. I don't know what he did, but it took the pain away."

Ben nodded shakily. "Okay. Good. Let's just finish this up then. Lord Tarkenta's office is close."

# Stones

Sami caught him in the stairwell as he made way to his barracks. His stomach did a cartwheel on seeing her, and he struggled to keep his expression even. He was still not sure what to make of Ben. He had witnessed the beginnings of something. Something that could be good. But what was his intent? Was his interest more than some carnal sense, a desire for companionship...a relationship?

He wanted to tell Sami about him, to give voice to what had transpired just this afternoon, but she didn't give him time.

"Hey buddy!" she said. "Stones tonight?"

"Sure." He said. Wait though—"

"Can't. I'm late for a date. Ariana and Peter said they got some of that Mirrhvalian wine all the nobles are raving about."

"O-okay."

She passed him by on the way down.

He watched her go, the words drying up in his throat. She was lost around the barrel shaft wall of the spiral staircase.

## Stones

"What time?" he called after her.

"Eighth bell. We'll play until curfew. Just don't blow it for us, okay?"

"I'm not the one—"

"See ya later!"

He deflated. "See ya!"

He marched up the stairs. If he knew her at all, there would be no romance in the intervening hours. There would barely be any preamble. Sami was not the type to entertain long standing relationships. He could not remember a time when she had been involved with anyone for more than a couple of weeks. As soon as the glamor and sparkle wore off, she would be onto the next one, and another girl's heart would be broken.

He sucked his teeth. *I guess I'll tell her later.*

He passed the second floor, and thought briefly of visiting the barracks there. Ben had said he could find him there, but it was too soon. He did not want to come across as clingy. He let the moment pass, marched onward.

*Give it a day at least. Maybe two.*

There was that exchange with Lord Aren to think about, too. Ben needed time to think that over, to decide whether it was worth getting entangled with someone in such a precarious position as he currently was. If he was honest with himself, he needed time to think it over, too.

He met his friends in the usual place. A storeroom somewhat removed from the kitchens. He could hear Ariana and Peter chattering away just inside, but he hesitated outside the entrance.

*How do I tell them?* He thought. "Oh hi. Yeah, Ben was the one from the showers. The one I embarrassed myself in front of...no, fuck that. I sound like an idiot.

"Hey guys! I met a boy. Yeah, it's him. It's Ben...stupid."

"You can come in any time!" Ariana called.

*Shit. Did they hear all that?*

He stepped across the threshold.

Dry goods populated metal shelves throughout the expanse, and candle light emanated from a corner near the back of the room. Beans and rice, potatoes, onions, whole heads of garlic and assorted spices were neatly arranged in burlap sacks, wood crates and shallow trenchers along the shelves, all there to remind him of his stage in the kitchens and the expectations of Ariana and Peter that he would eventually see sense and choose to work under them.

He didn't know how to approach that subject either. He couldn't tell them what Lord Aren had said. The general had been clear enough about that. He couldn't very well place himself in the kitchens where couriers were abundant and constantly jumping out of shadows, either.

*I'll cross that bridge when I come to it.* He still had his stage in the furnaces to think about. Some time before he need make a final decision. Once it was over, he could broach the subject, address the elephant in the room. They might not take it well. Peter would understand, but Ariana was a different matter. She might fight him over it.

*Who am I kidding. She* will *fight me over it.*

He negotiated his way around a tall rack loaded down with leftover bread from the day which would be repurposed the following morning.

His friends were sitting around an overturned crate in the corner. A wooden game board with a tight grid inlaid into its surface was situated on top of it. The fat candle they were using for light was seated on a nearby rack, together with two small sacks which housed the glass beads they would be playing with.

He edged around the board, and took a seat on the far side, next to Ariana.

"Oh, no. Absolutely not. You two can't play together."

## Stones

Peter protested.

"Why ever not, honey bunch?" Ariana batted her eyelashes innocently.

"Because both of you are cunning little shits. That's why." He said.

"Well then you might learn something." Lance said.

"Where is Sami, anyway." He asked.

Ariana reached behind her and snatched up a clay jug. A crimson wax seal held the cork in place, and it was unbroken.

Lance rolled his eyes. "She's off fucking some chick in the Teacher's Tower."

"She better hurry her ass up." Ariana said.

"Don't be like that." Sami materialized around the corner.

"Fuck off. You're late." Ariana groused.

Sami glanced at the board, at Lance and Ariana seated on the other side of it. "So I'm babysitting."

Peter glared at her. "I'm not that bad."

"No, of course not." Ariana said. "You're just too sweet for strategy games."

Sami snorted. "Something like that."

"I did tell them they couldn't play together." Peter said.

"We could do girls versus boys?" Sami said.

Ariana shrugged.

"We did that last time." Lance protested.

"Okay fine. I'll play with the lump."

"Hey now! Is that any way to talk about the guy who got you wine?"

"*We* got them wine." Ariana broke the seal on the jug.

Lance looked around. "What no cups?"

"Is that a problem?" Ariana said.

"I guess not." He said.

"Can we just get into it? Sami, take a seat. Since you made us wait, you can go last."

"That's fair. Besides, I need to wash my hands. See! Smell." She shoved her fingers under Peter's nose.

# SPIRIT OF SHADOW

He reeled back, screwing up his face in disgust. "Ewurgh!"

"Relax, I'm only kidding. Lance would have a heart attack if I touched those stones with pussy juice all over my hands." She said. "See! Look at his face!"

"You should wash up anyway."

"Already did. Shower and everything. It was fun, by the way. Real good time. Not a lot of talking."

"You're depraved." He said. "Can we get to the game?"

"Oh, fine." She took her seat next to Peter.

The bags of stones were upended and the stones divided four ways. Each of them made their first move, setting a stone on the quarter of the board that would be their individual domain. Lance took an aggressive stance, near the center of the board, while Ariana hung back. Peter's chosen position was neutral, neither far back nor far forward, and Sami edged her piece in close to the perimeter of his domain, in easy reach for an eventual block if it was needed.

And it would be needed.

"So, you know what I've been up to. What have you been doing since the last time we sat down like this?"

Ariana took a pull from the bottle. Her nose wrinkled, eyes squeezed shut as she swallowed. "What the fuck...is this shit." She coughed. "It tastes like piss."

"Care to tell us how you know that?" Sami glanced at Peter, a smirk touching her lips.

"If anyone has firsthand knowledge of that, it would be you." Peter said, taking the bottle from his girlfriend.

Sami shrugged. "Things get messy sometimes. And when your face is...well anyway. You don't want to hear about all that."

"What's her name, anyway?"

"You know I never found out."

"I met—" Lance started. He was immediately cut off by Ariana.

**Stones**

"I see what you're doing, sugar bear, but it's not going to work." She was eying Peter's growing array with shark-like hunger.

He took a pull from the bottle, and grimaced. "I see what you mean. Why is it that strong?"

"Maybe it's not really wine." She said.

"Mistress Dina said—"

"What does she know? She's never used it before. She's probably writing out a list of new insults about it as we speak."

"You might be right. Either way, it tastes like hot ass."

"Isn't that Lance's department?"

Sami and Ariana cackled.

"Speaking of—" Lance said, but no one was paying attention to him.

The bottle passed into his clutches, and he took a pull. Wisdom told him to take it in small doses. It tasted oddly sweet, and at the same time like it would be better utilized as floor cleaner. The back of his throat burned as he swallowed, and his stomach felt as if it had shriveled up and died when it hit. In the aftermath, a comforting warmth spread through him.

He passed the bottle to Sami. "Take it in sips."

"So, I'm not a bitch." She said, and knocked back a mouthful. She gasped.

"Bad, right?" Peter said.

"It's doing a job, though." She said. "But back to you guys. What's new? What's hot?"

"Well, it's your move for one thing." Ariana said.

"I—"

"What's new is Lance staged in the kitchens." Ariana said. *Oh not this.*

"And he did good. Mistress Dina said she was going to pass her recommendation for apprenticeship to Lady Tamalsen."

"She'll love that." Sami said sarcastically.

"I mean, what are the other choices realistically. Working with your friends, or sitting on your ass all day."

"Or running errands for the nobility." Peter supplied.

"And the military." Sami added.

"I still have a stage in the furnaces." Lance said.

"But you're not going to choose *that!*" Ariana said.

"I don't know. I might like it." He shrugged.

"Just say you don't like us. I can take it." Ariana took another swig from the bottle. A dark flush swept across her cheeks. She was grinning like a madwoman when she set her next piece, capturing three of Peter's stones in one sweep.

"BOOM!" she smacked her leg. "Love you, loser."

"Okay." Peter said. "*Okay.* I see how it is."

He took the bottle from her.

"Hey, I wasn't done with that!"

"It's called, um, sharing? I think that's the word." He took a long swig.

"I met a boy!" Lance said, the words tumbled out of him in a rapid string. "Ben. He's the one from the showers and I thought I'd done something to make him uncomfortable because I was staring at him, you know, and I really *really* wanted to avoid him but then he was everywhere I was and he kissed me.

"He kissed me. I don't know what it means."

A brief silence.

"What the fuck, Lance." Sami said. "When were you going to tell me?"

"I tried when I saw you earlier, but you had other things on your mind." He said.

"Well that's good." Ariana said.

Sami took her turn, daintily set a stone in a position aligning with the array Ariana had just captured, and took two of her pieces as a result.

"Damn you." Ariana said. "I had something going there."

"I do have eyes." Sami said.

"Anyway, I think I'm going to see him again."

"You should. He's nice." Ariana said.

"Do you think he's just in it for—"

"Trust me, he's not a whore. Not like..." she looked at Sami, hefted her eyebrows.

"I am ethically non-monogamous, thank you very much." Sami gestured airily. "Happily unattached, if you will."

"Well, anyway, how long do I wait?"

"Three days." Peter said.

"Fuck off. That's how you almost lost me."

"But I didn't. Which means it worked."

"It just pissed me off. And since your memory's so bad, let me remind you I approached you after a day and a half and asked *you* out. Because you were clearly too much of a punk to do it."

"Is that how you remember it?" He snickered.

Lance took another pull from the bottle. "This game is moving at a glacial pace. We only have until the tenth bell."

"Says the guy who just couldn't wait to tell us all about his new boyfriend."

"He's not my boyfriend. He's just a person of interest at this point."

"You sound like me." Sami said. "Which is good. You really should stir the paint more often."

"What does *that* mean?" he asked.

Ariana rolled her eyes. "She means you should dabble before you settle on one person. I disagree. If things work out with this guy, you're not missing anything by sticking with him."

"You guys are getting way ahead of yourselves." Peter said.

"Thank you." Lance grinned at him. "I was just going to say."

"I mean, you're talking about them like they're a thing

# SPIRIT OF SHADOW

already." Peter went on.

"They *are* a thing already. They kissed. Didn't you hear him?" Ariana said.

"One kiss. Probably not even a real one. And did you hear the part about the awkward shower scenario. You didn't pop wood, did you?"

"N...no. Why would you...I mean he's cute but...."

"I'm just saying it must be so hard for you being surrounded by naked men every morning."

"I'm not attracted to everyone that moves, you know." Lance grumbled. "I have standards."

"So you're going to see him again." Peter said, changing the subject.

"I think so. I don't really want to suggest the Teacher's Tower. I think he'd read into that too much."

"Go to the Core."

"Isn't that where Lady Therien's been—" Sami started.

"Is any part of the palace safe from her escapades?" Ariana cut in. "It's nice there. The gardens are always in bloom. There's a water feature you can sit by—"

"And braid each other's pubes." Sami said.

"Would you be just a little more serious?" Ariana growled. "It's his first date. Ever."

"Okay, slow down. I've been on a date before."

"With who?"

"No one you know."

"Bullshit."

"So the Core?"

"Best place you have access to if you want to set the right tone. He can shadow walk, so I suppose you could go up to the Royal Garden if you timed it right, but you'd have to ask him and that might be pushing your luck."

Lance blanched.

"Did I say something weird? I'm sorry."

**Stones**

"No. I'm just new to this."

"HA!" Ariana said. "I knew it!"

"So what is it about him?" Sami asked. "What makes him special?"

He shrugged. "I don't really know. I mean...I don't really know him. That's kind of what the date is for."

"Gotcha." She said. "Just keep it loose then. But do your kegels. No one wants it loose."

"Would you please shut the fuck up!" Ariana snapped.

Sami gestured at the board. "If you'll stop hedging and make your move."

"I'm strategizing."

"You're procrastinating."

"It's your own fault. You fucked up my rhythm."

"That's kind of the point, isn't it?"

"Pass me that bottle. It's going to be a while." Peter said.

Rolling his eyes, Lance handed it to him.


Sleep found him in the deeper darkness of a moonless night. His eyes drifted closed as he watched the stars beyond his window. The spider was absent this night, a good omen after a day filled with complex happenings, only some of which he had a clear eyed idea of what to do with. In slumber, echoes of coming dreams flitted across his mind. He was immersed in fleeting scenes with broken narratives, which blended together at their edges, obfuscating details and masking faces, so that he was left with no lasting impressions, would forget all of their myriad details by the time he awoke again.

The dreams blended together, collapsed like sand in an hourglass, pouring out of him and leaving vacant space to be filled with something else. Something morose, even painful, which would sit with him for many days thereafter.

A dull roar aroused him from a shallow slumber. Red glow

# SPIRIT OF SHADOW

filled the lone window in a room that was not his. A low wainscoting smoldered in places near that window, and outside, a hundred year oak was ablaze. Wide, burning fangs gnawed at the night sky. Vibrant tongues rolled over a manicured lawn at its feet. A peacock bolted across the yard, every eye in its long tail ablaze. It's screams were lost beneath the raging crackle and roar of the blaze.

He curled up against the wall, his bed an oasis underneath him and the room as hot as an oven around him. The fires had not reached him, but smoke pooled under a wooden door, promising a descent into the Pits of Amorahiya was forthcoming.

Someone was beating on the door. Pounding inanely against it and calling to him. A girl's voice, shrill with panic.

"Lance!" she hollered. "Lance are you in there! The door is blocked! I can't lift...climb through the window if you can!"

A groan as she labored at something outside. She was crying.

"I'm sorry, I can't lift it. I can't lift it."

"Andrea, I'm scared!" he said.

He was a child. Maybe three years old, all knees and elbows. His round face was scrunched into a mask of raw terror, golden eyes wide with worry. Black shadow loomed under the posters of his bed, and he was sure the Nepherim—servants of Seraphel, Immortal Shadow of Judgment—had come to pull him into the pits. Had come to claim his soul.

*Did I do something bad?*

Surely he had or the demons would not have come. The fires would not now be consuming his home. Where was his father? His mother? What had happened to them?"

"Lance, please, listen to me." The fight was leaking out of his sister's voice. "The roof collapsed. There's a beam in front of your door and I can't lift it. I need you to open your window. Climb out onto the roof. I'll try to get you down."

**Stones**

"O-okay." He whined. "They won't get me will they?"

"Lance, there's no one left. It's just you and me. No one is going to get you. Just climb out your window, okay. I'll meet you downstairs."

"You promise?"

"I promise."

He climbed over the edge of his bed and dropped onto the floor. The house groaned around him as he bolted to the window. A shudder ran through the floor. He pushed against the windowsill. It slid up a few inches. He pushed again with all his might. It wouldn't budge.

"I can't get it!" he shouted.

Tears streaked down his face. Smoke filled his nostrils, climbed down his throat. Harsh coughs wracked him. He shoved at the window again. It budged another few inches.

"Can you get out?" she asked.

"I'm trying!"

He shoved again, and it budged enough he thought he might be able to get through. Head and shoulders, he scrambled to get through the gap. The windowsill grated against his back.

"I can get out. I think I can!"

"I'll meet you outside, okay. I'll meet you outside."

"NO DON'T LEAVE!"

"I'll see you in a moment, okay, Lance. I need you to be brave. Can you be brave for me."

"DON'T LEAVE, DON'T LEAVE, DON'T LEAVE!"

Her footsteps carried her away in a rush. Thunder shook the house. He wiggled through the window. His chest was free now, chubby legs kicking at air behind him.

Cold washed over his thighs. Cold and firm pressure.

He screamed.


And bolted upright, gasping.

*What was that? Where am I?*

# SPIRIT OF SHADOW

He wiped thick sweat out of his eyes, cast about him, made sure he was safe. The fires were gone. The peculiar room in some far flung place was gone. He was in his barracks. He was safe.

*What was that?*

The girl's voice filled his ears, an incessant refrain. *I need you to be brave. Can you be brave? I need you to be brave. Can you be brave for me?*

*I'm losing my mind.* He looked out the window past Laramy's bunk. The spider was absent. Thousands of stars dotted the sky. On nights like these, he thought of foxes. The stars belonged to the foxes, the first lords of fire. But their fires purified. There was nothing pure about what he had just experienced. Just fear, and loss, and pain. And the melancholic echoes of a trauma he thought he might have lived.

# A Promised Path

The moon peaked out from behind downy, lavender clouds. Its light crossed over the bridge of Lance's nose, awakening him. It had been three days since the new nightmare had found him. The spider was back in its web. Spider and web alike were identical to the one that had been there before, and he was beginning to think he was seeing things.

A quiet voice whispered in his ears, and he could make out some of the words it spoke, though he could not understand them. This was not the language of Shadovane. It was no language he knew. And yet those whispers spoke of strain, of a quiet argument between their originator and some other who remained silent.

"Tedeltia iyal an! Eya anelfara, decenter omo zentov. Gan amilia speltion aena speltor a goyal ains tilsamav eyal?"

"Who's there?" he whispered.

Silence for several heartbeats.

"Eyo rocom valadi mi?" came that fraught whisper.

"I don't understand."

The person to whom the voice belonged, if it could be said to be a person, cleared his throat. He spoke in a guttural voice, heavily accented, but used plain language. Language Lance could understand.

"Am I to understand…that you can hear me, child?"

# SPIRIT OF SHADOW

"Who are you?"

"Were I to tell you, it would fall on deaf ears. Are you the one who tortures me so?"

"I don't know what you mean?"

"You are one of those people…always pulling on my limbs, yanking at my essence, tugging it into shape according to your whims with no regard for the pain it might cause, or whether I wish to come to your aid at all."

"I…I don't…I don't know what you mean."

"Then perhaps you are worthy. One of those rare ones who will listen to the voice behind the cries. Then chew on this for me, and do so diligently. There will be others now, if you care to listen, and those that come will give words for you to puzzle over. Know them. Know me, and perhaps we will abide you for a time. Perhaps you will find friends among us. So, too, you will know my name then. You will not be deaf to it.

"Know me in my essence."

*I've lost my mind. I'm hearing voices. I've completely lost my mind.*

"The sun stands to one side of a mortal. I lay to the other. All things have this in common. The sun shines, and I hide. In plain sight but full of secrets, able to frighten when seen in unexpected places, to divide myself twice or thrice, but always I lay in opposition to the sun. At night, I am at my weakest, and still I hide, for the moon and the stars draw me out, but I mustn't be seen directly by either."

A chuckle slipped out of him. *I am truly going* mad. "Is this a riddle?"

"Contemplate my words. Know my name. There will be others." The whisper faded.

He climbed out of his bed and dressed himself. As he buttoned his shirt, he glanced at the window. The spider in its web was gone. *Was it ever there? Right, then. Just a trick of the eye.*

He ventured into the bowels of the palace, beyond the maze of pipes overhead, across an eroded section of floor where a small pond had formed. Then it was into the furnaces to face the master of the department.

He kept his expression placid with some effort, but anxiety lay festering under the surface. When he saw the servants at work, the

## A Promised Path

numbness pulled back to reveal another feeling he didn't quite know what to do with. Envy.

The Master of the Furnaces was a servant like Mistress Dina. He was a kitune—with deep red skin and conical, tufted ears, and a broad, smashed-looking nose. His head was shaved bald and his beard—a burly frock hanging like a curtain over his jaw—was more silver than umber. Tight wrinkles around his eyes and a body made all of sinew and bone revealed his age.

"Lance?" he asked, his voice gruff and deep. He shifted a wad of chewing tobacco from his lip to his cheek.

Lance nodded.

The Master of the Furnaces held out his hand. "Gregor."

Lance took it, and Gregor squeezed with enough force to fold his fingers together.

"We've got two kinds 'round here. Burners and breezers. Burners ought a thing for fire. Breezers ought a thing for air. We 'on't take folks is bad with either. No water. No earth. Got it? They're useless. And I 'on't need staff's just down here to look pretty."

"Understood." Lance said. "So, what can I do for you?"

"Tonight you're gonna shovel coal. Shovel coal, clean pipes. Whatever I tell ya really. I'm not gonna test ya in magic yet. That comes later. Now ya just do the shit work so my regular folk get an easy night for once. They deserve it the work they do here."

"Okay." Lance said.

"Shovel's there, coal's that pile there." Gregor pointed to a small mountain of glossy, black rocks with a shovel planted in one side. "People come around with a bucket. You fill that bucket. Now get to it."

He clapped Lance on the ass. Lance trotted off toward the pile of coal. No sooner than had he picked up the shovel, a pair of kitunes arrived with a bin fit for the launderers.

They looked expectantly at him. He looked confusedly at them.

"Fill…the *bucket.* " One of them said. She was diminutive, with her hair cut almost to the scalp and a scowl on her face that seemed permanent.

Rather than risk the wrath of what he thought might be a future coworker, he started shoveling. With minor exception, he didn't stop until he left for the night. When the pile began to dwindle, a worker struck a button on the wall and a deluge of rocks came shooting out of a

# SPIRIT OF SHADOW

door in the ceiling. Lance had been standing directly in the path of the falling stones the first time, and was forced to somersault out of the way. No one thought to warn him. He learned to keep an eye on that button while he worked through the rest of the night.

He had already sweat through his shirt by the end of the first hour. By the end of the second, he'd abandoned it. Every now and again, someone offered him a flagon of water that he knocked back quickly before returning to his work.

The workers never seemed to stop moving. As he shoveled and filled buckets and dodged out of the way of falling rocks, no one tried to speak to him if they didn't have to. No one asked questions or tried to make friends.

As he worked, he fell into a rhythm. Shovel, fill, dodge. And as the night went on, he found the space he needed to think.

*What if I wasn't imagining it.*

Shovel, fill, dodge.

*What if that voice belonged to someone. Maybe someone hiding in the shadows. Can the Wraiths speak through them?*

Shovel, fill, dodge.

*What would they want with me? And why give me a riddle, then? Why bother asking me to figure out their names. Most of them would give them freely if I asked.*

Shovel, fill, dodge.

*Of course, I wouldn't ask. Too much of a coward for that.*

A servant, a Burner or a Breezer, he was not sure which, came by to take the push cart away. Another replaced it with a fresh one.

He went back to his labor, allowed himself to be swept away by his thoughts again.

*I did see that spider. Almost every night over the last week or so, I've seen it. Never mind that means whoever's been cleaning the barracks isn't doing a very good job. It was there. I didn't imagine it. It was right there.*

There was the dream of fire and chaos of a few nights past, too. It had been absent then. *Was it trying to shield me? What purpose would that serve?*

And the other dreams. A child alone in the dark and filthy. A food tray materializing now and again. A pile of shit watered down with piss in the corner and rashes breaking over his body. His clothes dirty, his hair caked with oil and grit.

Eyes flashed across his mind. Eyes, the bridge of a nose. Their owner's pallor was dark, the nose broad. The eyes were a violent shade of blue, like lightning. They were there and gone in a heartbeat, and an itch formed between his shoulder blades that had nothing to do with the motes of sweat pouring down his back, the sodden shirt clinging to it.

The night wore on. He lost himself in the rhythm, and the confused tangle of his thoughts leveled out in slow degrees. Everything seemed to swirl around that spider and what it meant. The voice and what it had said. Even when he considered how he had collapsed in Lord Aren's office—

"There was a word." He whispered. "A word I couldn't understand. Was it a name?"

He stepped clear of another wave of coal as it cascaded onto the heap, breathed out slow. *That language.* "It was the same."

Master Gregor marched down the channel between monstrous, bronze boxes. The furnaces proper framed him on either side, and fire glow touched his skin at interval as he passed open grates on his way back to the pile of coal.

"Come down from'ere." He said. "Want to chat with ya 'bout some'n." He spat sleuce on the poured stone floor.

Lance negotiated himself free of the mound and joined him at floor level. He stuck the shovel in the pile, and Master Gregor guided him through the chamber.

The furnaces towered over him on either side, cut a sharp corner and continued. Servants worked in teams to blast raw fire into the grates. They used magic to do it, a magic not dissimilar in its composure to the magic the couriers and the Wraiths used to travel through shadow, and yet in their presence he was not afflicted by those too familiar headaches, any waves of fatigue. He felt hale in their presence, even as their magic abounded everywhere around him.

Master Gregor eyed him. His expression was unreadable.

"My Burners get most o' the fun work through 'em winter months." He said. "Breezers're handier in'a summer."

"They're pretty good at this." Lance said.

"Better be! S'not like they have a choice."

He nodded.

# SPIRIT OF SHADOW

They climbed up a wire-mesh staircase and onto a catwalk which was positioned high above the furnace heads. Broad, square ducts climbed toward the ceiling to one side of the catwalk, robbing all sight of it from a quarter of the way around down. That exposed quarter was occupied by a poured stone block inset with a bay window, which served as an office for the Master of the Furnace.

Inside was a long desk peppered with schematics and tools.

"Sometimes things need reparin'." He said. "Part o' the job."

He leaned up against the desk. Gestured to a chair near enough by. "Take it."

Lance seated himself obediently.

"We need to talk about yer future here, don't we. Not a conversation I like havin'. Usually, the young'uns come 'ere with some baggage. You'an keep it to yerself if you want, but you'll find out fast 'em fuck ups down there aren't big on secrets. We're a family here. No one'd judge you for being a little screwy. Sky Lord knows you'd fit right in.

"So are ya in or are ya out?"

"Sorry what now?"

He cleared his throat. "Do you want…a job here?" He said, annunciating every word a little more than was necessary. "Lord Aren sent me…" he rummaged through the scattering of papers, plucked one from the heap. "Here it is. Sent a recommendation. Said you'd developed a *sensitivity*." He bit down on the word. "And you'd be better off here where it aren't a lot of shadow walkin' happening.

"Now I don't know 'bout no sensitivity. Don't much care for hundred mark words like 'at. But I do know 'bout good work ethic and ya got it. Just need'a get the business out the way first, ya know?"

"I think so."

"Great. Good." He said. "Look, s'not glamorous work, but it can be rewardin' enough, I guess. You keep yer nose clean and you'an go far here. But we do have rules."

"Okay."

"First an' foremost. What happens here stays here. You'an tell yer friends about the work yer doin' but we got some sensitive business in'is place and s'gotta stay here. That's gonna be people's personal business mos'ly, and also how we do magic. Couriers…really any department works wit' magic's bound by the same rules. You get caught tryin' to

# A Promised Path

teach it to people don't already know, they'll kill ya. I'm serious, they will. Wraith abduction. Then cold blooded murder. No exceptions. Same's true of trying to teach someone knows magic magic 'ey don' know already know. Trade secrets or somethin' like 'at.

"You agree to that, and I'm willin' to offer ya a spot on my team. Jus' need to send Lady Tamalsen a note sayin' you're giving the ol' fuck you to the other places ya staged at."

"Lance grimaced. "I don't know if I'd put it that way. But I like the work here. I'll take it."

"She'll fight ya." He said, grinning. "Ya just put up with her shit a little longer, an' I'll see ya in a few weeks."

"Will it be bad?"

"Always is. On'y people she thinks so low of as to recommend 'em to me are kitunes. Jus' racism. Thinks we're idiots by nature.

"But you seem like a stubborn 'un. She'll throw a dry run at ya to see if you'd like somethin' she likes for ya, so ya do what she says. But when time comes, remember I want ya here. Think ya'd get along great with my guys. 'Specially Duardo. He's the welcome wagon."

He held out his hand to shake. Lance took it, and braced his hand this time.

Master Gregor smiled. "S'more like it. I'll see ya."

"Thank you for the—"

"Oh, knock it off with the polites, kid. We 'on't do all 'at formality nonsense here. Jus' go get ya some sleep."

"A-alright." He climbed out of his chair, passed Master Gregor by. Master Gregor clapped him on his ass on the way out.

He jumped a foot into the air.

Master Gregor chuckled. "See ya soon, kid. We'll start ya off on 'at *logistical* learnin' soon as you're all clear."

# A Lady's Wisdom

*t hides from the sun.*

The riddle left to him by that stranger in the night had become a crutch of a kind, a puzzle he turned to when he needed to distract himself from the more pressing complications in his day to day life.

*Hides from the moon and stars, too.*

A short way off was an office and a meeting he did not want to have. He had been summoned to it. He hadn't even had the time to take breakfast before the time of his appointment, had barely enough time to wash.

The message was made clear with no need for extrapolation from its carrier. This was to be the beginning of the fight Master Gregor warned him about. At its end was a potential for peace. A chance at a quiet life, free from prying eyes and forced civility. A life in which he was no one to anyone who mattered. He need only see the coming argument through to its end.

A short walk. A conversation he did not need. A verbal drubbing at the hands of a woman who had been the closest thing to a mother he could have. Then, he could have his freedom. His nerves were on him, and the peculiar puzzle was there to keep his mind away from it. Strange that it should supply some relief when its origin was so imperiled. What gave a man comfort needn't make sense to anyone but him. It was fitting, then, that the one so plagued by terrors in the night, who  had spent his life jumping at shadows, would find resilience in trying to parse out a riddle given to him by a spider.

*He's at his weakest in darkness. That rules out darkness itself.*

He had arrived.

He tapped the knocker. Lady Tamalsen's missive came before he had set it down again.

"Enter." She snapped.

*Here we go.*

He pushed the door open, found her seated behind her desk and waiting for him, with all of her various papers set aside. It seemed she intended to give him her full attention.

She gestured sharply to the chair before her. "Sit."

He obeyed.

"I want to know why a sitting general on the Council of Liam is recommending you to the Furnaces." She said. "And *please* don't tell me you intend to choose them."

"I apologize for any insult I may have caused Lord Aren." He said. "I will accept whatever punishment you see fit to give me for my indiscretion."

"Oh, I have no intention of punishing you." She sat back in her chair, folded her hands together in her lap. The look she set on him was hawkish. "As it happens, all four department heads you staged for have submitted requests to add you to their teams. Lady Therien gave you a glowing recommendation for the Office of the Couriers."

"Then...pardon me for saying so, but I'm confused."

"That makes two of us. Have you settled on a choice?"

He hesitated. *How to proceed? If I tell her the truth, she'll be furious. If I lie, she might see through it and be even angrier.*

"I haven't made a decision, but I know I don't want to work in the Treasury. I don't think the kitchens would be a good fit either."

"You're considering the couriers?" she lifted a thin eyebrow. Her hope was palpable. He could almost feel it as a physical force, a low, insistent wind buffeting him.

"I don't know. It has its merits, but..." he fidgeted with his hands in his lap.

The moment's reassurance evaporated, was replaced by a stony regard.

He eased back in his seat, an inane bid to put more space between them.

"Let me place you on a follow up with them." She reached for a pen, took a fresh sheet of paper from a drawer. "Something a bit more stimulating. If it's down to the couriers or those greasy pigs in the furnaces, well, it should be an easy choice. Lady Therien will be glad for the extra hands."

"When should I present myself to her?"

"Time and date will have to wait until I hear back from Lady Jain. She grinned. "You'll be on one of the crews handling the Emperor's reception."

His breath caught. *Sky Lord's mercy, how do I reject her after that.*

"Lady Jain's office is taking helm on everything related to his visit. We haven't seen an event of this significance since we received Lord Rakhna down from Ash Island four years past.

"She will assign you to one of the crews on the welcome

**A Lady's Wisdom**

ceremony, and I will send someone with the details. Does that sound good?"

Her grin was wide and inviting, but there was a competitive edge in the gaze she set against him. She was confident she would have her way, which would only make matters worse when he tore her narrative to shreds.

He did not want to hurt her, but for all that he thought he would enjoy this task, and for all that the idea of being in such close proximity to an immortal out of legend—*the Shadow Queen, too*—it would not sway him. At the end of this tunnel lay a promise not of magical learning, but protection from its ill effects, and he wanted it. Yearned for it.

He needed it.

# HE
# SHINES
# LIKE
# THE
# SUN

# Watchers

Lady Therien hated children. It was the singular thing she detested more than any of her other duties that she should have to attend to the palace nursery.

She might have a less negative view of this *chore* if the children she need supervise were noble born, or even elven, but Queen Meredith was not in the habit of keeping blooded children in the palace. The old Teacher's Tower was long abandoned, a byproduct of a change in leadership when Meredith rose out of the slums and Queen Tania, her predecessor, died. She hadn't liked the old crone much either, but at least she had been of high birth, a professional.

It was not lost on her that the current queen didn't much care for her—and the feeling was mutual—but that did not give her justification to cast a high lady into the bowels of the palace in order that she ought to take care of dirty, snot nosed kids from so many corners of the world where culture was in short supply and those haunting, vacant-eyed stares were so damned common.

## Watchers

There was a logic in her decision, of course. There always was. Whatever their feelings for each other, she must acknowledge there were no others within the palace, at least not within the noble caste, who could do what she did. She might take that as a compliment if she was of a mind to, but then she would have to acknowledge that woman was right about something. That she may even be a competent ruler.

She traveled a hall close at hand to the dungeons, an expanse cast in those offensive, washed out shades the glow bulbs that spiteful bitch had insisted on installing everywhere the servants walked. The enchanting work had been done by a crew down from the Ring of Fire, all kitunes and all, to varying degrees, loyal to the Shadow of Lies. Better work could be found in the Eleventh Ward, and in particular within Aranor, where the Whiteheart family had dominated the market for generations, but to bring them here would have risked inviting rumors to spread across the ward, and into others along the borderlands where Shadovane and Mirrhvale alike were viewed as the product of a string of popular myths.

She stopped outside a door with a black triangle fired into a lone tile next to it at waist level, an unassuming sign which nonetheless demanded certain clearance be granted before one could enter. Shadow walking would be impossible here, which was another mild insult. She'd have liked to emerge just within the chamber she needed, and avoid those common beasts altogether. The enchanting work that prevented her doing so was far older, dating back at least to Queen Anastasia, as the rooms beyond this door had originally been her safe house, a necessary hideout during a time of great conflict, when even the shadows could not entirely be trusted.

She pushed the door inward, and whipped it shut behind her.

On either side of a narrow corridor were poured stone half walls fitted at their heights with glass pains that rose to the ceiling. Within those rooms, women doted on toddling vermin, or taught them lessons in reading, basic math, life skills they would need when they matriculated from this place into the Servant's Tower and the palace halls, where they would take on responsibilities as servants....

*Janitors, really. For a few years.*

Chewing her lip, she breezed past those rooms, her gaze trained intently on the end of the passage, dodging as much of what transpired in those classrooms, sleeping chambers, the quaint dining room where the kids would be allowed a modest meal three times a day.

The hall broadened out into a final chamber, the windows clamping against poured stone walls that rose to ceiling height and blocked direct lines of sight from that last chamber into the classrooms. Those were newer than the viewing windows, were mostly unaffected by the cracks and fissures the older work contained. Bitter lessons had been learned early in this enterprise, lessons which necessitated their construction.

What lay here was not strictly legal, nor was it precisely wise. Purpose driven to a fault, the true task set against her was not in maintaining these children. Noblewomen of low birth who could keep their mouths shut would suffice for that task, but they could not be expected to deal with the mechanism which upheld this new system, this convention of the last twenty or so years.

Arrayed against the far wall were men and women who ran the gamut of races and ethnicities haling from the Thirteen Imperial Wards and the Free Lands. A kaleidoscopic array of individuals who had one thing in common. Every one of these people was born with a Gift of the Blood. All of them were Watchers, and as the only Shield in Shadovane, she was the only person in the city who could resist them.

She panned over the dozen figures arrayed across that wall. Shackles bound their wrists and ankles, and heavy chains connected those shackles to thick bolts staked into the wall. Enchanted cadmium was threaded into the cuffs, together with thicker bands of silver to boost its effect. The shackles were all that was needed to suppress access to magic, to mute the sounds of the Cosmic Orchestra, that driving force behind all sorcery.

It was enough to keep the other women safe, to keep these savages bound in place, and yet it could do nothing for that cursed gift, the one thing in all of the world her emperor feared. Mere eye contact with one of those creatures would rob any of those women of conscious control over themselves, would expose every memory they had ever put away and open the possibility that their histories, their perceptions of them, might be altered. False memories might be inserted, true memories might be purged. Their personalities may be restructured, or they might just become hosts for these Watchers for a time.

She sneered, an ugly thing. *Yet they can do no such thing to me. All because of a quirk in my soul.*

When she had first discovered her gift, it had been by mistake. It had not been proximity to a Watcher but a Whisperer, one of those peculiar people who could make any lie they told ring more honest than the very truth they obfuscated. The Whisperer, sent to bargain with her late father over some trade dispute with a foreign lord from Ozos, had spoken his pack of lies, led her father by the nose into a duplicitous conspiracy which would have seen him handing over half the family estate in exchange for next to nothing over the following decade. She had picked up on his tone of voice, that snake oil salesman's grin, the unchecked greed, the elation in the way he looked at her father, as if he'd won without having tried at all. She had felt the lie in her body, had known it for what it was, and had called him to task with a battery of questions which left her father first furious at her, and then at him.

# SPIRIT OF SHADOW

Balance was for those chosen few who could call themselves of The Blood, who by some accident had come into such gifts. Balance in that each gift was countered by another, and all of them together might cause a great unraveling. She had known the liar for what he said. It had taken time for her to come around to the understanding he was so good at lying because of what he was.

By the time she rose to high lady of her house, she had not needed further explanation for her gift. It was a part of her, baked into her flesh, housed in her spirit, and she had grown accustomed to using it to great effect.

These Watchers could not touch her, would never violate her. But she could, with enough pressure, compel them to do her bidding...Queen Meredith's bidding.

"You look ill." She said to the one centered before her.

He was Jua, dark-skinned and bald as an egg. His eyes glowed a violent shade of blue, like lightning, as he set his placid regard against her.

"You look just as well as you usually do, she witch." He said.

Several of the others looked away from her. Those had been beaten down over the years, had learned it was in their best interests to be silent.

"What will it be today, woman?" he said. "How many children am I to infest with the latest narrative? What *is* the latest narrative?"

He waggled his wrist impatiently, the chain links tinkling together as the chain wavered to and fro.

"Bring them!" she barked. "Quickly now, I do not have all day!"

A woman rushed into the hall. A small cluster of children followed her like shadows. All of them were eleven or twelve, old enough to be let into the palace but only just. It would be some months before they were left to themselves, and in that time she would need return to this place periodically to ensure they were treated properly.

"Go now, kids. Go to Lady Therien." The woman gestured them forward, not daring to step into their path.

Lady Therien marched forward. A deep shadow coalesced against the palm of her hand. She stood before a Watcher, one of those who had been thoroughly broken, and grasped his neck lightly, bringing his head up so that he looked directly into her eyes. A black eyed gaze peered out from the face of a kitune, and there was fear in that gaze. Fear and obedience both.

"Do it." She said to the Jua man.

"Again, what is this latest narrative? What are they to remember?"

"Just feed them the usual garbage. Start with their early memories. Work your way up from there." She tensed her fingers against the kitune's throat.

"If I play with their earliest memories, it will make for an unstable base on which to build this, if you'll pardon the analogy, house."

"Excuses, you old prick, are like assholes. Everyone has one. Now get to work."

At the behest of the woman, the first child stepped forward. The Jua man bored into his eyes, and the child's head snapped up. He pitched forward onto his knees, and crashed to the ground.

The Watcher worked his jaw as the boy righted himself and stepped obediently down the hall to rejoin the woman.

"No funny business now. You'll only earn this one's death."

"D-don't kill me. Please d-don't...."

"That is not up to me." She cooed. Her gaze shifted to the Jua man. "It is up to him. As long as he does the correct thing, you needn't worry about the state of your life."

"You are truly a disgusting creature." The Jua man said.

# SPIRIT OF SHADOW

"And *you* are wasting my time. Get on with it."

He mumbled something under his breath, a curse for her which she ignored. He complied, and one by one those children fell to their knees, slumped onto the ground and then returned to their handler.

When it was done, she released her hold on the kitune's neck. By then, silent tears were running down the woman's cheeks, and the lady wiped them against her dress. She marched away.

On her way past, the Jua man spat. A thick glob of phlegm sailed across the intervening distance and struck the back of her head.

She spun on her heels, a brutish scowl on her face, her gaze hard and dangerous. "You foul piece of—"

"A parting gift, my lady." A shallow bow, for it was all the chains would permit him.

"Just for that."

She marched up the hall, took up a cleaning towel from the nearest classroom and returned with it. She tied it around his head, blocking his vision, and forced him onto his knees.

Should any of you seek to help, you will be next." She warned them.

"WOMAN!" she bellowed.

The one who had taken the recent graduates from their class to be pacified emerged from the classroom.

"Bring me the hardest, most offending cane you have in this hovel."

She hurried off and returned with a blunt instrument as thick around as her middle finger, and she set to the work of punishing him. Beat him over every inch of his body as the other Watchers shied away from her, refused to look at them as the damage was inflicted.

When she was done, she dropped the Cane on the floor and kicked it out of his reach. She marched away, leaving him a broken ruin against the poured stone.

"Half rations for him until the moon is full."

"He'll die."

"He can be replaced."

She stamped down the hall, swung the door open and slammed it behind her.

"Insolent bastard." She mumbled to herself as she marched off. "What was so wrong about the old system...*why* do we even *need* this blue-eyed scum!"

# Aldeirel

Thorn emerged from the shadows at the foot of Lord Aren's desk. Dressed in black reliefs, the collar of his form-fitting shirt hugging his neck and his trousers neatly pressed, he might have just come from his quarters, but Lord Aren knew differently. He had been expecting him.

The Thorn saluted, his gaze darting to the shepherd's hook hung just behind his master's head. His gaze shifted to the general, and his arms snapped to his sides.

"Your report?" Lord Aren said, setting aside his work. He folded his hands together in his lap, and fixed a stony regard on the Thorn.

"Lady Therien's movements betray a complication to us."

"More of her philandering?"

The Thorn shook his head. "No. That is being dealt with."

"Speak plainly, then."

"I've just come from the Servants' Tunnels. A reach near the entrance to the dungeons. She entered an area that requires certain clearances. However...I have never seen the symbol before."

"The color?"

"Black."

"I see." Lord Aren tapped his knuckles against his knees. "Were you able to learn anything from her?"

"The area does not permit shadow walking. It refuses entry...even to open a doorway."

"Yes, then there is enchanted quartz somewhere inside. A substantial amount."

"I *was* able to glean something. When she returned from that chamber, she was furious. She looked as if she'd just endured some strenuous activity. No, I do not think it had anything to do with the affair.

"She did also say something I thought odd. Something about...'blue-eyed scum."

A chill swept through Lord Aren at that. He kept his expression even.

"You are dismissed. Leave this matter to me. Tell no one of what she said."

"Understood, sir."

The Thorn saluted, and slid back into the shadows, leaving Lord Aren to himself.

"Blue-eyed scum, huh." He mumbled. *How much damage does that woman intend to do. So close to the Emperor's arrival, no less.*


He emerged in the dungeons, an gloomy expanse. Glow bulbs shed strong light at regular intervals, but the spacing of those glass orbs allowed for deep shadows to pool in between, the better to invite a rapid response in the unlikely event of a prisoner escape.

Rebels occupied most of the cells in this stretch. Some were retainers from the lost times of Queen Tania, deemed too close to her to be trusted under the new regime. It was, perhaps, not common for a newly emerged queen to jail her predecessor's agents, in particular her elites who often had ties to high houses; but then it was not common for a lowborn youth to rise to the station of Shadow Queen either.

It would be so much simpler to do away with the old tradition, to establish a regime which expressed its power matrilineally so that power was inherited and not simply given, but Shadovane could not afford to be so short-sighted...so frivolous in their expression of power. No, there was power in the way they conducted this business. It just happened that power was volatile, and the current expression of it was, to put it politely, antisocial.

It was no secret to him why the old regime had been pulled down. Nor was it any secret why Lord Elise, a man barely into his thirties who had served as a Bloodless for a handful of years, was not their ruler. No secret either why she tolerated Lord Cree's frequent attempts to poison his more problematic subordinates, or the occasional low-born nobleman who got on his bad side. The queen had proven to be politically savvy, yes, but she was more a monster than any who had come before her since at least Queen Mariah's time.

He marched through the dungeon, his bronze-shod boots beating a rhythm as he passed by those rebels, many of them who he had known in his youth. If he shared little in common with his queen, he knew what it was to be born in the slums. A boy in the Second Turn had few choices if he wanted to escape the extreme poverty so common to that area, a problem that had only gotten worse with her rise. He could join the military, or he could leave...venture out into the world in hopes that he would escape the attention of the Wraiths and Thorns who would undoubtedly pursue him. He *might* find himself in a place of safety, in the Ring of Fire perhaps, if he could find his way to Star Island on the northern side, or to Amsol. If he was lucky, he might get to

**Aldeirel**

Daemonheim and the dense forests around that ancient relic, the Norenberg, but that posed its own complications.

Join the military, or run away and hope he could find a place of safety. The easy option was also the hardest one. Many of these were men who would have made fine Wraiths, or Mauls...who might have become Thorns under his lordship if they proved themselves worthy. Yet they had chosen a different path, to defend their city from itself, to save it from one of their own, and time and again they had witnessed failure. Had been pulled into the shadows, their secret meetings broken up, their ploys to assassinate this tyrannical queen thwarted. Much of that had been by his own hand, something he had come to treat with ambivalence.

He recognized the faces of those elder, who had grown up with him, who had risked everything for their cause. Emaciated ruins of their former selves, some bearing dark, yellowing bruises where they had been beaten at some point in the recent past, or wounds of other stripes.

He had been like them once, and he had chosen his path. Not for nothing, he respected them for their tenacity, but it was all useless in the grand scheme. A new queen would rise when the old one was deposed, and so the cycle continued, and it was all because of a pendant. A silly trinket which legend said housed a fragment of a goddess's soul, which chose who would become queen, as an extension of Her will.

He turned corner, followed an adjacent hall almost to its end. There were no more prisoners in this section of the dungeons. None within ear shot of the man who had, for much of his life, commanded the highest price among them, the greatest priority for his capture.

He halted in front of Aldeirel's cell. Safe behind cadmium bars, he could not hope to use magic, to pull down the Cosmic Orchestra, as the uninitiated called it, for his use. But it was not his command of magic that made the man dangerous. Here was a man who bled hope from his veins, who inspired others with the power of his voice, with his sermons in the slums along the cliffs. Here was a man who had become a Thorn in the side of the crown, who had only recently been captured...not for the first time.

Lord Aren stood on one side of the bars, watched as the man labored to get his feet under him, to approach them from the other. His back was bent horribly under the labor of keeping himself up, and he clutched his knees as arthritic joints worked to move his feet, to slide one and then the other forward. With the use of a cane, he might be able to make greater progress, but even then he was disadvantaged by advancing cataracts that had left him nearly blind.

His voice came out reedy and thin when he spoke.

"This is a rare treat." He said. "You coming to call on me. What might you be after, old friend."

"That you still see me as such holds its own virtues." Lord Aren said.

"Were it that I believed you were infatuated with this regime's philosophy, Silas, I would perceive you very differently, I suppose. But you were never that man. Not susceptible to the propaganda they feed the young ones.

"Have you thwarted the great rebellion, yet?"

Lord Aren bit his tongue.

Aldeirel nodded. "I did not think so. Well, out with it, then. You would not have come here without a purpose."

"Amaia seyan ojahs ar'delantia, lothor." He said.

"Do you think he will answer?"

"I know he will."

"Ah, but there is another complication floating about in this palace, isn't there. Another one who can hear him, who might just steal away his loyalty."

"You sense him from this distance."

"Like a bonfire, Silas. Like a bonfire. Such warmth...it is a comfort, I will not lie. It has been long years since I witnessed

**Aldeirel**

the arrival of a Seem."

"Not since you yourself were born, yes?"

"Oh, it would not be fair to say as much as that. It is a rare thing, though, isn't it. Perhaps he shares the blood of Laula."

"Perhaps, but that is of no concern just now. I have come because I believe you may know something of a certain program. A certain woman's role in it."

"Ah ha ha." Aldeirel chuckled. "What do you want to know."

"Do the words 'blue-eyed scum' mean anything to you. As spoken by her."

"Perhaps. It may be that she is useful to the queen in an oblique way. In supporting the overall...*environment*...she needs in order to maintain her hold on the city's elites. On their hearts and minds. Comfort, after all, goes a long way in enticing others to put up with bad behavior."

"The scum she speaks of?"

"Watchers, I think." Aldeirel turned hard eyes on Lord Aren then. "A wasted opportunity, if you ask me. If you know where they are, why have you not sought to use them. You have an entire supply of patsies at your disposal, don't you? You might have cleaned house a long time ago."

"If I could gain their trust." He said. "I must wonder how *she* succeeded."

"Oh, I doubt its anything as innocent at that. Gifts of the Blood are Five. Just that. You have been exposed to two of them just in this conversation. Then there are the Whisperers, who may be of some use against Watchers, but must inherently be unreliable for their ability to convince others of mistruths. Then there are Seers, but they have little bearing on the matter at hand. And last, Shields, who serve as a perfect counter to the Watcher's gift.

"If she was one of mine, I suppose I might have made use of her somewhere down the line." He gestured airily, and smiled crookedly, his teeth clamping together, making the effort seem painful. "But then she is not, is she?"

"This has been...enlightening." Lord Aren said. "For your cooperation, I will see to it that you are compensated. A nice meal. Perhaps a wash."

"For all of your many faults, you were always fair." Aldeirel acknowledged.

He turned on his heels and marched away, a scheme half-formed in his head.

# The Core

Lance stood in front of a mirror, looking himself over while the off-color music of snoring night crew workers drifted up from around a bend in the barracks wall. What few servants were still around were nearly all snug in their beds with their coverlets pulled over their heads to block out the noontime sun drifting through the windows, just beginning its trek toward the evening low.

By the light of that very same sun, he looked himself over. Golden eyes stared back at him from within a pale, angular face. His nose was slender and slightly crooked, his cheekbones low and broad. His hair dripped with water from a poured stone basin, which was cast in a mold so that the working along the edge resembled briars. He gripped it with white knuckled fists.

Soon enough, chicken feathers would begin to creep out of the mass of straight, silver-blonde hair. He might think about smoothing them, then, a nervous habit. He hoped he could maintain his cool.

Ben had invited him to join him in the Core, had passed the message on through Ariana just that morning. He suspected the location and time were Ariana's suggestion. He had intended to do the asking himself, of course, but time and all of his worries had gotten away from him, leaving him uncertain whether he should make the first move or wait for this would be suitor to take the initiative.

# SPIRIT OF SHADOW

*If it could just be like this all the time.* He thought, looking himself over.

He touched the side of his neck, where a wound so old he sometimes forgot it was there at all stood out in a darker shade against the skin. He could not remember how he had come by it, but it must have happened in early childhood. If he remembered so much of his life in the palace, those earliest years were a different matter.

Letting his hand drop, he turned from the mirror, and headed out of his barracks.

*Time I got to the Core.* The thought that Ben might not be there when he arrived, that he might not show up at all, crossed his mind. He pushed it down forcefully, yet it lingered in the periphery, waiting for the first sign he had been duped to come storming back into the fore, where it would put down roots and invite all of his great and small insecurities back into him. Right now, he was feeling brave. Brave enough, certainly, to entertain this...whatever it was...*date?*

*He'll be there. He wouldn't stand me up like that.*

Halfway across the palace from the Servant's Tower and his barracks, he entered a cylindrical garden through a wrought-bronze gate designed in the image of peonies and plum blossoms. The garden was full of trees and bright flowers, a broad array of different kinds which suffused the air with their perfume, quite unbothered by the chill air or a bitter winter looming just over the horizon.

Gardeners, a class of servants with some knowledge of horticultural magic, kept the flowers in bloom and the leaves on the trees whole and green in defiance of the natural passage of seasons. While the world beyond the palace walls descended into autumn, and the leaves on oak, maple and birch turned vivid red and yellow, then dropped from their bows, the gardens and the flowers scattered throughout the halls of the palace remained, heralding a never ending spring.

He closed the gate behind him, and traveled away along a winding, river stone pathway which took him toward the garden's heart. The Core was called, by the nobility, the Hall of Glory, and was originally designed to be a cunning trap in wartime, for the defense of the palace, which was meant to look like an easy regrouping point for an invading force. The bricks had been laid at angle, similar in some ways to a tortoise shell, with ridges protruding from the bottoms and slick faces

## The Core

which tapered near their height to become flush with the walls. They were designed to provide the illusion of hand-holds for climbing, and rose to level with a series of windows on each of the four floors framing it.

From the windows, soldiers might lob from narrow windows along those curved walls. They could weaponize every tree and shrub with fire, lob projectiles of all kinds at the enemy, and the enemy would be helpless as long as they remained there. What was more, the halls immediately surrounding the garden had no direct connections, no conveyances which might lead from one floor to another, and some of the doors in those hallways were false, leading into nothing but poured stone.

If they were nothing else, the Shadovani elves of old were cunning. This garden had been modified some four hundred years in the past, when times in the Sun Empire were tumultuous, and rebellion was becoming a common feature in the north lands. Since then, the Hall of Glory, the Core, had become a place of quiet ambiance for those who wished for a moment's peace to reflect and enjoy the scenery. It had become a popular place for servants to meet, in the colder months, as the nobility seldom ventured beyond their halls except to travel into the countryside.

It was, he reflected, a perfect setting to get to know someone. Be it Ben's idea or Ariana's, they had chosen well.

Lance walked the spiral pathway toward his destination. The most obvious place for them to meet would be at the garden's heart. He came around a bend in the path, and latched eyes onto something he should not see. Something which would, nonetheless, be burned into his mind's eye for some time, unshakable for its absurdity.

A lady lounged on a park bench, her arms spread over its backrest, her fingers twined in the bars. She wore a dress with a plunging neckline which exposed her supple, milky breasts. Her eyes were closed and her head upturned.

She gasped. Her chest heaved, and her hips shifted backward, ground into the backrest.

Lance looked down the front of her dress. Her skirts were flared outward, and a third and fourth leg, turned outward with knees set against the ground and draped in light-gray cloth, peaked out from underneath them. A man was settled between her legs, and the skirts twitched with the movement of his shoulders. Her own legs were propped on top of them, her moccasins carving twisting arcs through still air.

He recognized the woman—he had seen her not so long ago—and lingered for a moment, wondering who her latest toy was. Had Ben not said this latest beau was a military man, a young soldier? He wondered if it was anyone he would recognize; and, fearing he might be caught up in her antics, that he may face harsh punishment over it, he moved on.

Lady Therien's head descended, and her eyes fluttered open.

Lance ducked behind a shrub, avoiding her eye, but she seemed to suspect something anyway, and pressed her skirts down around her suitor's shoulder.

Her skirts parted as the suitor threw them off of him. He cast about for what had disturbed her, and Lance fixed him in his sights. He did recognize him, and suddenly understood why Ben had been so insistent on exercising caution with this one. Indeed, if her husband discovered them, things would get messy not just for her, but for anyone who was perceived to have known what went on between them.

*Lord Tarkenta?*

He was a man that minded of a statue, with chiseled features, high cheekbones, a beak of a nose and somewhat sunken eyes. His hair was streaked with iron-gray strands, which had pushed in from the sides so that the original black was less than a handful scattered under the gray.

"What? Was it too sloppy?" He asked her.

"No." she said. "I thought…never mind. You may continue."

He plunged back under her skirts, and she tilted her chin up once more, closed her eyes and purred while he did his work.

Lance took the opportunity to leave.

*That was close.* He thought, amused and at the same time aware he had narrowly avoided a trip to Lady Tamalsen's office for a caning. *To think she'd take the risk. With all of those windows.*

He found Ben sitting on the ledge of a fountain. The fountain's centerpiece was a sculpture made to look like a cliff with several disk-like rises climbing along its sides, forming a spiral with roads like catwalks connecting one rise to the next. It was meant to be a model of Mirrhvale, where the Emperor lived, and it had not always been there. The centerpieces in the Core's fountain changed with the seasons, with sculptors submitting their proposals for consideration and one high lady or another lord approving the design for any given season. The winter's design had been postponed for something more intimately associated with the coming event, and so a piece of Mirrhvale had come to live in Shadovane, to delight the palace residents and its visitors with notions of a far away place, and all the romance it offered.

Fish of various kinds flitted about in the moat. Minnows traveled in schools among rocks and reeds while fat carp drifted lazily along with the current.

He watched as Ben thrust his hand into the pool, water and foam spraying away from the sight of impact. Harassed fish darted away as he came out empty handed, and followed their travels with a sad look on his face.

Lance approached him, wondering what he meant to accomplish with this strange game as he repeated the action, again coming up empty handed.

He sat next to him. "Hi again."

Ben spun toward him. He overbalanced and fell into the pool back first, catching himself in the knee-deep water on both arms just before his head submerged.

Lance chuckled. "I didn't mean to scare you."

"You uh…it happens." Ben said.

"Are you okay?" Lance held out a hand that Ben took, helped him onto the ledge.

"I'm fine. A little wet"—he gestured at himself— "But otherwise good."

"What were you doing?"

"I was tryin' to catch a fish. I did it once before. I wanted to see if I could again. Is that weird? It's weird, isn't it?"

Lance shrugged. "It's not the weirdest thing I've seen today."

"What is?" He pulled his shirt over his head—revealing again his slender torso, coin-sized nipples, eggshell skin—and set it aside.

Heat flooded into Lance's cheeks.

He grinned. The sun touched his eyes and added its warmth to them, bringing out the red beneath the brown.

"When you said Lady Therien was seeing a soldier…."

Ben guffawed. "You saw them? Are they here?"

"They're just past that bend." Lance said quietly, pointing up the direction he had come.

"We should probably take this somewhere else, then."

"The laundry, maybe?"

He looked himself over. His pants were still sodden, and his shirt—now hung over his arm, streamed water onto the tiles. He shrugged. "Maybe."

"It's closer than the Servant's Tower."

"Yeah, and I'd be short a uniform if we went there anyway. Bright side is Mistress Rosaline is usually willing to part with a fresh change no questions asked."

"You've had to do this before?"

"Yep."

"Is there a story there?"

"Nothing crazy. Just occupational hazards of the work I do. Sometimes something spills…or explodes all over you."

A brief but pointed image flashed across Lance's mind. He stuffed that down, too. "Shall we?" he gestured down a path that led in the opposite direction from which he had come.

Ben led the way, past apple blossoms and then into the warmer reaches of the halls. He shivered as they crossed the threshold, the warmth reminding him just how much colder the garden was than the halls.

"So…about the other day." Lance said.

"I don't mind." Ben said too quickly. "I haven't told anyone what happened and I'm not going to. Besides, it's not your fault you have a…well, anyway."

"You're sure?"

"I'm sure. But let's put that to bed. I kind of hoped you'd show up."

"Ariana came up with the idea, didn't she?"

"She was really persistent. I was going to ask you today, anyway, but she wanted details. Plans. Thought I couldn't handle coming up with an idea on my own, apparently."

"So, she settled on the Core?"

"No, that was my idea. She floated the Teacher's Tower."

"That's unlike her."

"Well, it makes a kind of sense. No one bothers the servants there, and the views from the top level are spectacular. Especially around sunset."

"Maybe next time then." Lance said.

A shadow of doubt darkened Ben's expression.

"Shit, sorry. I don't mean to…I mean…I just put my foot in my mouth, didn't I?"

"It's okay. I just thought…never mind."

"We're okay?"

"Of course."

They talked at length as they ventured through the corridors, took the first opportunity to exit into the servants tunnels. They were no glamorous place to travel, but they provided a necessary measure of discretion. It did not do to be seen in such a state of disrepair as Ben currently was by the nobility. Word would get back to Lady Therien or Lady Tamalsen or both before long then, and he would be punished, trivial though the reason was.

They arrived at the laundry. Ben did not mention the need to take the slower, more mundane route to get there, did not mention the strange sensation that stole over Lance when he was exposed to shadow walking, seemingly even small doses.

The laundry was a cavernous space not unlike the Furnaces in its design, except that instead of giant, metal boxes, wide-mouthed tip kettles occupied most of the space, and on elevated rises were drying lines populated with noble wears. The servants' uniforms went into tumblers which one servant spun while others blasted air and raw heat into the chamber.

Ben led him around these contraptions to the back, mounted a narrow, wrought-bronze staircase to an elevated rise where a lone desk rested. The Mistress of the Laundry reclined in a wingback chair with her feet resting on the edge of the desk.

Mistress Rosaline was of Harua descent, but taller than Ariana by a head. She was middle aged, not as old as Mistress Dina or Master Gregor but still older than most servants by at least a decade. Planar cheekbones were drawn down over a round chin, and jet black hair was tied in a neat tail behind her head. She wore the white uniform of a servant, not the black more fitting of a woman of her station, but then no one was going to come to call on her about it. No one of consequence ever bothered to come down here.

Her eyebrow quirked up at the sight of Ben, a complete lack of

# SPIRIT OF SHADOW

surprise traced across her fine features.

Her gaze shifted to Lance.

"You brought a friend."

"Yeah…well, I kind of embarrassed myself."

"Should I even ask?"

"It's not a very good story."

She cocked her thumb in the direction of a series of racks against the wall, all loaded down with fresh linens and changes. "Take what you need."

"Thank you, Mistress Rosaline."

They ambled over to the racks. She followed them with her gaze. "You know I'm not used to seeing a guy coming in looking like that. They usually don't bring their *friends* with them either."

"Oh shut up!" he groused, as he poured over the shelves in search of a new shirt, undergarments and trousers. He selected out the items in his size, pulled them down and started undressing.

Lance turned away, a bright flush creeping across his cheeks. He met Mistress Rosaline's eye and shied away.

"Never seen a naked guy before?" she asked.

"It's just…we only just…."

She nodded, her tongue pressed against her cheek. "Yeah. I can see that."

"Could you cut the guy a little slack." Ben said.

"It's really okay." Lance twisted round to mollify him, caught him pulling on a new pair of socks. He was otherwise naked.

He twisted sharply around to face Mistress Rosaline, his face beet red.

"Fun date?" Mistress Rosaline asked Ben.

"It's getting interesting. That's for sure."

"You gonna go for a second round."

"This *is* the second round."

"So you like him?"

"Y-yeah. I suppose I do."

"Good."

"Good?" Lance echoed.

"Good." Ben said. "As long as you like me too."

"I-I do. S-so far. A-are you decent?"

"Decent enough." Mistress Rosaline said.

Lance turned around again. Ben was there, standing a few inches from him with a clean shirt in one hand and his pants securely on. He backed up a step. "Are you okay?"

"Sorry, I just…."

"Stop talking, please." Mistress Rosaline said. "You can see he's trying to go for it, right? Just let him kiss you."

Lance froze, cast about at several objects, avoiding looking at Ben far too long. Ben laced his fingers into his, drew him closer. "It's okay. She's just messin' with you." He said. "Wants a performance she's not gettin'."

He looked to her over Lance's shoulder, a grin spread across his lips.

She stuck her tongue out at him. "You're no fun.

"Put your shirt on. Get out of here."

He slipped into the shirt, turned around and made a rude gesture at her.

"Should you be—"

"Don't worry. We're friends."

"All…alright."

"So, you want to see me again?"

"Yes." Lance said, deflating.

"Good. I want to see you too. Let's plan next week."

"I can't."

"Why not?"

"Lady Tamalsen assigned me to the reception ceremony."

"Well great! She'll have you workin' with us. I can see if Lady Therien will put in a word to have you placed with me."

"You'd do that?"

"Of course." He grinned. "How else am I going to convince you of my merits?"

Lord Aren emerged from the shadows. It was not his way to involve himself in affairs better handled by others, but there were so few in the palace he could trust absolutely. There were those he tolerated, even liked, among Shadovane's elites, but trust was such a fickle thing. If he was discovered to be involved in this current task he would, at best, be court marshaled. But then, if this operation was successful, he needn't worry overmuch about what those posh aristocrats and peacetime generals thought of him.

He wondered what the Emperor would do were he to discover the Shadow Queen had been harboring Watchers.

Certainly, whatever punishment he doled out would be handled in private. The common rabble would never know anything was amiss. Even those closest to her would only have conjecture to rely on. Sudden shifts in her affect, an occasional outburst maybe. She was not a long tempered woman.

Would he have her executed? Quietly replaced with a loyal ally? Or would he satisfy himself with having her watched, lorded over by a hand selected sitter, to ensure she would engage in no more scheming without his express knowledge.

It occurred to him that the emperor may even know of her plots, be they intended to mollify the nobility or to undermine him. This use of a Watcher's talents was so frivolous. He could almost believe she was so small minded, so ignorant to the abstract potentials of these beings. Had it been Queen Anastasia or Mariah, he suspected they would have wielded the power of those captives openly against that ancient creature, would have carved a path across the empire as they carved a path into his mind, and forced him to his knees.

But to do so in their time would have invited a greater discord. In this time as well.

*They would have doomed themselves, then. She would now, if she saw fit to rail so hard against him.*

He held a grimoire in his hand, a book of black magic. The melodies and harmonies contained in that book would invite the subtlest expressions of death onto whomever fell victim to them. A servant would never dare to be found in possession of such a tome, and that was precisely why he had chosen it. Death rites were not the provenance of any outside the military. He supposed some of those more conniving nobles may have made a study of the rites, may even have gleaned some useful insights from them, but even they would be few. Politics in Shadovane was not the deadly game it had been some four hundred or so years back. Lady Christine, Daughter of Queen Anastasia, had not risen against her parents yet. Had not carved out her oasis, invited her mother's jealousy.

Danger and wrath, twin prongs of the tuning fork, had come from inside. There had been no great threat from outside the city in those days...so the histories said, anyway.

He stood before a servant's bed. The servant was sleeping, unaware of her visitor, and he made a point of keeping it that way. An almost lyrical sentence formed in his mind's eye, and he spoke the words in that ancient language first taught to the stone people by the spirits, who commanded magic. The words, once spoken, drew power from the elements, suffused the air with them, a request of one spirit, whose dominion was dreams and sleep.

"Bagani oman, Chara." *Spin your threads. Hold her in your embrace until I have departed.*

"*She is not yours to hold.*" The spirit answered.

"She will not be harmed. Only used." He whispered.

"*Still.*"

He traced embossed lettering against the grimoire's leather face with his fingers.

"Someone must draw their eyes." He said. "She is one of those who poses little risk. And *they* will see in her...hope. Will you not embrace her, because I have asked."

"*This once, He Who Remembers the Way. But tread lightly, lest I draw you into my embrace. Eternally.*"

He nodded. "Thank you, Spirit *Chara*. I will not forget."

Warmth bubbled forth from him as he pressed his thumb to the sleeping servant's forehead, bled into her, bound her into what he hoped was a pleasant dream. He retracted his

# SPIRIT OF SHADOW

hand, and slipped the grimoire under her mattress.

# The Teacher's Tower

ance!" Ben shouted. "Lance, you in here?"

He had never been in the fourth floor barracks. There hadn't been much incentive to climb so high with his own bunk on the second floor and his friend, Rashanna, hulled up on the first. The scattering of romantic entanglements he had entertained over the span of his short life had mostly been matters of convenience, with men who were in close proximity to him. Most of those bunked in the same quarters as him, the only one who hadn't had been an ill conceived foray into the workplace affair, with another courier, and he had never come to call on him.

Each floor was interchangeable with the next. Bunk beds were arranged around the barrel shaft at the heart of the tower where access to the staircase and the subterranean levels where the canteen and the showers were kept could be found. A Wraith was posted outside at all hours of the day, and their shift changes occurred at predictable intervals. The walls were all heavy slabs mortared together around tall and narrow windows, a relic of wartime since outfitted with glass panes and wooden bars to lend a certain, utilitarian ambiance to the expanse, and though there were far more servants milling about in this quarter, they were nonetheless mostly reading or napping after their shifts.

Some few huddled atop or around their beds in clusters, chatting away about the day's events, but those clusters were uncommon. Most servants here seemed to favor other reaches for those activities, just as they did on his floor.

For a moment, he wondered if he had the wrong time. If he had misremembered when Lance told him to meet him. Evening painted the sky in fiery shades, and fat clouds drifted across horizon above a series of cliffs that blocked all sight for the sky, the sun and the moon from sight on his floor.

He envied Lance that view.

He had lived in the shadow of those cliffs as long as he could remember; was only able to lay eyes on the open sky when he visited the Core, or the Royal Gardens, or the Teacher's Tower...but those latter places weren't always safe, and he rarely ventured into them before dark. He supposed it was a privilege of a kind, traveling through the shadows, being able to engage in the limited rebellion he could...what the Wraiths turned a blind eye to. He was not so bold as to think they did not know what the Couriers got into at night, but then sneaking off into some quiet reach of the tower, pilfering the kitchen storerooms for treats and the occasional drink was hardly criminal behavior.

"Lance?" He halted halfway down the hall, looked to the interior side first, and then the window. A smile touched his lips. "There you are."

Lance was snug in his bed, awake but with a book propped

against his knees and a thoughtful expression on his face.

He approached the bed, and sat beside his feet. And waited for him to notice.

Lance looked over the top of the book, a startled expression was quickly displaced by a returning smile. "Fancy seeing you here."

"What are you readin'?"

Lance turned over the book, showed him the cover. "Tales of the Five. As far as the titles they'll let us have go, it's my favorite."

"You ever thought about asking for somethin' else?"

Lance chuckled. "I don't see Lady Tamalsen being very helpful with that."

"You'd be surprised. I have a copy of The Collected Works of Sura tucked under my mattress right now. I've had it since I chose my path."

"Did she give you that *because* you chose the couriers, or was it out of the kindness of her heart." Lance closed the book and set it aside.

"Probably because of my decision. She was pressurin' me into it pretty hard." Ben said.

He patted Lance's knee. "You ready?"

"Sure."

He waited as his suitor tucked the book away and climbed out of bed, as he slipped black moccasins onto his feet and then dusted his hair into a more uniform shape. It proved a useless effort, as the chicken feathers simply chose different directions to lay.

They left the Servant's Tower together, Lance reaching out and lacing his fingers into his before they were well out of the fourth floor barracks. The Wraith stationed there favored them with an amused half grin as they departed, which he did not miss. He laid a kiss on Lance's cheek as they came to the door onto the stairs, and Lance's face turned scarlet.

They took the long way, through the Servant's Tunnels,

and he was glad that they did. Though it would have been more expedient to make use of the shadows, he found himself quite engrossed in conversation as they navigated the palace underbelly on their way to its northeast corner.

Conversation came easily now, and flowed until they had reached their destination. They talked of Lance's coming choice and the Emperor's arrival, of their friends and how they had met them, and a host of other foundational subjects.

Arriving at the Teacher's Tower saw a soft silence descend over them, and he thought it might be anticipation on Lance's part. That perhaps he had thoughts for what this adventure meant, the frontiers they might cross. He was not oblivious to the reputation this tower had, either; but he was not ready for that just yet. Today was about building trust, about getting to know each other better, and if something more did happen...well, that was just as might be.

"It's kind of a hike getting up there." He said as they approached the entrance onto another staircase.

"About the same distance as getting from the canteen to my barracks, right?"

"The Servant's Tower is a little shorter than this one. Maybe by a floor or two. I don't usually take the long way."

"So that's *eight* floors?"

"If we're goin' to the top. The views up there are spectacular."

"I'm not opposed to it. My calves, you see..." Lance thrust out a leg and twisted it theatrically. "...are pretty well developed."

Ben chuckled. "Good to know."

He pulled open the cedar door onto the staircase. The old servant's entrance to the upper floors sawed back and forth along the posterior wall, and windows let in light from the outside at each landing. Old cupboards were situated on those landings next to back entrances into the halls within, which would have allowed the palace janitorial staff of old to enter unseen by the children of Shadovane's elites. With the main entrance blocked off, it was the most convenient means of accessing the upper floors, and the shortest.

"Sometimes I wonder why Queen Meredith closed this school down." He said. "With her temperament, you'd think she would want as much influence as she could have over her peers kids."

"You're assuming it was by choice. A lot of those kids probably belonged to country lords."

"Who pulled them out when she rose to power." He rubbed his cheek. "It makes a kind of sense.

"Anyway, we're here."

The came to a halt on the final landing. A narrow staircase rose higher from the broader steps climbing down from this floor, and bottomed out against the ceiling, where a trap door was situated.

"Is that where we're going?" Lance asked.

"No. No, no." Ben shook his head. "That's the roof access. Maybe if it was summer it'd be nice to go up there, but its bitter cold this time of year."

He tipped his chin in the direction of the door in front of them. "This is the entrance."

Lance reached for the knob, pushed the door inward. They were met with unrelieved darkness on the other side, and Ben took point as they entered.

Lance lingered in the stairwell until the first shafts of light broke through the gloom. Ben worked thick, velvet curtains aside, sending motes of dust skirling away into the air.

He returned to the entrance when the last of those curtains was parted, took Lance's hand, and led him into the chamber.

What furniture had served whoever occupied this chamber remained, a call back to a time when it had been inhabited, at least temporarily, by someone. A heavy, ornately tooled desk rested before the bank of windows on the western side, and a wine-red, wingback chair sat behind it. The feet of the desk were made of brass, and an ornate seal was fixed against its face. The seal was encrusted with jewels—topaz and peridot, onyx, turquoise, and diamond—and Lance was fixated on it.

Along the walls were other fineries, trophies from who knew where, relics to show off the wealth and wisdom befitting a person of influence. There was a hide buckler with several feathers dangling from it, a boxy, personal vault situated atop an ebony table, and a harp which began plucking notes of its own accord when he passed by it.

Lance jumped at the sound of the music, and Ben squeezed his hand to comfort him.

"It's okay." He said.

"What is this place?"

"The Headmaster's Office. I don't know much about him, but they say he was a gifted enchanter. Some of this was his work."

"Wh...where is he now? I'd think I'd have heard of him...if he was still here."

"Probably dead. It's been a long time since Queen Meredith took office and shut this school down. If he's alive, I bet he lives out in the country somewhere."

"They just left this stuff here?"

"To be honest, I don't think they care much what he had squirreled away up here. That vault doesn't open. I tried, but it burned my fingers as soon as I touched the lock."

"Ouch."

"The harp is nice, though. Kind of comforting when you get used to it. And the desk is really fun."

"That's enchanted, too?"

"Yep."

"What's it do?"

Ben led him around to the chair behind it and helped him

into the seat. He positioned himself behind it. "I don't know what it does when you use other kinds of magic on it, but...just watch."

Lance grit his teeth as he went through the motions of performing the limited bit of magic he knew. The humdrum sounds of the harp playing its notes, the wind whistling against the windows, drifted away, leaving a pocket of silence to be filled by something else. From the silence came a chaotic tangle of other sounds, instrumental noises all clashing with each other, each one seeking dominance over the others, succeeding for a brief moment before being crushed under the weight of all the others.

He listened for the ones he needed, and dragged them out of the cacophony, the Cosmic Orchestra, yanked hard with his soul as if he were fishing, and compelled them to him. The other sounds died away, leaving just a broody harmony, a thread of music through which ran dark power.

He pressed his hand to the desk with the harmony playing in his ears, a harmony heavier with two elements than any others, *sa* and air. He heard them as percussive, vibrant, almost electrical sounds, with woodwind accompaniment.

The desk was spurred to life. Light punched out of its face and struck a blank patch of wall across from it, just above that vault. Colors shifted, arranged themselves into the image of a shadow elf, a Wraith clad just in his loincloth, with bands of script running across his torso, slithering around his bicep. Missing was the image of another elf who might be kin. Instead, ornate script in the language of Shadovane formed an intricate knot where the image should be.

"Watch."

A gruff voice spoke as the image began to move through simple forms. The Wraith stood in place with its eyes closed. Its shadow deepened from the usual shade to matte black, and then he dropped into it. Darkness swam around the Wraith, and with his eyes still closed, he navigated through it.

# SPIRIT OF SHADOW

"Shadow walking is a delicate dance." The voice claimed. "For the unpracticed, it poses significant danger, as the practitioner, unattended by a more experienced instructor, may be exposed to the Dark Heart, those ill feelings in mortal beings, which in shadow possess power to harm the body, and the spirit. A wary practitioner must learn to embrace silence, and thus form a pocket around himself in which their voices cannot be heard, for speaking is the purest essence of the Dark Heart's power."

Ben removed his hand before the disembodied voice could say more.

"It keeps going." He said. "But I don't want to risk showing you more until you've made your choice."

"Lest you be killed." Lance mumbled.

"Yeah. Something like that."

"Master Gregor told me about all the risks of working in a department that uses magic." Lance twisted around to face him. "And I made my choice, by the way. Lady Tamalsen assigned me to the emperor's reception ceremony to try to talk me out of it, but I want to work in the Furnaces. I think it's for the best that I take Lord Aren's advice."

Ben shrugged. "They're good people down there. A little rough around the edges, but that's okay. Just watch out for Emma. She's kind of a cunt."

"Emma?"

"Tiny thing. Short hair. Looks like she chews rocks for a living."

Lance nodded. "I met her. She didn't tell me her name...didn't really introduce herself, in fact. I see what you mean."

"She's also second in command after Master Gregor down there, so you probably shouldn't piss her off."

"Good to know. So this view."

Lance climbed out of the chair. He turned around to face

the windows, slid his arm around the small of Ben's back and pulled him close.

It was Ben's turn to blush. "It's somethin' isn't it?"

"Yeah."

The windows revealed a sprawling view of the outside world. This high up, they were almost at the same height as the cliffs. From the roof, the tops of them were plainly visible, an expanse of plains lands crawling all the way to the horizons.

Along the cliffs were homes carved directly into the rock. Narrow staircases zigzagged back and forth and broader paths were planed out against the sheer, broken faces. Down below were the homes of commoners, all wooden structures, some with tiled roofs still intact though most were fitted with straw where the tiling had fallen to ruin. A network of narrow channels and broad thoroughfares formed a web spanning from the feet of the palace outward, the radial avenues providing the best routes for trader's carts, and the connecting side streets closer, more intimate.

People populated those streets, and all of them were elven. Children played on dusty avenues, mothers washed linens in tubs in quaint yards and hung the laundry to dry on thin lines which spanned the distance between houses. Merchants and farmers brought in wares for the common folk to quibble over, though most of the wagons marching into the city from beyond the first turn did not stop for them. Most came directly to the palace, where they would find better prices for their goods—or perhaps they were bound by agreements to service the palace and all of its nobility, it staff, and the military before attending to the needs of the city beyond.

He would not have called that city beautiful, tried not to look too closely at those dilapidated homes or the state of health and dress those people were in. He looked to Lance, to see in his face what he thought of the city in twilight, what he thought of those high cliffs and winding passes etched into his face.

He was comforted to find the same wonder there as he had experienced the first time he ventured into this place.

"It's incredible." Lance said, turning to meet his gaze.

"There's nothing quite like it." Ben agreed.


Sami awaited her date in an old classroom in the upper levels of the Teacher's Tower. The last flame had guttered and died quickly, and a new spark had been kindled in a woman who worked in the Palace Treasury. She was eager to meet with her, anticipation and a scattering of salacious thoughts already warming her in that peculiar way they always did when she was approaching first contact. Static surges flared across her nerves, and a heady fog had settled in her mind as she contemplated her surroundings.

The classroom was her favored place for trysts of a less than wholesome persuasion. A heavy carpet lay on the floor, and writing desks were stacked and pushed in from the walls, so that narrow channels created the impression of a maze with her chosen spot at the center. Some time after the tower had been abandoned, someone had taken the initiative to move those desks out of the other classrooms on this floor, so that those were largely empty and this became a storage room all the brick brack that once helped them function. Bookshelves broke up the stacked desks, and those, too, were mostly empty, but she had taken several candles from a storeroom in the Servants' Tunnels, which now populated those low shelves, the flames wavering with subtle breezes, occasionally crackling as they chewed up their wicks.

Close quarters made for intimate encounters, and as the moment drew near, she arranged herself on the rug, tousled strawberry blonde locks to give herself that fresh out of bed look that made so many girls swoon, and unbuttoned her shirt, tossing the collar off one shoulder so that her cleavage was obvious, not hinted at but on full display.

Her liaison would be here any moment now. *She's probably climbing the stairs by now.*

A small basin lay behind one of those desks, a rag nestled into cold water. She had taken it from the same storeroom months ago, for the event she or her partner wanted to wipe down before they left. Sometimes, these conquests turned messy. When the clothes came off, and the fun was well under way—fingers and tongues roving over bodies, squeezing soft breasts and asses, and exploring other, warmer and wetter places—they could get messy, indeed.

The door fell inward, a slice of harsher light cutting through the gloom in that direction, painting a bar of orange light against the floor tiles. She adjusted her pose, pulled her shirt lower onto her arm, rearranged her breasts. She pursed her lips, then, thinking better of it, tried on a different expression, something more casual. A smile alighted on her lips and then fell away. She wanted to be attainable, inviting, but not too inviting. She wanted to be seen as a sexual being, but she did not want to be perceived as a slut.

"Laurel?" she asked. "Is that you? I'm over here."

No answer.

*She likes to play games.*

She liked games. She liked breaking games.

The door warbled closed, the bar of light receding, leaving them in the room together, to play this game of hide and seek by candlelight before the main event transpired.

"Don't keep me waiting too long, now. I've been so patient waiting for you, but I don't know how much longer I can—"

A hand clamped over her mouth. A scream welled up in her throat and then died. The hand was soft, the palm wide and the fingers delicate. Its pair traveled over her midriff, hooked around her flank.

Cold.

All at once the lights were snuffed, as if a gale had blasted

# SPIRIT OF SHADOW

every flame away, leaving her in absolute darkness. The floor gave way from under her.

*Wait. This is wrong.*

A sense of vertigo stole over her as she was dragged down, and away.

Lance jerked his head to the side, causing Ben to miss his lips and plant a kiss in his hair instead.

"Did you hear that?"

"Hear what?" Ben asked.

"Someone just screamed."

"Someone's probably gettin' it on down below."

"You can hear that all the way up here?"

He shrugged. "Depends on how close they are."

"It didn't sound like...maybe...maybe you're right."

Lance turned away from the sound, met Ben's eyes. There was the look of longing in them, of poorly suppressed desire. He moved inward, taking charge, pressed soft lips against his and drew his mouth open.

Hot breath gusted into him, tongue flickering against tongue, rubbing over its ridges as passion burned into him, a mutual exchange.

As tightness built in his trousers, his lips vibrating, head full of hot air, Lance drew away.

"Do you want to?"

He shook his head. "Not...not yet."

"Are you sure?"

"No, but I think..."

Lance leaned in, planted another of those passionate kisses on him, laced slender fingers into loose, chestnut curls and tipped his head back. He bit softly at his lip and dragged it back. Releasing his hold as he drew away, golden eyes fixed on him, his free hand traveled over Ben's body, down his side, up under his shirt.

**The Teacher's Tower**

Ben reached out to drag his hand away, but he could not deny the tension pressing against his pants, the building pressure there. He could not deny that he wanted deeper contact, to feel him.

His hand dropped away, allowing Lance to explore his belly, his chest, to play with his nipples and then trail away down and down, into his pants to palm his ass and *squeeze.*

Sensation rippled through his body, climbed out of his legs to settle around his navel, and his hands found purchase beneath Lance's shirt.

"Okay." He whispered against Lance's lips. "Okay. We can...we should...."

Lance unbuttoned his shirt, and he reached for Lance's pants, unfastened the buttons there and drew the fly open, then dragged them down just enough to expose his underclothes, blond hair, slender thighs.

Lance drew the shirt open, dragged the sleeves down, kissed his neck, and sucked.

"No, no. Don't do that."

"Okay."

Sucking reverted to tender kisses.

"Lady Therien would kill me if I..."

"It's okay. I promise."

He leaned into those kisses, unbuttoned Lance's shirt and helped him out of it. Lance's pants dropped to his ankles of their own accord. He stepped out of them, leaving him naked except for his small clothes—tight, white briefs.

His rock hard cock pressed against them, a slight curve in the shaft inviting wild fantasies to bubble forth in Ben's mind's eye.

He wanted this. He wanted it bad.

He seized it, drew closer until his chest was pressed against Lance's chest, the warmth of their bodies playing off each other, driving away the subtle chill on the air around them.

# SPIRIT OF SHADOW

Hot, passionate kisses. Lance's hands roved over his body, found his pants and yanked them down, in the same motion forcing him back against the desk. He played out a power fantasy, and Ben indulged him, allowing him to drag his pants off him, to yank down his small clothes, crawl into the space between his legs.

He tipped his head back and closed his eyes at a renewed tension as Lance gripped the base of his cock and began stroking, looked down to see his member in a pallid hand, its girth rising two inches past the knuckle, the added length disappearing, reemerging, as he reached down. Down. As he dragged the edge of Lance's waistband back and under his sack, ran his fingers up the length of a cock nearly the same size as his, thick at the base and tapered, the curve tilted upward, the head sheathed in foreskin slender, somewhat pointed.

He gripped onto it, worked up and down as Lance worked on him.

Lance's tongue ran circles around his nipple, then carved a path across his chest, his stomach. He kissed, and bit at Ben's flank, his belly as he made slow, sensual progress down, brushed thick, pubic hair with his chin, ran his wet tongue up the length of Ben's shaft and then....

A groan issued from Ben as his lips parted, as his foreskin was pulled back and warmth and wetness climbed inch over inch down the length of his shaft.

Lance stopped short of the base, breathed out through his nose, traveled back up again. His fingers kneaded beefy testicles heavy with unspent seed as he worked over his tongue slithered back and forth against the head, then the shaft, back again.

Ben's eyes rolled back into his head. He pumped faster, his grip firming on Lance's shaft as the other man worked him with his mouth, growing clumsier as time went on but nonetheless giving him filling him with maddening pleasure.

He gasped, the muscles in his perineum seizing, cock tensing as fresh, hot cum slammed against the back of Lance's throat—once, twice, thrice.

Wet, cloying heat spattered his fingers and his wrist. He looked down to see Lance's quivering cock in his hand, the head still oozing, thick, white liquid splattered across his hand, his wrist and forearm.

He leaned forward, slid from the table into Lance's waiting arms, and held him, his chin on his shoulder, sweat beading his brow and a hollow sensation in his balls like he had not felt in some time.

"That was good." He whispered, as they lingered in each other's embrace, catching their breath. "That was good."

# Rashanna

The canteen was alive with activity when Lance entered the following morning, but none of his friends were there. When he approached the window to take up his breakfast from Janice, he found Peter and Ariana both toiling away among the kitchen workers. Ariana, situated in the passe, was screaming at the hot line cooks to get their shit together, while Peter was behind the line helping someone who looked on the point of tears. The cook was young, probably having just made a choice of his own path, and he looked as if he was regretting his decision already.

He took his food and navigated the aisles in search of a familiar face. Sami was usually here by now, getting her first meal in before her shift in the armory started. It was odd, her not being here, but then he supposed with the influx of orders from the military and the occasional nobleman, she had probably made quick work of eating before departing to start her day. Lord Halan might even have ordered his charges to show up early.

"Hey!" Ben waved him down his place at a table near the

back.

Smiling, he walked over to join him.

He was seated at a table with a portly, Jua woman. The woman was perhaps a handful of years older than Ben, and wore a stony, unreadable expression as she set eyes on him. Her tray sat untouched in front of her, and she steepled her fingers, her elbows resting on the tabletop. She did not welcome him as he sat down.

Ben embraced Lance in a half hug when he was seated, and made the introductions.

"This is my friend Rashanna." He said. "And Rashanna, this is Lance."

"Your new boyfriend."

"I..." Ben winced. "I don't know if we're there yet."

"I don't either." Lance said.

"But we've been seeing each other."

"I gathered." Rashanna said tonelessly. "You fuck him yet?"

They exchanged a look.

Rashanna nodded. "Okay. So how long is this one gonna be around—"

"Rashanna!" Ben said. "Don't mind her. She's always like this."

She patted buoyant curls, a sly grin cracking her teeth. "I am who I am. And I won't apologize."

"No one asked you to." Ben said.

"Rashanna works in Lady Jain's office. She's on the reception crew, too."

"Then I might see you around then." Lance said to her. "Lady Tamalsen assigned me to it."

"I doubt it. I won't be at the ceremony. I'm stuck on the setup crew, getting things ready for her *heinous* to receive the lord emperor."

"You mean her highness?" Lance asked.

"I said what I said."

# SPIRIT OF SHADOW

"Rashanna isn't a fan. She's had to work around Queen Meredith before." Ben explained.

"She's a cunt." Rashanna added.

"I thought Ariana would be somewhere around. Or Sami, I guess. Peter usually works the morning shift, doesn't he?"

Lance shrugged. "They alternate. They're both in the kitchens right now, though. I haven't seen Sami either, but she probably just decided to get an early start. The armory has been—"

"The Pits." Rashanna cut in. "So I've heard, anyway." She tucked into her breakfast. "Half the noblemen in the palace have been submitting orders to have old breastplates let out and polished up. I bet they think they're gonna impress our guests, but I think they're gonna look like idiots."

"They usually...look like idiots." Lance agreed. "Especially Lord Bran."

"The lush." She rolled her eyes.

"Where's your girlfriend, anyway?"

"Alesha?" she shrugged. "We broke up last night. I might get back with her tomorrow. I needed a break."

Ben snorted. "You could just leave her for real this time."

Rashanna laid an ambivalent side eye on Lance. "He hates her."

"She's such a bitch."

"I guess it's too bad I decided I love her then. You'll just have to deal with our whirlwind romance until she decides she's had enough. And who *knows* when that'll be."

"Lesbians." Ben groused. "Takes five minutes for them to get together, and five years to break up."

So, how long have you two known each other?" Lance asked.

"I'm gonna go." Rashanna said. She climbed off her bench, picked up her tray. She had only eaten half of her food. She carried it away, leaving them alone with each other.

## Rashanna

"Is she okay?" Lance asked.

"She's just kind of like that." He said. "It's what I love about her."

"And this Alesha person?"

"Just rubs me the wrong way. That's all. They fight like cats and dogs, break up every other week. I think they do it because it keeps things spicy, but I end up in the middle of it a little too often."

"Hopefully Sami never ends up like that."

"She doesn't really *do* relationships, does she?"

"No, not so much."

"So, I'm thinkin' I'll ask Lady Therien if she can place you with me for the reception today. I think she'll bite."

"That would be nice."

"Do you...not want to—"

"No. I mean yes. I do. If I can. I just don't know how that's going to work with the headaches."

Ben grimaced. "Right. I forgot. Maybe its best if—"

"No, please ask. I can handle it. I want to."

"Okay. I should be going though. The emperor's coming next week and Lady Therien's been heaping the work onto all of us lately. It's just going to get worse until he gets here."

He gave Lance a peck on the cheek.

"See you later?"

"Tomorrow?" Ben asked. "I've got plans with Rashanna tonight."

"Tomorrow." Lance agreed.

Ben took his tray and left.

With his shift concluded, and all of the drudgery work done, he made a stop by the kitchens before retiring for the evening. Peter and Ariana were still there, overseeing the clean up and a shift change for the evening meal, and Mistress Dina had finally arrived to replace one or both of them.

# SPIRIT OF SHADOW

He waited outside for them to get off. Ariana arrived in the hall then, while Peter stayed back with Mistress Dina.

"Is he working a double?" he asked.

"Yes." She said. "I hoped he wouldn't have to, but we have all this extra shit to do. I mean sure, the military's kitchen is helping us out with the more tedious stuff, but even with both of us on this stupid ceremony, we're still overplaying our hand. I guess Lady Jain thinks we can just make puff pastry happen. The shit takes seven hours!"

"That's too bad."

"It's fucking terrible!" she said. "You want to get out of here? I'm tired of looking at these shit heads. They've been giving me grief all morning."

Lance climbed to his feet. They ambled off together.

"What do you want to do?"

"Nothing specific. I just need to get away from here for a minute."

"Maybe the Core then?"

"Too far. Let's just go up to the barracks."

"Alright. Mine or yours?"

"Mine is closer."

"Okay." Lance said. "Have you seen Sami lately? I feel like I haven't seen her in days?"

"Now you mention it, no. I mean she said something about going to the Teacher's Tower yesterday and I haven't seen her since. Usually she pops by to brag about the new ones."

"Maybe she found someone she likes."

Ariana cackled. "No way. She doesn't do feelings."

"Yeah, you're probably right." Lance chuckled. "I met Ben's friend today. She was kind of rude."

"Who is she?"

"Some girl. Rashanna's her name. She works for Lady Jain."

"I know her." Ariana said. "Well, kind of anyway. She's on

my floor. She's actually really sweet once you get to know her."

"Is she? I couldn't tell."

"She's kind of like me, I guess. She doesn't like people. Especially *new* people."

"So, how do I win her over?"

"You that serious about this guy?"

"I don't know. Things are going good I suppose, but its still early."

"Then what's that shit eating grin about?"

"Nothing." He said too quickly.

Her eyebrow twitched.

"Really, it's nothing. We just went up to the Teacher's Tower—"

"You fucked."

"No."

"You did *something*. You're beet red."

Heat vented over Lance's collar as he thought back to the last evening. He stuffed those thoughts down, fearing he might tell on himself in other ways.

*Lady Jain, Lady Jain, Lady Jain.*

"Fine. We did stuff. Not *that* stuff. But stuff. And it was nice. It was really nice."

"Stuff like?"

"I sucked his dick. Happy?"

She cackled. "Very."

They mounted the stairs.

"So you like him."

"Yeah. I do."

"And he likes you too."

"Maybe—"

"That wasn't a question. He introduced you to Rashanna. The guy has a lot of acquaintances, but he's not close with that many people. I think she's his best friend."

"It was kind of a coincidence. None of you were free, so I

had breakfast with them."

"You think he would have invited you over there if he didn't want to take things farther?"

"I see your point. I guess I haven't formally introduced him to you guys yet. Maybe I should."

"He's met me."

"And Sami. But that's different. That's work." Lance shrugged. "Maybe we can do a stones game. I can invite him."

"It'll have to be after the reception." Ariana said.

"Alright. Then we'll do it after the reception. The usual place work?"

"Sure. I'll tell Peter." She said. "If I find Sami before you do, I'll tell her, too."

# The Power of a Name

Sami awoke in a jail cell. The bars, shimmering on this side with raw energy, spoke the tale of what had happened, that she had been abducted by some entity—the Wraiths or the Thorns, that someone within the military hierarchy had seen fit to seize her.

Panic welled up inside her, a flurry of thoughts for what she might have done. Who she might have offended. What law or rule she had broken so baldly she they had seen fit to take her.

She had heard of other servants disappearing, those who in their hubris or with a flippant disregard for the iron law had chosen to teach others what magic they knew, or solicited them to teach what they should never learn. She had heard the whispers when a servant simply ceased to be seen in the halls, the quiet truth spoken with derision at the character flaw which had landed those servants in hot water. Which had seen them whisked away.

If she was here, then she would be dead soon. Once they had satisfied themselves that they knew every detail of how she had come by whatever forbidden knowledge they believed she had, they would kill her. The law was absolute, every servant with a command of magic, every servant who had chosen a path that would never see them learn, knew what lay at the end of violating the rule. Heads of department told their charges never to step out of line, never to invite the attention of the Thorns, and she had *listened*.

*What could I have done? What do they think I did?*

She had gone up to the Teacher's Tower on many occasions throughout the years. It had almost become a routine. But so many other servants did and never faced any repercussions for their small indiscretions. Sure, it wasn't strictly in bounds, but with so many venturing that way, using abandoned classrooms for all sorts of extracurriculars activities, how could it be that just one of them was pulled down and the rest left alone?

There was some injustice in that.

*Maybe it's not that I was there at all. Maybe it's something else. But I can't do magic. They'll see that if they question me.*

She winced.

Questioning. A euphemistic torture that belied its true nature in the means by which it was done, what it avoided saying about the process. She would be tortured. She might tell lies in the hope they sounded like the truth just to get it to stop. Even knowing death lurked at the end of the tunnel, she would be helplessly at their mercy, the understanding burned into her mind with every passing moment, every terror inflicted upon her, that it would not end until they were satisfied there was nothing left to tell, that if what she told did not fit with their narrative, she would remain alive, but not whole, until it did.

But there was nothing to tell. No hidden truths lurking behind the veil. She had gone up to meet a woman. To anyone looking at her in those final moments, her intent should have been obvious. She had worked under close supervision, had enjoyed an amenable, even casual relationship with Halan. Surely, he would not have sold her into this...this....

She stuffed the thought down, and began to cry.

"There is nothing to fear for you." Came a reedy voice from the cell next door. "Nothing for you to worry about just now."

"I...I don't...you don't understand. I didn't *do* anything. They're going to kill me."

"Oh, now, they would not have placed you here if they intended to do so. There is the matter of pretense, certainly. They will use that to whatever effect they see fit to, but you need only comply with their demands. These Thorns...some are reasonable. Not all, but some."

"You don't know what you're talking about."

"In fact, I know a great deal more than you." He said.

She scoffed. "You're in prison. What could you know."

"My name is Aldeirel, child." He said. "I've been with this city since Queen Tania rose to replace her predecessor. I was a child then. Her rule was...different, I suppose. For one, your kind were not present in those days."

"W-what?"

"It was not the way back then. I suppose the elder servants remember. A time when they were not *bound* to serve, but chose to. They came from many places then. Some even lived in the city.

"Of course, those days are behind us now. I would not be upset to discover some of them were dissatisfied with this latest regime."

She sat in silence, tears streaming down her face, a hard block supporting her as she curled her legs up, hugged her knees to her chest.

"Not all is as it seems, miss?"

"S-Sami. My name...is Sami."

"Not all is as it seems, Sami." He said. "There is rebellion in the city always. The rebels will rest, I think, with the arrival of the Emperor. They will not want to invite violence while he is here. And with me here, it does not serve them to engage in such violence. They will not have my mind behind them, you see. Nor my other gifts.

"But there is resistance in its many forms. There is the active resistance you see in hard charges at the gates, in riots when our governors have gone too far. Then there is the quieter resistance. Stealing foodstuffs from the fields, hiding it away in secret cellars where it can be used to feed our hungry. Providing them with the care they need in whatever way we can. Our people mend clothing, provide healing where they can. They tend to each other when the crown will not provide.

"I fear this winter will be a hard one with the demands of the palace so much more pressing. They glut themselves in the best of times, but there will be more mouths for them to feed with the coming of mirrhvale's elite."

"What do I care what happens outside. I'm a servant. I'm loyal."

"And your loyalty has seen you framed for a crime you did not commit, the nature of it unknown to you. You are not the first to suffer this fate."

"But...but...."

"No, child. It is not fair. But I suspect I know what they want from you, and though it will be unpleasant, it will see you through to a brighter future, I think. If successful, your kind may become more whole, and in that wholeness, angered. Think for what you can accomplish from within the palace, the resistance you might provide. You may be forged into something we have never had before, and then, perhaps, our collective suffering can end.

"But know, too, we are more alike than we are different. We common men and women, and you servants of the crown. We are both, I think, treated with contempt by our betters, who choose to handle us, but do not love us. If there is one thing I can say, it is that I do not hold your relative state of wellbeing in contempt. My suffering and yours are not so different, and the hand who carries the cane is the same for us. It is a hand who's touch I know well.

"But rest. They will come for you when they choose, but it will not be just now. When they do, comply with them. Do not resist. Do not lie to them either. They will know."

She buried her face in her knees, tried to drown out the sound of his voice. As her thoughts returned to all those critical uncertainties, she could only lay there, and let his words wash over her. They brought her no comfort.

The moon loomed in the sky outside the window, a thick crescent closing in on half full, and the spider and its web were back again. Soft whimpers rippled through the air, barely audible to him as he examined it, looking for differences in its construct from the last time he had seen it. He noticed nothing out of place, but then, his recollection of it was less than trustworthy. Having nothing with which to record its shape, he had nothing reliable to compare it to, only his memory.

The spider's legs twitched, its abdomen contracting and expanding, seemingly with the labor of breathing, and words in that peculiar language broke through the whimpering on occasion, words filled with quiet rage.

He watched the spider twitching in its web, the way its mandibles played against the strings, reached for it as if to take the fat, ugly thing into his palm. The urge lingered, though he was not brave enough to do it in truth. Whether his imagination played tricks on him, or that spider was there, present and in this pitiful state, he did not think it wise to take it from its home, did not know if this creature had venom. If it was capable of harming him.

He listened to those whispered curses, and wondered at what they meant. A question formed on his lips, and he spoke it into the ether, only half convinced he would receive an answer, anticipating silence.

"Why do you keep coming back?" he asked.

The spider's mandibles stopped moving. Its legs stilled. Its abdomen clenched tight and relaxed as it sat there.

*"Why do you care?"*

"It's just...well I see you there struggling every few nights now. Almost every night really. I think the one time I haven't was the night of the new moon."

*"I do not like the dark."* He said. *"It hunts me."*

"But you keep coming back to *this* window. There must be a reason."

The spider, he was convinced that voice belonged to it, grumbled something under its breath. Something that defied his understanding.

It's mandibles twitched, hooked around a silken thread.

"What kind of spider makes black threads, anyway?" he said.

*"You can see me?"* the spider asked with a tone of surprise.

"Of course I can. Is that strange?"

*"It is...exceedingly uncommon. Can you see others?"*

"I don't know. I suppose not." He kept his voice low, so that if anyone in the nearest bunks awoke, they would not hear him. He hoped they wouldn't. *They'll think I'm insane.* He wasn't convinced they'd be wrong.

"Actually, now I think about it, I had an imaginary friend when I was younger, I think. The memory is hazy, but I have the impression I once knew a weasel. He had a funny name,

## The Power of a Name

too. Used to talk to me, not unlike you do. My older brother...."

His mouth clicked shut.

"Is something wrong."

"Just...I don't have an older brother. At least, not that I know of. But I recall a face." He rubbed the palms of his hands against his cheeks, his gaze shifting to the ever watchful moon.

*"There are those in this palace with power over memory."* The spider said. *"They are few. They should not be here at all."*

"Like Watchers? Those people from the story books?"

*"Precisely those. People who bear witness to the deep reaches of the mind, who manipulate memory."*

"Where are they? I thought they were outlawed."

*"It is hard to eradicate what is given by birthright with simple words on paper. They are here. They should not be. They nonetheless are."*

"How many?"

*"Twelve, currently. There have been more and fewer in the past."*

Lance's thoughts hung on that for a moment. He asked the question that seemed most obvious; hoping, at the same time, to distract from that peculiar sense of a family he had no connection to, that he thought he might only be beginning to remember.

They had brought him here, his parents. Perhaps he shared some relation with another servant, and if he did, the connection was lost in early childhood. If it was so, there was little point perseverating over it. It did not change much anyway.

"Have you visited other parts of the palace?"

*"I have known all parts of this palace save two, which possess a poison to me in their midst. I avoid those places. The Watchers are in one of them, I think. I have seen them smuggled into the palace in crates meant to conceal them, but*

*each time I witness their arrival, I am blocked from seeing where they go."*

"I wonder."

The spider's limbs drew inward compulsively, its thorax bowing toward its abdomen.

*"I WILL KILL YOU! I WILL KILL YOU ALL!"* it bellowed.

"Shh." Lance said. "Someone will hear you."

*"I promise you they will not. They are immune to the sound of my voice. Have been..."* it groaned, its body unfolding. *"...for generations."*

"Really, what are you?"

*"I am a spirit. Of the elements. One in particular. But I have told you this in so many words. Remember, I set you to a task."*

"The riddle."

*"Yes."*

"I forgot. I'm sorry."

*"You recall the words I spoke."*

"Well yes. For the most part. I've just been distracted. I haven't put much thought into it recently. But I think if you can see so far into the palace, you must know every corner of it, right?"

*"Every corner. Every dark thought and whispered curse ever uttered within it. All exists in my domain."*

"Every...dark..." Lance mumbled. "Can I ask you something? Apart from knowing you, what happens if I guess the answer to that riddle?"

*"I suppose you will have made a friend. The beginning of a friendship anyway. I may see fit to help you in your endeavors, if you do not force me to serve you."*

"I can do that?"

*"I advise against it. Pulling on me would only cause me pain, and I would resent you for it."*

"But you would help me if I asked you to. If I knew what

you were."

"Yes."

"I've been wondering something. You see, one of my friends has been absent. I haven't been able to find her. I suppose I could look harder, but with you knowing so much about this place, maybe it would be easier if I asked you to help me instead."

*"I may be so inclined."*

"Do you know where she is?"

*"There is no one in this palace I cannot see. At least, no one I haven't seen before."*

"Alright. Well I've been thinking." He said, observing the web. Its peculiar makeup, the threads all cast in silhouette, inviting notions of the very darkness the spirit would claim to hate. "And maybe I'd have gotten it wrong if not for something you just said. That thing about dark thoughts and whispers.

"There is a place I've been that has something like that. They call it the Dark Heart. And if that place belongs to you, I think maybe...well, maybe you're a shadow."

*"I am all shadows, boy. All of them. I am the pure essence of shadow. And my name is Lothor."*

*"Lothor."* Lance whispered. At once his shadow stretched across the bed, pooled against the mattress behind him, and deepened from its usual shade to matte black. Cold washed over his back, and he twisted round to see the offending portal clear before his eyes, a vacuous pool hugging the contours of his body, which drove animal fear into him.

"Get it away! Make it stop!"

*"The word is zente."* Lothor said. *"It means end. You need only speak it."*

"Zente. Zente!"

The peculiar sensation fell away, and with it his shadow retracted, the shade of it lightening rapidly.

"You know I could be executed for knowing you.

# SPIRIT OF SHADOW

Knowing...knowing how to do that.”

*“There are others here who can do the same, though the names they know are different. Most of those share kinship with fire, though some do entertain a spirit of air.”*

“O-okay.”

*“You have a request of me. To find this friend.”*

“Y-yes. If you could.”

*“I will try.”*

“Thank you, um...if I say your name again, will that happen...will it happen every time?”

*“Simply speak the command together with my name, and I will come to you.”* Lothor explained. *“But you must learn to command my power in truth if you are to resist the dark hearts of mortal beings who guard me. Now, this friend. What is its name?”*

“Her name is Sami. She works in the armory. She has strawberry blonde hair and blue eyes. She’s tall. Not as tall as me. Maybe a head shorter. But tall for a woman anyway.”

*“I will see to it you know where she is.”* He said. *“But rest. A first calling is hard on the soul. You must sleep.”*

# A Necessary Sacrifice

etal shod boots clanked against the poured stone floor, alerting Sami to the arrival of a newcomer. She peered through the bars of her cell, watched as the shadow of an elf crossed the corridor.

*It's time. It's going to happen. They're going to take me now.*

She thought about fighting. About scratching and biting whatever chunk of exposed flesh she could find, blinding her handler and sprinting off to somewhere, anywhere, where he might not reach her.

Flight would be hopeless, of course. There was nowhere to run once free. She didn't know how she had come to this cell, by which avenues, and the Thorns had the shadows. It would not take them long to locate her, and when they did, they would be that much more furious.

*I'd be as good as dead then. If I'm not already.*

"Remember, dear girl." Aldeirel said as the figure closed in. "Do not struggle. Comply."

He fell silent as the guard came forward, and was surprised to find she was looking into a familiar face. The face of a man she had done work for recently.

Lord Aren looked into the cell, found her there and gestured her closer. "Come now, girl. We haven't much time."

She did not approach. Even with Aldeirel's advice to guide her, she did not trust herself to approach those bars, did not think she would abstain—if pushed to it—from fighting. Knowing who he was did not change the nature of her thoughts. She could struggle against him, a sitting general on the Council of Liam who had served in the armed forces longer than she had been alive; or she could go quietly. If she struggled, she would die, but in her death there would be relief. That last scrap of knowledge, as life left her and her soul drifted away to face its day of judgment along Amorahiya's heights, that she had escaped torture. That she would not have to endure ceaseless pain, the preamble to her eventual demise, as this man questioned her.

"Come!" he commanded.

She sat bolt upright.

He unlocked the grate and slid it aside, and as he did, she stood and walked over to him—as obedient as a dog.

"If you're going to...just...do it now, please. I can't take...can't take—"

"Quiet." He said. "I will permit you to walk freely, knowing you have no knowledge of magic, but if you force my hand I will place you in shackles. Do not think I will show mercy because you have served me before."

She followed in his wake, counted the turns, paid attention to the direction they traveled in at each intersection. Though the halls marched on straight for some distance after they arrived at any one intersection, he took a winding path with many turns, an effort to muddy her sense of place, deny her any ease with which she might find her way out the next time she was taken from her cell.

Glow bulbs provided light to see by, and dark stretches filled the space between them. In those stretches were housed many prisoners, who slithered back from the bars as the general passed, shielded their eyes as if they had been struck by sudden light.

She lost count of the turns they had taken, lost track of where they were in relation to where they had started. She thought this was somewhere southeast of the point of origin, but it was impossible to know for certain. She had not known where her cell was in relation to the way the palace above was situated, and yet when they arrived at the entrance to the dungeons, the scattering of interrogation rooms near the bronze barred door, she thought—if she put her mind to it—she might be able to find her way out. Might use the faces of familiar prisoners to see herself at least this far, though to arrive here would be a dangerous pursuit for its own reasons.

Lord Aren did not take her into an interrogation room, but instead disengaged the lock on the dungeon door, and ushered her into the hall outside.

"Is this some kind of...mistake?" she asked.

"What did I say?" he asked. "Be quiet."

He marched down the adjoining hall, which was better lit but in a state of greater disrepair. The telltale signs of ware were present in hairline cracks along the walls, narrow puddles and trickles of water from leaky pipes overhead. Down the adjoining hall and then another; they arrived at an unassuming door. Next to it, about halfway up on the wall next to it, was a single tile with a black triangle glazed and fired into it.

She had some familiarity with the codes the military used for their various levels of clearance, but she had never seen a symbol this color. Even the chamber where the Council of Liam met only had a blue triangle. She had thought it to be the highest level of clearance. She was mistaken.

"Before we enter," he said. "I know you have committed no crime. This is not personal, you understand. You were just in the right place at the right time. It was easy to craft a narrative surrounding you which might see me to my ends."

"I'm being framed?"

"Yes." He said. "For the good of all of us who still have a sense of justice. My Thorns found the grimoire I planted under your bed, a grimoire of death magic, and they have since returned it to me. If it ever came out that I was the one who planted it, I suppose I would be executed. At least, that will be the end for me if I fail here.

"Which leads us to you. Inevitably, you will be missed by someone, and that someone will come looking for you. You will be in control of yourself much of the time, but you mustn't be seen in those times. You must never be found, you understand.

"What I am giving you in return is a chance to become whole. A chance to remember what your betters compelled you to forget."

"Do I have a choice?"

"I'm afraid not. Now, let's get this over with."

He pushed open the door, then nudged her through it, and closed it behind him.

Several queer looks were cast onto him by the various women in these chambers. She was surprised by how many noncombatants were involved. More surprised by the small flocks of children they doted over. Some of those children were still of toddling age, while others were much older, and still the eldest couldn't have been more than twelve.

A point of irony, as her own memories became hazy around that age.

## A Necessary Sacrifice

Lord Aren led her forward, ignoring the expressions on those women's faces, the ones so intent to accuse him of some wrongdoing. To lump her in with him for her mere presence here.

One hustled out of what appeared to be a classroom. The tables and chairs were all pitiful things, tiny and unkempt, and toys and blocks covered the low shelving along the walls. The children sat at their tables with oil pastels and paper board in front of them. Some scribbled intensely on their boards, and the scenes they depicted were invariably dark. Homes rendered in dark shades with jagged shapes guttering in bright oranges and reds; animal forms, horses and cattle, with haunting, white eyes and blood leaking from their necks and flanks; and stick men with ropy piles of sickly yellow and green tumbling from their stomachs.

The children expanded on those images, fixed them in place. Her stomach tied itself into a hard knot at the sight of them.

"What the fuck?" she whispered.

"Indeed."

The woman approached, blocked them from going any further.

"Hi, sir. Are you here on official orders?"

"Is anything about this place official?" he replied.

"I...I see your point. What I mean is did Lady Therien send you?"

"Lady Therien has no bearing on my being here."

"Then I think I need to ask you to—"

He clamped his hand onto her shoulder. Black shadow passed under his palm, and Sami just caught the edge of it as it traveled across her clavicle and faded into the base of her neck. She collapsed, eyes wide and dull, mouth still open around the unspoken word.

*Leave.*

She wanted to.

# SPIRIT OF SHADOW

More shadows spiraled out from under Lord Aren's feet, thin lines that zigzagged cross classrooms, stopped just short of the other women there, pinned them against the walls where to flee would be almost impossible.

He marched forward, dragging Sami along with him, until the arrived at a broader chamber at the end of the short hall.

He looked to one side of it, and she followed his gaze to a mass of solid quartz which rose to level with her hip. Every facet and bar glowed with a blue-tinted light. His gaze clawed across the floor to settle at their feet, and she saw they cast no shadows. A dozen men and women were shackled and bolted to the far wall, and they did not cast shadows either. They were all of different races, some human and some not, and all of them shared the same violently blue eyes, eyes like lightning.

"You have taken a great risk in coming here." The central figure among them, a bald, Jua man said. "You may have staked your life against it."

"We have a common enemy, Watcher. The one who did this." He gestured to Sami. "I would see her pulled down, if you could be convinced to help me."

The Jua man chuckled. "And how do you expect me to do that?"

"By riding her."

Several gazes shifted to her, each beset by curiosity.

"What will come of our bodies?"

"I will deal with them."

"And them?" the Jua man cocked his chin in the direction of the classrooms. "Your witnesses are many."

"I believe you are capable of handling them. It need only appear I was never here. Long enough that they presume you all to be dead."

"But we will not be?"

"You will appear to be for a time. And your bodies will be

moved into a safe place when they have seen fit to dispose of them."

"And the woman? The Shield?"

Stony anger displaced the placid expression on his face, and the Watcher smiled at that.

"You didn't know." He said.

"No, I'm afraid I didn't. We have a plan for you, if you'll hear it?"

The Watcher shifted his position, planted his fist against his knee. He sat cross legged, leaning forward to get a better look at the general, ignoring Sami completely.

"Who is *we?*"

"My agents operate from within and outside the palace. Some under another man's control often conspire with us. I need you to kill a certain few—"

"I know of whom you speak. I have seen it."

*That fast.* Sami thought. *They were able to read a sitting general that fast. What will they do to me?*

*Comply.* The word listed through her mind in Aldeirel's thin voice. *Do not struggle. Comply.*

"Will you handle them, then?"

"What's in it for us?"

A cold grin spread across Lord Aren's cheeks, a grin that did not touch his eyes. "Freedom."

"And for you, I suppose it will be...regime change."

"Nothing so straight forward, no. Rather, in exposing her secrets, I intend to put a leash on her. She will not be able to move as freely in the wake of the work you do, and we will all be better for it."

The Watchers' gazes, one after another, shifted to Sami. Her head snapped back as if struck by twelve arrows. She collapsed first to her knees, and then to the floor.

Lord Aren bent over the servant's prone form. Along the wall, the Watchers slumped over, each and every one falling face first onto the ground.

He checked the girl's pulse, satisfied himself that it was still there, that she had not been driven into shock by the invasion of her body by twelve foreign souls, the minds that accompanied them.

He stood, and marched over to the wall, where he examined each of those lifeless bodies, concocted a narrative for them.

Behind him, the girl climbed shakily to her feet. As he turned toward her he found a woman whose eyes shone lightning blue like any of those Watchers, an unnatural, unsettling shade.

She leered at him. "You might regret this, you know."

"I have many regrets in this life." He responded. "What is one more?"

She nodded, and ambled down the hall as casually as if she was taking a stroll through the garden. On her way down, she looked to each of the women in those rooms, and one by one they were struck down by the Watcher's gift, their memories of these happenings erased.

Lord Aren called on the spirits, the Celestial Choir, listened for answering echoes from those he needed.

*"Tanc seyan absires, Olae, ab a eyo, Simiel, miyo speltet elrarat, gairo seyan grundanas. Zente, orang mi, Ravana, mor grundael dem eya draem languyae tehirian sei. Mas sei ojian gan miyo secairet sei ojiv."* He whispered in a rush.

Song blasted through him, and power leaked out through his fingertips as he placed his hands on each of the bodies, repeating the instruction to the spirits each time. When he was finished, he walked away, leaving each of those bodies a corpse for whoever found them.

He would find some way to have their bodies apprehended, some pretense for setting his Thorns on their path, perhaps. Or there were those rebels in the city.

## A Necessary Sacrifice

*It may be time to let Aldeirel out of his cage.*

# Six Nightmares

song of great sorrow descended over Shadovane. In the song was contained mortal pain and longing, a dirge to fill the silence. A spirit crept through the streets, invaded dilapidated shacks and spun threads around those who lay on lumpy mattresses filled with sour straw and old cotton. Whole families lay in single rooms, and with her coming, sleep took them.

She traveled through the streets, inching along and spreading satin threads throughout to drive those destitute common folk into the dream, for in dreams lay the truest expression of her power, and this night called for a greater silence.

A column of priests, soldiers, nobility and their servants marched into a narrow, closed on the city on the last stretch of their long journey from the imperial capitol, Mirrhvale. With them came a being who was just a boy in her memories, a boy born into the body of a man, who had grown into himself swiftly and become something entirely unfathomable to those mortal beings, as close to a god as they could conceive.

He came in her wake; the dream, a last mercy paid to those who had struggled too hard for his sins. He came to visit upon a wife who was no empress, a wife who did not love him but hated him, for their marriage was not born of kinship or closeness, and no true attraction lingered in their souls. In him, an infatuation with the one whose essence she carried. In her, a politically necessary coupling, one of many traditions she detested.

She entered the palace, traveled down pristine halls and up staircases, into reaches where servants slept, and drew them down into sleep also. The dreams they had may haunt them, but they were not new to nightmares. And in those dreams lay memory, which had been suppressed, concealed behind a veil she cast open, for those briefest of moments while her power held.

The dream came first to Sami, who slept off a recent transformation within a storeroom in the palace bows. Though the woman slept, her eyes remained open, and others watched in wakeful silence as she rested. Others with their own agendas.

She was just a girl. Her dress was a simple thing of linen; dyed blue and cut like a gunnysack, the hem dangled around her ankles. Dirt and grass stains were ground into the knees and back of it, the byproduct of her wrestling with a brother a year older than her. The brother sat on a low stoop outside a barrel-sided house with a tiled roof. A window near the open door let onto a kitchen, and the savory aroma of a stew her mother had been cooking suffused the air as thin threads of steam drifted into open air from their source, a pewter pot on the range.

Cattle dogs caromed about the city outskirts, and fields broke against that first line of houses of which hers was one. Dirt avenues traveled between her home and the fields, where cattle and sheep grazed, brayed and lowed and huddled together.

A proud bull was sequestered in his own field. Its coat shimmered black in the evening sun as it tested the air with curved horns. Alone, it grazed, for it was not yet time for breeding. Those cows had only recently birthed their calves.

Dust licked at the horizon in the distance, and she jumped up from where she had been toying with the grass. She craned her neck, a futile effort to get a look at who was coming, whether it was her father and his horsemen come back from wherever they had gone.

Horses and riders materialized at the far end of the field, coming round onto the road and slowing. In their midst was a carriage drawn by a pair of stallions, the stock that had given Trom its name. The wagons loomed black as a shadow on behind them, and she wondered who it carried.

Her father did not travel that way. He had never been one to ride covered, even on his treks into the deserts in the south. When she and her brother were permitted to go with him to Shadal, they were taken in a wagon drawn behind his horse, together with their effects, but he preferred to travel light, to carry with him only as much a burden as his horse could tolerate. A bedroll, a change or two, his weapons.

As they neared, she noted he was not among them, that though the other figures looked familiar, and road Tromite horses, he was not in their midst.

She wondered at that. It was not common for him to send his men ahead of him. She had never known him to do so before.

The riding party and the carriage rolled past the field and along that first line of houses, and the wagon came to rest near her home as the rest of the riders disembarked for reaches far removed from them. Her mother peeked her head through the doorway as a fox-faced driver with long limbs

**Six Nightmares**

and a hump in his back hopped down from the doorway, and called out to them as he opened the door.

"Sami, come here." She lifted her son onto her feet. "Go inside."

A bouquet of tiny, white flowers was painted onto the wagon side, and a man dressed in a garish, five piece suit climbed out of the wagon, ignoring the offered hand of his driver. Top hat, coat and trousers were all canary yellow, the shirt underneath was pinstriped and a powder blue pocket square peaked out from its customary place. His mustaches and beard were a sooty gray, shot through with darker streaks to remind of fleeting youth. Age lines crinkled the corners of his eyes, and he walked with a slight limp, though he went without a cane.

She goggled at him. He looked like something come straight out of a story book, one of those posh schisters from the stories of Anastasia her mother sometimes read to her.

He smiled at her as he passed, but that smile did not warm his cold, silver eyes. His gaze slid over her, up to the house and her mother.

"Come inside, Sami. Come get some supper with your brother."

She looked over her shoulder, stepped away from the stranger. Her mother stepped out of the house, her hand hidden behind her back, and Sami wondered at that, too.

"Don't make this ugly, Loraine." The man said. His hand clamped down on her shoulder, and he moved in front of her. "Put her in the carriage for now."

The driver plucked her off the ground.

"Let go of me!" she screamed. She bashed him over the head with tiny fists, kicked at every part of him she could reach. "MOM! *MOOM!*"

He tossed her into the wagon.

"Now, Hugo, I think we have a misunderstanding. If Markus is with you, maybe we can—"

# SPIRIT OF SHADOW

"I'm afraid Markus is dead." The man in the suit cocked his head to the side, his gaze unfocused. "He's been dead for quite some time."

"I know you for your lies, Hugo. If he's dead, who killed him?"

"Well." He nodded. "Yes, that's right. I did."

Her arm thrust out from behind her back, and she dropped the kitchen knife she had been holding.

He looked down at it, where it lay in the grass.

"Oh, come now. You didn't think you could do me in with that little thing." He drawled. "Surely you have something else up your sleeve."

The driver closed the carriage door, and locked it.

She kicked at the door, screaming as muted conversation passed between the man in the suit and her mother. As her mother's voice rose in pitch, and she began speaking very rapidly.

"It is unfortunate, isn't it." He said, as the fight leaked out of her. As she stopped kicking. The tears streaming down her cheeks were accompanied not by screams but whimpers.

"Mom. *Please. Don't let him take me!*"

"I quite liked Timothy, but you must understand a man in my position cannot simply let something like this slide."

"So you're taking my daughter?"

"I'm flattered that you have so much faith in me." He said. "Yes, I think I will. As for you and your son...."

Red glow painted the shade drawn over a window in the carriage door. Footsteps over gravel, the wagon rocked as the driver resumed his seat. The door swung open, and Hugo climbed in. He took his seat, revealing a last image of Sami's home.

Her mother lay in the yard, her limbs spread at odd angles around her. Her home was ablaze.

## Six Nightmares

The dream drew down Ariana's eyes, and she was dragged into a world within, a nightmare that tasted like a memory, of a distant place intimately connected to her heritage.

She was a girl, perhaps six years old and already a firebrand like her father. She played in a coy pond at the heart of an elaborate garden, a rooftop oasis in the city of Haru, which was framed on four sides by long houses with tiled roofs, each of them outfitted with an array of sliding, paper doors. Across those corrugated doors were painted images in vibrant watercolor, grand murals depicting scenes of summer, autumn, winter, and spring, and their corresponding animal guardians.

An eland milled about in tall grasses, the white stripes along its flanks helping it blend in with shadows cast by warty trees whose canopies were verdant and full of life in summer. Smaller creatures peered out from behind low shrubs and ferns, and all seemed at peace in the creature's presence. Its horns were twisted like those lowest, sweeping bows, and a thick waddle dangled under its neck, and almost touched the ground as in stasis, it dipped its head to take its meal.

A salamander lounged on a rock amid trees to reflect those in the summer scene, and the leaves were cast in fire colors to reflect the evening sky breaking through where those heavy boles parted. Ink black and far larger than any newt she had seen, of size with a horse to her eyes, its tongue slithered out from a wide, toothless mouth, and fire rippled across its spine.

In the mural on the northern side was a forest deep in winter, with heavy snows blanketing the earth and fat snowflakes drifting down amid bare branches. A white bull stamped its hoof in the center, its body splayed across doors on rollers which let into her uncle's chambers.

The last, a spring scene of cherry and apple blossoms, and budding leaves frosting twisted bows just liberated from winter. The earth was bare and brown except for those ferns, and scattered ice and sleet broke up the terrain. A boar tested the air with hooked horns, its steady gaze fixed on the bows, and there was anger, or perhaps passion, in its eyes.

The doors against which the Eland was posed spread open, and her father emerged from within. He was tall for a Harua man but would appear short when set next to someone from the surrounding city states of Trom or Duyaire Bense or Ashvein. From him she inherited the subtle tapering of her eyes, the way her cheekbones and chin made a vague triangle of her face, and hair like obsidian, glossy and dark. He dressed in a green tunic of fine silk, and black trousers today, and went barefoot as was his custom when he was home.

Several baubles and trinkets dripped from his wrists, and an ornate pendant outfitted with an aquamarine stone the size of a thumbnail lay against his chest. The gem trade ran strong in Haru, was the spine on which the Hoga family built their empire, and it was this dominance in the trade that granted them estates atop the tallest tower in the city, though she could see only the faint reflection of lights popping on throughout the city below, sure sign that evening was fast giving way to night.

Her father was not alone. With him was a man he shared only incidental resemblance to. Where her father was slender, the other, her grandfather, was round bellied and thick in the limbs. Where his face was angular like hers, her grandfather's was round, his eyes wider set and his cheekbones made less apparent by meaty cheeks and a blunted chin.

He was dressed as her father was, though more fineries dripped from him than his son, and his tunic was tucked into his waistband, snug behind a leather belt with a buckle in the shape of a fox's head.

"Ompa!" she shouted, and ran to her grandfather. She

**Six Nightmares**

could not remember the last time she had seen him. She vaulted down a river stone path and launched herself into his waiting arms, embracing him around the belly.

He ruffled her hair with a calloused hand, and as she looked into his face, her excitement was abated, replaced by confusion. The man, so often full of joy, wore a stony expression. So easy to make smile, a dark scowl touched his lips.

"What's wrong, Ompa?" she asked.

There. The smile came to his lips, but it not the easy thing she was accustomed to.

"Nothing, little girl. Nothing at all."

Her father stepped forward. "We're taking a trip, Ariana."

"To the mountains?" she asked, her excitement returning.

Her father and grandfather exchanged a look. There was something in it she could not quite place, a sense almost of dread.

"Yes, I think that is best." He said.

"We don't know if we can trust them." His father said. "It may be better to take her to Duyaire Bense. Or to Shadal. Priest Samos would not betray us."

"Jorin has his king's ear. She will be afforded all the protection Del Zaros can give her."

"They are still worryingly close to the border."

"So is Duyaire Bense."

"A different border. They are farther removed than us."

"And again, of uncertain loyalty."

Her father's grimace told her of his frustration. This was not to be the trip she wanted. Not a holiday outside the city, but something she had been told might become necessary just months past, when her grandfather had last been inside Haru the family estates. This was flight.

"The way to Del Zaros poses complications, as well. He will expect us to move for their protection. Shadal is closer, and we have close ties with the Giida there. Can I not convince you to reconsider."

"Hugo Silvanes will also have to pass through there. I have word from Trom that Timothy has been dealt with already. He might have spared him, but he will not spare me, which means you and your siblings will have to take up my mantle, secure your ties to the Cross, if I cannot best him."

He peeled her away from him, and passed her into her father's custody. "I'm sorry, granddaughter. But be brave. Our path will take us where it leads. You need only remember that the Hoga do not bend to the winds. We move with the changing seasons." he gestured expansively to the murals. "As we have always done."

Twisted columns like coral clawed at a night sky. Wide lanes all covered in red dust followed curved tracks amid those basalt structures. Kitunes marched down the streets, and Peter followed in their wake. He was a child, not quite five, and he followed in the wake of a cluster of other children, all orphans. The other children were older than him, and their leader, a boy who wore his hair long and tied behind his back, who dressed in thick wool despite the oppressive heat, carved a path through the city by side streets, looking over his shoulder now and again to see that no one was left behind.

The other children were of varying age, and none of them older than a dozen years. Most wore ragged linens, the last uniforms of their kind, what their parents had left them when they died, or abandoned them to this fate.

His belly ached, a sour sensation which had been days building inside him, which he had almost learned to forget. They marched along, and the locals watched them with suspicion and contempt, but they were not here for them. Who they robbed, for this was their purpose, would be foreigners. People of substance who were not so wealthy they could afford a dedicated guard, who were not poor either.

Their leader, Roach, knelt in the shadow of a building at the mouth of a narrow passage. A ramp and framing staircases connected this street to one lower in the bowl. A volcanic glow emanating from the city's borders and its heights robbed the sky of starlight. Night was a black waste above them to match the hole in his soul where his family had been. Darkness never fell on the city, yet it lived in the hearts of its residents.

"Quiet." Roach warned them.

"You be quiet." The halfling bastard of a prostitute grumbled. His father was merenern, from the lake city of Morgrotten down slope from the volcanic peak Ash Island occupied. His heritage from that fish-like people was made plane in light gray skin and dark, sinuous lines running down the sides of his neck, a ripple pattern across every exposed inch of him which reminded of scales.

He had seen the halfling exposed to water once, had seen the panic stealing over his face as his skin bubbled, rigid scales sheathing him in organic armor as the gills now closed against his neck fanned open, exposing ribbed, pink flesh in preparation for a descent into the lake.

His mother had abandoned him because he he was ugly to her eyes, a monster she had birthed when she could not find a proper healer to get rid of this unwanted life growing within her. He was the sweetest boy among them, and, so close in age to Peter, had quickly become his closest friend among this ragged group of vagabonds.

Roach gave the signal as a pair of human visitors passed the alley mouth, and they bolted into the street.

Peter and Night were to distract them while the older children stole what they could get their hands on, the coin purse dangling, so tempting, from the man's waist. The clamshell purse from the woman, and the bags of fresh produce they carried between them.

# SPIRIT OF SHADOW

He centered himself in front of them, putting on his most pitiful expression, clutched his stomach and collapsed at their feet. The unsuspecting woman leaned down to help him to his feet, and at that moment, Night appeared, dunked himself in a bucket of water situated outside the nearest home and launched out of it screaming.

A gloss layer covered his eyes, and his skin bubbled.

The man cried out as Roach snatched his coin purse and another boy cut the woman's purse from her shoulder.

The others swooped in on the bags of food and pelted away with them. Peter righted himself, darted out of the couple's reach and sprinted.

He slammed into a bulky figure and fell hard onto his rump. Filling his gaze as he looked up at the obstruction was the figure and the form of a monster. A legend.

The monster was clad in black wool robes from his neck to his feet, and his skin was the same blood red as a kitune, but tiny horns crept out of his forehead, and fangs peeked out from behind thin lips, thrust up from a blunt jaw.

He scrambled to get away from him.

The monster's finger twitched, and a blind mage came forward, fire already pooling against his fist, and he knew he was dead before the light left the mage's palm.

But the fire crashed against an invisible obstruction. Sparks showered the street in the intervening space. A woman placed herself between the monster and him. Gray hair framed her face, and her ears poked out through holes in a wide hood which shadowed her features. He saw that her eyes were milky white and unfocused, and knew what she was. That she had made a grievous mistake placing herself in the monster's path.

*Pyre Magus.*

His mind raced. He was frozen in place by fear.

"Run, boy. Fight another day." She croaked.

**Six Nightmares**

"You are prepared to pay the price for your betrayal." The monster growled.

"What betrayal?" she asked. "I see no criminal here. Only a starving child."

He nodded.

"I said run. No need ta waste time now. Get outta here."

He scrambled back on hands and knees, flipped onto his belly, started running before he was fully upright. He bolted past the awestruck couple and past, and the face of that woman was burned into his mind. A Pyre Magus standing up to the Shadow of Lies, for a child. A thief. A boy who no one wanted.

Rashanna plunged into the dream and was met with a confusing scene. She was a girl not unlike herself in her features, but here she was happy. How rare, for her to be so animated, to be dancing among people who looked like her, dancing to the music of drums and woodwind instruments as men and women chanted and sang in a dusty circle amid stone structures. How strange that she should know the words to this song, being in a language she could not remember learning.

The song suffused the air with power. The spirits were here with them, adding their song to the songs of the mortals who played with them. Her hair was bound in pigtail braids, not yet the hip-length things of those older than her, and peacock feathers were laced into them, so that the rib formed the core of the braid and the eyelet poked out against the end. Her braids bobbed and swayed as she worked through the steps of this intricate dance, and a bonfire burned at the heart of the circle of others, children and men and women all dressed in ceremonial attire with their faces painted to reflect the animals native to the region. Her own face was painted like a tiger's, and her brother wore a paint made of white ash reminiscent of the bone snakes that lived in the jungle.

# SPIRIT OF SHADOW

Broad feathers bobbed over his shoulders, and his chest was bare, exposing a newly laid tattoo, the shape of it signifying a power he was deemed ready to carry. This ceremony was for him, an Atreiya family tradition for he had just become a man, would have gained the right to take a bow from the Tree of Life, were it not so damaged. The tree had not grown a leaf since her grandfather's time, a curse which was slowly fading, which had left the lands in jaukali and the neighboring territories inside the Sun Empire where her city was centered into a period of drought lasting more than a decade.

They danced, for the drought had lifted. For her brother was a man and had earned a fluted flower set over his chest on the right hand side. The mark was an auspicious one, for by itself it held little power, but were he to draw on it in the presence of a Watcher, a Whisperer, one with a gift such as those, it would draw them into a soothed state, drive them to him, lull them into a sense of complacency.

A strange gift, one which would take time to master, it was nonetheless a mark with utility, if he found himself in the presence of those who would influence his mind.

He found her among the dancers, smiled and hopped his way over, spinning as he came to join her. The skin around the tattoo was still puffy and dark, ridges marring the image of the flower. It had been done just that morning, when the sun was still rising over the horizon, had been tested that afternoon, when he was exposed to a Watcher's gift.

Light broke the night darkness deeper in the village. Torches drove back the dark to her eyes, and her feet froze under her, her arms dropping to her sides.

He followed her gaze, the good natured grin falling from his face as he stopped dancing too.

Others, seeing the coming lights, froze in their steps to contemplate the new arrivals.

**Six Nightmares**

All at once the scene was changed. Fire flashed amid houses, screams filled the air. Shadows flickered unnaturally back and forth as creatures out of legend stormed in to break up their circle, to put an end to this ceremony.

Signs in an ancient language, a language that predated what the Jua people spoke, bloomed radiant against the bodies of armor-clad soldiers, burned black into the soil. Soldiers fell in dozens, and dozens more spilled into the circle, laid slaughter with sword and sorcery. More spilled from the shadows, and she was taken.

Drawn down.

Into darkness, and away. Away from all she had known.

The dream came to Ben, and he was plunged into a chaos of another kind. Fires raged around him. Men and women who looked like his people but were not streamed through the streets. Gold lamps and lanterns hung from their hips, and ghostly entities streamed in their wake. Their ghastly familiars lashed out with clawed fingers and sharp teeth, blooded his kin, felled his cousins as his mother dragged him through the streets.

He was just a boy, perhaps four years old, and he was frightened. The Temple of the Sun, Lazul's shining jewel, loomed at center city, and ahead of them the great wall, so long a bastion of protection against all of those who loathed the Lazuli Giida was manned by foreigners. At its height were three figures, who observed the unfolding chaos with cold ambivalence as down below, Jua men blocked its towering gates, gates laid open, a challenge to the people to make their final bid for freedom.

He was clad in a hooded robe, the hood drawn up over his face and a sunburst died across the chest, sign of the people, the last of the Owl King's charges. Jua women wielded their scripts, burning sigils into the sands, bleeding them into stone roads at crossroads, and people fell to their insidious traps, too.

His mother dragged a pendant in the shape of a cross free of her robes. Fitted with topaz and peridot, he recalled the moment his father had given it to her. Somewhere deeper in the city, he lay amid rubble and ruin, had been among the first to die at the hands of these invaders. The Ozites in their vibrant silks, their loose-legged trousers, with their ghoul harboring vessels fixed behind broad scimitars with serrated edges. The Jua people, dressed in straight leg trousers and dashikis that emulated colors found in nature.

She held the pendant high over her head, a thick, gold "x", ornately tooled across its face, peridot frosting the tips of each bar and a larger piece of topaz suspended in the puzzle-piece joint at their heart. A Jua woman stepped aside, let her past, and a man of the same tribe received her.

"I'm...never mind who I am. Take the boy. Take him!" she demanded. "He is not part of this.

"Take him to Lord Silvanes. Take him to Henry. Whoever is left of the Hammers."

She shoved him at the Jua man. Vice-like grips held him in place as she liberated the pendant from her neck and passed it into his hands.

"You will be okay. I promise you will be. Keep this. Keep it safe. Show it to their leader."

She pooled the fine, silver chain into his palms and folded his fingers over it. And she retreated.

"Maman!" he screamed. He struggled against the Jua man's grip. "MAMAN!"

She retreated into the masses, into the chaos.

"To think we have been reduced to this." The Jua man said to the woman who had let her mother past. "Slaughtering *children.*"

"What would you have us do?" the woman said. "What happens here...it could happen to us."

## Six Nightmares

The dream crashed around him, faded into dissolution, and he was left was left with a cold ache in his chest as his eyes fluttered open, memory of it rippling through his mind, remaining to remind him all was not well.

It was the same dream of fire and chaos, of a bed yet not burning, oppressive heat pressing against the wall behind it, that greeted Lance in sleep. The same dream, but a variation of it. The essence of it the same, and yet extrapolated on to reveal new details not present in its first iteration.

There was his sister screaming outside, there was his sister losing the fight, pleading with him to flee through the window onto the roof, promising to get him down once he had won free.

There was the oak tree with its swing in the front yard, its canopy ablaze. There were the screaming peacocks running away toward a wrought bronze fence as fire lashed at their plumage.

He wrenched at the window, heat building against his toes, the balls of his feet. It gave. Gave some more. He scrambled through it, his back striking the sill, legs kicking at open air.

A vice grip clamped down on his calf. The assailant wrenched him back.

"ANDREA! SOMETHING'S GOT ME!" he screamed, tears blurring his vision as he was thrown back into the room, as his tiny body skidded across the floor like a rag doll.

A Wraith loomed over him amid the flames, rendered a demon in fire light as the bed finally caught.

"Somebody help me!" he cried. As the Wraith closed in on him, a weasel cast in silhouette darted out of the smoke fast filling the room, lingered just above them.

His gaze latched onto the creature, and he cried out to it.

*"Aughere!"* He gasped, bolting upright as the dream

# SPIRIT OF SHADOW

crashed into dissolution.

Smoke billowed around him, coming from nowhere he could see. There was no fire in the barracks, not even a candle to produce the cloud. Atop it lounged a weasel all in silhouette with eyes that glowed raw white.

"Long time no see, friend." It snickered. "I thought you would never call."

He looked to the window. The spider, Lothor, was still there in its web.

"A silkworm has been here." The weasel said, following his gaze. "And you, huh? Wouldn't your mistress be upset if she found you lurking about?"

"No more than your own." Lothor grumbled. "Now leave me to myself. And let go the smoke. He will be noticed."

"Ah. I suppose you're right." The weasel's gaze shifted to Lance, who watched him intently. "You remember me, don't you?"

"As the product of a dream, yes."

"Memory. Such a fickle thing. It does like to flee when it is not well tended." The weasel snickered. "You remember my name, at least. You just uttered it."

*Aughere.* He thought. "Yes, I think I do."

"Well...I don't want to bother you when there is so much fun to be had on the horizon. I'll leave you with your peace. But call me if you ever feel a need for better company. Or a simple service."

*"Aughere zente."* Lance breathed.

"Oh, not that's not very nice." The weasel disappeared, along with the gray cloud it had been riding.

# Who Shines Like The Dawn

auls, Shadovane's infantry, marched down the streets in the city. Their bronze-shod boots beat against the dirt roads, creating a harsh music as they roused the common folk. Dawn was still north of an hour off. The farmers who lived atop the cliffs would be about their errands on a normal day, but those errands had been postponed.

"Line up!" A soldier roared. He was marked out by wooden badges dangling from his pauldron as their captain. .

The common folk hustled out of their hovels. Bare boards clung to the eaves of those homes.  They were bloated and bowed, and some were beginning to fray as downward shifts in the homes' infrastructure increased tension against foundations. Whole sections of some dwellings had fallen through, leaving behind gaping holes in the walls and ceilings. Where roofs existed at all, they were a haphazard mess of old, chipped tile and rotten, straw thatch.

Poverty hung on every man and woman here.

# SPIRIT OF SHADOW

The Mauls corralled them like cattle, herded them toward the main thoroughfare that led from the edge of the city, beyond the Third Turn, to the palace in all of its glory. They shoved or kicked the ones who moved too slowly. Some of those elves were rickety elders, hobbled and gnarled and bent, but they were few. Their juniors were mostly working age, and they were gaunt, emaciated, as often wearing repurposed gunnysacks as honest raiment, and where they could afford true dress, it was riddled with patches of cheaper materials, whatever they could get their hands on. Their skin was sallow and oily, their hair unkempt for they had not had time to piece themselves together, wash in waters dragged from the well or a nearby creek in the high passes, shake off recent sleep and bring the vigor back into their joints.

The use of magic took energy from the body. They had so little of it to spare. Where disease was present it ravaged the body, and the elder among them were left with cancerous tumors, goiters, sores. What few did know a bit of the art were too feeble to conjure more than a candleflame, or the simple rite to soothe an itch. In their state, they could not defend themselves, nor heal their fellows of their more serious ailments, and so they were resigned to this life. What foodstuffs they could come by went to the children, to keep them healthy. What was left went firs to the rebels keeping them safe, then to the parents, and then to everyone else. There was never enough, and with the emperor's arrival, they knew they would witness bitter days.

Some of them remembered the rule of Queen Tania, when they could eat enough to live and be happy, and their children were healthy and playful. In their memory, there was music in the streets, and there was strength enough in the people that the roofs remained in good repair, and clean water was never hard to come by.

Those days died with the rise of Queen Meredith—a bitter irony for many still remembered her as a girl. With her came a shadow so deep and gluttonous it sucked the very spirit out of the city, and left its people to drift along, meaningless, forgotten until the moment they were needed.

They arranged themselves along that thoroughfare and obediently dropped onto hands and knees, grinding their noses into the dirt, and when they were in position, it began.

A brilliant light crested the horizon. The first trumpets sounded, and

## Who Shines Like the Dawn

then the drums began to beat. The light filled the distant canyon passage on its way to the second turn, and those commoners brave enough to snatch a glimpse knew what it meant.

It had been a decade since the emperor last visited, but he had come. He came with the dawn, as tradition demanded. When he left at the beginning of true winter, there would be little left for the common man. This would be a winter for starving. It would be a winter for dying.


"First Bell!" The Wraith stationed guard on Lance's floor bellowed. He stood with his hands cupped around his mouth—the shadows playing with his pallid skin—and repeated his call.

Lance launched out of bed. He wrenched open the drawer under his bunk as Fat John stretched and yawned, and Laramy hauled himself out of his own bed.

*It's finally time! He's here!*

He rummaged through the drawer, pulled free the dainty, highly polished, black slippers, the snowy reliefs and, with extra care not to wrinkle it, a black tabard emblazoned with the seal of Shadovane in thread of violet —a raven clutching thorns with its skeletal feet. He liberated a towel from near the back of the drawer, and then joined the short line cuing up in front of the door.

He rushed through his morning shower, dressed as quickly as he could and tried to brush his hair into a uniform shape. It lay flat for ten whole minutes before the first chicken feathers snapped up.

He found Ben before anyone else when he arrived in the canteen. Ben had chosen a bench near the back of the hall, as usual. Rashanna sat with him. Her girlfriend, if she had rekindled her romance with her, was not present.

He set his tray down and joined them. "I'm so nervous I could die."

"You and me both." Ben said.

Rashanna rolled her eyes. "When are you supposed to go in, anyway?"

"Six, I think."

"It's five thirty."

"And?"

"And you're already late. Everyone has to go through a security check before they get on with their duties today. Didn't you know?"

# SPIRIT OF SHADOW

"Fuck." Lance smacked his forehead. "That means I'm even later."

"Need to go see Lady Jain first, right? I would take you up there, but I'd rather eat my breakfast. Hope you understand." She said.

Lance vaulted to his feet. Ben eased back from the bench, and they left together.

They deposited their food in the trash. Lance took his toast with him. He'd at least have something on his stomach before this started.

When they arrived at the entrance to the Servants' Tunnels, they parted ways.

"I'll see ya in a bit." Ben said.

"See you." He hurried off in the direction of the Office of Operations, where he was to be briefed by Lady Jain.

He stood in line outside the Little Hall, where the queen met with minor nobility when they sought an audience with her. Through the open, oak doors he could see the throne had been removed. The chamber was tiled with matte-gray ceramic that had taken on the character of centuries of erosion, and skylights in the ceiling shed narrow threads of light here and there to touch the leaves of plum trees forever kept in bloom by the gardeners.

He could just see the edge of white hair near the heart of the chamber, where Lady Jain was positioned. He was getting closer.

The cue moved at a sluggish pace as Thorns handled security checks, an unwelcome departure from the usual norms. He did not love the Wraiths, but even less did he want the attention of Thorns, those perpetually fixated on amassing information and doling out judgment, on him. Sami had still not materialized, and he was beginning to suspect they had something to do with it. That she had broken the law in some way, earned their attention. He did not like to think too long on that. Not least because she did had never seemed the type.

He had not had the chance to ask Lothor, yet, either. Having not seen him in the night in some time.

As it was, he had little time left to report to Lady Therien for how long the checks and briefing took. Lady Jain had not minced words, had handed him a badge denoting his station in the grand scheme, and dismissed him.

The palace was in chaos ahead of the reception. The kitchens had been working double time these last days, and the cleaners and

## Who Shines Like the Dawn

launderers were barely able to sleep for all of the waxing, and dusting, and scrubbing, and washing, and pressing that needed to be done. The nobility was mostly dressed in their finest garb and yet even they—haughty and arrogant on the best of their days—seemed nervous.

He arrived at the Office of the Couriers with no time to spare before his assigned time, and Lady Therien greeted him with a tart expression.

"I'll expect punctuality if you choose this path." She said. She tapped a pen against her lips as she examined a ledger, flipped a page and panned over it, her dark eyes darting back and forth rapidly as she hunted for his name. "You'll be at the queen's side for most of the morning with Ben. Lady Jain seems to believe having someone less seasoned, and I suppose less arrogant, will be good for this task. The queen does like her servants green. Ever one to pick them apart, as she is.

"Do not embarrass me today."

Lance's heart fluttered. *By the queen's side...for most of the morning...* He couldn't believe it. It was a rare treat to serve the queen herself, one he had not dreamed he would be called to.

A Wraith approached Lance from the back of the room, where he had previously stood with several others dressed in the same loincloths and warpaint as himself. It seemed even they had taken a little extra time to ready themselves for the ceremony. Spirals and streaks in red paint and what looked like coal ash dressed their faces, making them look even more intimidating than usual.

He patted Lance down from neck to slippers, a second pass he had not anticipated after being cleared by the Thorns, ran his fingers through Lance's hair and then patted it back into shape, and rummaged through all of Lance's pockets. He even flipped Lance's tabard over, both front and back panels, searching for any weapons or enchanted trinkets he might have stashed there.

He kept himself from wincing with some effort. If there was one thing in the world he would have preferred to avoid, such intimate contact with the Wraiths was something he did not think he would ever get used to.

None of the servants would ever think of harming the queen or the nobles, of course, but the emperor's arrival meant special attention needed to be paid. He imagined all of this was reserved for the event that an assassin made an attempt on the emperor's life. It would be foolish to even try.

"Report to the kitchens. Present Mistress Dina with this. Show her the badge you obtained from Lady Jain. Ben?" she called.

Ben hustled over. "Is it time?"

"It is." She said. "Take the boy with you. And please mind your manners. Lady Jain has you serving the queen her *grapes*. As if she can't…anyway. Hop to it. If there's one person you don't want to keep waiting, its *her*."

His insides writhed, but there was a lightness in his step and an easy smile on his lips when he thanked her and walked away.

They arrived in the kitchens half an hour later. The stink of boiling fish sauce was the first thing he noticed as he entered. He hurried past the pot throwing up those fumes and onward down a line full of shining metal cookware and wooden counters where cooks furiously chopped vegetables and hammered steaks so thin he could almost see the cutting board through them.

Two servants worked a slicer in the far corner. One cranked a hand wheel so hard his arms blurred together while the other pushed a frozen hunk of meat through, picked up the thin disk that fell out of the bottom and set it on a plate already loaded down with identical disks of the same stuff—bass judging by the dingy pink-brown striations in the meat.

Still other cooks prepared sauces, floated thin steaks in hot oil, pressed plantains flat against the countertop-like surface of a monstrous, wood-fire grill. Salt flew from hands in huge quantities and everyone seemed to have a jar of seeded citrus fruits of one kind or another on hand. He noticed a whole, dark-fleshed bird rotating on a spit. A tray collected the drippings rolling out of its skin and funneled them into a clay pot.

He breezed past the chefs, calling his pockets as he navigated the line in search of Mistress Dina. He tried not to draw too much attention to himself, but several of the cooks greeted him as he passed. Ben was a favorite, it seemed, and when they arrived at the Mistress's post, it was to find a subtle leer on her lips.

Mistress Dina watched her charges with the same predatory gaze she had favored Lance with when he shadowed under her. The look of her could crush boulders into dust all by itself.

Lance slowed when he saw her, and approached like a prey animal

## Who Shines Like the Dawn

unsure of what it was confronting, even as Ben moved past him to greet her. He clasped his hands behind his back as he closed in on her, and bowed.

"Honor to you, Mistress Dina." Ben said. "Lady Therien said you would have duties for us."

Mistress Dina held out her hand, but her gaze was not focused on him. She panned over everything in the kitchen, everyone. Lance pressed forward, guilt boiling through his intestines. He fished his badge out of his pocket and placed it in her upturned palm.

"Don't you dare, fuck head!" she snapped. Lance whipped around as one of her charges—a boy a little older than him with light brown hair and oily, broken skin—snapped to attention. He shifted the pot he had been stirring to a position far from the round burner at the center of his grill. "That's better. Low and slow to the finish. If you fuck it up, I'll have you in the corner with a dunce cap and a kazoo to play with your ass cheeks until service ends, you hear me?"

"Yes, Mistress Dina." The boy said meekly.

He was suddenly certain he had chosen right by not pursuing this path.

She examined the badge.

"Duties for the queen eh?" she said, her gaze shifting from one to the other of them. "I bet you're excited. Probably think you're something special." She shoved the badge at his chest. He scrambled to catch it before it dropped.

The barest, most malevolent grin broke across her lips. Her eyes flashed ominously. "You best not fuck it up. The queen is merciless, and if you embarrass her…well.

"Do as you are told. Mind her boundaries. Do not break decorum, even for a second. And for the love of all that is sacred, don't speak unless *she* asks you to."

Lance suddenly felt like he would rather be anywhere else. He did not waste time on questions.

"Grapes!" Mistress Dina shouted. "Cheese and crackers! Now!"

Lance flinched at the tone of her voice. Two cooks sprang into action, hurriedly plating an assortment of cheeses and other accoutrements for the queen's consumption and bundling them into two platter with wooden lids carved over with thorny vines and snapdragons. They brought the plates to him as quickly as they could without outright running.

He took one from them. Ben took the other.

They saluted Mistress Dina, who observed them as if they were worms wriggling atop dry earth. They retreated.

"Take the stairs. Wait for your bell to ring. It will ring once to draw your attention. Again to alert you that it is your time. Do nothing until the second bell sounds. Then hurry, but don't appear to be rushing. Kneel to the queen's hand. Do not look at her. Do not *touch* her. Do not ask questions if she commands you to do something. You are the dirt beneath her feet. Bile in her throat. An unpleasant reminder of how her pleasantries come to her. Act like it."

"Understood, Mistress Dina." They said in unison.

"Smart boys." She said. "Now get out of my sight."

They hurried off, mindful of the trays so that they didn't shift overmuch as they navigated the treacherous line on their way back through the kitchens.

They dipped through the entrance and veered toward a narrow staircase, which was bright with the cold, impassive light of a series of glow bulbs recessed into the walls above the polished, oak railing. At its height, it opened onto a small, well-lit chamber whose ceiling was obscured by a system of copper bells, pulleys and cloth streamers. Each streamer was inked with a name.

A series of benches lay against tiled walls, and two doors rested parallel to each other at opposite ends of the room. One led into the labyrinth of palace halls where the nobility too inconsequential to be invited to this audience were undoubtedly gathered, waiting to catch the very slightest glimpse of the emperor and his party when they arrived. The other led into the Grand Hall, which was reserved for the receptions of only the most important dignitaries throughout the Empire. The last time it had been in use was two years previous, when the Immortal Lord of Ash Island, far to the north, had come to call upon their queen.

Lance located his name on a streamer, and Ben's situated next to it.

He thought of the terror that had awoken him in the night. The spirit—so unlike Lothor, so playful—had known him. Had remembered him from a time before the palace, and that dream. If it was a memory, he may not be the lone survivor in his family. There may be a sister somewhere out there waiting for him.

## Who Shines Like the Dawn

He was not sure what to think about it. A sister he would never meet did not change the nature of his life. He was here, had no idea where to find her, and could not leave the palace besides. What good did remembering her do, if the memory of her had no tangible impact? If he could but explore the meaning of a traumatic event which felt so impersonal, even as it settled in his mind's eye, a challenge to the narrative he had long known as truth?

They found seats between two servants on a long bench. He knew their faces, but he had never spoken to either of them. They sat with just enough space between them to accommodate two others, and refused to look at each other.

Ben leaned into his ear, spoke low so that neither of them would hear. "They dated. It didn't end well."

Lance made casual observation of both of them in his periphery. He did not want them knowing he was looking them over, spinning a tale that might fit with their circumstances, their demeanor.

The girl's bell rang. She got up and exited through the entrance into the Grand Hall, toting a small plate with a burnished, bronze lid. A number of others left with her; their bells having sounded.

The boy sighed. "Women. You'd think they would let go eventually."

Lance tried to ignore him, but he kept talking. He was attractive enough, with straight, umber hair, and dark circles under his eyes that gave him the appearance of someone aloof and mysterious.

"You know, we didn't even date that long. It was three months. She was so possessive, and well I…it doesn't matter." He said. "The point is she's crazy. She put a live rat in my bed, you know…"

Lance let the boy's grousing wash over him. He was aware of the rat situation. Rumors spread rapidly among the servants, especially those younger, but he did not know what possessed her to go so far. There must be a reason. After all, it was not in the nature of people to seek petty revenge of that magnitude over something trivial.

He suspected the boy had cheated on her. He was not alone in that belief.

Ben squeezed his hand, and the boy pressed on until their bells rang, twin chimes, for the first time.

Their bells rang for the second time, as the boy pressed on. Ben interrupted.

# SPIRIT OF SHADOW

"I'm sorry, but that's us."

The boy nodded. "Thanks for the company."

He sprang to his feet, the wooden box in hand. Lance followed him through the servant's entrance to the Grand Hall.

It didn't just dwarf the Small Hall, it eclipsed it. A series of skylights ran the length of the ceiling, shedding light on a wine-red carpet that ran the length of the room. Pillars held up copses to either side of the central pass. Everything was done in granite and gold—floors, pillars, walls…even the ceiling. A pair of double doors with an intricate knot worked to look like five creatures chasing after each other was the only exception, and that made of smooth, poured stone. The creatures were the Five Saints from story and myth—a peacock; a wyvern; a great, whiskered serpent; a falcon; and a fox with nine tails.

Together, they represented the endless passage of time, and all of the change that came with it. The first mortals believed they were real, but Imperial wisdom said otherwise.

The throne rested beyond the reach of the last beams shed from those skylights, alluding to its owner's title, her association with shadows. At no audience was the queen ever in direct light. Tradition in Shadovane mandated that she never touch the light in the presence of those who came before her.

The throne itself was a forbidding thing. Its back and sides were petrified wood gleaming in an array of vibrant colors. Amethysts dripped from its twisted branches, and threads of fine silk connected the thickest bows high above the queen's head—a spider's web and a porcelain spider nestled into it. Its abdomen was the largest amethyst of them all.

No one but the queen herself could have sat that throne without being consumed by it. The throne was magnificent, but it lacked the subtlety of her beauty. She was the diamond in the dross that was her domain. Her skin was pale as porcelain, her dark-as-night eyes framed by thick, dark fans. Her nose was a subtle prominence over full lips stained so dark they were almost black, and her buxom, curvy frame was more than even Lady Therien—known for her beauty if for nothing else—could claim.

The high nobility gathered to either side of the carpet running from the great, heavy doors to her seat, dressed in their finest, taking

**Who Shines Like the Dawn**

refreshment from a number of servants, pretending not to see her. She drowned their grandeur, cast it away behind the veil of her perfection.

Following Ben's example, Lance made his approach on sure feet. His guts roiled inside of him, but he kept the worst of his nerves off his face and hoped none of it showed that she could see. They crossed from the pillars behind her throne, and knelt at her hands. He kept his eyes forward as he removed the lid and held it behind his back, offering the tray to her armrest in silence.

She peered at it, plucked a green grape from the vine and slipped it past her lips.

*Am I doing this right?* Mistress Dina had said not to talk, but as he watched the queen, he thought he should say something. Anything was better than complete silence.

Two guards stood at Queen Meredith's flanks. They were both members of the Council of Liam. Near Lance, boxing him in, was Lord Aren—his hair almost completely silver, his cheeks pooling under his chin, with sharp, silver eyes that seemed to see everything at once. The other was Lord Elise, whose own eyes projected a kind of slow madness, a disquieting rage. He was younger than any of the other seats on the Council of Liam, having risen high in a very short time.

Lance thought back to a conversation in the armory, how Lord Halan had been reluctant to send any servant to him, and realized that he could believe the Councilman capable killing someone over almost nothing.

Lord Elise was a time bomb. He wore an easy smile that contrasted with the darkness lurking behind his eyes, bringing that madness out even further.

Both men wore the plate armor that all of the Bloodless did—made to look as if smoke had been forged into the metal, with black and violet sashes wrapped around the waist and spaulders crafted to resemble the heads of ravens.

Lance made a point not to look directly at either of them.

"Lord Elise?" the queen said. "You will have to have someone take these children's trays back to the kitchens."

"Theodora!" he shouted.

A girl froze with her plate held out to a nobleman dressed in black silks. She scurried to the throne.

"Take their trays *back* to the *kitchens*." If she was afraid, she didn't show it. She took Lance's burden from him, moved over to take up

# SPIRIT OF SHADOW

Ben's as well, and rushed off toward the shadows and safety.

"Thank you." The queen said. She turned toward Lance. He averted his gaze. "Fear not, young one. All of these other servants will be dismissed shortly. The emperor will want the hall cleared. He is greater than any king or lord, and the forms must be respected, for propriety's sake.

"Still, I cannot be seen to have no one at hand. Should the need arise, you will take up whatever duty he desires, though I think he will not need you."

A shiver ran up Lance's spine. He savored her words, hoping beyond hope he had not misunderstood her. *I'm to serve...him?*

He met Ben's gaze, saw the subtle grin spread across his lips, there and gone in a flash. There was the edge of envy there, as well, a softer kind, for he must want to be seen in this hall like him. Seen by this impossible creature.

Even if his services were not needed, that meant staying through the entire audience. He considered that this honor should have gone to someone older, wiser, with more experience under his belt. It would have made far more sense to select someone who had, at least, gone through their test and set onto their life's path. But he wasn't going to complain, nor was he going to point any of this out to his queen. He intended to bask in this moment, and remember it for all of his life.

Rumors upon rumors framed the emperor in an improbable light. He was bliss incarnate. He was the tallest elf who ever lived. His eyes were wreathed in flame. No, he had no eyes. No, they were made of solid gold, and he radiated light from every orifice. When he spoke, all things became silent. The very wind stopped blowing. No, it blew at his back wherever he went. The sound of his voice raised the dead. No, it healed all illness. No, that was the sight of him.

Lance wondered what he was about to see, and also feared it. The emperor was immortal. He was born on the day of creation, and he had not aged a day since.

*Is he a child then?* Lance wondered. *Or is he stuck in some other age?*

He didn't have to wonder long. A Bloodless dislodged himself from his team at the forward gate, spoke briefly to Lord Elise before walking away. Lord Elise whispered something into the queen's ear.

## Who Shines Like the Dawn

"The servants are dismissed." She said in a carrying voice. "The time of the emperor's arrival has come."

The servants scattered into the dark like rats. Lance resisted the urge to join them. He was not worthy of this honor and he knew it, like they did.

He remained in his place. Dull pain ran through his knee, down his shin and into his ankle but he ignored it. What was coming was far too important for his comforts.

With the servants gone, the nobility lined up to either side of the throne along the first third of the carpet.

Thunder rolled through the chamber almost as soon as they were assembled. A pair of Bloodless marched away from the doors. Another eight filtered in from various places throughout the room. They formed a line to one side of the carpet, joining the nobility there.

The first rays of sun peeked through the series of skylights, brightening the scarlet carpet running from poured stone double doors to throne, washing out the stormy grays and lightning-bright lines in the granite floor.

The doors cracked open.

A different light danced with a series of tapestries hanging between the columns. As the doors continued to roll apart, the sliver of light broadened, encompassed everything before the throne, which resisted its glow by some magic Lance did not know.

Figures streamed through the entrance amid the sound of beating drums and symbols bashed together; echoing, adding to the ambient tension that stiffened the backs of every member of Shadovane's nobility. The first figures to cross the threshold were dressed in plate mail which had been forged with a pearl-like cast set into the metal. Their sashes and capes were gold and sky blue, and they wore bell-shaped helmets with a great, yellow disk painted in the center of their foreheads.

Lance had heard of the Enlightened. They were Mirrhvale's equivalent of the Bloodless, the most feared and cherished force throughout the Empire.

They marched across the carpet, a drumbeat marking every step, until they came to rest opposite the ten Bloodless. After them came the smell of incense from swinging thuribles held in the hands of burlap clad monks from the capital's temples. Every elven head was dressed in falls of golden hair, every eye green or grey or blue. Lance had expected the Mirrhvalians to look different, to dress in different garb certainly, but he had not expected the contrast to be this stark—like night and day.

The monks were followed by Mirrhvale's nobility. By comparison, they made the Shadovani in their opaque silks and woolens dyed in deep and dark colors look prudish. The men went sleeveless, with their collars covered in falls of gold chain and fine bangles of gold and silver dripping from their wrists. Their silks were so sheer Lance could almost see through them and the women left little more to the imagination. They wore bangles and tiaras, rings on every finger, jewels large enough to purchase the loyalties of whole courts in the borderlands and dresses that clung and flowed in the most flattering ways, of materials as sheer and transparent as the noblemen.

They filtered in as a double file and positioned themselves accordingly. When all of those who came with the emperor had taken their places, silence descended. If the mood of the room wasn't tense before, it was alarmingly so now.

The anticipation was making it hard to focus. He was too aware of who was next to him, who was guarding her. The circumstances demanded he not break from decorum and tradition, and yet he wanted to run from this place, flee from the Grand Hall and the castle and Shadovane, never to return.

The true event was marked by the piercing cry of a horn—one clear, carrying note that touched Lance's heart. Gooseflesh crawled over his skin and he knew, in that moment, that he would never witness something so great as this moment, so terrible as what transpired here and now.

The note died. The drums beat anew. Every man and woman stood at attention. He had never seen them so apprehensive. Light spilled into the room. Like the reflection of the sun beneath water it fractured and pulsed, spread across the walls, the floor, embracing everything, yielding to nothing. It spread across the throne, breaking the magic of its enchantment and washing the Shadow Queen over, revealing her in her every detail.

And then *he* came.

A guard stood at each compass point, boxing him in, and Lance knew who they were too. They were called Prophets. They were the

## Who Shines Like the Dawn

emperor's honor guard. If they had been standing next to anyone else, they would have struck awe into him, but the emperor was all consuming, pushing them out of his mind along with every other aspect of the room. In the moment he set his eyes on the emperor, all that surrounded him bled together, the corona surrounding the sun, and he couldn't look away.

He was impossibly tall, perhaps nine feet, willowy and commanding in pristine, white linen that glowed with the light that emanated from his skin. His eyes were vacant, silver rings in milky oceans, bearing a terrible knowledge that would take any mortal man under, into chaos. He wore no adornments save a stole with a great, yellow sun emblazoned at each end, and a brilliant, rose-gold crown, broken and bowed at the front in an approximation of a beetle's mandibles, with teardrop cut turquoise and sapphire dangling from its edges.

He halted with his guard before the gathered figures. The high, youthful voice of a boy still in the throws of puberty came from behind him. Lance heard the struggle in the boy's voice, the strained effort to keep it from cracking.

"Welcome the emperor, the Immortal Light of Bliss, the first creation of the Sky Lord who is God, Lord of the Thirteen Wards, Wielder of the Light Well, first and last defender of us all. Welcome him. Emperor Conan of Mirrhvale. Welcome him."

The gathered nobility, soldiers and monks threw themselves to the ground, pressed their foreheads to the carpet.

"All hail the Lord of the Morning." They recited in unison. "All hail his holiness."

"May the light shelter you." The emperor said.

"And may the shadow preserve *you*." They responded.

The elves stood gracefully. The queen and the emperor held each other's eyes. There was electricity there, a bond forged in love or in power. It was a fearsome thing the look they set upon each other.

The emperor's eyes drifted to her chest for a fraction of a second, where a pendant lay in the valley between her supple breasts—a silver spiral with a soft, green gem suspended in its twist.

A more experienced servant would know better than to watch the emperor, but Lance was clumsy, unaware. Those eyes, drunk with the knowledge of the ages, reported anger in that moment, and if Lance didn't mistake it, the barest hint of fear.

# SPIRIT OF SHADOW

*What could he have to fear from a pendant?*

It was hard to conceive of someone with the degree of both political and real power he possessed fearing anything. He wielded it so easily—as if he was quite unaware of who he was. It was good enough that his subordinates knew that for him.

He knelt by Lance, until his lips were at Lance's ear. Lance froze, suddenly unsure what to do. The urge to run as fast as he could away from the man, the throne, the chamber resurfaced. There too was the nagging feeling that doing so would almost certainly dishonor the queen, and tarnish the reputation of Shadovane.

"I understand you are frightened, child." The emperor whispered. "It would please me greatly, however, if you stepped aside."

Lance's bowels went to water. He could feel heat rising in his cheeks and hoped he wasn't blushing noticeably. He stepped back and to the side until he was clear of the throne. The emperor took his place, standing at the queen's right hand.

He cleared his throat, and when he spoke, he spoke with confidence.

"I am honored." He said. "Shadovane has been an ally like no other throughout our history as the greatest power in the world. It will forever be the jewel of the Sun Empire, a place of poise, of restraint, a pillar of infallible support in a world increasingly plagued by violence and discord.

"It is my honor to return here, to the birthplace of the Mother of Night, daughter of the one true god, the Sky Lord, whose name we do not utter. Ten years is long to be so distant, and while I have enjoyed news come from your leader, Queen Meredith, there is something in seeing a thing in person that words cannot quite capture, however articulate, however pure in their intention.

"I come to you with my most trusted, and my most loyal, that we may again know each other. So long an absence has made us strangers where we were once family. I would have my family returned to me. And so, I am honored by the kindness that has been shown, the clear effort apparent in this reception. May we come to know each other better in the coming weeks, and rekindle the kindred spirit we once enjoyed."

The gathered nobility applauded. They dragged their clapping on for an age, smiling while they darted acid glances at each other. The highest among them—Lord Giram who helmed the Council of Liam; buxom

## Who Shines Like the Dawn

Lady Therien; Lord Haman Bran, descendant of Queen Mariah who was the most famous queen of Shadovane; Lady Jain, who sat atop a horde of gold and silver; and old Lord Aren whose network of spies and questioners made even the nobles nervous—were the first to rest. Beyond them all others dragged their applause on and on, until finally the emperor held up his hand for silence.

The queen rose as their applause died down.

"It is our humble honor to serve in your Empire." She said. "To serve in the construction of your dream."

She stepped aside. The emperor positioned himself before the throne, and took his seat. He sat so tall in that chair that his head blocked the porcelain and amethyst spider in its web. The queen took his previous position. Electricity entered her gaze.

*Was that anger? That look...could it be hatred?*

He wondered who else had seen it. Who had noticed? Was he the only one? The gathered nobility, soldiers and monks gave away nothing.

The audience proceeded from there through a series of formalities including the offering of a number of extravagant gifts including Tromite horses from the Free Lands and furniture hewn of the Lafia tree, a variety only found in the deepest reaches of Juakali, with roots that reached for the sky—or so the nobleman who presented them claimed. When the last of them were given, the emperor gave thanks for the gifts he had graciously received. He rose, and his honor guard fell into step with him.

"A ball is to be held this evening in honor of our emperor's return." The queen announced. "Until then, you may consider yourselves dismissed."

Lance waited by her side while the double file of nobility, clergy and soldiers followed the emperor out. As the last of them left, the queen tipped backward on her heels and vanished through the place where her shadow touched the granite floor.

Lance stared at the place where she had vanished. For a wonder, it seemed even his queen had forgotten he was there.

*What did I just see?*


When he passed through the holding chamber, it was to find it empty. The servants who had been there, awaiting their turns to pass hor d'oeuvres into the waiting hands of the nobility and soldiers gathered ahead of the reception, had been cleared away, leaving not a trace to remember them by.

He passed out of the chamber and into a hall which was alive with chatter and banter, as the gathered nobility of little consequence passed rumors back and forth, and some of those in attendance recounted the events just transpired to peers who clung to their every word.

He navigated the hall to its end, being careful to avoid bumping into any which one of those people, thinking of Ben and the conversation to be had between them. He was excited to tell Ben all he knew of the emperor, and anxious to recount the strange flashes as of resentment that had passed between their queen, and him.

He followed an adjoining hall away. The nobility were sparser here, so many of them choking the hall he had just been down, but a few of those Mirrhvalians also lingered in this hall, evidently catching up with old friends among the Shadovani.

He slipped past them and down the first hall he could find, intent on getting away from them, taking the shortest way to the Servants' Tower he could find. Ben would be waiting for him there in the canteen, and if he wasn't, Ariana and Peter should be finding their way out of the kitchens soon, a brief reprieve before preparations for this ball the queen had announced were needed. They would want to hear his tale, too, though he suspected they would not believe him.

He thought of Sami then. For all the pomp and spectacle, of rushing through a hectic morning, he had not thought much for her. He was alone now, following a hall with a familiar flavor, which bred an itch into the joint between his shoulders.

*Is she avoiding me, or has something happened to her?*

There was that chance he could find her, given his recent

discovery of the shadow spirit's name, his nature, the sudden shift toward camaraderie between them. He decided to call on him.

"*Lothor?*" He whispered.

"*Careful, now. You are exposed.*" The spirit said.

He looked around, found the familiar spider crawling down a nearby door frame.

"I just wondered...have you found her?"

"*Your friend is hiding. No, not from you. She is nonetheless dealing with complicated designs, and is only half aware of the weight they carry. She will, I think, resurface soon enough. Though she will not be welcomed back among you. She has been gone too long.*"

"Where is she?"

"*She moves, yet she is always within the palace. Always inside the tunnels your kind use for transit. She is nonetheless unharmed.*"

"T-thank you." He said. "It doesn't do much to put my mind at ease, but at least she is safe. Wherever she's been."

"*As you say.*"

"Zente, *Lothor.*"

He pressed on, and within a few steps found himself standing before a familiar gate, one crafted of bronze and embellished with flowers, behind which descended a staircase, into deep shadow.

He reeled back reflexively, a bitter dream of darkness and grease and rank odors surging forth, freezing him in place.

A hand settled on his shoulder, and he spun into its owner's grip. Lord Aren consumed all of his vision, and the look on his face was like fire.

"Where did you learn that skill?" he demanded.

"Learn...what? Learn what, my lord?" he said.

"You know precisely of what I speak. Where did you learn to call him?"

"Am I...am I in...are you going to—"

# SPIRIT OF SHADOW

The fire left Lord Aren's face, and he settled a cold regard on him. He could not read what lay behind that expression as the old general knelt. "Do not ever show what you have done to anyone. Do you understand me. It is a rare talent. Particularly now, it will see you into difficult circumstances, and I cannot protect you."

"Protect...you're not going to have me executed?"

Lord Aren shook his head. "Have you taken up with Master Gregor?"

"We've talked. I accepted his offer."

"Good. He alone may know of what you've stumbled onto, you understand?" Lord Aren said. "No one else. Not even your friends."

*More secrets.* Lance thought. *What's going on with him?*

Lord Aren released his grip. "As long as we understand each other. Your talents are uncommon and dangerous. Not dangerous by themselves, but dangerous if others find out about them."

He climbed to his feet, turned to leave.

"I can see them." He said.

Lord Aren froze in mid step. "A spider. And a weasel once. They are all in silhouette, with white eyes. They come to me."

"Tell no one of this." He marched away.

# AWAKENING

# Choice

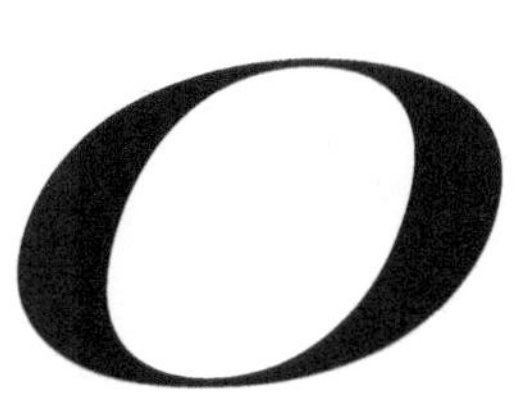

ne last talk. *Then it'll be over.* Lance thought to himself as he lingered outside Lady Tamalsen's door. If he succeeded in whatever testing Master Gregor required, he would take his place among the furnace workers, and he might never have to see her again.

It was a bittersweet thought. As much as he was ready to move on—was ready to leave behind the janitorial services the palace demanded of its younger servants—he did not enjoy the idea of leaving Lady Tamalsen on a bitter note. He wondered how spiteful she would be, how angry when he told her he had made his choice and it was nothing she approved of; but then he had already known he would work for them before the emperor's reception. Had known he would face a fight, yes, but had made his decision nonetheless.

As he rapped the knocker against the door, he found he had no regrets. Calm stole over him, stilling his nerves, as she said: "Enter."

He pushed the door inward, entered her office, and took the offered seat without protest.

## Choice

She set her gaze on him, steepled her fingers together in front of her. Her papers lay in neat piles next to her elbow, and for the first time in his memory, the desk was otherwise clear.

"Did you enjoy yesterday's events?"

"I did."

A warm smile alighted on her lips. "Good. Then I take it you've made your decision."

"I have."

"For the couriers?"

A long pause as he formulated his thoughts.

"I appreciate the time you took to pull whatever strings you did. I really do. That ceremony will be one of my fondest memories, I think. But—"

She held up her hand to stop him.

"You're greasing the shoot, but it will lead to the same place whether it is freshly oiled or dry and peppered with glass." She said. "You're rejecting the offer, aren't you?"

He grimaced. "I am."

"Why?"

"Well, I—"

"When your life would be so much less complicated, why not choose the obvious path? Why not live and thrive among friends and peers who understand you, who are of similar *intellect* to you?" she demanded. "Why bother choosing a path which can only bring you hardship when you are qualified for something far better, far more practical...even *honorable!*

"It does not make sense to me?"

"I'm sorry, I—"

"Just go." She gestured sharply at the door, her regard cold against him. "Go to your pitiful life."

"I'm sorry, Lady Tamalsen. I had hoped this parting would be on better terms."

Her lips twitched.

He stood and bowed, then shambled to the door.

# SPIRIT OF SHADOW

"What is it that so charms you about those people?" she asked as he reached for the handle. "No. Never mind. I do not want to know."

He drew the door open, and exited.

As soon as it was closed behind him, a smile crossed his face, bunched his cheeks into tight balls as he did a little dance in the mostly empty hall. A servant washing the far wall with a thick sponge chuckled. He had been watching him as he left the office.

"You pissed her off, didn't you?" he said.

"I promise I didn't mean to."

The servant snorted, went back to his scrubbing.

He hopped away, elated now it was finally over.


Lord Aren paced the length of his office, the bone-white shepherd's hook above and behind him, his wardrobe soundly closed. He ran his fingers along the edge of his desk, absently playing with the tooling there as a scribe waited for him to dictate his message to her.

The scribe was a newly risen servant, and he did not trust her. The more seasoned among them knew the importance of keeping their mouths shut, but the younger...well, they gossiped. He had chosen her knowing she would, a politically necessary move in order to ensure he was not seen to be withholding information from the other generals on the Council of Liam—chief among them Lord Cree, who would pose a complication to him if he began to suspect they were not aligned in their goals.

He thought about how to frame the messages he needed to send, how to word them so that their meaning was not lost even as little might be parsed out by those he did not want scrutinizing his activities.

He started with Lady Therien.

"To the Lady of House Therien, I commend you for an

excellent showing with this morning's activities." He said. The scribe set to work. "However, I must forewarn that you send a courier to my residence on the morrow. I am in need of a draw from my accounts. Please do send the one who served me some days ago, I cannot remember when. I found his service was exemplary, and believe he is worthy of this greater measure of responsibility in my affairs.

"I would quite like it if you entertained the idea of sending him to me as a dedicated servant in the future, if he continues to show this high measure of competence.

"Yours, Silas Aren."

The scribe finished with the letter, let the ink set and then waved it to finish drying. She slid it aside, selected a new piece of parchment, and set down to wait again.

"To Lord Giram." He said. "I am aware of your desires of me; however, I have nothing new to report. Activity in the city has slowed, as we expected, and the vermin have gone to ground. My Thorns continue to watch for changes, and I will report when any change occurs."

The servant signed the letter, let it dry, and set it neatly atop the first.

"To Master Gregor, my chambers are a bit warm at the moment. Please pause the heat coming up to them for a time. Have your boys see to it that I am not roasted alive. Take whatever steps necessary to ensure they comprehend the delicate balance between a bonfire and an ice shield."

The scribe repeated her ritual with the last letter. When she was finished, she folded the parchments and pushed them to the edge of the writing desk she sat behind. He crossed to her with a pot of heated wax in hand, and dribbled a little of the powder blue substance on each. He impressed his seal, the ringlet of blackthorn, into the wax on each of them, and she let it set before housing them all in a satchel at her ankle.

She picked up the leather case, bowed to him. "The shadow preserve you, Lord Aren."

# SPIRIT OF SHADOW

"You are dismissed." He said.
She took her leave.

# Burners & Breezers

hen Lance arrived in the furnaces the following night, it was with a new sense of determination. The smell of soot and earth hung on the air, and the uniforms of the workers were dirty and gray with coal and sweat wiped away from calloused hands. The shovel was stabbed into the hill of black, misshapen rocks across from the entrance where it lay under a wrought-bronze balcony, which overlooked the pit where the servants labored.

Lady Tamalsen had not yet given up on turning him away from this path, he was sure of it. Tonight would hand her a victory if he did not succeed. She had done everything short of beg him not to squander his gifts, but she did not know what he did. Did not see the necessity of this for the secrets he hid from her.

She did not see him in his barracks, staring across Laramy's bed at the window from which the moon's glow fell, hunting after a spider whose name he now knew, whose power he could call upon be it for his benefit or otherwise. She did not know about the monster inside of him that refused to stay quiet when all else was still—the nightmares that bubbled forth, promising windows into a past he did not want to remember. He needed this place, for the distraction it provided him, for the promise made by Lord Aren that he would find among these people—most of them kitunes placed here as a byproduct of Lady Tamalsen's prejudice—understanding.

Master Gregor was waiting for him when he arrived in his office. He held a letter in his hand, and another was open and laying atop the mass of other items scattered across his desk—tools and missives and other dross.

He lounged on his chair with his boots resting on the desk's edge, glanced at Lance over the letter as he entered.

"Close the door, will ya?" he said. "Got some things ta discuss wit' ya."

A sleuce can sat next to his free hand. He spat into it without looking. Chew spit ran into the vessel, not a drop spilling across the desk's surface.

"She give ya trouble?" he asked.

Lance nodded.

"Sit, sit. Yer makin' me uncomfortable."

Lance took the open seat across from him.

"She sent this 'ere." He flapped a letter at him. "Hot load o' garbage, in'it, but I s'pose it shows she cares."

"What's it say?" Lance asked.

"Lot o' stuff 'bout how I should be shamed for askin' you to take a job here knowin' yer too smart for it. Little bit 'bout how disappointed she is in ya fer choosin' these 'ere louts over *posh, disciplined* people." He gestured at the bay window, a series of thick pipes blocking sight of his soon to be peers. "She *really* wanted *you.*" He chuckled, exposing several missing teeth.

"Oh, wait, 's my favorite."

He cleared his throat, glanced at Lance, a mischievous look on his face as he settled back in his seat, adjusted his feet atop the desk.

In a shrill imitation of Lady Tamalsen's voice, he read: "'It *boggles* me that such a gifted young man would *elect* willingly to work among *loud*, dirty *vagabonds* like you. But I suppose I am wasting my words. You don't know what half of them mean, anyway.'

"Ya see, I can't quite tell 'f she means *boggles, elect* or *vagabond* but the tone is clear enough. She thinks ev'ry damned kitune in 'is place 's an idiot." He saluted with two fingers. "Jus' goes ta show what she knows."

"So she's mad." Lance said. "I gathered that when I talked to her yesterday."

"Maybe she ought a point. Ya do talk like one o' them snooty bitches."

"Thanks."

"I 'on't mean nothin' by it." He said. "Jus' bustin' yer balls. But tha's not what I wanted a private moment wit' ya 'bout. There's 'is other business ta settle."

He tossed Lady Tamalsen's letter in a trash bin and picked up the other one. The seal was still clinging to the paper, a ringlet of blackthorn in blue wax.

"Ta the untrained eye, this'd be a request to stop pumpin' so much damned heat into the vents up Lord Aren's way, but I ain't got one o' those. My vision is sharp as ever ya see, and I know what Lord Aren came from. My question is, do you?"

"I'm afraid not, Master—"

"Told ya to call me Gregor, didn' I?"

"Right."

"Well, see, Lord Aren come's out o' the slums 'bout thirty

# SPIRIT OF SHADOW

aught years ago. 'Bout same time I showed up in 'ese parts. Was lookin' fer a change, ya see, an ain't a lot o' places you could earn much outside the Ring in 'ose days. S'neither here nor there." He waved it all away. "What's important 's Lord Aren's a friend. Came up as a Wraith, he did. I 'on't envy 'em who take that way into the army, but he an' his brother had plans an' damn if they didn't make good on 'em.

"Almost forgot. *Lothor,* yoldord sei iyel."

*"You have always been a coarse bastard, you know that."* Lothor grumbled.

"Call me what'cha want, but ya do right by me. Like a little privacy while we handle delicate business."

Lance looked in the direction Lothor's voice had come from, found the silhouetted spider crawling across a messy stack of papers on the desk.

"What'cha lookin' at 'ere, friend?" Master Gregor asked.

"A spider." Lance said before he could think to stop himself.

Master Gregor ran his hand across his scalp, and whistled. "Never thought I'd see the day. Makes sense o' what Lord Aren was hintin' at, though, don' it?

"You can see 'em. The spirits."

"Is that not normal."

"Look kid, 'ere aren't many people out 'ere can *hear* 'em anymore. Really hear 'em. None of that music 'ey make when 'ey're all in pain, their voices. What 'ey *say*. I can't say I ever met anyone who could *see* 'em. There're stories, o' course, 'bout a king in the Free Lands, but nothin' anyone can verify. Empire suppresses infermation like 'at anyway.

"But look, s' nothin' ya shouldn' be proud o'. S' not normal, but—"

*"It is a gift."* Lothor said. *"One which comes but once in an era."*

"Lord Aren told me not to tell anyone." Lance said. "When

he found me by the staircase.”

A dark chuckle escaped Master Gregor. “Best ya leave ‘at place alone fer now.”

“What’s down there?”

“Nothin’ you want ta see. But come on.”

He hopped onto his feet. “We got a test fer ya ta pass. An’ let me tell ya, everyone ‘ere knows tha old way. Can ‘ear em like you can. Well…mos’ly.”

He led him around to the door, opened it and followed him through. They marched across the bronze catwalk and down the stairs into the pit. Then around to a metal cone shaped like a cornucopia. Several furnace workers followed their progress to the fluted contraption. Its wide end was fully three man heights high and situated so that it faced them, and its narrow end was connected to a duct that cut a path into the ceiling.

“We use this fer testin’. ‘Bout time any heat blasted in it gets anywhere it dulls out enough doesn’t affect much, but in the before times it was the primary means of heatin’ the palace corridors.

“Yer task is ta blast heat into it, by makin’ use o’ the spirits, but ‘ey’re a testy bunch. Won’t come willin’ly unless ya figure out their names, and ya have ‘till the end o’ the night to do that. I ‘on’t expect it to take too long, given the circumstances.

“Now, let me call on tha one ya need.”

His lips framed a silent word that Lance could not read, and in the wake of it, a spirit materialized, alighted on the vaulted rise before the cornucopia where he and Master Gregor stood.

The creature was a fox, resembled those in some of the friezes he had seen throughout the palace. His gaze shifted to it, and it set a steady regard on him.

*“We approach the end of an era, and order is restored.”* She said, her voice a soothing contralto. She looked to Master

# SPIRIT OF SHADOW

Gregor, whose gaze was fixed on the cornucopia. *"Is this one who sees?"*

"Should be apparent what he is, lookin' at him." Master Gregor answered.

She turned her attention back to Lance. *"Then know my nature, and wield me, Seem."*

"What is a Seem?" he asked.

A soft chuckle from the fox. *"Where there is fire, I am there also. Not naked to the eye save in the presence of my sister, but there always, when she is not. When embers crackle in the hearth, I am there, and weaker than when my brother brings the flame. Always, I am there when the sun touches the land, yet in shadow I may rest. In winter, I may sleep, until again the fire emerges. Know my nature, and I will grant you my name. Know my essence, and I will pass unto you my power."*

He did not have to think long to comprehend her true nature. It was there, pressed against his skin, the principle purpose behind the work these servants did. He did not flinch away from this truth, but spoke it plainly for the spirit to hear, voiced her nature, and awaited her name.

"You are heat." He said.

*"And my name is Phia. The command you shall call to me, when you need, for the simplest expression of my power. Call for me and say...dabi benigne mi."*

He positioned himself before the cornucopia. Master Gregor helped him set his stance, one leg back to brace himself, his hand forward, trained on the fluted pipe.

"Do it." Master Gregor said, stepping back to a safe distance. "Put all ya got into it."

"Dabi begnigne mi, *Phia.*" He said.

Many of the servants down below stopped what they were doing to watch, more than a few looked impressed. He suspected it was not common for someone to pick this up so swiftly, but he had practice. Had called two spirits already.

## Burners & Breezers

Phia leaned back on her hind legs, lowered her muzzle almost to the floor. Her power surged into him, and raw heat blasted from his palms, blasted on a high wind into the pipe.

Master Gregor took another step back and shielded his face as the heat surged forth. As it rumbled into the pipe and banged against its narrower end.

"Stop!" he shouted over the noise. That's good, now stop!"

"Zente, *Phia.*" Lance said.

*"As you wish."*

The heat subsided, the rumbling dying down as the last of that terrible wind flew up the shoot.

Down below the servants cheered, some slapping each other on the back and laughing as he turned round to face them.

He didn't quite know what to do in that moment, and when Master Gregor came to his side, clapped him on the rump, he jumped. "Ya got a gift, kid. Ya got a gift.

"Now get down 'ere and help 'ese assholes out. Ya just earned yer spot wit' em."

"Come on, Master Gregor, 'on't scare 'im away now!" A kitune among the servants down below shouted. He was doughy around the middle, with dark brown hair and silver eyes. He might have been a year or two older than Lance, but no more than that, and the smile he set upon him was warm and broad.

"Would you shut your fucking trap, Duardo." A woman, the one with short-cropped hair who Lance had seen briefly on his stage, snapped.

Duardo glared at her, but he kept his silence.

"Come down 'ere and join up wit' me. I'll see to ya tonight."

"Go on then. Duardo's a good 'un. He'll take care o' ya." Master Gregor pushed him toward a staircase descending into the pit.

"Did I not tell you to—"

"Both a ya could learn a lot from shuttin' up." Master Gregor snapped. "'S his testin'. Give 'im a minute, yeesh!"

Silence descended with the finality of a hammer stroke.

He joined Duardo in the pit, and the kitune led him to one of the various metal boxes, the furnaces, where he set him before the opening.

"We take it in shifts, but 'cause yer new, you 'an go right now. I'll come behind ya wit' a nice breeze ta give it some body. We work together like this an' 'at's how heat gets up to the upper floors. Got it?"

"I think so."

He settled back onto his hind foot. Phia remained where she had been, watching as he began his work. She lay at Master Gregor's side as he sat, the kitune unaware of her, as her power was drawn into the waiting hands of others. Another fox materialized next to her, and lay down at her side. He suspected that one served as much purpose here, was another spirit of fire.

"Alright, go." Duardo said.

He called to Phia, and an answering surge of power ran through him. As if from a vast distance, he heard a song in her voice, and was surprised to find it was joined by other voices. A light, male voice, and a lilting melody joining them which was familiar to him. He looked up to the rise once more, and found a weasel had joined them. Aughere's presence made him falter for a moment, before Duardo nudged him back toward the open door of the furnace, guiding the direction of his heat into the furnace itself.

As he grew used to the rite, and worked himself into a heavy sweat, an ache formed behind his eyes. It worsened the more he used it, forcing him to put in more effort to maintain his focus, and in spite of himself he found his mind drifting. The ache made him think of thorns, like those carried in the balled up feet of the ravens on Shadovane's banners, and those that prowled the dungeons and palace halls—that struck fear into the servants, Wraiths and noblemen alike—who were controlled by Lord Aren.

He thought of the fire, too. Of the raging currents inside the furnace. Of the fires that plagued his dreams. Of Aughere, where he floated above the two foxes, both of whom ignored his presence, seeming annoyed.

Duardo's hand on his shoulder drew him up.

"That's enough." Lance found the other boy smiling at him. He let go of Phia's power, and stepped aside. "I 'on't want ya to burn out. Using magic like that too long or too much will kill ya if you're not careful."

"What do you want me to do, then? Shovel coal?" Lance asked.

"I want ya to get to bed. Need ya fresh for yer next shift."

So, Lance left the furnaces, smiling at Duardo as he made his way out. Something in him suggested he would find camaraderie with the excitable but good natured kitune in the future.

When he finally found his bed, stripped off his clothes and climbed into it, and all thought for the Thorns and those fires had gone in his exhaustion, his thoughts turned to Sami, and he wondered at where she had gone. Whether he would ever see her again.

Sleep took him, robbing him of what remained of his concerns, and plunged him into a dream.

# Shadow Queen

An elf stood guard outside Meredith's chambers, but his shift was close to its end. She lounged against an ornate, uncomfortable couch, a lively fire burning behind the grate in her hearth, painting her body in red glow and shadow. A pink, silk robe was draped over her, the panels open and exposing her breasts, the contours of her hips, a soft, inviting flash of leg.

She waited at rest, her pose carefully selected, for she knew a suitor would be arriving soon, and when he did, she would tempt him.

Outside, soft footfalls alerted her to the coming relief. She looked to a clock on the mantle, saw its hands poised just shy of midnight, the seconds ticking away silently as delicate enchanting work propelled it ever onward. How she had marveled at those devices when first she had come to this palace, not as a pauper but its queen. She had never seen something so mesmerizing, so beyond her comprehension in those days, as the memories of all of those women who came before her awakened within her. In those molting days, it had been the study of enchanters' crafts that kept her stable—as her mind was flayed apart by the power of Celesti's Soul, as it stitched itself together.

The pendant lay across her supple breasts, a smooth, green stone held fast by a spiral of silver. The tooling of the pendant was simplistic, almost crude, and she had thought more than once to have it reset; but to be apart from it felt dirty, as if in letting it pass into another's hands, even to have it fixed into a clasp more befitting of a queen, was to taint its legacy, the gifts housed in those other womens' memories.

More footsteps carried the old guard away, and a pause in his replacement's motions made clear to her that he was waiting for the other man to fade. There was no shortage of prying eyes in her palace, but shadow walking was forbidden here, in this hall, where the emperor's betrothed slept.

Thinking of him, a scowl spread across her face—there and gone as the door into her chambers swung inward, inviting better company. There stood an elf who was just taller than her, whose hair swam across his back and shoulders, a curtain dark as ink, and as smooth. He was dressed in gray military reliefs, and a knife bound In a leather sheath rested at his hip. He removed it, together with his belt, and set them on a table as the door fell shut behind him; then stepped into the firelight.

She feasted on him. Her gaze traveled from those manic eyes—the smirk quirking his thin lips—along the edge of his throat as if she traced it with her own blade. Down to linger on his chest and shoulders, as he unbuttoned his tunic and let it slide away from thick biceps, across long, slender fingers. Down, then, across pallid flesh which rippled over a hard, defined core, to wait as he drew down his slacks. She followed the retreating material over thighs whose muscles bounced as he pulled first one bare foot and then the other free, and then cast aside the obstructive garment, leaving him just in white briefs, a welcome sight.

# SPIRIT OF SHADOW

"I was overdressed, wasn't I?" he said.

"You were." She agreed. "Now come to me."

A wicked grin spread across his lips, revealing a flash of straight, white teeth. "I think not, woman. If I am to be of service, it will be on my terms."

Her eyebrow twitched upward. "Really, now. And what might those terms be?"

"You will come to me, I think."

"And if I don't?"

"Then you will be punished."

"The punishment?"

"Depends on the severity of the infraction. I am growing impatient. Now, *come*." He clapped his hands together.

Her features twisted into a snarl of indignation. She shifted her position, her robe spilling over her shoulder, exposing clavicle and nipple. "Make me."

His sneer broadened. Black shadow coalesced across his palm. He dropped onto his haunches and pressed one finger to the floor. Several inky lines darted away from his fingertip, zigzagged away in different directions and came together again at her throat, across her breasts and midriff.

"Parlor tricks?" She said.

"You don't think I would do it?"

"Fear is for lesser creatures, my lord."

"Ennui is for the gods." Lord Elise whispered. "Yet it is I who grow bored with these games."

A throaty chuckle. She climbed to her feet, drawing the silken robe back over her shoulder, and as she crossed to him, those tracers dissolved. There were few things she enjoyed more than seeing a confident man shaken. Lord Elise may believe he was her match in power or better, but she was not like her predecessor. She had not grown up in the palace, and she had never believed her rule would be calcified under her without shedding some blood along the way.

## Shadow Queen

Power was for those who relished wielding it, who found exhilaration in the throws of doing what they wished because they could. She had no illusions about her relationship to it. Whether by birthright or a random act of fate, she had been blessed with a power like few in the world possessed, and it had been given to her freely.

Lord Elise leered at her, but she could see the workings of his mind in eyes that remained, for the first time, fixed on her. The will not fleeing but redoubling, like a mountain cat faced with a rare uncertainty, that his chosen prey may be too great a challenge for him to overcome.

"Can you hear them screaming?" she cooed, her lips at his ear. She wrapped delicate hands around his waistband and teased his briefs away, feeling a tangle of wiry hair grinding against her fingers as she drew them slowly down.

"Screaming into the silence?" She whispered.

Her words, an echo from a distant past. The memory belonged to one of her predecessors—the mightiest among them, her favorite.

Lord Elise's cock was an iron rod, hot in her palm as she dragged it free. His breath came out in rapid flutters, carrying on it a fragrance of cinnamon. She slid it between her thighs, along the contours of her labias. Up and down, denying him entry, teasing him as he fell into her gaze, and his body went rigid under her press.

"Do you want it, my lord?" she asked.

She pulled away. He stood at attention, all of the good soldier, as she backed away from him.

"Then come to me."

He obeyed, followed her to the couch.

"You are a strange beast...woman." He said.

She took him by the cheeks. "I am as close to a goddess as you will ever witness." And dragged him onto his knees, set his lips against her cunt.

"Serve me." She whispered.

# SPIRIT OF SHADOW

Obediently, he set to work.

# Blood on the Floor

Sami walked the halls of the palace. Through her eyes, she saw a world of white tiles, of fine pottery, of flowers and paintings. She saw the steps she descended, the poured stone and cold light of the avenues the servants used. When others passed, she dipped into vacant rooms, or used the shadows to conceal herself, and though she tried to scream, to cry for help, nothing slipped past her lips. No sound to alert others of her presence. Her screams remained inside, and useless.

She tried to compel her body to act in some way that would alert those others to her, but her body was not hers to control. Every attempt to will her arm to rise, to knock over a vase, to step a little wider in order to dislodge some trinket from its perch and send it crashing down, was met with resistance. Those others inside her, those invaders from that orphanage behind the black triangle, were in command, and she a passenger within herself.

She was the shadow she hid within. She was the silence of her steps. Her movements came without her control. She wanted nothing more than to make it stop, but she was their prisoner, held in their hands to wield as they saw fit.

She had never felt so helpless.

*If I had only resisted when I had the chance. If I had just listened to my gut.* As if she stood at one end of a long tunnel, her thoughts echoed—a dark whisper in her ears, building in volume and intensity as they traveled, until they sounded like accusations.

She paused outside a door on the main floor of the palace, passed it by, paused outside another. In one hand, she held a knife she had stolen from the kitchens in the night, when the servants were sleeping.

With her free hand, she pushed a door open. She felt the grain of the wood against her flesh, the grit of dried lacquer, just as if she was the one guiding her body's motions.

There could be no greater betrayal. Her body, reminding her of the command she had taken for granted, reminding her of how easily she had lost it to these Watchers. What greater crime against a mortal woman could there be? They had taken her autonomy.

She was in an office. A silver pitcher sat next to a crystal glass on the desktop. The desk itself was ebony chased with gold. The walls were bare save for a tapestry in violet with the Raven and Thorns in black thread embroidered over its surface. A series of swords was arranged on a bronze rack. Each sword was sheathed in a scabbard of a different kind of wood—cherry, mahogany, ebony, cedar, elm. All of them were chased with silver or gold.

The articulated pieces of a suit of armor not unlike what the Bloodless wore rested just beneath them. A black

## Blood on the Floor

breastplate embellished with silver tooling, and a matching set of pauldrons was mounted there and framed by coverings for each of its owner's limbs. She had worked on that set before, would know it anywhere for the grief it had given her.

She stood just inside the door—waiting, dreading the moment the waiting would end.

It arrived too soon, and though she tried to squeeze her eyes shut, to deny what was happening before her, she was forced to be witness to it. A bystander unable to flee, an accessory who wanted no part in this crime.

What lay in her path filled every recess of her vision, and there was no reprieve for her. Were it that she was sleeping, she would drift among her darkest dreams, for even there she would know a kind of relief. Relief in that she would not have to know how those gifted beings used her.

Her hands flashed out. Light danced along the flat of the blade. The muscles in her arm strained behind the knife as tension built against it. Blood welled over her fingers, and though she could not retract them, she could feel the heat, the sticky, thick fluid spatter the back of her hand, leak between her fingers.

She was rummaging through the pockets of the still twitching corpse, coming up empty. She scoured the study, knocked over neatly stacked papers, wrenched open desk drawers, spilled their contents across the floor. Paper rippling, trinkets clattering. They were the sounds that greeted her in the dark. Frenzied accompaniment for this theft, first of life, and then of the deceased's possessions.

Her hand closed on a ring, pulled a set of keys free. She held them at level with her eyes, blood cooling against her skin, congealing, glue-like, against shirt sleeves stained red and clinging to thin forearms. She shoved the keys in her pocket, took a last look at the corpse.

Ugly, cruel, it was the face of Haman Bran that looked up at her through glossy, vacant eyes. The very man she had

# SPIRIT OF SHADOW

expected, who may even have deserved this fate; his limbs were splayed around him, knees oddly curled. Blood pooled in the space between his limbs and chest, kept orderly as it eddied away from him. She met that gaze, and spat on his cheek.

She was running, then.

Away from the sight of the crime, for it was not yet time to reveal herself. There were other affairs that must be seen to, other crimes to commit. Running, because the Watchers demanded it, though if they were lurking down some corridor within her mind, they hid in deep places. She could not see them, and they did not see fit to speak to her.

Running back the way she had come, leaving Haman Bran's corpse to be found by those who cared for him. Running toward a place of safety. Somewhere the Wraiths and the Thorns would never think to find her. To a place the queen herself did not know.

# Hot Gossip

hen Lance arrived in the furnaces for his first real shift, it was to the sight of clustered workers engaged in animated conversations, some dripping sweat as they labored to inject renewed heat into the massive ovens that supplied the castle, while others watched on and chattered excitedly among themselves. Some migrated from one furnace to another, picking up the threads of what was being discussed where they had left off, delivering their thoughts to new ears.

He caught snippets of their conversations as he passed on his way to check in with Master Gregor.

"They found him on the floor in his office."

"I bet it was alcohol poisoning."

"His chamber was a mess."

"I'd hate to be the servant who had to clean that up."

"Do you think they'd leave it to one of us? I bet the military got called in."

He navigated the pit on his way to the metal staircase, and climbed to the second level. Behind the bank of ducts, he found Emma and Duardo standing just outside the open door to Master Gregor's office, and the man himself could be seen lounging in his swivel chair with his boots resting on his desk, through the bay window.

He joined them at the entrance.

"Yer early." Duardo said, smiling at him.

"Thought I'd make a good impression." Lance replied. "Is it alright if I...."

He gestured toward the door, but Duardo was shaking his head.

"We know yer here. Jus' go down 'a way an' join one o' the crews. I'll be down in a second."

"Nah, no." Master Gregor waved him off. "You two give me a second. I ought business to attend to wit' 'im."

"Yeah?" Emma said. "What business is that?"

"None 'o yers. That's what."

She glared at the Master of the Furnaces, and shuffled off. "Come on Duardo. He doesn't need us anymore."

"Oh, don't be like 'at. S'not like he's threatenin' yer post."

"Shut the fuck up, Gregor!" she called.

His remaining teeth cracked around a sly grin.

"Come in 'ere." He gestured for Lance to enter. "We ought business."

Duardo lingered in the doorway as he passed him, and remained until Emma called after him again.

"Come the fuck on, you dumb fuck!"

"HEY! DON'T TALK TO ME LIKE THAT!" he shouted, but he followed her away.

"What do you want to talk about?" Lance asked as he took the seat opposite his new master.

"Well, you mos'ly." Master Gregor said. "But put a pin in it for a sec. Lord Haman Bran turned up dead s'morning. Murdered, so 'ey say."

Lance's breath caught.

### Hot Gossip

"Now, now, nothin' fer ya to worry 'bout." Master Gregor waved it away. "Jus' a fact o' life. Nobody liked the guy. Was only a matter o' time 'fore someone got nasty wit' 'im.

"Mainly, it presents an opportunity to talk 'bout somethin' a little complicated. So...how do ya feel 'bout the nobility?"

"Given what you told me about Lord Aren—"

"Leave 'at out o' yer mind fer now. How do *you* feel 'bout 'em. Are you happy wit' the way yer treated by 'em."

"If I was, I wouldn't be here." He said. "Lord Aren asked me to take up work here because I was having trouble being around shadow walkers, but that isn't a problem now."

"Ol' Lothor's playin' nice, then."

"I suppose."

"So, what's yer take on 'em."

"This conversation isn't going to get to anyone else?"

"Can't promise 'at."

"Who do you plan on telling?"

He shrugged. "Relevant parties an'at. No one dangerous to ya."

"So...."

"We're friends, buddy. I'm no fan o' the Thorns, whatever my thoughts on Lord Aren."

Lance nodded. "I find them hostile. Most of them anyway. Lord Bran was a monster. Lady Jain and Lady Therien are, too. I have no ill will toward Lady Tamalsen, even if we don't agree on everything. Is that sufficient."

"Sufficient for my purposes, I s'pose." He said. "Sets my mind at ease. I'm gonna teach ya some more advanced stuff. Want to test ya like I did wit' Duardo and Emma...few other people here. Most of 'em, actually."

"Test me how?" Lance asked, suddenly nervous.

Master Gregor chuckled. "I'm givin' you a night off. Three nights from now. Camp out wit' a friend. Take someone up ta the tower past curfew. Someone ya trust. Need ya to have a plausible out if things get tricky."

# SPIRIT OF SHADOW

"What is this about, M—" he hesitated. "Gregor?"

"'S More like it. We're friends. S'how we talk to each other." A queer look crossed Master Gregor's face. "Now what this is about'll be made more plain later. We'll talk at length somewhere away from pryin' eyes. If ya trust me, you'll be 'ere. Wit' a friend. Someone you trust. No one ya think'd rat ya out."

"You're not giving me confidence."

"Tha's good." He said. "Jus' be there, and be quiet about it. 'On't want ya gettin' caught up in somethin' ya can't handle."

"You realize I should take this to Lady Tamalsen. Or someone else."

"But ya won't."

"You're confident in that?"

"Yer askin' questions. Framin' hypotheticals." Master Gregor gestured airily. "Not the kind o' stuff ya'd be doin' if ya intended to go 'ere."

"What *would* I be doing?"

"Keepin' quiet. Observin'." He said, raising his eyebrows. "Goin' along wit' what I say wit'out restistin'. If ya weren't askin' the right questions, I'd think ya meant to go to someone, but I 'on't. Yer too curious. And tha's...well tha's good fer me."

"O-okay." He said.

"Three nights from now, tenth bell. Come by way of the shadows, and tell Lothor to keep you out o' sight. He 'an do 'at in his domain. Has control 'at way. Jus' don't be seen, okay?"

"Okay."

"Now get on wit' ya. Got work to do." He wagged his wrist toward the door.

Lance climbed out of the chair, and exited.

*I wish Sami was here.* Lance thought. Whatever Lothor

said about her, he did not want to think about what she might be doing. Why she was in hiding. Going down that path led to too many complicated feelings, but he wished he knew how to find her.

It had occurred to him more than once that she might be involved with whatever Master Gregor and Lord Aren were doing in some way, that she had been coerced into performing some duty for them. She *was* an armorer. She had regular contact with shadovane's military...even some of their elites. It would make sense for her to become embroiled in some conspiracy to undermine the nobility. It seemed that was Master Gregor's intent.

*None of that is going to help me, though. Is it?*

He waited outside the kitchens, just in the poured stone corridor outside the antechamber that led into them. He would have liked to be somewhere less exposed. Watching other servants pass by on their way to or from their departments ramped up his anxiety. They couldn't know anything of his intentions, wouldn't note him sitting there as anything unusual. It was hardly the first time he had taken post outside the kitchens waiting for one of his friends to get done with their shift.

Still, he felt exposed. Vulnerable in a way he had never felt before. Knowledge, even as oblique as he possessed, was proving enough to rattle him. He had hedged about choosing someone, had run through so many scenarios in his head, costs and benefits of going to each of those he was close to, or trying to become close to, with whatever this was. He was still not sure he understood what Master Gregor's intentions were, how he fit into the man's designs.

Ben was too new to him. He may have his opinions about the nobility, and those may be largely negative, but how much trust could be had for someone he had known for so little time. Then again, there might be some benefit in bringing this to someone he had been entangled with for so little time.

# SPIRIT OF SHADOW

Ariana...she might handle all of it well, but she would see herself as his protector. If she went along with him, showed up in the Teacher's Tower at the predetermined time, she would do so out of a sense that she needed to make sure he was safe. That he wouldn't just disappear like Sami had.

Lord Bran was on his mind. Any number of people might have wanted him dead, but the important ones were not without opportunity. They could have done him in subtly, should have long before he died. But Sami's disappearance lined up too closely with his death. Absent evidence, there was no way for him to prove it. However weak it was, she did have a motive. He couldn't see her as a killer. He had never thought of her as violent. But then *why* had she disappeared?

*If the Thorns were involved....*

Peter emerged from the antechamber into the hall where Lance sat. His gaze fell on him.

A moment's awkward silence, and Lance climbed to his feet.

"I need to talk to you." He said. "Somewhere private."

"Store room." Peter said.

Lance nodded. "That works."

They walked down the corridor to the dry storage room they so often used to play stones in the waning hours of the day, building up to curfew. Peter unlocked the door and gestured him through, falling into step behind him. He closed it, and secured the lock in place.

"What's up? Are you okay?"

Lance grimaced.

"Did something happen?"

"Kind of."

"Nothing to do with that guy you've been seeing."

"No. That's going okay." Lance said. "No, this is more complicated. To be honest, I don't really know how to start."

"Did you—"

**Hot Gossip**

"Ariana doesn't know anything about this. And she *can't* know. You can't tell her anything, okay?"

"Well, now you're scaring me." Peter eased onto an overturned crate near one of the many racks that populated the room. He leaned his elbows on his knees, fidgeted with his hands. "You're, uh...you're not in trouble or something...."

"I don't think so."

"It's just with Sami..."

"I...."

"Maybe it's better if I don't know—"

"No!" Static vibrated through Lance's chest. What was he doing? He should just tell Master Gregor he couldn't do whatever it was he wanted him to. Bringing someone else into this was a bad idea. It didn't matter who it was, this could only end badly.

He had chosen Peter because he thought he might know something about it. He was a kitune. Most of the furnace workers were too. Maybe his reasoning had been weak. His assumptions too presumptuous.

He leaned against the rack behind him, finding small comfort in its support. "I'm sorry."

"It's okay. I think."

"This was a mistake."

"You don't know that yet."

"I think I do." He sighed. "Master Gregor asked me to meet him in the Teacher's Tower tonight. He told me to bring someone I trust. I don't know much more than that. Just that he wants to meet with me and he doesn't want me to come alone."

Peter chuckled. "Must be a hazing thing."

"What?" Lance arched an eyebrow.

"It's not unheard of. Mistress Dina does it with her sous chefs. It's a whole thing. Ariana was ready to piss herself when her time came due. I couldn't tell her anything, of course. Mistress Dina would have been pissed if I ruined the surprise."

"What...what did she...?"

"Nothing I can tell you about. It's a kitchen thing." Peter waved him off. "I've never heard of an interdepartmental thing, don't get me wrong. But if it's something like that, I'll be there."

"Your sure?"

Peter nodded.

He felt somewhat more at ease, though he didn't think Peter had the right of it. There was the matter of the odd line of questioning Master Gregor had lined up against him. Why bother asking him what he thought of the nobles? Why bother with any of it at all if it was just a pretext to get him to show up for some right of passage?

"Okay." He said. "But I can't promise you won't regret it."

"You can't promise I'll be safe either." Peter said. "But I'm sure it'll be fine. Like I said. It's not unheard of.

"When do you need me to be there, anyway?"

"Tenth bell."

A crooked grin. "Count on it."


"He was murdered, Conan!" Queen Meredith slammed her fist against the table.

The Emperor sat on the edge of a small couch, as prim as an Ozite whore. A vase full of snapdragons—the last still in bloom in the palace—rattled under the force of her blow. "Inside *my* palace. Right under our *noses!*"

White-hot iron burned inside her skull. Shadow Queens past had never known such a fury as she felt. Not even Anastasia, when she came to sack the kingdom her predecessor's daughter founded.

Yet Conan was as calm as she was shaken, as cool and collected as she was angry.

She could have guessed he would behave this way. That he

would not come to comfort her, or seek to abate her anger.

He did not love her. He was in love with an idea, an ancient one he hoped to revisit, which would never return.

He had never loved her predecessors either. The queens of Shadovane were a weapon in his hand, nothing more, but that he would see them as tools did not give him the right to treat her as he did now...with such ambivalence.

Her house was on fire. With his almighty power, he could put it out in moments, but he refused.

"You will help me find whoever is responsible." She breathed. "As a guest in my house, you will do this."

"Bold tonight, aren't you." He said. "Have you forgotten your place already?"

She glared at him.

He sighed, squeezing the bridge of his nose. A low fire chewed on the last remnants of a few, slim logs in the hearth, and he stood with his back to it. A soft light emanated for a finger's width around him, but the aura was uneven, filled with pits and valleys.

"Put this matter to bed, Meredith. Lord Bran was unimportant." He said. "Many had grudges against him. It should come as no surprise he met his end through violence. He was an arrogant prick and a drunk, and his house will be better off without him."

"It is not who was murdered, but the act itself that bothers me." She growled. "It is only a matter of time before others become involved. If there are no more deaths, there will still be that uncertainty lingering in the minds of his peers. If I could not keep him safe, what of them? Some may even believe I sanctioned it."

"If you are that concerned, call on the Council of Liam. Let them deal with it." He said.

She turned her back on him. It was the simplest means of masking the burning in her gaze, the easiest means of keeping him in line. She remembered their last argument. She did not wish to repeat it.

"I want them found." She whispered. "I want them slain where every noble, and every servant, can see. And when it is done, I want you out of my palace, and my city."

"Trust I have no desire to be here. I would not be, if it was not so clear your people needed a reminder of who is in charge." Conan said. "This cycle will continue beyond you, as it has before you. That pendant you bear does not make you special."

Meredith kept her features smooth, mirroring him as she at last met his gaze. She did not have two thousand years of practice in keeping her composure, but she knew the burn of acid.

He made her skin crawl. In the memories of those other women had been lain a pattern for her to witness. Manipulation of the weak among them, control through hostility for the defiant, subjugation through abuse for those who flew too close to the sun...the ones who he acknowledged almost as equal were the malicious and the cunning. Those who understood how to wield their power softly, from the shadows.

She harnessed her venom, and put every bit of it into the look she set against him.

"Celesti never loved you, Light of Ignorance." She said. "For all of your pining over her, she could not see you as anything except an obedient dog hoping one day to be her equal. But she was a goddess, and you were no god. You saw the contours of who she was, but you could never see her truth.

"What I find myself wondering so often...why have you wasted so much time hoping she awakens in us, when you know deep down there is nothing you can do to make her yours."

Conan surged toward her. His hand flashed out, took her

by the throat. There was true anger in him—smoldering, toxic—as he clamped down hard enough to bruise, cutting her air supply down to a trickle.

"I know...why you keep...coming back." She groaned. "To monitor me...because you think...you think I will awaken."

Spots darted across her vision, and darkness crept in at the edges. If he kept up like this, he would kill her.

"Like you believed Mariah would. So much...so much...that you raped her."

His grip loosened, the anger replaced by something harder to define. A mix of resentment and sorrow. She would survive this time as in all times past. He needed her—to believe in this fantasy of his, that if she performed in the right ways, perhaps she would unlock some secret her predecessors had not, and fade away to make room for the woman whose soul inhabited that pendant.

He reached for it, hungry longing in his eyes, a desperate, obsessive need which would never be sated. Twitching fingers stopped short of touching it.

"You will remember your place." He whispered. "Beneath me with the worms and the vermin."

They both knew he could not touch it. In all of those memories conferred to her by Celesti's Soul, that fragment of stone so like jade, he had never touched it. She had never understood why it was so, but he drew away each time he came close. Those memories went back millennia, encompassed all of the history of her city beyond the fall of the Mother of Night. She remembered that hunger as seen through their eyes, the way it ebbed out of him as his fingers retreated, twitched inches from her breast, and then fell away.

Mariah was four hundred years dead, but her legacy lived on. She had been Conan's favorite, the one who most resembled the Celesti of his memories.

She had also been his greatest mistake.

Now, watching those slender fingers contract, those eyes burn with crazed hunger, she wondered if he would do to her what he did to that other woman. One more he did not love, the unwilling mother of his heir.

His hand slid away from her throat.

"Find who did this. Kill them." He said, as if she had not been telling him this was her intent, as if it was a command. "I will leave when I am ready."

He stormed out of her apartments. She heard the door click shut down the hall. Only when he was gone did she lay fingers on her neck, test tender flesh and measure the damage.

It would bruise before morning, and she would deal with it then.

*I'll have to call on a healer.* She thought. *Call on my generals. Lord Giram will keep them in line, and Lord Elise will be there to ensure he is not too merciful. And when this is over, maybe I will invite that bastard to the dungeons. He will know his place, then.*

# The Council Of Liam

The sun bared down on Lord Aren's shoulders, beams cast from skylights cut into the ceiling of this highest level of the military compound. Shields were scattered across the walls in this reach, each calling to a different nation. His gaze flicked from one to the other of them as he made his transit over a river of granite. He lingered longer on those of most consequence, those who had given Shadovane trouble at one time or another, waged wars against her, or made attempts at her ruler's life.

Here were the silverfish of Morgrotten, a beacon of resistance for the elves of Shadovane were not accustomed to marine battles, and the city had won out in the end. Here was the sun and rays of Lazul, wiped away by the combined might of Zankal and Ozos, and that only recently. Their first skirmish with the Sun Empire had proven disastrous for both sides, not least because the then queen Alice had been no general, had nonetheless inserted herself into the affairs of her soldiery, undermining their leaders. Lessons in humility and humiliation lingered in those shields, and while certainly Shadovane's forces had proven victorious over many more states than they had lost battles to, in each loss was a lesson to be learned. Something new to be gleaned from settled conflict, which might prove useful in the future.

Here, the lynx of Gourum. The nations sophistication in the art of enchanting proved time and again their savior. In all of known history, the wall there had never been broken, their armies never defeated. A curiosity, for their ruler was, as tradition demanded, a child. And there was Kore's coiled serpent, its sinuous body following the edge of a round shield, forged into the bronze. Kore's sign was alone among those representing the Ten Kingdoms, those terrible lands in the east. It was there, not because Shadovane had waged conflict with that nation, but as a reminder of all of the bloodshed and chaos their empire had endured at the hands of God's Legion, those who traced their service to the imprisoned Sky Lord himself.

He hoped never to see the day that conflict was renewed. Too much would be lost if war broke out between the Sun Empire and the Ten Kingdoms. It had almost happened once, just more than a decade ago, when a citizen of empire brought his wrath to the border of Gorozoan. Had been put to rest by his most cherished friend, so the intelligence said. For that, Lord Aren was grateful.

A last shield stuck out to him. It was there, just next to the door he needed, and he paused before it, thinking for the details behind its capture. A sickle moon loomed against the center of the kite shield. That and nothing more. It was all that was needed to remind those who served on the Council of Liam of their greatest and longest standing enemy, the one who had nearly done the empire in.

Lun, ruled by the emperor's own daughter, had been a jewel carved out of the Empire, a place of peace and prosperity. Those who ruled were so often jealous guardians of their lands, and when the territory sought independence, when they declared their sovereignty, war soon followed. The place once called Lun was sacked by the daughter's father and his concubine, the entire region cursed and burned to cinders. The Shadow of Lies, Rakhna, took over then, and the lands, now desolate, were turned into a prison for the empire's most dangerous criminals. Where Lun once stood, the Ring of Fire arose, and what peace it had known was shattered.

He moved past it, and halted at a door flanked by two Bloodless in full armor, the Raven and Thorns bold across their chests, reflected in the design of yet another shield to the right of one soldier's shoulder. Another—the metal cast with a pearl-like finish, the raised hand of Mirrhvale emblazoned in burnt orange across its face—rested against a bracket opposite it.

The Bloodless saluted, eyes forward, as he passed into the waiting chamber.

The room was barely larger than the oblong table which occupied it. Six, wing-backed chairs with black, velvet cushions were situated around it. Three of them were occupied.

Atop the table was painted a map of the world, with silver figurines in different shapes scattered across it, reflecting the real-world movements of enemies and allies throughout Etherel.  Too many of those pieces were clustered along the border between the Free Lands and the Ten Kingdoms. Omari's headhunters were moving into the mountains of northwest Jarra. Baris's Grimwok were amassing near Darkridge, a handful of days' journey from the free territory of Haru.

But they were just posturing. The Ten Kings wanted an

end to their truce with the Empire as much as the Empire wanted to violate that truce itself. One would not move into the Free Lands before the other, as it had been for the two millennia, since their compact was ratified.

More problematic was the series of cross-like figurines which had moved away from their home in Aranor and spread into the Free Lands around Ozos and Nimrodel.  Those represented a criminal enterprise which had been a thorn in the side of the Empire for nearly two decades. It had been their former leader who nearly dragged the empire into war with the Ten Kingdoms; their current leader, who had stopped him. And yet, this new one defied comprehension. His plans had become erratic of late, and there was that matter so many years past, a genocide in Lazul Lord Aren strongly suspected he had been involved in.

They had performed necromancy that night. To what end, he could not claim to know. It was a dark mark on the empire's reputation, one of those few they had not earned themselves.

"You seem troubled, today, Lord Aren."

He looked to the source of that high, cold voice.

Lord Cree observed him over a long, pointed nose. His dark hair flowed down his back, gray only just creeping in at his temples. He wore a bored expression, but Lord Aren knew better than to trust in what Lord Cree displayed outwardly. Though he had never been traced directly to any crime, rumors swirled around the general, suggesting—but never outright proclaiming—that he had murdered his way into his position through a combination of hidden knives and poisonings. Matters which Lord Aren had turned a blind eye to upon his counterpart's ascension to the council. Whether he was responsible or not, Lord Cree's enemies, those who had offended him, did have a habit of dying under mysterious circumstances.

## The Council of Liam

"There is much to find troubling of recent." Lord Aren said to him, matching his even tone. "That is why we are here, is it not?"

"But surely you are not so concerned with the death of one nobleman. In particular not Haman Bran. Asshole that he was." Lord Cree gestured toward the cross figurines. "These are the matters which concern me. Movements among our enemies. Happenings in the borderlands which threaten our control of them. Truly, what is Lord Bran to any of us?"

"I do not fear their posturing, Lord Cree. Any more than I fear what may come of the Cross's intervention in the Free Lands. Their leader does not intend to revisit what his predecessor did."

He took his seat at the table, next to Lord Tarkenta, who studied the map with a vacant expression.

The last of those gathered here was Lord Elise, who sat with Lord Cree on the table's other side, just as nature intended. Though sometimes misguided, Lord Tarkenta had something which resembled a proper moral code. Lord Elise was more a monster than any of the other Councilmen, and Lord Cree behind him only because he possessed the restraint and intellect Lord Elise lacked.

"Have you any thoughts on the servants?" Lord Tarkenta asked. His gaze flickered over the map, taking it all in. Of all of them, he would have the most reason to worry over Shadovane's recent problems. The Wraiths were his charges. It was with him responsibility for the apprehension and training of the servants lay, at least in part. And he did care deeply for them, in his way, though Lord Aren disagreed with him on the nature of his work.

What Lord Tarkenta called a mercy, he saw as a means to an end. Servants must always be a part of the fabric of Shadovane's culture, lest the nobility begin to cannibalize each other, but they could not be taken from the ranks of common folk, whose resentment for the upper class burned

# SPIRIT OF SHADOW

with a slow intensity. Lord Tarkenta had not been born among them, and could not understand the way common men thought. Lord Aren had escaped his poverty, his disease-ridden hovel, and had done at great cost. He had no desire to go back to that life, but that did not mean he could not empathize somewhat with what lay behind this rebellion in the lowest caste of Shadovani society. Were his own involvement discovered, he would surely be immolated. Subtlety must always be his priority, even if it meant he must occasionally perform acts that weighed on his conscience.

"I do." He said. "I will, however, hold my tongue until the others arrive."

"They do like to make us wait, don't they?" Lord Tarkenta chuckled. His crooked smile looked wrong on his stony face, out of place.

"Have you been well of late?" Lord Aren asked.

"Better."

Lord Elise sneered. "The missus is putting out again, then?"

Lord Tarkenta glared at him.

"Of course it's all over the palace. The rumors are—"

"Quiet, Elise." Lord Cree snapped.

The door opened, admitting a rather feminine man who walked with his back so straight one might think a rod had been rammed up his backside. His cocky grin was a permanent feature, as was the swagger in his step.

Lord Bertram seldom appeared to treat anything with the gravity it deserved, but he was discerning, and thoughtful, and good with both the sword and the knife. A few of those who offended him had found one or the other of his blades sheathed between their ribs. Less than half of those deserved it.

Following short behind him was Lord Giram, who helmed the council. His hair was as white as Lord Aren's, but cut almost to the scalp. He was short, and broad-shouldered, with a barrel chest and the scar from an old burn white against his neck, which he refused to have properly healed.

"Everyone is here?" he panned over the other five from his seat across from Lord Aren's. Lord Bertram sat to Lord Tarkenta's other side, his hands folded together, resting against the edge of the table.

Lord Giram drummed his fingers against its surface, his eyes on Lord Aren. "Well?"

"Queen Meredith will not be in attendance, then?" Lord Bertram raised his eyebrows, his lips a thin line.

"You really are as bad as Lord Elise, you know that?" Lord Giram said.

"Oh, not quite, I think." Lord Bertram replied. "Perhaps if my appetites for things best left on the shelf were stronger."

Lord Elise snickered.

The queen had long shown the lord over the Bloodless an unusual degree of favorability, but Lord Aren suspected his counterpart was little more than a set piece in her life. He would not be surprised if Lord Elise felt the same for her. Certainly, no true love could exist from one monster to another.

"We did not come here to trade insults." Lord Giram said in an icy tone. "We came here because the queen ordered it."

"Ever the one to reserve judgment, aren't you?" Lord Bertram mumbled, earning him glares from Lords Giram and Tarkenta.

"What do you have, Silas?" Lord Giram asked Lord Aren.

"As of right now, very little, though my Thorns are working tirelessly to gather more information. What we know is that a grimoire of death magic was found under a servant's bed. That servant frequented the Teacher's Tower, mostly for the purpose of meeting up with other women."

Lord Elise snorted.

He pressed on. "My men took her into custody several

days prior to the emperor's arrival. They made the oversight of placing her in proximity to Aldeirel, violating my orders, and at some time thereafter, she escaped. I do not know how."

"Even with a command of death magic, there is no means by which a servant could escape those cells." Lord Cree mumbled. "The bars are lined with cadmium and silver. She would not have been able to hear well enough to draw on the Cosmic Orchestra."

"Which implies she had help from outside." Lord Tarkenta said. "But my Wraiths have yet to uncover anything that would preclude the involvement of those rebels in the city."

"It may not be them." Lord Aren set his gaze on the cross figurines.

"Oh, you can't be serious." Lord Bertram turned his nose up at the prospect. "How could they even know of us. Our predecessors did their due diligence wiping records of our existence away. They believe their rulers to be human in the eleventh ward. What possible—"

"It is only a suggestion. The one who calls himself Headsman is known to be religious. It is possible he believes the stories so many others call myths."

"Then why Lord Bran?"

"I do not know."

"He's a pain in the ass, but he is not—"

"Important, yes." Lord Giram cut in. "No, if this is an outside job, it would be one of *hers*. I do not think it has anything to do with those Crossmen.

His gaze shifted from the map to Lord Aren. "Her proximity to Aldeirel is troubling." To Lord Tarkenta. "Keep on those rebels. Sooner or later, they'll let something slip."

"In the meantime." Lord Elise said. "What do we do about her? The queen feels—"

"I think we are all quite aware of what and how the queen

feels." Lord Giram cut in. "Unless you plan to undress her for us."

He opened his mouth to speak. Lord Giram pressed on, ignoring him. "So, we know next to nothing and we haven't found her hiding place. What we do is what we were already doing, then. The Thorns and Wraiths will need to work together in these matters until we have uncovered her. Set them to search everything the shadow touches.

"In the meantime, Lord Aren. I would like to question Aldeirel. If she was positioned in ear shot of him, he may have gotten into her head. It would not be the first time. Lord Bran may have been a significant target for him, even if the rationale behind taking him down does not make sense to us."

"He will resist." Lord Aren said.

"Then we will use force." Lord Giram supplied, spreading his hands.

*Another complication.* Lord Aren thought, but he nodded. "I will see to him myself, then. He will be in interrogation room D when you want him."

"Good." Lord Giram said. "This is over, then."

He negotiated himself free of his seat, and lumbered out of the room.

"It must be so hard torturing an old friend." Lord Elise said.

"No harder than pretending to love your meal ticket." Lord Aren replied.

Lord Bertram cackled. "That is just the bit of comedy I needed. With that, I think I will leave you to it. Unless you intend to fight?" He looked hopefully from one to the other of them. Both men wore stony expressions. "No? Just as well. Toodle-oo."

He waved goodbye, and marched out of the room. Lord Aren rose with Lord Tarkenta, and they left after him. Lord Cree and Lord Elise were not far behind.

"You don't think it's revenge, do you?" Lord Tarkenta

# SPIRIT OF SHADOW

asked as they marched down the hall outside. "She *is* a servant."

"Yes, and it may well be that. But she would have to remember something of her former life for a revenge plot to make sense. Even then, she chose a weak target. Someone who was likely mean to her. I do not think her targets include anyone of consequence. Not yet."

"If she is speaking to Aldeirel, it is only a matter of time before bigger targets fall into her lap."

"You have Wraiths stationed outside his cell?"

"Would you be offended if I did?"

Lord Aren patted his shoulder. "Not at all, old friend. If she meets with him again, we will know. Won't we?"

Lord Tarkenta nodded. "Yes, I think that is best."

They parted ways at the end of the hall, and Lord Aren navigated back to his chambers. He would go to his office later. For now, he needed seclusion, a little time to think.

# Moon & Shadow

I t was nearing the tenth bell. The servants whose activities concluded with the day were all in their beds and most were on their way to sleep. Those whose duties required them to toil way through the night were already in their departments, and most of those in the bowels of the palace. Quiet conversation filtered to Lance from distant places in the barracks, but Laramy and Fat John, at least, were well and tucked into their beds, ignoring all that transpired around them in favor of a blissful night's rest.

He looked to the window by his bunk, saw there the spider in its web. The spirit...or whatever he was...lounged near the eye, his forelimbs twitching against the threads, his abdomen contracting rhythmically as he groaned against a pain which defied Lance's understanding.

*"Lothor?"* he whispered.

*"Yes?"* came his baritone growl.

"Can you open the shadow cast by my bed?"

*"With ease."*

"And if I asked you to keep the Wraiths from seeing me,

could you do that, too?"

*"If there is such a need."*

"Then...then I think you should. If it's not too much to ask."

*"That you ask is enough, child. It is enough."*

Motion at the edge of his bed drew his eye. He watched as the shadow extended and deepened, knew Lothor had opened a portal into his domain. As the moon shed its light through that window, cast silver beams into the barrel-shaft chamber, he pushed back his coverlet, and rolled over the edge of the bed.

Cold embraced him as he plunged through shadow, and arrived in an abyssal realm in which sight was lost to him.

"I don't know where I'm going." He said.

*"It is not my place to guide."* Lothor said. *"Not alone. But there is another. One who will answer if you seek her."*

"But this is your home. Isn't it?"

Lothor chuckled. *"No. Home is a place far from here. This is but an expression of who I am."*

"Then—"

*"We work together, those of my kind. In all things, we must. There are those I will refuse to work with. You should know this. But they are few. Who you seek is a spirit of guidance. I am merely a spirit of place."*

"But she's here?"

*"Yes."*

"Where?"

*"Call to her."*

"I don't know how."

*"You have a need."*

"If I stay here too long—"

*"The heightened resistance those others feel is my will railing against them. It is reciprocal, this pain. That they should, in their hubris, seek to compel me to do as they wish...I*

*cannot stop them, but I can make their passage more difficult. Were they in my home, I could keep them from using me, but we are far from there, you and I. I am not as strong in this place.*

"*She is the same. But call to her. Express your need.*"

"O-okay."

He seated himself on the ground, not trusting himself to keep from wandering off within the shadows.

"I want to go to the Teacher's Tower, but I don't know the way." He said. "Where is it?"

A lilting, alto voice broke through the quiet and the gloom. "*Know me, and I will come.*"

"Who am I to know?"

"*In the autumn I fly away from cold and toward it in the spring, but always I know where I am going, and where I come from.*"

*I'm never going to get this.* "Are you summer?"

A soft chuckle.

"No, that doesn't make sense." He said. "Maybe you're time. But that doesn't help me."

"*You have a need.*" Lothor intoned. "*But it is not my place to express that need.*"

"*He knows you?*" the newcomer asked.

"*He has seen, friend. Seen the way. Seen it in truth.*"

"*Then he is friend to us.*"

"*He is.*"

"What am I going to do." Lance mumbled. *I don't have time for this. I should have asked Peter to meet me here, in my barracks. He could have taken me straight there.*

"*A different perspective.*" The newcomer said. "*If you should hide from me, I will find you. If you should lay in one place, I should know. If you should move, I will feel it. Wherever I have been, there is the way back. Wherever I should go, I arrive without fail.*"

"There is a way back?" Lance said. "You know where

you're going."

"*Yes.*"

"You navigate."

"*Yes, yes.*" She giggled.

"Then you use directions."

"*I am!*"

"What is your name, spirit?"

"*It is Shana. Call me, and I will answer. Always, I will answer.*"

"Shana? Will you guide me to the Teacher's Tower. To Master Gregor."

"*I will.*"

As if the petals of a flower unfolded around him, a new sense bloomed in his soul. Lothor's energies merged with those of this new spirit, and thin lines were thrust forth from his feet and the top of his head, angling down with the distance until, at the edge of his vision, they merged together. He felt something tugging him in one direction, and climbed to his feet, the space between those lines dilating and the angle sharpening.

A few steps. The angle inclined, became steeper. A few more and the pull shifted in a different direction. He followed it for a few more steps, and was met with a vertical line which emerged almost at his nose.

"Is he here?"

"*Reach?*" Lothor said.

"*He is here.*" Shana added.

He lifted his arm, touched darkness above him. Shadows pulled apart, revealing a snatch of the world outside. A dimly lit room devoid of furnishings. He touched that window, and shot through.

He arose in an abandoned classroom. Ambient light was provided by candles arranged in a rough circle along its perimeter, and the it was otherwise devoid of furnishings.

The classroom Master Gregor had chosen had no windows to look out on, no need for curtains to block out the outside world. A brass chandelier still clung to the ceiling. Slender tines caught firelight, exposing tarnished bars and cobwebs to his eyes as he glanced this way and that, expecting to find....

*What exactly.* He wasn't quite sure.

A door to his left opened onto a slice of the servant's access, and Peter stepped through. He looked around at the ring of candles, found Lance standing near the center of the room, and approached him with a knowing smile on his face.

"See. I told you. Just a hazing thing." He said.

"Where do you think they are?" Lance asked, his gaze returning to the candles, the long shadows pooling between them.

"Probably just waiting outside somewhere. They'll want you nervous, right?"

"They've already succeeded—"

Two figures arose from the shadows at opposite ends of the room. Another pair arose behind each of them. As they approached Lance and Peter, the details of their identities were made clearer. Master Gregor, together with Duardo and Emma, closed the distance from one side. To the other, Lord Aren. Behind the general were two Thorns, both of whom pointedly avoided looking in Lance's direction.

Lance froze. Nearby, Peter took a half step back toward the servant's access.

"Don't be afraid." Lord Aren made a warding gesture. His gaze shifted to Master Gregor. "You didn't tell him?"

"Tell me what?" Lance asked.

Master Gregor shook his head. "Might be able ta block 'em Wraiths watchin' from the shadows, but who knows who's got a trick fer gettin' 'round what 'ese days. Didn't want ta take any chances.

"Watch it bucko!"

# SPIRIT OF SHADOW

Peter froze in mid-step. He was making slow progress toward the exit, a bad move given the Master of Thorns and his companions had seen him, knew who he was.

"I-I don't understand. We haven't done anything. We're not—"

"Not what? Criminals? Rebels?" Lord Aren said.

"What's going on here?" Lance asked. "You told me not to tell anyone—"

"Our position has changed. It occurred to us that you might fair better with a companion in which to confide. Especially given what we intend to ask of you."

"To ask...of *me?* I'm just a servant."

"That in't entirely true." Master Gregor said.

"He can 'ear 'em." Duardo said. "Same as the rest of us."

"Quiet Duardo." Emma warned.

"Listen. 'S no safer place fer ya 'an in my furnaces." Master Gregor said. "An' I'd be glad to keep ya 'ere f'it was up ta me. But it in't. S' his."

He cocked his chin in Lord Aren's direction.

"We've been working together for some time." Lord Aren said. His gaze shifted from Lance to Peter. "How do you know the boy?"

"I don't! I mean...sorry, it's just a..." he grimaced as his gaze fell on Lance. "We're friends. But I don't know anything about what he's been up to. Or your, uh...stuff."

"Our stuff." One of those Thorns chuckled. He turned to the other. "They always like this?"

The other Thorn shrugged. "Some of the tougher ones get a little defiant. It makes no difference as long as they don't try to attack."

"Why we chose a room wit' nothin' in it." Master Gregor said. "Lessons learned an 'at."

"Really, what's this about?" Lance said, exchanging a look with Peter. *Don't piss them off, please. Just ride this out.*

*Maybe we'll get away with our skins.*

"This would be so much easier if the girl was here." Lord Aren mumbled.

"You mean Sami. You abducted her, didn't you." Lance said.

"You know each other?"

"Why the tone of surprise." Peter mumbled. "Don't your people know everything—"

He cut off as he realized who he was talking to.

"What did you do to her? *Lothor* told me...shit! Zente, *Lothor.*" He said, noting the black as pitch shade of his shadow.

"You haven't taught him control?" Lord Aren said to Master Gregor.

"What did you just say?" Peter's gaze was on Lance, his eyebrows climbing into his hairline.

"We'll get to that. If you choose to work with us, you will receive training in these arts. Just the same, I believe Mistress Dina will be glad for it. Her department is far less unified than his." Lord Aren gestured airily in Master Gregor's direction.

"And if I don't you'll have me killed."

A Thorn chuckled.

"I am not without mercy." Lord Aren said. "You will disappear, certainly, but I believe you will want to remain here for a time. Those gaps in your memory ought to be incentive enough. The dreams that feel so terribly familiar...have you not wondered why they should have a quality as if you have lived them before?"

Peter stiffened.

Shaking his head, Master Gregor sighed. "Might be best we get ta the point. All 'is hedgin's gonna make 'em shit 'ere pants, and I can't handle the smell."

"Could you be serious for two seconds?" Emma growled, and smacked him upside the head.

"Ouch!"

"You deserved that." She said cuttingly. "Do we even need him? He doesn't look like much."

"He picked up on the old way faster 'an I've e'er seen." Duardo said. "'F anything we 'an use 'at kind of talent more 'an you might think."

"He knew what he was doing before he showed up in our department, idiot." She said. "He's been doing magic longer than any of the other ones had."

"That might be true." Lord Aren said. "Though not for near as long as you would like to think. Shortly before he entered your service, he started having a reaction to the spirit of shadow's Dark Heart. I intervened, as I have done on the rare occasion I witness one of yours in such a state.

"I believed he possessed a Gift of the Blood, a rare affinity for the spirits which, by birthright, made him more able to detect their voices, and their essences."

Duardo cocked his head to the side. "Is 'at not wha's goin' on 'ere?"

"Not quite." Lord Aren said. "Not entirely."

He may very well be a Seem, but that is not all he is. If I am correct, this boy's birth marked the end of an era, the beginning of a transitional period as we crawl toward the next. We have not seen such times as these since the days when our Emperor was born."

Lance's breath caught.

"You can't be serious." Emma said into descending silence.

"It is strange, isn't it?" One of the Thorns said, stepping forward to join Lord Aren. "He was taken from Aranor, wasn't he? Back when the Cross was having its troubles."

"He was the son of their leader." Lord Aren said. "The one who was slain to make way for the current head."

"Then the Headsman...he's his uncle?" the other whispered. "How in the Pits did he end up here?"

A cold grin spread across Lord Aren's cheeks. "I wish I knew.

"Given the nature of his lineage, I doubt it was any great accident that he found his way to us. You would not have been made aware of what transpired in that day."

"We nearly went to war with the Ten Kingdoms, didn't we? Is that not why Queen Meredith ordered the Wraith Core to infiltrate Aranor?"

"Story for another time." Lord Aren said. "The important thing is Hugo Silvanes sits at the heart of a web whose threads reach all the way across empire. Into the Free Lands, too. And his nephew, as it happens, claims he is one who sees."

"What now?" Emma asked.

"This boy claims he can see the spirits. Not simply hear them, but see them as physical manifestations."

"I never said that." Lance said, at last finding his words.

"But you *can* see them."

"I don't know that they're physical *anything*, Lord Aren. All I know is they show up looking like common animals. A pair of foxes in the furnaces. A spider in the window by my bed. A goose in the shadows...don't...just please don't look at me like...." He sighed, deflating under the hawkish gazes of everyone in the room. Everyone save Peter, who had backed himself up against a wall, and was now looking at the floor, avoiding all who stood around him.

"There was a weasel, too."

"You know their names?"

"Most of them."

"We should test him. Make sure he isn't lying." The Thorn who stood at Lord Aren's side said. He looked uncomfortable, which was not something Lance was accustomed to from that unemotive cast.

A curt nod from Lord Aren.

The Thorn moved forward.

# SPIRIT OF SHADOW

Peter slid down the wall. He cupped his hands over his mouth, watched intently with worry in his eyes as his friend was set against this questioner, to undergo a trial of unknown character.

The Thorn spread his hands, mumbled words neither Lance nor Peter could read in a language neither had learned to speak. Not in the way Lord Aren or Master Gregor spoke it.

Before Lance's eyes, several figures materialized to linger in those shadows. There was a bull, stamping its hoof against the tiles impatiently. There, too, a fox of a kind he did not recognize, who was far smaller than either of the others, and whose long and broad ears twitched as it settled onto its rump. There, very near where Peter sat, a peacock to remind of those burning others he had seen one night in a dream. Among them, it was the only creature not cast all in silhouette. Rather, the peacock was cast in light shades, its body white and glowing with silver light that reminded him so much of the moon on a clear night.

He felt its pull on his soul, a peculiar feeling as if he should know this creature. Had met her before.

Ambient, silver light filled the room, driving back the lower light of those candle flames. It filled the space, an even, sourceless glow which pushed the shadows back to the corners of the room, denied them their hold.

Lance's gaze settled on each of those spirits the Thorn had called.

The peacock strided forward on narrow legs, its short tail carving arcs in still air as it approached him.

*"How long it has been."* She cooed. *"Since one of my own has so readily identified me. Go now, to your homes in that other place. I will suffice for this."*

The bull dipped at the shoulders, and vanished. The fox jogged through the closed servant's access door. The light held in their absence.

Quiet had descended over the gathered others. All of them were watching him now, though to see their expressions, their posture, they needed no more confirmation than this. Whatever test the Thorn had designed for him, it was useless now. Cast out along with every other plan he might have entertained to ensure Lance spoke true.

*"My words are for you and only you, child."* The peacock shifted form. Molted feathers danced across the room. Her legs thickened, her back curved upward and her neck shrunk in on itself. In the stead of the elegant bird was an old woman, who was naked and cast in marble hues, her eyes a vacant white, matching a fall of curly hair which traveled over her shoulders and down her back.

*"I am the moon, child. And you are mine. I am first of a dying era, and last in these newborn times. Trust these men, for they cannot harm you as long as you wear my mantle in your soul. Trust their aims, if you do not trust the means. Find the way out. The way by which those who walk in shadow cannot follow.*

*"They will know. If not the way, then the means to find the path. They will know."*

She cupped his face in her hands, and her touch was warm. She guided his head down, to meet her eyes, and held him there as images flashed across his mind, forgotten things brought surging forth to remind him of dark tidings, of all that had transpired to bring him to this place.

She released him, and strode away. She paused to take Peter's head in her hands, to meet his gaze, and then faded into the ether, to be seen and heard no longer.

Lord Aren sank onto his knees. Peter stared blankly forward. Master Gregor stepped back, and Duardo stepped forward to stabilize him.

"What...what just happened?" he asked.

"You didn't call her." Lord Aren asked the Thorn at his side. "Did you?"

"N-no. I called for light to fill this space. That was all."
The Thorn who had performed the rite replied.

"You see, then, why we must protect this boy. Why he
matters." Lord Aren said.

Emma's regard shifted from Master Gregor and Duardo to
Lord Aren. "What do you need from us?"

"To teach him control. To guide him." Lord Aren said,
accepting help from his Thorns to regain his feet. "Just that.
Until he is ready, we will have to rely on the girl...Sami. We
will have to rely on Sami to see our ends met."

"And she can do this?" Master Gregor said.

"She's not alone." He said.

"Lord Aren?" Lance asked.

The soldier's gaze landed on him.

"Are there places in this palace you can't go?" he asked.
"Places that you can't shadow walk into?"

"Y-yes." He said.

"I think...I think there's a way out of here. In one of those
places."

The Thorns exchanged a look.

"I remember...remember when I was a kid—"

"No." Peter said. "Don't. Please."

"It's okay, Peter. It will be, I think."

"How could they have done this to us." Peter whispered.
*How indeed.*

He remembered every vicious trespass against him, every
harm he had endured before his twelfth birthday, before he
looked into those lightning blue eyes and his childhood was
lost to him.

And going back further, he remembered Aranor. A brief
but better life there than he had ever known here, a family
who loved him. A brother and a sister. A father who he bore
little resemblance to, and a mother whose features were
much stronger in him. He remembered the uncle who had, by

Lord Aren's own reckoning, seen to his father's death. Remembered the streets of a city a world away, and beyond that, vast desert, dunes and improbable cities. And a passage that led into a cliff, a waterfall come crashing from somewhere sheathed in darkness, and a strange arch which looked to have been poured out of a kettle and frozen in place, a veil like an aurora rippling in its pearlescent frame.

He had seen it but once, as his family was ushered along for what must have been days, ushered through cramped tunnels and away from a city on fire, whose streets teamed with ghosts and men and women cloaked in flowing robes who ran in terror for anywhere that might be safe. Ran away from death, ran away in desperation.

"I will have my loyalists search for such a place." Lord Aren promised. "You focus on your training. Learning control. Without it, you cannot hope to do anything for us. Be that leading us out of this place, or saving us from the hell it has become."

"I'll do that." He said. "Peter will, too."

"I-I will. I'll do whatever you want. Just don't...don't kill me. Please don't kill me." Peter agreed.

Lady Tamalsen scratched out a report to her queen. Her cramped handwriting already populated half of the page, the ink drying in stages as new text soaked into the parchment, its finish dulling while she contemplated what else to add. The last few nights had seen a great deal of progress made in Lady Therien's work. Though her mood worsened with every passing day, a byproduct of the Emperor's visitation upon her, Queen Meredith could only be delighted by the recent happenings.

She certainly was. A new batch of servants to guide meant new challenges. No two were exactly alike, and each new batch provided her with myriad puzzles to solve, selections to make, and paths which would follow them through the rest of their lives to set. If they were lucky, those lives would be long and fruitful, in the way they could be.

*If* they were lucky.

*The bitch needs something to keep her occupied. She has been dwelling on these rebels far too much.*

Her doorknob rattled and the door came open. Without looking up from her report, she said: "I have a knocker for a reason."

She scribbled a few more words, dropped her pen into the open ink pot beside her message, and then looked over the silver rim of her glasses at the newcomer.

Anger welled up inside her.

The woman who loomed before her was dressed in a uniform stained with various kinds of grime—the most alarming, a splotchy mass of blood stiffening the wrinkles across her chest and sleeves.

She had known the brats would send someone for her eventually, and had no intention of going the way Haman Bran did.

"You." She breathed.

Sami observed her through lightning-blue eyes, her expression cold and impassive. The girl let the door fall shut behind her.

The electrified whisper of a death rite hung like a cloud around Lady Tamalsen. She held it ready, a bead of darkness clinging to the underside of her lacquered fingernail.

"They must think to have set you up for a great win with me, young woman." She said. "But they have grievously miscalculated."

She launched herself over the desk.

A blast of wind struck her in the chest, slammed her against the wall. At the same time, the melody filling her ears faltered. Papers fluttered in the air around her, cascaded whimsically to the floor.

"Where did you learn magic, armorer? They don't teach your kind." She said, reaching for the rite again.

The melody remained well out of her reach. She could no more will it forward than she could will herself down from this wall.

*Silenced, too.*

"Who do you work for? The emperor's bitch daughter? The Cross?"

"You oversaw the conditioning of those children your people stole, alongside the late Haman Bran." The words issued from Sami's mouth, but it was not her voice that came through. She watched from within as the Watchers riding her body closed the distance, gripped the edge of Lady Tamalsen's desk with her fingers. "For the countless deaths on his hands, the *failures* as you call them, we slew him. For your part, in releasing them, you will be spared his fate."

"You expect me to believe you will not kill me?" she said.

Sami shook her head.

Her eyes pulsed brighter, and the wind broke.

Lady Tamalsen slid onto the ground.

Her body moved of its own accord. Her fingers unbound the buttons holding her bodice closed, as electrified light flickered behind her irises. She peeled her dress off, turned her chair backward and mounted it, resting on her knees, leaning over the backrest, clutching it in both hands.

*What is this?* She wondered. Her faculties rapidly caught up with her. She looked again into Sami's eyes, recalled their usual color. It had not been so long ago that the woman before her was a girl readying to take her place in what department would have her. She had been successful in steering her to the place she would be of most use, a decision met with levity from the servant. A servant who was no longer in control of herself, who was as clay in the palm of another entity...or several. *Surely she couldn't have found that place. They wiped her memory.*

# SPIRIT OF SHADOW

Yet clearly, she had. Even those that knew about the nursery were not permitted to enter it except under very specific circumstances. Lady Tamalsen had never so much as been beyond the entrance. No one with any knowledge of it was ever to be in the direct line of sight of the Watchers enslaved there, so how did this girl find it? How did she find them?

"You're possessing her." She whispered coldly, and was surprised at the ease with which she spoke. "You unnatural beasts are using her. Manipulating an innocent girl."

"As have you, more times than any mortal could know." Sami crossed the room to a tall cupboard, wrenched the door open. Inside was a series of canes of various sizes. She took one out, tested it by bending it. It yielded rather easily. "You've terrorized hundreds of children, forced them to believe the very people who captured them are their saviors, that those who murdered their families are protecting them."

"I gave them better lives than they could have dreamed of. Most were in poverty when our Wraiths took them. Half would have died within the year." Lady Tamalsen said. "You know nothing of what they have been through!"

Sami replaced the cane, removed another and tested it.

"And the other half?"

Her jaw clicked shut.

"Yes, we thought so. It is all right there in your mind's eye. You have no secrets from us. Your Wraiths work often with poachers. Poverty...perhaps they were living in squalor, but they were free then. Able to live on their own terms.

"The rest, and do not waste our time with falsehoods, were prisoners. Hostages. You took many from important families to secure their compliance with your demands. No different than Gyarval or Arganon were your aims. To crush dissent in the borderlands. To prevent more allies from amassing around the one you call Reaper. To see that man dead in favor of his psychopath lieutenant when you could not keep him under control."

She returned the cane she was holding to the cabinet, removed another. This one was as thick as her thumb and beveled along its length, not unlike the leg of a chair.

"You beat them with this?" she asked, shedding a look of hard judgment on the lady.

Lady Tamalsen held her silence, glared back defiantly.

"Yes. I suppose it is better if you do not lie to us." She gave it an exploratory swing. It made a *whooping* noise as it sailed through the air.

She moved around the desk, positioned herself behind and to one side of Lady Tamalsen, so that her dominant arm was on the outside, ready to dole out pain.

"What do you think to accomplish?" Lady Tamalsen watched the cane as Sami brandished it. "Beating me will change nothing. Nor will killing my associates. You could kill the queen herself and the cycle would remain, untouched save for a superficial changing of faces."

Sami sneered. "We require a witness, Lady Elira of House Tamalsen.

She swung the cane hard, earning her a pained yelp from Lady Tamalsen. The cane came down again. A sheet of tears blurred Lady Tamalsen's vision.

Again.

*Again.*

*Again!*

With each brutal swing, Sami flinched away from the image cast in front of her eyes. She could not look away, could not ignore this violence. Could not flee into herself and thus avoid bearing witness to this cruelty. The Watchers held her before the event, compelled her to remain still and watch as they executed judgment on the lady who had raised her. The closest thing to a mother she had ever known.

Lady Tamalsen's jaw clenched tight around the scream she

# SPIRIT OF SHADOW

refused to let loose. The pain must have been unbearable. The degradation humiliating even in these private quarters, in this intimate, dangerous setting.

Again and again the cane came down, driving rational thought to a far corner of the lady's mind.

*What a way to die.* She thought absently. *Beaten bloody with her own cane.*

The door to her study burst open. There, standing in the doorway, looking terrified, was Rashanna.

"Help me!" Lady Tamalsen screamed.

Sami dropped the cane.

Rashanna pitched out of the way as she bolted from the room.

"L-lady T-tamalsen." Rashanna stammered.

"Run girl. Find a Wraith. Alert the guard. She is still close."

Rashanna did run, then. She did not go immediately to any Wraith or Thorn, anyone who might help the woman. She pelted down the hall until rationality caught up to her, until there was room within her to process what she had just witnessed, to recognize the danger was well and far removed from her.

Panting, she leaned against the wall near a crossing where two halls met. "What in the Pits. What in the name of...."

She straightened up, shook herself. *A Wraith. Need to find a Wraith. Let them know what I saw.*

# The Staircase

Lady Therien arrived in the nursery with a clay jug in one hand and a wine glass in the other. If it was her purpose in life to see to it these Watchers were kept in hand, she would do it on her own terms. She did not much care to entertain them sober this night, and had polished off half the contents of this jug of Mirrhvalian wine before descending into the palace bowels to attend to her affairs.

There was another affair she intended to entertain when this was over, and she quite liked the idea of handling that in a fitting state of inebriation, as well. Lord Tarkenta would mind little. He did not question her habits, and she did not question his. It was all just physical anyway, a temporary foray into the strange and new which would end when it ended, with her husband none the wiser.

She twisted the knob on the door into Queen Anastasia's old safe room, and hip checked it open. The door thumped against a poured stone wall as she passed it, and she kicked it shut again.

# SPIRIT OF SHADOW

The staff were mostly engrossed in preparing the younger children for a night's sleep. Some fussed over bottles filled with tinctures to incapacitate the little cretins, and others fussed over bedsheets and coverlets or read stories out of books of myths to their stubby charges.

She breezed past those chambers, left the women to their work. There was the bastard on her mind, and she wanted her taste of revenge. An hour or so, if she could be bothered to remain her so long, spent beating every inch of him into a bloody ruin would do her good. She would be over it then, might even spare him the remaining days of his miserable life spent eating less than might keep him alive until the moon rose full once more.

"We must show them mercy on occasion, mustn't we." She mumbled. "Else we will never break—"

The jug crashed against the tiles, and sobriety stole over her as shock abruptly displaced the middling drunk storming through her.

The Watchers, all in their line, were slumped along the wall. All of them were, by every appearance, dead.

Gingerly, she set her wine glass on the ground, ignoring the shattered ruin spread across the floor, and approached them. She tested the Jua man's neck with trembling fingers.

*No pulse.*

She moved to the one next to him and repeated her analysis to find the same result. To another.

*Sky Lord's mercy.*

She turned and ran out of the chamber, ran until she was well clear of the door and the silencing effect of the chunk of enchanted quartz in its corner. She drew on the Cosmic Orchestra and opened her shadow, flung herself into it and away.

She thought of the queen as she ran through a sightless world in search of Lord Tarkenta, no longer intent on a foray

## The Staircase

into that so pleasing world of adultery, but in need of him in his official capacity. *She'll be furious! What are we to do without those blue eyed freaks? Start over?*

A needed outing brought Lance to the canteen for lunch for the first time in several days. With his shifts in the furnaces all transpiring at night, he had little incentive to awake before afternoon was well underway, and then it was to sit for dinner, spare those few hours he had for his friends or for Ben.

He had not seen *him* in some time, either. Too much lingered in his mind's eye to place much focus on the little things, good or otherwise.

He had agreed to lunch with Ben because he felt he was neglecting him. With everything so new, he did not want to come across as dodgy, did not want Ben to think he had lost interest, that he was contemplating breaking things off before they had gone much farther than digging out a basement to support the house he intended to build.

*If everything could have just stayed simple....* he thought dejectedly, as he passed under the great clock, its pendulum swinging to and fro just over his head. His tray was populated with simple offerings. The kitchens had been stretched thin with the demands of the nobility of two cities to contend with, and their offerings had become much less inspired as a result.

He should be happy they hadn't elected to serve wheat gruel three times a day. As it was, he approached a table where Ben sat by himself with boiled sausages and a baked yam to contemplate.

He took the saved seat across from him, set his tray down, and picked up his fork.

"How've you been?" he asked.

"Decent, I guess." Ben said. "Lady Therien's been on one with the Mirrhvalians here...and that business with Lady

# SPIRIT OF SHADOW

Tamalsen. I think she's taking it personally what happened."

"What *did* happen?" Lance asked, meeting his gaze.

"She was flogged. Beaten to a bloody pulp. Rashanna was on duties for Lady Jain to clue her in on...something...and she saw...." Ben trailed off, a concerned expression stealing over his face. "Are you okay?"

"Just tired. I'm not used to being up this early." Lance said. He tried on a grin. "So Rashanna?"

"You're sure?"

"I promise I'm fine." Lance said.

Ben nodded, but the expression on his face only ratcheted up Lance's concern. *Why didn't I take you with me? It'd be so much simpler if I could just tell you what's going on.*

But he wouldn't. To tell Ben anything would only invite more complications into his life.

"Right." Ben said. "So Rashanna walked in on what was happening. She was the one who reported it. She's still pretty shaken up over it."

"Sky Lord's mercy." Lance breathed. "I'm sorry she went through that."

"She'll be okay. She wasn't hurt or anythin'. She's just in shock over it all. It was...well, I guess she said she wasn't sure what she saw. But she swears she recognized the person who did it."

"Did she say who?"

"Y-yes. I don't know if I should tell you if I'm being honest."

"Someone I know?"

"Sami, actually."

Lance flinched.

"You said you hadn't seen her in a while. Well, it's lookin' like she probably did Lord Bran in, too. I'm really sorry."

"It's okay."

"It's a lot of things, but I don't think—"

## The Staircase

"It's okay, just...can we talk about something else?"

"Sure."

There it was. Another complication to add to the small mountain of problems facing him. Those memories recently pulled loose by a spirit whose name he didn't know—whose nature was made known to him even as she chose to withhold her identity, to deny him her aid—skittered across his mind. Harrowing perils tap danced across the spongy tissue of his brain, leaving him more confused than he could remember being, and with too much to process besides.

There was the problem of Peter and his block. That he couldn't hear the spirits voices seemed something Lance was personally responsible for, and whatever solution came along to mend that wrong needed to come from him, or he would never be relieved of his guilt.

They shared the same problem, if its manifestation was different for each of them. They were bonded now in their silence, a need for secrecy. His friends had, almost overnight, become little boxes for him to stash away secrets, with no two of them knowing everything he knew, and he hated it. Peter did not know how he had come to arrive in the furnaces, why it was deemed necessary for him to be there. But Ben did.

Ben did not know what Master Gregor and Lord Aren were up to, or what they claimed Lance was. This alien entity who might, if he could learn to harness his power, save them from something they had been less than forthcoming in defining. But Peter did.

Sami knew something of the perils he was embroiled in, too, or why had she gone rogue. What had made that sweet if rebellious woman turn murderer? Why had she chosen to single out Lady Tamalsen, of all people, for a lesson in humiliation? She must have stumbled onto something, and he could not stop thinking about a staircase behind a metal grate, a place he had happened upon first when in the company of the very man sitting across from him. Which inspired such palpable anxiety in him that he would rather be anywhere else.

He could not stop thinking she had gone down there. That whatever had driven her to cold blooded murder was housed at the other end of it.

They made idle chitchat as they tucked into their food, avoided all talk of her, of his condition and what it might mean. Ben kept things on light notes, did the heavy lifting of keeping conversation flowing. And if he thought Lance was acting strangely, he might attribute it to having just learned his very best friend was a killer.

He thought of Ariana, too. If she knew Sami had attacked Lady Tamalsen, she couldn't be in good spirits, either. Knowing nothing other than a friend who had disappeared had resurfaced a violent criminal, one at large and with an agenda that seemed inspired by vengeance, she could not be doing well either.

He walked with Ben to the spiral stair leading to the upper floors of the Servant's Tower, took him to his floor, and kissed him goodbye. Then, he traced his steps back the way he came.

If Sami had been driven to such violence by that place, he would go there. If that place had nothing to do with her sudden shift toward cruelty, he would still go there. In that secret reach lay answers to at least some of his questions. If nothing else, there would be a confirmation there for some truth he held close, that not all in this palace was as it seemed.

He listened at the entrance at the height of the stair until he was certain it was safe, and then proceeded down the steps.

He sucked in a deep breath and let it out slowly. *The best way to overcome your fear is to confront it.* Maybe the other servants were okay with not knowing what was down there, what the truth behind this secret was, but he needed to. This place elicited the same palpable fear in Ben as it did him. He suspected most servants had a similar reaction to it. Animal panic, bereft of reason. A memory in the body of dark times, which the mind refused to identify.

Some disease brought small truths to the surface in the servants in those vulnerable moments when they were frightened or defenseless. Something needed to be forgotten for them to accept their place in the palace. He might regret knowing, but it would be like replacing one regret with another. He was convinced the source of his madness, of all of their madness, lay here, at the other end of this staircase.

He steeled himself, pushed his fear aside, and kept going. He pressed his hand to the wall as a guide through the darkness, navigated the steps by feel. An ache formed in his temples as he descended, and the air grew progressively colder. He halted halfway down, and closed his eyes.

He was a child—maybe three years old. He sat in front of someone atop a beast with a neck extruded from a fleshy hump covered in coarse fur. As far as he could see in any direction, there was only sand. He was thirsty, but the bladders he knew contained water hung out of his reach on the animal's saddle, and the person behind him wouldn't help him with it.

Memories like this one had become a frequent intrusion on his daily life since that ancient woman who called herself the moon looked into his eyes. She had unlocked a door within him, and the terrors in his past had come spilling out, but they had not all come at once.

He opened his eyes, started moving again. In the distance, lights flickered, warm and yellow-orange, the afterglow of a

# SPIRIT OF SHADOW

fire.

He closed his eyes again, paused where he stood.

He was a child in someone's home. *My home.*
Low flames flickered in a hearth near his seat on a broad strip of velvet carpet.  People sat around a pile of neatly wrapped parcels. They wore sweatshirts tooled with fanciful designs and slacks to mark the formality of the occasion. A boy with his dark hair slicked back surveyed the parcels through hungry, storm-gray eyes. The older people laughed and sipped at drinks, their cheeks red, eyes glossy.  There was the man that matched the boy, a woman with eyes that matched Lance's. There was another man with them—with silver eyes and salt and pepper hair, dressed in a fuchsia, four-piece suit. Then another walking in from somewhere else with a tray in hand. He was coal dark, coconut headed with round ears and wiry hair. Two older children sat on a couch with a green-eyed girl that looked somewhat like the younger boy. The daughter, darker than the son, was of an age with the green-eyed girl. The son was a few years older, maybe fifteen.

They looked so happy—all of them gathered together. And he knew he had been happy with them once.

When he opened his eyes, the chill on the air was in his bones, cold water filling him, stiffening his legs, pressuring them to resist as his brain signaled the march forward.

He kept on.

The light intensified. The silence deepened. He stopped on the last step. This time, he didn't close his eyes.

The room that crawled out from under that step was a simple expanse, with floor and walls of poured stone. A blocky prominence with a door marked a holding room of some kind. In the recess next to it, a trough full of dirty water sat beside a pile of plates and trays arranged willy-nilly atop a ragged looking stool. A table framed by bench seats filled the space in front of it. A kitchen knife lay on its surface, and it was covered in grease.

Across from the recess and the holding room and all down a hall that fell out of sight were panes of mirrored glass with columns of poured stone between, each a hand's width thick.

He stepped into the room. The weight of rumor and story was with him as he ran his hand over the rough surface of the table, the wall of the holding chamber where a torch burned in its bracket. He touched its handle to make sure it was real.

Finally, having summoned every ounce of his courage, his skin crawling with static, he set himself in front of those mirrors.

He reached out with shaky fingers, pressed his hand to the glass. The glass cleared, fog on the window chased away by a sudden wave of heat. The clarity spread to its corners, revealing what lay beyond. Where his reflection had been looking back at him, a cell appeared. His stomach roiled. A lump in his throat threatened to choke him.

There, waiting for him to find, was a boy. He was no more than four years old. His hair was a matted, dirty mess. His skin was coated in grease, and salt, and soil. His fingertips, where they clung to his shins, were crusted with dried blood, the nails chipped and grimed. He huddled in the far corner under a wall scratched over with so many overlapping marks there was no telling where one prisoner's desperate attempt to keep time ended and the next one's began. A pile of feces took up the corner furthest from the boy, whose only garment was a pair of briefs gone yellow and crusty, if not from urine then from sweat and dirt.

Lance felt the itch in his private parts, the burning sensation from defecating and having nothing to clean up with. He felt the oil on his skin, could smell, suddenly, as clearly as if he was the one in that cell, the sour, onion-and-pepper odor of his own, unwashed body. His scalp itched and his eyes watered. He couldn't remember when he started crying, but soon his breath hitched in his throat; and anger, and pain, and fear battled with each other inside of him. He felt sick, like nothing in the world would ever be right again.

He closed his eyes.

Fire burned everywhere. He was surrounded by it. A broken timber blocked the door out of his wood-paneled room. He sat on his tiny bed, watching the fire burn, inhaled smoke and listened to his sister scream and bash the door.

She couldn't save him. Young as he was, he knew that he would die before she got to him.

Cold hands wrapped around his shoulders. He fell backward through some unseen barrier, into darkness.

One memory gave way to another.

Light poured into a darkness he knew concealed a fate like that of the child in the cell, and a woman stood in that light. She was tall in his memory, with full lips and black hair done into a neat bun at the back of her head. She wore a lilac and obsidian dress, with skirts that hugged her figure. A pendant with a green stone set into its woven, silver frame hung between her breasts from a fine chain.

She claimed to have saved him, and he loved her for it. The Shadow Queen, Meredith, whom he knew now had imprisoned him after she ordered him stolen from his family.

He stumbled, caught himself on the edge of the table. The door to the holding chamber burst open. A Wraith—dressed in an oil-skin loincloth, a band of script running around his midriff, another broader coil over his heart, stood inside the doorway, holding the door against his forearm.

## The Staircase

"You're not supposed to be here!" he shouted.

All of the rumors came unbidden to Lance's mind. *No one comes back from here. They never come out again. They'll execute you if you go down there...or worse.* He searched for a way out, but the Wraith had seen his face. A ball of flame coalesced against the Wraith's palm. He cranked his arm back, readying to throw it.

Lance panicked.

He snatched the knife off the table. The grease made it slippery in his grip.

He screamed, charged, the knife held in front of him in both hands.

The Wraith hesitated. The knife slammed into his throat, above the collarbone.

Lance recoiled as the elf stumbled and fell over. Blood ran from the wound in his neck. Lance stood there dumbly as the blood pooled under the elf and spread.

Then, he ran—up the stairs, across the hall, through a door into the servant's tunnels and down. He ran until his legs wouldn't carry him and then slowed, stopped.

He ducked into a storeroom. He was near the kitchens now, his legs and lungs on fire.

"What did I just do?" he breathed.

His hands shook violently. He couldn't believe they were capable of such violence, couldn't comprehend how he had just...*killed someone.*

"What did I do?"

He pulled himself together. It took some time and even when he had his composure it felt as if one wrong word would pull him apart again.

He stripped off his clothes, tossed them in a mop bucket full of dirty water that he used to scrub his hands and forearms clean. He wiped his face with the untainted back of his tunic, and left the storeroom in his underwear, hoping—as he navigated the tunnel, ducking into storerooms or taking a new path whenever he heard another servant approaching—he could get back to his barracks unseen. He was certain that if he was caught, he would be immolated.  Thought for anything else was ephemeral.

# Peter

He arrived in the headmaster's office within the Teacher's Tower, found Peter already there and waiting for him. He looked unkempt, as if he couldn't be bothered to keep himself up, but there was some relief to be had in seeing him in that state.

He had been struggling with the revelations the moon spirit had left with him, the sudden resurfacing of so many lost memories, of forgotten places in the palace and the events that transpired within them...and other things.

There was the matter of all of that guilt and sadness that followed him from the dungeon rooms where he had been kept as a child, certain confirmation his worst nightmares had been truer than his best memories of this palace. Everything that had befallen him, every small victory, every word of encouragement from Lady Tamalsen, from all of those others of the noble caste he had received any kindness whatever from, were recast as condescending reflections.

His light was dimmed. Darkness lurked behind everything, there if he could only have seen it.

# SPIRIT OF SHADOW

He sat in the headmaster's seat, behind the desk, flirted with imbuing the desk with some essence of a simple magic he had learned, to see what it might do. He stayed his hand, instead focused on his friend, who sat with his back against the wall, the harp playing softly to push back the quiet.

"What did she show you?" he asked. "Your memories...what were they like?"

"Does it really matter? I can't change what happened. All I can do now is try to forget about it."

"That's not going to help either of us, and you know it." Lance said.

"Remembering didn't help Sami." He said.

Lance stiffened.

"I know you want to believe we can get out of here somehow, but what if we can't? This whole thing is crazy, Lance. Did you not hear what Lord Aren said when we met with him. Before that *thing* awakened this...this...."

"It all just seems so useless." He turned his gaze to the floor, rubbed his hands together in his lap. "I don't even know who I am anymore."

"That's why I'm asking you to share your pain with me. Maybe it'll be an easier burden for us both to carry if we don't have to do it alone."

"But none of this helps us escape. We could try to shadow walk out of here, but the Wraiths would just hunt us down, and they're so much stronger than we are. And what about our friends? They'll be stuck here. I don't think I can stomach the thought of leaving Ariana behind, whether she knows the truth or not."

"I feel the same way." Lance said, easing back against his seat.

"We shouldn't trust Lord Aren." Peter said, finally looking at him out of the corner of his eye. "He might be friendly to us now, but he'll throw us away as soon as we've served our purpose."

"You think so?" In truth, Lance had been feeling the same way. He didn't quite know why he was so averse to trusting Lord Aren. Maybe it was because he had helped him find his steps, had given him a solution to a persistent problem when he was still ignorant to Lothor's name and nature. Maybe he felt he should trust him on that basis, but he was not sure of the man. He was not entirely sure of Master Gregor either. They had their own wants, and those wants did not seem to align with his.

"You heard what he said about Sami. He knows what happened to her, and he's not telling us everything. I think he might have been responsible for it."

"He made it sound like she was working with him, too." Lance said, trying to sound as if he believed his own words.

"Why wasn't she with him, then." Peter said.

"I don't have an answer to that." Lance admitted.

"Look, if you want to know what happened to me before...well, can you just go first? I'm not ready to...well. I don't want to talk about it just yet."

"Fair enough." He ran his hand over the desk's surface, smearing dust around. He wiped it against the underside of his shirt. "I was born in the Eleventh Ward, and that's where I spent the first three years of my life. I guess I'm lucky it wasn't longer than that, because I don't remember much. Maybe it would be worse if I did.

"My father took us on a trip to the beach somewhere in the Free Lands. I don't know where. And my older brother was abducted while we were swimming. I never saw the person who did it, but my parents were...well, it isn't surprising how they took it. When I was three, someone set fire to my family's house. The roof caved in. My sister tried to save me, but she couldn't get the door to my bedroom open. I tried to get out through the window, and a Wraith dragged me back. Took me into the shadows. Next thing you know, I was in a cell in this palace.

"You know the rest. You lived it."

Peter flinched.

"Your turn." He said. "If you don't tell someone what happened, you're going to explode. So out with it."

Peter grimaced. "Fine, then. You're right, okay. It's just...I never had any family. There's nothing out there for me to go back to."

He nodded. "Okay."

"That's it?"

"That's it."

"I'm from the Ring of Fire. Ash Island. I don't know who my mother or my father were, but they couldn't have liked me much because they dumped me on the street. I fell in with a bunch of other kids whose parents abandoned them for one reason or another, and spent the first few years of my life robbing tourists to keep myself fed.

"There was a woman who saved me from certain death once. She was blind. She sacrificed herself for me. Didn't matter much in the end, though. Some poachers got me and sold me off to the Wraiths."

Clapping from a corner of the room startled both of them. Master Gregor rose out of the shadows with Emma just behind him.

"Ash Island in't easy to live in, kid. I'd know. 'M from 'ere myself." He said. "That blind lady yer talkin' 'bout was a Pyre Magus. Weird thing 'bout kitunes. We've got some quirks other races 'on't have. Mos' 'on't even know 'bout 'em. Bet you never been burned before." He cracked a toothless grin, his silver-eyed gaze settling on Peter.

"Thought so. Yer not immune ta fire, 'on't get me wrong, but 's a fair bit harder to burn a kitune 'an any aught other people. 'Ere are merenerns all over 'at region, too. Can breathe under water. Swim pretty well, too. 'S why 'ey were never conquered. Lands around Morgrotten were taken by this empire, see, but seein' as 'ere capital's at the bottom o' that lake, wasn't much 'em elves could do but box 'em in and pretend 'ey were part of this lovely empire all along.

"'S neither here nor there, though. Best thing kitunes ought goin' fer us 's a byproduct of blindness. All 'em Pyre Magi're blind as bats. Some're born 'at way. Some come by it other ways. Blind a kitune, you unlock ten fold the power she might 'ave otherwise. 'At woman gave a lot more 'an you know to save yer skin. So maybe she didn't *love* you, but she sure did keep yer ticker goin' 'in't she?"

Peter stared into his face. A soft chuckle escaped him.

"Wha's funny. 'M bein' sympathetic." He elbowed Emma in the ribs. "'A's the right word, right?"

"You're an asshole." She said. "You can't see he's going through it?"

"'M jus' trying to lighten the damned mood. 'S that so wrong?

"Anyway, I'll leave ya to it. Emma's teachin' you stuff today. I might pass Duardo the torch one day, but we'll see. Kid's a good 'un, but he's spacey. Forgets a lot o' shit."

He opened his shadow and slid back into it, leaving just Emma in the room with them.

She panned over Lance and dismissed him. "Neat desk."

"You're kind of a bitch, aren't you." Peter said.

"Your girlfriend is worse." She replied. "She's still one of my favorite people, though. I was hoping this piece of shit would bring her for our little rendezvous the other night, but beggars can't be choosers." She shrugged.

"Don't talk to him like that." Lance said.

"Or you'll do what?"

He balled up his fists. There was a lot he could do if he was so inclined, but if he didn't play her game there was every chance it would get back to Master Gregor, and then who knew where he would land himself. Whatever peculiar ability he possessed, he was still her subordinate as far as the furnaces were concerned. And he did not have the command over magic she did, either.

"Relax, Lance. I can defend myself." Peter said.

"So...that's actually what we're here about. That one's gonna sit this one out." She cocked her thumb in Lance's direction. "You're the star of the show today."

"Shouldn't I be doing something?"

"Well as you can hear the spirits already, no. In fact, you should not be. Right now, your friend needs to unlearn some bad habits so we can get him back in their good books. Otherwise, we're all fucked. See how that works, muffin?

"Now get the fuck away from that desk. I need it."

He obeyed, took up a chair from a stack of them by the wall, and seated himself.

She took up his old seat.

"Thanks for warming that up for me." She spared him an insincere grin, and thumped her palm against the desk's surface. He heard the echoes of a voice on the air, which he did not recognize.

"Fun fact." She said. "Something Master Gregor left out when he was explaining about racial quirks and stuff, actually. We all have different elemental affinities. The elements are divided into five houses. Different affinities are more common across races. Kitunes mostly align well with fire spirits. That's the norm. It's not always the case, but you throw a rock into a crowd and...you get the point. So that's where we'll start."

An infographic image materialized in the heart of the office. A disembodied voice launched into an explanation of an aspect of fire magic.

"Do your people always use this space to train new recruits?" Lance asked from his corner.

"Most of the time. Unless we run across someone like you

who's already been dabbling."

"I wasn't dabbling." He said.

She rolled her eyes. "Anyway. We're doing the learning. The learning is king. Let's all listen to the dumb ass who put this lesson together, shall we? It's important."

He nodded.

"One must simply sit in pensive silence until such melodies as define the cosmic orchestra reveal themselves to his ears. To sit too long in this chaos places pressure on the mind and soul, opening the possibility for serious injury. As such, it is imperative that the practitioner of magic act decisively to compel what melody he seeks into his direct control."

"Wrong." Emma said.

"At which time, and under his guidance, he can manipulate it with his will."

She removed her hand from the desk. The image collapsed, and the voice was silenced.

"That's about what you learned, right?" she asked Peter.

"Pretty much." He said.

"Yeah, so that's the problem. Those sounds you hear when you try to shadow walk are actually cries of pain. The spirits don't like being manipulated that way. Sure, you can do it just like that, and you'll get consistent results that way, but you shouldn't be using that method as a first resort.

"The *only* time it's appropriate to force a spirit to comply with you is when it refuses to and you're in danger. Got it?"

"Sure." He said. "So, what am I supposed to do instead."

"Learn to call it by its name. Understand what the thing you're trying to use *is*. That is has feelings. Once you've got a handle on that, you *might* be able to call on it without too much resistance.

"And that's the other thing. Those spirits you're trying to call...the reason you tap out so fast when you do call on them is because they're actively trying to resist you. They can't do much, but they can make it harder on you when you try to use their power, which means the shelf life for how long you can draw on it is a lot less time, and you'll be a lot more tired when you finally let them go."

"Okay." He said. "Still don't see how I'm supposed to pull them in if I can't hear them."

"Well, honey bunch, you're in luck. Because I can. And so can he. And that means we can, between the two of us, get those little bastards here for *you* to conversate with.

"So, without further preamble, and because I'm wasting a perfectly good day off teaching you manners, let's begin, shall we?"

She called the name of a spirit, and the little fox Lance had last seen when the Thorn had sought to test him materialized at the foot of the desk.

"Figure out what she is, and she'll tell you her name. That's the basic concept." Emma said.

*"A new one, huh?"* the fox snickered. *"Well, I suppose Phia isn't of much use in* this *environment."*

"Exactly why I chose you."

"Are you talking to one of them?" Peter asked.

"She is." Lance answered. "One I don't know."

"Which means you can't help your buddy." Emma thumped the desk. "Isn't that just so delightful?"

*"Do you hate everyone?"* the spirit asked.

Lance guffawed.

Emma glared at him. She turned her gaze on Peter. "Just...listen. Try not to judge. And if you bumble fuck your way into that stupid tidal zone that sound like a bunch of soloists playing on top of each other, lean into it. That's where the magic happens."

"Literally." Peter crossed his arms. He leaned back against his chair, and closed his eyes.

*"I am here. I am waiting."* The spirit said. She repeated

those simple statements like a refrain.

Lance watched intently as Peter navigated the channels of what magic was known to him. It was no brief thing, him coming around to the truth, hearing what was plain to everyone else in the room, and Emma did not seem surprised by this. If Lance's apparent aptitude for these dealings had revealed itself swiftly, it was a fluke of his being who, and perhaps what, he was.

Peter screwed up his face, hunting for something which ought to be plain before him.

*"He is distracted."* The spirit said. *"There is a block."*

"What kind of block?" Lance asked.

The spirit turned her gaze on him. *"He is no Seem. No, I should not expect it to be so simple a thing, him coming to hear my voice. But there is something in his soul. I can feel it. Instability in the connection, which lives in his mind."*

"He's still..." Lance climbed out of his seat.

"Let him work." Emma said.

"No, I don't think I will. Did you not hear her?"

"I certainly didn't." Peter grumbled.

"Should I be mad?" Emma said. "I think I should. I should be very mad."

"You clearly are." Lance said. "But you're missing an important detail in your calculations, here. Peter wasn't aware of any of this before he was struck down by that woman."

"I'm sorry."

"The peacock."

"Still not sure I—"

"Look, I realize you don't remember much before they shunted you out of that place in the dungeons. I wish I didn't know how to get there, but I do. Same with the other place. There are things in this palace that you should be glad you don't remember. I think that's what's holding him back."

"I'm right here, you know." Peter said.

# SPIRIT OF SHADOW

Lance sank onto his haunches.

"It's okay." He said.

"Is it?" Peter relaxed a hair, accepted a small measure of comfort from his friend.

"There's no defense for what they did. I don't blame you for feeling the way you do about it. And maybe...maybe some petty success isn't what you need right now. This can wait. Right now, I think you need to process what you're dealing with, and figure out how to cope with it.

"This will still be here when you're ready."

"So I'm wasting my time." Emma groused, scowling.

The spirit shed a glare on her.

*"Everything in its own time."* She said.

"Before you go," Lance said to the spirit. "The spirit who did this. Who is she?"

*"I'm afraid it doesn't work that way. I cannot give you her name. It is hers. She is the ruler of the House of Sa. That is all I can say. All else of her nature, she has told you."*

"Thank you, but that's not why I asked."

A pause as the spirit contemplated him.

"I wondered if she could help him."

*"The mind is not her domain. That spirit will not help him either. Strength from within is the most stable kind. It requires no aid to sustain itself."*

She faded away, leaving just they three to fill the room.

"She's gone." Emma said dejectedly.

"You summoned the wrong spirit, anyway." He said.

"Who would have been better?"

"Someone he's already familiar with."


Lothor was in his web again, nestled in the corner of the window just the other side of Fat John's bunk. Lance listened to his curses as his abdomen scrunched in on itself and his

## Peter

legs performed a dance against the strings. If he could, he would alleviate the spirit of its pain, but he could do nothing for him.

"Hey." He whispered.

He had been thinking of Peter, of the struggle he must be dealing with in trying to marry the image of his life with the truth he now comprehended. *I should have told him about the dungeons. That place behind the gate.*

He couldn't see how telling him of that place would have helped. Peter might have gone there himself, seeking the same confirmation as had given validity to the newfound memories rolling around in his head. Nothing good could have come from that. It was in control of the Wraiths, not the Thorns. And even if the Thorns had been the commanding presence there, how could he trust them? There were those loyal to Lord Aren, yes; those who knew the truth, but they could not all be of one mind. There would be those loyal to the crown, who answered to Lord Aren because he was their master, because they believed he, too, was loyal to the queen.

There were other things on his mind, as well. He put a pin in Peter's predicament. Decided instead to focus on what was in front of him. What he could control.

Lothor's legs stopped moving. His abdomen clenched and released rhythmically, but he was otherwise still.

*"What is it now, boy?"* the spider demanded.

"Lord Aren and Master Gregor. They speak a language I don't understand. Your language, I think."

*"The language is ilfeiya. It is the first language, which the spirits taught the stone people."*

"Who are they?"

*"Those created by god to alleviate his loneliness."* Lothor answered. *"You know them as Croni, if you know them at all. Born of earth, who dwell in earth. Most hail from the north, in this day."*

"They know this language?"

*"Some do."*

"How would I learn it?"

*"Your people write the important things in their books and on their scrolls."*

He nodded. "All of those are in the Royal Library. I can't go there."

*"Can't and won't are different things."*

He contemplated Lothor in his web, the silhouette cast in moonlight from outside the window. Light from a moon he now associated with a peacock and an elder woman, who were one and the same.

"If I go there, the Wraiths might kill me. Or the Thorns. They might jail me first. Torture me. Make me give them answers for everything I've learned. Lord Aren might—"

*"Lord Aren is of no concern to you. And if you were captured, what might happen? You would come before him. A sham interrogation. Then you would disappear."*

"Like Sami did."

*"Yes and no."*

"Where do the ones who don't go along with him end up?"

*"Away."* Lothor said. *"Abroad."*

"But alive?"

*"Yes."*

"There are books on this language in the library?"

*"There are books on many subjects there. Finding them might prove difficult. Without help."*

"Where would I find that help?"

*"You know the name of the spirit."*

"And if I did not want to be caught?"

*"You know the name of that spirit, as well. Though I have no great love of him. He is annoying to me."*

*Aughere. And Shana.* He thought.

Peter came to the fore of his mind again. If there were books on the language the spirits spoke, perhaps there were

Peter

those that might direct him to how to help his friend as well. And if they were there, he might be able to mend a great wrong Peter had encountered with a testing intended for him. He had never meant for him to be hurt.

"There are grimoires there, too."

*"Old tomes. From before your people forgot us."* Lothor agreed. Strangely, he sounded happy.

"Then maybe...maybe I should. Go there, I mean."

*"Alone, you will certainly be caught. How much time have you to locate all you need. Go in two directions and you will have traversed a great distance. And I cannot save you should the weasel's good graces dry up. He is erratic."*

*I'll take him with me. If he doesn't find anything that helps, maybe just looking for something will get him out of his funk.*

"Thank you." He said, and twisted around in his bunk. "Goodnight. Sweet dreams."

Lothor chuckled. *"I know her well."*


Ben's duties took him to the kitchens—to fetch a meal for Lord Aren, who had taken a shine to him.

He wasn't sure what possessed the general to ask Lady Therien for his direct services, but since the message had been sent, almost all of his duties centered around the general. What little time he had to spare was spent running messages for other military men, most of them sergeants, who he supposed treated him well enough. The lady seemed content with his newfound placement. Seemed to take it as a badge of honor that he would be chosen so early in his career for such a high honor.

He had no illusions about her relationship to Lord Aren. He had long believed the two detested each other, even before he had been tasked with these duties.

But that was of little concern to him. The dealings of Shadovane's elites were far and away not his business, until they entailed who was fucking the lady and where. But Lord

# SPIRIT OF SHADOW

Aren had no interest in her. If his friend on the Council of Liam was entranced by her, so be it. What could a servant do about any of it.

He waited for his turn in a pass situated some way back from that window where the servants dished up. Ariana was there, adding garnishes to plates before they were fitted with domed lids and passed to the couriers who would take them where they needed to go.

His number came up, and he approached the window.

"Fancy seeing you here." She grinned.

He returned the gesture. "New duties. I'm likin' them so far."

"Oh really now."

"Lord Aren asked for me to be his personal servant. Most of what I'm doing now is just bringing messages back and forth."

"I love it." She said. "He's not a dick, is he?"

Ben shook his head.

"How are things with Lance?" she asked.

"To be honest, I haven't seen much of him. We're on opposite schedules, though. I guess it makes sense. I was hopin' we could get together, soon, though. Maybe in the evening before he goes to the furnaces."

"Has he been acting weird?" she asked.

"Maybe. I don't know. This is all still so new."

"I mean he's not acting like he lost interest, right? He talks about you a lot."

"Nothin' like that."

"It's just...Peter went up to the Teacher's Tower with him. He said something about a hazing thing. I guess the furnace workers do that to the new guys. She shrugged. "I can't judge. We do that shit here. But he's been acting like a little bitch since then. Moping around. If I didn't know any better, I'd say he's depressed. But he won't talk to me about it."

**Peter**

"I'm sure it'll pass."

"Lance isn't being weird like that, though?" there was a kind of pleading in her gaze, an almost desperate need.

He shook his head. "I don't know. Like I said, I haven't seen much of him. I can ask him what's goin' on."

"If you see him, please do."

"Wait." He took his tray from her. "*You* haven't seen him?"

"Not in a few days."

"Maybe I should be worried then."

"Just let me know if you find anything out from him."

"I will. But you do the same, okay? I don't want to think he's been suffering in silence and I've been too much of an ass to notice."

"Okay." She tried on a smile.

He said his goodbyes, and left with Lord Aren's meal.

# The Royal Library

*A grimoire. Something to help me learn their language. Maybe there's something in the library that can help me with both of those things.* Lance thought to himself as he dressed in the night gloom. He had chosen to leave when he might otherwise for his shift in the furnaces, but he had no intention of going there. If he succeeded here...if he could hide what he found well enough...he would have delivered a boon not just to Peter, but to Master Gregor and the furnace workers, as well.

He told himself he would.

*Anything that might help me find a way out, too. That would be helpful.*

He would go to Peter's barracks first. He hadn't told him of his intentions, but knew this task would be beyond him if he went it alone. He did not know how large the Royal

Library was. Didn't know how it was organized, either. There would be complications to his plans as soon as he arrived there, risks he would have to take if he was to get what he needed out of this misadventure. Even with Shana to guide him, finding anything of use would be an uphill climb.

*"Lothor?"* he whispered.

*"Yes?"*

"Time to go."

His shadow deepened at bedside, became a matte well roughly cast in his image, but longer, and somewhat wider than was strictly natural. He tipped forward, and plunged through it.

He landed softly on his feet in unrelieved darkness, and called on Shana, the spirit of direction, a guide on uncertain paths.

*"Where do you wish to go?"* she asked.

"To the second floor barracks. But stay close. I need you to take me somewhere else after that."

*"As you wish."*

Silver lines unfurled before him, one at his crown and the other crawling away from his toe tips.

"Hide me, *Lothor*. I don't want to be followed."

Lothor grumbled something he couldn't quite make out, and he hoped the spirit had complied.

He traveled forth until the threads intersected, and then pulled at a substance that felt at the same time like silk and oil above him, opening a window into the world above, where a bunk bed hugged the contours of a sloping, windowless wall.

He emerged, saw Peter soundly asleep in his bed, a complicating presence cupped against his body. Ariana had chosen this night to share his bed with him.

He slid his hand over Peter's mouth, and braced himself as the kitune stiffened.

Ariana shifted next to him. "Something wrong?"

# SPIRIT OF SHADOW

Lance pressed his finger to his lips, gesturing for silence as Peter set eyes on him.

"Come with me." He whispered.

Peter nodded, and he removed his hand from his mouth.

"Nothing's wrong, babe." He said. "Just...bathroom."

"Don't fall in." She said, and drew the coverlet tighter over herself as he crawled out of the bed. He marched a short way off and Lance followed.

"What's this about?" he asked.

"I need you to help me with something?"

"Something involving—"

"Yeah. Just...we need to be quick."

"She'll notice if I'm gone that long."

Lance grimaced.

"O-okay. Just let me get a shirt."

He crossed back to his bed, drew open a drawer in its base and pulled out shirt and moccasins, which he carried away with him as not to further disturb his girlfriend.

As he dressed himself, Lance called again on Lothor, and opened his shadow.


Ariana rolled over. Through vision slightly blurred with recent sleep, she watched as her boyfriend dropped into pooled shadow together with another man.

*That lying sack of shit.* She ground her teeth together, suddenly very alert. *Where the fuck does he think he's going.*

*Was that...was that Lance?*

She rolled out of the bed. Dressing was a jagged, hurried dance, and she approached the site of their disappearance on tiptoes as she wrenched the hem of her pants up around her hips.

There was nothing there to remember their passing, but she was sure she had seen them go. Off somewhere without her, to do who only knew what.

*Ben's on this floor, isn't he?* She thought he was. They didn't often cross paths within the barracks. There were only so many Wraiths that would allow her to sleep here, and when she did it was with the intent that she be well within her own barracks before sun up, ready to go to the kitchens before anyone knew she'd been gone.

*If Lance is here...where the fuck could they be going?*

She traveled the barrel shaft corridor, hunting for the courier, and found him on the far side, well removed from the entrance and near the low carve out where this floor's toilets were housed.

*He really got the shit end of the stick, didn't he?*

She nudged him awake.

"Whassit?" he yawned, arms stretching catlike as he put himself together.

"You said to let you know if I heard anything from Lance." She said.

"Ariana?"

"Who else would it be. Now come on. He just took Peter into the shadows. If we're quick, we might still be able to catch up with them."

"Why would I want to—"

"Look, are you going to help me or not? They've been acting weird. You said it yourself. Time to figure out why."

He nodded. "Okay." And rolled his clothing drawer open, pulled out what he needed, and then pitched sideways onto his feet.

"Let's go."

"You're not gonna—"

"Don't have much time. I'll get myself together on the way."

"But you're—"

He waved her to silence. "Not a reason to wait. I'll do the honors."

He opened a portal into shadow, pulling down a lilting,

dark melody out of a chaotic storm of other, instrumental sounds. The shade of his shadow deepened and drew itself wide, allowing enough space for Ariana, reluctantly, to step into.

He followed her through, and the shadow collapsed behind him.

"How do we find them?" he asked, once they were safely inside the Shadow World.

"The same way we find anything in this place." She said.

He nodded, and drew another melody to him, one with a percussive, light cadence which sounded akin to a pianist playing to inspire hope.

"I'm used to doing this to find a place. Not a person." He said.

"You sure you don't want me to do it?"

"You've done this before?"

"Once or twice." There was a defensive edge in her voice.

"Not all is well in paradise, then." He let the melody drop.

"It's nothing like that." She said. "The old sous before me...well...I may have...anyway it's water under the bridge."

Ben whistled.

"Done."

A silver line ran away from her feet, a second cast in scarlet streamed away from her crown, faded into obscurity within a few inches of her.

"That's odd."

"It'll grow as we follow it."

He made a noncommittal sound in his throat. She wrapped her arm around his, and they set off into the gloom.


The sound of fabric tearing brought light into the shadows. Candles floated through the air beyond the portal, between bookshelves that soared toward a high ceiling. Ladders rested against them, and in the distance, Lance saw balconies where still more candles floated.

He had not imagined the Royal Library would be so vast. It rose for six stories, with walls of weathered stone covered in ivy. At its height was a mass of clocks of all different shapes and sizes, attached to gears and pulleys and cranks and levers. The contraption was obscenely complex, and likely only understood by those few scholars who existed among the noble houses.

He touched the portal, and shot through into the dimness.

"Where are we?" Peter asked, emerging from shadow behind him.

"The Royal Library." Lance answered.

"Oh, no, no, *no!* Absolutely not!" Peter said. "Have you lost your fucking mind? If we get caught here—"

"Keep your voice down." Lance said.

He quieted. "What could you possibly hope to accomplish here?"

"I think we can find some grimoires. Something about how to do magic the right way. Maybe we can get you past whatever's stopping you from hearing the spirits if we have a guide."

"We have Emma, Lance. I don't like her, but she's a capable person."

"She can't help you with this."

"And this will? If we get caught, they'll torture us. They might even kill us. We'll end up just like Sami."

"Sami's alive." He pointed out.

"She's *ill*." Peter said. "Whatever happened to her clearly—"

Lance rounded on him. "She's our friend, for fuck's sake. She's a good person!"

"Okay, calm down." Peter made a warding gesture.

Palming his forehead, he sighed. "I'm trying to help you. Can you just—"

Lance's gaze snapped to Peter's shadow. It had darkened

several shades, and a pair of figures were rising from it.

*"Phia."* Lance whispered, but he held himself back. The uniforms were wrong. Not the loincloths and bare skin of the Wraiths. Not a Thorn's blacks either. Both of those figures wore white from their neck to their shoes. "Zente."

He watched as Ben and Ariana materialized, as Peter spun round and set eyes on his girlfriend.

"What the fuck, Peter!" she snapped.

"Shh." He said.

She sneered indignantly at him. "Don't *shoosh* me! Where do you get off sneaking around—"

Ben clapped his hand over her mouth. She struggled against him, and then stilled as the weight of where they were, what it meant, slammed into her.

Ben released his hold on her.

"What the fuck." She whispered. "What the actual fuck."

"Blame Lance, okay. This wasn't my idea."

"I can't explain everything right now." Lance said. "You two *need* to go back to the barracks. You're in way over your head."

"We're not going anywhere." Ariana  clapped her fists against her hips, preparing for a stand off. "Right, Ben?"

"Ariana, we're in the Royal Library. We're not allowed to be here." Ben said in an harried attempt to reason with her. He couldn't know how stubborn she could be. Nothing he said was going to change her mind. "If we get caught, we'll never see daylight again. Best case, we're jailed for the rest of our lives. Worst case—"

"Exactly. Which is why you need to turn around." Lance cut in. "We'll explain what we can later, but you have to *leave.*"

"Absolutely not. You're going to tell us what's going on with you two, and you're going to do it now."

"Ariana. Now is not the—"

## The Royal Library

"Shut the fuck up, Ben. We deserve answers."

Lance rolled his eyes.

"Don't be a—"

*"Aughere."* He said.

A confused expression stole over her and Ben.

The weasel materialized almost at his shoulder, swimming through air as if through water.

"Can you hide us? Keep us from being seen?"

*"For a time. You are not strong enough to spread that influence far for long just yet, friend."*

"Then do what you can. These are friends. We can't be caught here."

*"As you say. The request, should you need, is tanc alge. In your language, hide us."*

"Tanc alge, *Aughere.*"

Smoke spilled forth from the weasel and embraced them.

"Will this keep us from being heard" he whispered.

*"That is not my domain, friend."*

He nodded. "We'll need to be quiet, but if anyone's watching, they can't see us."

"Wh-what did you just do?" Ben asked.

"Magic. A kind I'm not supposed to know." He answered. "Now, we need to be quick about this. We're here to get some grimoires. Books on a language called ilfeiya. Anything that might help us get out of the palace. If you won't go back, then help us."

"Only if you tell us what's going on." Ariana insisted.

"Fine." He groused.

He explained as much as he could without wasting all the time they might have with Aughere drawing on his strength to hide them. About Lord Aren and Master Gregor, their quiet rebellion in the palace. What he suspected about Sami's role in all of it.

"How the—"

"No time for questions." He said before Ariana could get

# SPIRIT OF SHADOW

started again. "Are you going to help us or not?"

"O-okay. Fine." She exchanged a look with Ben.

Ben nodded. "We'll help you. As best we can."

"Remember. Grimoires. Books on language. Anything that might tell us about the queen or the emperor, or a way out. Anything that could help us. Even if it doesn't seem all that obvious."

"This place...it would take days to search through all of this." Ben looked around at the upper levels, the balconies and shelves lining those walkways, the intricate clock at the center of the tower.

"Weeks." Peter agreed. "Maybe months."

"We should split up." He said.

"That seems like a bad idea." Ariana protested.

"No. He's right." Peter said. "If we meet under that clock in...say...twenty minutes, we should be okay."

"That's not gonna be enough time." Ben argued.

"We'll meet at the top of the hour." Lance said, looking at the clocks. I think I can keep us covered that long, but it'll be a close thing. I'm still not used to doing this."

*"You'll be cutting it close, old friend. Best you shut their mouths swiftly. You've already wasted enough time."* Aughere intoned.

"That still isn't—"

Lance cut across him. "We could spend hours getting lost in here and find nothing. We're already taking a huge risk. If we spend too much time here...."

"Fine. Just don't do anythin' stupid and if you all run into trouble, shout for help." Ben said.

"Let's get a move on. We're wasting time." Peter said.

Lance squeezed Ben's hand. "I'm sorry I didn't tell you. I didn't know if I could trust you with this."

"It's okay. Just...no more secrets. *Please.*"

He panned over them. "I'll see you soon."

# The Royal Library

"At the top of the hour." Ben agreed.

Lance walked away, turned at the end of an aisle and started his search.

He turned into a new aisle, noted a low crate filled with long scrolls on his way by. A narrow sign denoted the subject matter in the books this aisle contained.

"Sha—"

*"No."* Aughere said.

"Will you not work with her?"

*"Nothing of the sort. I quite like the old goose, but you are already stretching yourself thin. Call on her, and you will not have enough energy left to sustain me for the allotted time. You might not anyway."*

He turned back to the shelves.

"What is anthropology?" he mumbled as he scanned them.

*"A behavioral study. Or...a behavioral approach to history, I think. Your people's ways are not so terribly clear to me."*

He began to pour over titles as he walked. Societal Implications of the Ascension. He wondered at the title. *What does it matter what society thinks if they can't change the thing they're thinking about?*

He left the section and buried himself in another aisle some distance further off. A candle floated by at eye level. He sidestepped it.

He stooped and read another title. The Great Houses and their Symbols. He looked to another book, higher on the shelf. Queens Past and Present. That one was so dusty and battered as to fool no one. The last queen it had seen added to its ledger was likely dead a hundred years and more.

A ladder rested near enough to that book. He pulled it into a new position and climbed until he was near the height of the shelf, some two stories into the air. He scanned the bindings of those books, took in the smell of paper and dust and pine.

*I could really spend my life here.* He thought.

# SPIRIT OF SHADOW

"The Legion of the Sky. That could be something." He pulled it out and settled it into the crook of his arm. A short distance from it was a book bound in powder-blue leather that he took up as soon as he saw its title. Immortals and Ancient Things.

*This isn't a leisure trip.* He reminded himself.

He started down the ladder, and stopped midway into his descent. The book he set eyes on was a simple thing bound in brown leather, its title faded and worn so much that the only legible word on its spine was "Compact." Outwardly, there was nothing in particular appealing about it. It was thin, flimsy and ancient beyond reckoning, but it tugged at something inside him. The sensation building in him was almost akin to that which he had experienced on seeing the moon spirit. He eased it off the shelf. It's cover seemed to vibrate against his fingertips as he slipped it under his arm.

"How strange." He whispered.

*"Oh, but that shouldn't be here."* Aughere said. He flipped around in the air, then sniffed at the binding. *"It smells like him."*

"Who now?"

A shrill cry pierced the air, drawing his attention back the way he had come. He adjusted his bundle of books against his hip and ran for the source of the sound.

"I thought you said—"

*"I have no power to keep people from hearing you children."* Aughere said, interrupting him. *"She may have made a sound. Or exposed herself in some other way. What happens now is not my problem, nor my doing."*

Lance glared at  him.

He dodged between candles and around corners, heedless of the danger he ran toward, and emerged in another section.

Ariana lay curled around her stomach on the floor. A Thorn stood over her, and for a moment he believed he might

## The Royal Library

be in sympathetic company. He wore the black on black ensemble they all wore—tight, restrictive, oppressive—and his hair was cut down to a quarter inch of black fuzz that made his sleek ears look longer and sharper.  His steel-toed boot was pressed against her cheek. The thick tread pushed her lips into a pained "O".

"How deep does the infestation go?" he demanded, and Lance thought again of the Wraith in the dungeons. Ariana's tears stained her cheek, ran over the bridge of her nose. She pleaded by some telepathy conveyed through her eyes for Lance to do something.

Books and scrolls lay scattered around her. She had done her duty. He was responsible for her fate.

Ariana was going to die if he didn't do something.

The Thorn's boot pressed down harder. She gasped, squeezed her eyes shut.

Candles floated by, illuminating the Thorn's face and his. He fumbled his way through a list of spirits, trying to recall the name of one who might help him. None came to mind.

Panic clouded his thoughts, drove him further away from the solution when it should be drawing him toward it. He dropped his books, vaulted forward, latched his hands around the Thorn's slender neck, and squeezed.


Ben charged around the corner. He had found what he needed. Grimoires abounded in the crook of his arm, weapons made useless at the sight he came upon.

He saw the Thorn, saw Ariana and Lance.

The Thorn's boot lifted off Ariana's cheek. He twisted toward Lance.

Lance reeled back, losing his grip.

Ben reached out on instinct, drew in the first melody that came to him, indiscriminate, knowing nothing of its nature.

Song filled his ears, loud and aggressive and woody, and he hurled that magic at the offending soldier.

# SPIRIT OF SHADOW

A breath passed through Ben's teeth. The Thorn loosed a gargled scream. Blood sprayed from a gash in his chest. Ben slammed open his shadow. Ariana scrambled to pick up her books. Lance scooped his stack off the ground.

"Move it!" Ben hollered.

They launched themselves toward him, and into the waiting portal. He followed them through.

"I never wanted to be like this." A man whispered.

Lance snapped his head in the direction the voice had come from.

"Was that a—"

"No." Ben said. "I-it's the Dark Heart. I can't push it back."

"You can't treat me like this!" A woman sobbed.

"Are you insane?" Another voice said. Then another added. "I don't deserve this."

"I can't...I can't suppress it. I'm too...." Lance said.

"You can't run away from yourself?" another voice crooned.

"Give me a second!" Ben whispered.

"Where is Peter?" Ariana moaned. He isn't..."

"Lothor!" Lance shouted.

*"Yes?"* came a guttural whisper.

"Can you do something about these voices? Where is Peter?"

*"The Dark Heart stands as a defense against my pain. A pain these beasts are causing. I will do nothing."*

"Fuck." He whispered.

He approached the source of Ben's voice and took hold of a bundle of cloth.

"Just follow me. We'll get through this. We'll get out."

"I just killed someone, didn't I?" A warble entered Ben's voice. His cheek was wet when Ben found it.

"I hope Peter made it out safe." Ariana said. "I couldn't

live with myself...."

Lance found her, took hold of her hand, and helped her to her feet. They started walking.

With every step they took, the voices became more earnest.

"Such delicate things, these creatures."

"Kill you."

"I'll kill you."

"Kill."

He picked up his pace.

"Now would be a good time to get rid of those voices." Ariana said.

"It's not that easy, okay!" Lance snapped. "I can't. The spirit...he's angry with you. Or Ben. Maybe me for bringing you into this. I don't know. He won't listen to me. He's too angry!"

"Maim."

"Hurt."

"Destroy."

"You're going to have to try." Ariana said.

"I am!" He shouted.

"I'll make you bleed."

"I'll never forgive you."

"Am I dead?  Is this what it feels like? Where's the light?"

"What hell is this?"

All at once those soft whispers became a chorus of screaming voices. He ran. Lance held on tight, running after him.

They pelted through darkness. Lance had no idea where he was going, only that anywhere was better than here.

He spared no thought for whether Ariana kept up with them. Getting out of the Shadow World came first. Everything else was secondary.

The voices drilled into his ears, pressing in from all sides with their messages of sickness and loathing, for themselves and for others. Sometimes even for him.

*"I hate you!"*

*"I will hunt you to the end of the world!"*

*"You're going to die!"*

*"You deserve to die!"*

"Make you bleed, crimson and red. Make you bleed until you're dead." A chorus of voices sang together.

"Knives are so primitive, so intimate."

"If I can't have you—"

A hole rent in darkness, a shaft of light pierced the shadows. Dim glow met gloom. Lance felt himself hauled upward as he pressed his hand to that window. The shadows remained, but the voices failed.

He let go of Ben, crawled away across rough, stone blocks too coarse and uneven to be the tiles they used for pavement throughout the palace. He dropped his books, put his back to the wall, drew his knees up and rested his head between them.

He listened to the silence, willing the voices to go away, leave him alone. Inside of him was a turmoil like none he could remember experiencing. His nerves fired off random signals, drilling panic deep into him that held his guts in vices.

"It wasn't real." He told himself as he rocked on his heels. "It wasn't real. They can't hurt me."

*Snick.*

Light emanated from a candle flame. It touched on curtains of heavy velvet drawn closed against the moonlight. When Lance looked up, he found he was in a classroom.

Dead snapdragons rested in a pot, a sparse assortment of skull-like seedpods hanging from their woody stems. A heavy desk—stained mahogany, covered in veins of light green paint that imitated ivy—sat before the central window.

Ben touched the candle flame to another wick, and then

another.

Stacks of wooden chairs lined the walls, and smaller desks that were little more than nightstands appeared out of the shadows in a double file to either side of a broad aisle. The curvature of the walls created a semicircle, and against the flat wall, across from the largest desk, was an olive-green chalkboard.

"Where are we?" Ariana asked.

"The Teacher's Tower." Ben answered shakily.

He faced Lance now. The light and the good had gone out of Lance's eyes. The last remnants of his paranoia were ebbing away, but the going was slow.

"Are you two okay?" he asked.

"I'll be fine in a minute." Lance said. "Just...I thought we were gonna die. I was sure it was gonna happen."

"The Dark Heart—"

"It's not that." Lance said. "The Thorn. I felt so helpless. I saw it. I couldn't stop thinking about it. The dungeons. And then you came along and...you shouldn't have had to do what you did."

"The Dungeons?" Ben whispered.

"I...I went down the...the staircase. The one we passed when I was staging with the couriers. I...I killed a Wraith. I killed him."

"Is that why you've been so distant lately?" Ben asked. "Sky Lord's mercy. This doesn't feel good."

"Killing someone...I don't think the guilt will ever go away."

"He would have killed you if you hadn't—"

"It doesn't matter."

"Peter's still out there." Ariana breathed, drawing their attention to her. She leaned against the wall under that chalkboard, her head in her hands.

"He'll be okay. He'll find us." Lance whispered. Ben's steady gaze felt like an accusation. *You did this. You're responsible for this.*

Ben leaned forward, and hugged him. "It's gonna be okay."

"Ariana is alive because of whatever it is you did." Lance said. "I've never seen a rite like that before."

"I panicked" Ben mumbled. "I just *panicked.*"

"I don't want to talk about this anymore." Ariana said.

"I don't either." Lance agreed.

For a moment everyone was quiet. No one seemed to know where to go from here. Lance looked to his books.

"What did you guys find?" he asked.

"Maps, mostly." Ariana gestured to the scrolls. "I found a book about the military, and one about herb lore. I thought it would come in handy for after we escape."

Lance tried on a smile. It felt wrong on his face. "Maps of Shadovane?"

"One, yeah. Most of them are of the palace and the military quarters."

"That gives us an advantage." He said. "What about you?"

"I found grimoires." Ben said. "It's lucky I found them. I didn't think given the time I'd be able to find anythin' useful, but I got three of them."

He set three rather thin books, each bound in leather dyed a different color, on the desk with Ariana's. Each of the books Ariana took was at least twice as large, but the books Ben presented were still thicker than the one entitled "Compact". He saw uses in what Ben and Ariana found that he didn't think existed in his own discoveries. If he would have had more time, he might have found something better, but he had allowed himself to get distracted. Had come away with vapid nonsense for all the pain he had caused them.

"What did you find?" Ariana asked.

"A book on the Immortals." Lance said. "One on the Ten Kings." He held up the book entitled The Legion of the Sky. "And...I don't really know what this one is. It just kind of stuck out to me."

"So, History?" Ariana asked.

"The Shadow Queen is supposed to be an Immortal." Ben noted.

"I thought maybe there was something in there about the emperor that could help us." Lance said.

"Maybe." Ben scooped up the book labeled Compact and flipped through it. He landed on a random page, scanned it.

"This is weird." He said. "Really bad grammar, too." He flopped it onto the desk. "It looks like it was translated from another language, and not well."

"What does it say?" Lance asked.

Ben spoke, but no words came out. He cleared his throat, tried again.

"That's strange." Lance said. "It's like when I call on the spirits."

"I swear I'm not trying to...it must be spellbound." Ben said. "It's not like it makes sense, anyway. The stuff on that page was just gibberish."

"Good to know." Lance made a mental note to page through that book for himself the first chance he had.

"Anyway, we should get goin' before anyone suspects we've been up to no good." Ben said.

Ariana touched her belly.

*What happened before I got there.* "They saw us, Ben. We can't go back.

"But listen." He pressed on as their expressions darkened. "I think we should try to get everyone out. I think that's what Master Gregor intends to do anyway. If we can get the servants out with us—"

"They're happy not knowing what we know." Ariana cut in. "I don't think most of them could handle the truth, either. You know how it feels finding out your whole life is a lie."

"What if there was a way?" Lance insisted.

"Then we might be able to do somethin' for them" Ben

# SPIRIT OF SHADOW

said.

"You're with him?" Ariana asked.

"No. Not yet. But if he could convince both of us to do somethin' as reckless and stupid as what we just did, maybe he can find an answer to this problem." He explained. "We got what we came for, right?"

"I guess." Ariana sighed. "Some of us did."

"Peter will be okay. I can find him. Wherever he is."

"Then do that!" she growled. "If we've been wasting time beating around the bush when you've had the perfect ability to—"

"It's not that simple. You two pissed off the spirit of shadow. He's the one I need to call on to find out if Peter is safe."

"How the fuck is this our fault?"

"I'm not saying it is. Just that he's not happy. When you shadow walk, it causes him pain. It's like you're trying to pull his legs off. That's why we couldn't get the Dark Heart under control."

"So we can't do magic?" Ben said.

Lance sighed. "Not like that. Not ever again. That's why we were trying to find grimoires. I thought we could find something in them that would help Peter overcome what's been holding him back. The furnace workers were trying to teach him how to do this the right way, but he was having trouble. It was my fault, and I just...just wanted to help."

"And now he might be dead." Ariana said coldly. "Maybe next time you decide to help someone, you just stop. Maybe then no one has to get hurt."

"Call to this spirit, Lance." Ben said softly.

Lance nodded. He set himself against a desk, and called the name of shadow.

*"Lothor."*

In a shaft of moonlight which carved a line across the desk

where it broke through a curtained window, a spider materialized in silhouette. He focused on it, drawing Ben's eyes to the moonbeam.

"I'm sorry about earlier. I didn't mean for any harm to come to you."

*"You've been met with punishment."* The spider said. *"I am mollified. This time."*

"Can you help me find someone?"

*"The woman?"*

Lance shook his head. "The kitune I took with me to the library. I just need to know if he's okay."

The spider's mandibles played over the desk's surface. *"He is safe. Returned to the Servant's Tower and bed. He was not seen."*

A sigh of relief. "Thank you. You've put my mind at ease."

*"All is well, boy. Do not bring pain to me again."*

"I won't. I'm sorry. Zente, *Lothor*."

The spider faded away.

He turned to face Ariana, who was pacing the length of the room in front of the chalkboard, a steady stream of curses for him passing her lips in a hush. "He's in the Servant's Tower. No one saw him go. He's safe."

She deflated. "Thanks to the Immortals. I'm going to go to him."

She climbed to her feet.

"Don't." Ben and Lance said in unison.

"I don't have much choice. He's my boyfriend. I want to know he's okay."

"You already know that. But if you go there now, you'll only put him in danger." Ben said.

Lance sank against the desk. "He'll show up here eventually. He's still wrapped up in all of this."

"We'll just have to wait for him." Ben said.

"I fucking hate you." She said to Lance, and he could not blame her. All of this was his fault. All of the blame landed

# SPIRIT OF SHADOW

squarely on his shoulders.

She sank into a seat. "We can't live on air you know. We're going to have to steal food and stuff."

"We can handle that later. When the heat dies down." Ben said.

"We have allies. People who can get those things for us." Lance mumbled, plopping into a chair.

"Really, how deep does this conspiracy go?" Ben asked him.

"Deep." Lance said, and left it at that.

# A Path Forward

Distant screams filled Sami's ears. Unfettered rage come from somewhere beyond and below the rooftop she stood on. An unfamiliar garden loomed out of darkness around her, under a scattering of stars, the bulk of them hidden behind a brighter light emanating from the city's passes.

Woody stems clung to skeletal seed pods. The snapdragons had lost their flowers, for the queen had not been here in some time, and the gardeners had little reason to keep these flowers in bloom. The leaves on shrubs and trees to either side of a river stone path had long lost their vitality. A gnarled, old maple's canopy was touched with crimson where that light pressed against its leaves.

She flexed her fingers, and was surprised to find she could.

"Is this a trick?" she wondered.

She saw through her own eyes, moved on feet suddenly willing to heed her demands of them.

The shouts drifted over the edge where the garden yielded

# SPIRIT OF SHADOW

to nothing. In the distance, cliffs caught and held the shadows. Tiny dots of light drifted out of their gullets to join the fire in the sky, to call out to the coming stars.

*Your home is here*, those lights said. *Come back to us.*

Those shouts were the voice of unrest. Those were cries of rage and longing. There was pain in them.

She knew too much about that pain. In the days that had passed since she learned the truth, she had discovered the true meaning of helplessness.

*I should go.* She thought. *If they're done with me.*

There was nowhere *to* go. She had never learned magic. The Watchers had found some way to act through her, but they had left none of the tools behind for her to use.

She looked back over her shoulder.

Beyond the scattering of trees, bushes and dead flowers, the colors marching toward barren winter broke and were replaced by gray, stone slabs twenty feet to a side. The heath and soil washed over the edges for a graded finish that fell into lifelessness.

She thought again about leaving. There has to be some way off this roof. A tower window or something.

That vitriolic yelling floated on the air, enticing her closer to the roof's edge. Curiosity overwhelmed fear. She was already a dead woman walking. What was a few more steps?

"Why take me here and then let me go?" she mumbled to the bushes and the trees. "None of you are free."

She slid a hand into a pants pocket and came out with a set of brass keys. Dried blood flaked off the teeth of a few of them as they clinked together.

*My hands did that.* Her fingers trembled. She replaced the keys in her pocket.

The shouting—the product of hundreds of open throats all screaming at once—approached a climax. Rippling booms called back to them, and a tremor ran through the roof.  She thanked the Immortals that she was not standing closer to the edge. She might well have fallen off.

A voice she recognized came from behind her before she could step any closer to that edge.

"Why here?" a man asked. *Lord Tarkenta?* "The commoners are insufferable this time of day."

Sami turned around slowly. She could only guess who he was talking to.

Her suspicion proved accurate.

"That is why." Lady Therien cooed. She caressed his cheek. The low sun brought out the ridges of his cheekbones, the hard line of his jaw. He looked like a statue. The way Lady Therien looked at him, he might have been just that—a hunk of stone chiseled and polished, harrowed into shape just for her pleasure.

She pressed tender kisses against his collarbones. His hands traveled over her bodice, first untying and then loosening the thick, white laces binding it tight against her breasts.

"I want you to take me right here, to the music of the urchins' screams." She said.

He gave her a queer look, but her composure did not break.

Sami felt sick.

He ripped her corset down. Her skirts fell around her ankles. Everything Sami suspected about the woman was revealed in pallid relief against the autumn explosion of burning colors, the night grays and blues. Her breasts, the curve of her ass, her slender shoulders and small feet made Sami's cheeks burn with a fire to match the leaves of the maple tree.

"If they could hear us...." Lord Tarkenta growled.

Lady Therien guided his hand between her legs. He pressed his lips to hers, drew her breath into him as his arm stiffened. As he set to work.

# SPIRIT OF SHADOW

"Perhaps..." she fumbled over the gold buttons holding his coat closed, threw it wide.

It fell away.

He rid himself of his shirt, revealing a patch of curly, steel-colored hair over his muscled torso, a trail vanishing into his trousers, then slid his fingers back into her. His kisses traveled over her neck, across her breasts. He bit her nipple playfully.

Sami's stomach twisted, threatened to haul up everything she had consumed over the last day. She couldn't move or speak. Either risked exposing herself.

Suddenly, there was darkness, and then the dazzling light of her memories, windows into her soul. Her life played out all at once all around her, and the Watchers stood before her, in a line, with the Jua man closer to her than she cared for.

"You see why we fight?" he asked. "They are monsters. They revel in our suffering, and build their fortunes on our backs."

"They took care of me." Sami whispered.

"They *took* you." The elder Watcher spat. "They kill who gets in their way. They have no morality. They have only ignorance as their virtue." He held out his hand. "Come to me."

"Are you going to kill them?"

"They will kill you if we do not. Now come. We can save you."

"When this is over, will you let me go?" Sami asked.

"Soon." He responded. "When we are free. It is nearly time."

Sami approached him. She stopped short of taking his hand, eyed it like a serpent.

*This is only the illusion of choice.* If she let go, they would see her away from here. If she fought them, they would still get what they wanted in the end. She did not want to kill again, but then, if they took agency away from her, it was not really like she was killing at all. Her mind was not in control of her body.

"Is that why?" she whispered.

"We give you a choice." A woman's voice broke through the stillness. Her gaze turned in the direction of its source, a kitune, who even in spirit looked malnourished. "If 's moral, and necessary, it in't wrong to do wha' we do. This every warrior knows. Ya needn't take it upon yerself, nor d'you need ta watch."

"But then...."

"The choice is simple. Come willingly, or don't. All that is lost in your decision is who you choose to stand with. How you will come away from this." The Jua Watcher said. "But know that we do not act without cause. The high lady has, for years, forced us to take what does not belong to us, to remove the memories of those like you. The general has ordered every murder that placed one like you here, every abduction. They are guilty of crimes innumerable. This system cannot sustain itself without them. In particular without the woman, who is the only Shield among these people. The only one capable of resisting our gift."

"I don't have to watch this?" she asked, and hoped what he said was true.

"You need not watch any of it." He assured her. "But make your choice. To identify within yourself whether you stand for tolerance, or savagery."

"Why did you make me watch before?" she asked, meeting that startlingly blue-eyed gaze.

"We are not without mercy, girl." He said. "You were better served to see a truth unfold before you. To know we were not without cause in our treatment of those others. Neither were we without restraint. The Lord Haman Bran tortured you for no greater reason than to ensure the rest of his life was spent in a kind of comfort you would never experience. We spared the Lady Tamalsen for she was a lesser evil than the rest. There is but one more we must see to when these are gone, but she will not die by our hands either."

"One more." She whispered.

"Just one. The one whose idea brought all of this to bear."

He offered his hand once more, and this time she took it. "As long as I don't have to see it, I will go with you."

He nodded. Though she gave him what he wanted, he did not smile. His expression was grave, full of purpose.

She looked into those eyes. They were the last thing she saw.

# Decisions

Lord Aren scanned the contents of the letter a courier had brought to him. His expression soured.

His plans had been complicated with the disappearance of Lance and two other servants, one of whom should now be under his direct protection. A dead Thorn—not one of his loyalists, but one of those who blindly believed he was loyal to the crown—in the Royal Library, and several accounts from other soldiers on patrol only heightened his concerns.

Even now, his loyalists were keeping watch over the old classroom they had chosen to hide within. They would have done better to find a place deep in the dungeons, in one of those forgotten halls where dust frosted the stones and desiccated remains were all that was left to remind of the war prisoners once housed there, but they could not have known about those reaches. Would not have viewed them as safe if they had known.

He needed to find an opportunity to visit them in person; but these most recent tidings, though well intentioned, only served to complicate matters more.

He looked to the wall where his shepherd's hook rested. He had long found comfort in its presence, but it was not so now.

He crumpled the letter in his fist and pushed his chair back. Lord Giram had made it quite clear this summons was not optional. He was to report to the conference chamber of the Council of Liam immediately, likely to discuss the meaning of Lord Tarkenta's death.

Lord Tarkenta was one of those who visited the practice yards as frequently as the soldiers still in training. He sometimes played at swords or sparred with them. Sometimes Lord Aren crossed swords with him.

They were an even match.

That a group of children, with a bare handful of weeks of rebelling under their belt, had done him in was unthinkable. No, he was sure the Thorn had been them. The Wraith in those aged chambers behind their gate—bait for the ones who resisted their conditioning—was them, too. There could be no doubt about that.

But Lord Tarkenta and Lady Therien had been the work of those Watchers. There could be no other explanation. Lady Therien was not one to bow easily, either. They must have posed a challenge. Taking them down could have been no easy task.

Blessedly, the queen would not be in attendance to direct the flow of the conversation at this meeting. She would undoubtedly have led them down a rabbit hole of embarrassingly savage plots that suited her lust for blood, without thought for logic or reason. Lords Cree and Elise would have basked in those schemes, supplying a plethora of ideas so dark and gruesome they would have made Lord Aren sick, and without his closest ally and friend among them to dissuade her, it would have been nearly impossible to make her see the faults in their proposals.

*There is still a chance. If I can steer the conversation in a neutral direction, I may be able to buy some time.* He thought.

That Queen Meredith was to be absent was as cutting as it was convenient. That she had arranged a funeral for Lady Therien while Lord Tarkenta was to be buried without as much as a wake would be sitting about as well with Lord Giram as it was with him. Lord Bertram was more ambiguous, but he seldom agreed with Lord Elise on anything, even when Lord Cree supported his causes. He may still be worth something in this mess.

*We truly are dirt beneath her fingernails.* He had always guessed this was the final truth, but had not had proof before now. She was truly a foul woman. The worst kind of monarch. *What I would give to have Queen Tania back.* If he was honest, Queen Meredith's predecessor had not been much better. Less temperamental, less bloodthirsty, but also far less intelligent.

He left his office, and headed off down a hall under the light of an afternoon sun that streamed through a series of windows high in the ceiling. He took one of four sets of stairs to a higher level of the Military Complex, and navigated a hall to the chamber he needed.

He entered, and took his seat at the table.

Lord Giram cleared his throat. The other members of their order were gathered already. Even Lord Bertram, who was, by some miracle, on time. "Lord Tarkenta is dead, as you all know by now. Lady Therien, as well."

"Has anyone told her husband?" Lord Bertram asked.

It would be better, in Lord Aren's opinion, to leave the Lord Therien as ignorant to the details of her death as possible.

"You mean has anyone told him she died with Lord Tarkenta's cock in her cunt?" Lord Elise's grin was full of malice. "If it has been mentioned to him, it was not done by us."

"I still say we dispose of the servants who found them." Lord Cree said. "Given the nature of our greater problem, no one would question it if we told them the servants belonged to this rebellion."

"I would tend to agree." Lord Bertram said. "We don't need more loose ends, now do we?"

"Killing those servants gets us no closer to ending our search." Lord Aren said.

"Yes, about that." Lord Giram cut in.

Lord Aren gave him a warning look.

Lord Elise snickered. "It seems we are not the only ones who share a secret."

*Does he know something he should not?* Though Lord Aren prided himself on his ability to read people, he had never cracked Lord Elise's code, a fact that rankled him. It was nearly impossible to read that degree of madness with any sense of certainty. What did one so compromised want except to sew chaos into everything he touched? He was too unstable to predict, an all consuming mass of avarice wearing a man's skin.

"I simply cannot believe a lowly servant successfully murdered our friend and comrade." Lord Bertram said.

Lord Cree nodded. "Agreed. It is quite far-fetched, this notion that one of those little cockroaches killed Lord Tarkenta. Don't you think?"

Lord Aren closed his eyes. *My work is not done.* He looked to Lord Cree. "It would take extreme good fortune on the part of a servant to be able to take him down, but these are no ordinary servants."

He met Lord Elise's eyes, let a fraction of his anger for the other man show.

"What do you have from your Thorns?" Lord Giram asked.

"I too am curious." Lord Elise said.

"The servant who killed Lord Tarkenta and Lady Therien

is likely the same one who attacked Lady Tamalsen. We can assume she is also responsible for Lord Bran's murder. We have reason to believe she worked under Lord Halan in the armory before she turned rogue." He explained. "We also know who the ones who killed the thorn in the Royal Library are. We have positively confirmed their identities...all three of them having gone missing. One served as a sous chef in the kitchens. Another was recently risen, and took up work in the furnaces. The last was a courier who had recently been assigned as my personal attendant. It is my understanding they are all friends. The courier and the furnace worker may even be involved."

"They're fucking?" Lord Bertram said. "How typical."

Lord Giram rubbed his chin, his eyes unfocused as he thought mulled the details over. "A courier would be in a prime position to watch Lady Therien. It's no secret she leans on them to cover her tracks when she's fooling around with someone she shouldn't be. He would have known exactly where she went...could even narrow down the list of places she was likely to be vulnerable, leaving the way open for the armorer to attack."

"It makes sense the armorer would be the assassin, as well." Lord Cree said. "She has a direct line to observe soldiers while they're training. If she picked up the trick to performing magical rites early on, she might have sat on that knowledge while she eavesdropped on our men."

"Giving her enough to go on that she might figure out the rest herself." Lord Giram added.

"The courier would be similarly well positioned to learn what he ought not know." Lord Aren said. "And his proximity to me...it could well be these rebels have placed a target on my back. They went for Lord Tarkenta first because he was the more vulnerable target, but I am no friend to the rebels in the city. I have imprisoned many of them over the years, seen to no few executions. They may be leaning on the servants, doing *something* to wake them up. There could be no more perfect spies in all of Shadovane."

"You think they're working for Aldeirel's people?" Lord Giram said. His gaze was fixed on the map table, on the cross figurines positioned throughout the Free Territories and the borderlands. "Do you know the names of these fools?"

Lord Aren shook his head. "First names, but not surnames. Descriptions, but nothing definitive."

"Well?" Giram gestured for him to speak.

"The furnace worker is a boy named Lance. Gold eyes. Ash blonde hair. He's on the taller side. He's only nineteen. The sous chef is Ariana, who would have been pulled from Haru or somewhere near there. She is diminutive. Very well liked by the Mistress of the Kitchens. The courier is Ben, who is Giida of unknown origin. Average height, curly hair, walks somewhat duck footed." Lord Aren said. "Are you seeing something I am not?"

"You've just listed off three hostages Lord Tarkenta's men took around the time Lazul fell. The blonde boy is Lance Whiteheart. He was the son of their old leader. He is the nephew of the new one. The Giida boy...we're not entirely certain who's child he might have been, but we had reason to believe he was the son of the Hammer in Ozos, or the one who served in Lazul before it fell. He was found with one of their symbols in his possession. The last is the granddaughter of Shan Hoga."

Lord Aren's expression was stone. He looked around the table. Lord Elise alone seemed unaffected by these revelations.

"I'll make a suggestion of you, Lord Aren." Lord Giram said, meeting his gaze. "Expand your search to include their close relations. Friends and coworkers they had good relationships with. Identify if any of those have associations with the Cross. They may not be involved, but they will likely be targets for conversion. Aldeirel's men may have finally made contact with the Cross."

Lord Cree hissed through his teeth. "If their agents are here, we will need to root out the infestation quickly."

"Or take the fight to them."

"Any operation we seek to engage in which centers on the Eleventh Ward will need to begin here." Lord Bertram supplied, waving a hand fan near his face. He looked bored by all of this. It seemed the Cross's potential involvement did not bother him.

Then again, Lord Aren's own outward concern was farcical. He was, however, surprised at how readily the conversation had shifted away from the glaringly obvious prospect that these children were working with someone on the inside—a traitor to the throne. Even more that they had so easily taken the bait buried in Ben's proximity to him. They could just as easily have arrived at the truth.

"I will expand the net." Lord Aren said. "Perhaps bringing their friends in for questioning will give us some insight into who these kids are working with."

"That is all and well, but it would be much better to take them into custody themselves." Lord Bertram said. "Their activities having gone unchallenged for so long is an embarrassment. How do we face the Emperor given our circumstances, and claim to be the most elite army outside of Mirrhvale."

"I take your point." Lord Giram said. "Do you have any suggestions?"

"I do." Lord Elise sneered.

The general eased back into his seat, looking disappointed.

"We smoke them out." Lord Elise went on, gesturing airily. "Spill some innocent blood, yes? Not enough to inconvenience those pampered nobles. Just enough to draw the bad eggs out of their hiding place.

"We will rely on the conspirator's sense of moral piety.

# SPIRIT OF SHADOW

Hold sham executions before the servants all. They will come forward, I think, if they believe their actions may place the lives of close friends and lovers in jeopardy."

"Careful, Lord Elise, before you start making sense." Lord Cree intoned. "You might just earn your seat on this council after all."

Lord Elise scowled at him. "My qualifications are more than enough."

"Yes, we all know how *pleasurable* our queen finds your company." Lord Bertram intoned blandly.

"Nonetheless, your plan *does* make sense. Lord Bertram and Lord Cree, begin making preparations. If Lord Aren's investigation fails to turn up any leads surrounding their whereabouts, we will go with Lord Elise's plan."

"You're sure you want to—"

"Politics are a messy business, Lord Aren." Lord Giram said. "You know that better than most. Those servants may have done nothing to warrant their deaths, but we cannot take our time with this, either. Lord Bertram is correct. Our lack of forward movement on this is an embarrassment, and it will not be rectified until we have them in hand. The longer it takes, the more Shadovane's standing in the imperial order stands to fall. Our influence in the Empire is not guaranteed, and I will not be the Chief at Arms over the decline of our city!"

*You already are.* He thought. He bowed in his seat to his superior. "If that is all."

"Yes, I think we can wrap this up. Get out." Lord Giram cocked his thumb in the direction of the door, and the other generals picked up their effects, and left.


A Thorn approached one cell among the many in this mostly vacant expanse within the palace dungeons, produced a ring bristling with keys from within his reliefs, and thumbed through them until he landed on the one made for this door. A gleaming piece of topaz, ellipse cut, dressed its clover-like bow, and the bits were broad and perforated.

He slid it into the keyhole, disengaged the lock. The door swung inward at his push, disturbing the prisoner within it. The prisoner labored to right himself. His knees crackled as he stood up.

He shambled across the cell, an easy smile on his lips.

"Silas?" Aldeirel said, emerging from the darkness. "Has it begun?"

"Not Silas old man, but a friend." The Thorn said.

Aldeirel looked him up and down. He was reminded of his father, a man long dead by the time he ascended to his station. He understood, then, why so many chose to follow this broken old fool. To believe in his words, hold him almost as a messianic figure among them.

There was within him a sense of familiarity under the aged rebel's gaze, and though he knew cataracts had robbed the man of his sight, he was made to feel small before him. Small for his crimes against his own people, and yet reassured at the same time that what he had done was for a greater purpose. That it all fit into a grand design whose ends were, just now, within reach.

"It's time, Aldeirel. They are moving."

"What caused the change?"

"I was not made aware of the cause." The Thorn said. "Just that my master believes now is the time to gather your rebels. In the coming days, the armed forces intend to gather the servants, execute some in order to drive the others out of hiding."

"How many are involved."

"To my knowledge? Four. Though there may be more. There are three who stole several books from the Royal Libraries. Mostly studies of magic. Some maps, as well. We are still assessing the full scope of the damage they might

# SPIRIT OF SHADOW

have done. There is also the one who has been killing off nobles. Lady Therien and Lord Tarkenta are dead. They died together."

"Fitting, that." Aldeirel patted his chest. "How long do we have?"

"Month's end, sir. There will be a ball held that night. The servants will be gathered while the nobility drinks themselves into a stupor."

"Not much time at all then."

"Will you be ready?"

"To what end do you expect us to be? Are we to seize the palace? Eliminate the queen?"

"I know only what I've been told, sir. Though I believe it will be the former. The latter may prove too complicated given the nature of the times."

"With the Emperor still in Shadovane." Aldeirel said knowingly, his hand sliding away from the soldier. "We will be ready for what may come. Whatever may come."

The old man's shadow deepened and stretched, and he shambled into it. The Thorn swung the cell door closed and locked it. He marched down the hall and away.

# THE GATE

# Reunion

inding sleep had been a trial in the two days since Peter's narrow escape from the Royal Library, but no one had come looking for him. The Thorns and the Wraiths, it seemed, had not seen him, even after he discovered a dead soldier in the section where Ariana's screams had come from. *What about my friends? What about Ariana? Are they alive? Are they okay?*

Thoughts for their safety cluttered his mind, keeping him away from sleep. His eyelids drooped, threatening to pull him under, and feral panic drove him sharply into wakefulness again and again. If he fell asleep, he might die. They would come for him when his defenses were down, drag him away into the shadows and toss him in a cell somewhere to await questioning, which would inevitably drag answers from his lips that he did not want to give.

Lord Aren might save him, but his hopes in the general's ability to shelter him from harm were small things lingering in the periphery, as a storm of urgent thoughts—dark and novel beliefs—took priority.

## Reunion

How much could any of them trust the general? He hadn't come by his position without making sacrifices. It would take a few leaps of faith to believe his path to the Council of Liam hadn't seen its fair share of murders and abductions, and betrayals.

As he lay there, the shadow under his bed deepened, and a figure rose at his back. Hands crept over him, and he rolled sharply into them.

The Thorn mouthed the words: *be quiet.*

He nodded, though he did not trust the soldier. Could not know whether he was one of Lord Aren's loyalists or a pretender—if it mattered.

He climbed to his feet when the Thorn stepped away from him. Stepped into waiting shadow, seeing no other choice save to run. He would not get far with the Thorn standing so close, observing him through cold, ambivalent eyes, almost daring him to try it.

They arrived in the dungeons, outside a room with a bronze-barred door. A window set high into its face looked into a brightly lit room where a table and a pair of chairs were arranged and waiting.

The Thorn unlocked the door, and ushered him through.

"Wait there." He said, and closed it behind him.

The ensuing several minutes were the most tense Peter had experienced in his life. He wondered at whether he would be tortured. Whether this was all part of some scheme to see him safely away from here. Lord Aren had said he did not kill those who refused to comply with Master Gregor; but there was that nagging question, lingering in the back of his head. How far could a servant who knew too much really trust the military, who's job it was to protect their monarch and her often fraught aristocracy.

The door opened again, admitting a Jua woman he recognized. He had seen her palling around with Ben often enough, but he couldn't quite remember her name. She had never seemed all that pleasant to him, but Ariana spoke highly of her. They were on the same floor in the barracks, and knew each other. Maybe not well.

She took the seat next to him. She looked as nervous as he felt, played with the hem of her shirt and kept her gaze trained forward.

"Why are *you* here?" he asked.

"We shouldn't talk." She said. "They might be watching."

"If we don't have anything to hide..." he quieted as she fixed him with a heavy dose of side eye. She returned to her observation of the wall, her breath coming out in choppy, short exhales.

He fidgeted with the edge of the table, grimacing. "Okay."

The door opened a third time, and Lord Aren stepped through with two Thorns at his shoulders. They closed it behind them.

"Yalado gan speltov." He said.

There was a word there, at the end of his sentence, which Peter could not quite make out. Strain as he might, screw up his eyes as much as he wanted to, he could not as much as read Lord Aren's lips. He wondered if he would ever grow used to that.

"I've called you two before me under the pretense that you are to be questioned discretely in regard to what happened in the Royal Library." Lord Aren said.

The woman stiffened.

"Because you both share bonds with the servants who were discovered there." He went on. "There are some questions I would like to ask, if you'll humor me. Once our business is out of the way, however, I intend to have you taken up to the Teacher's Tower, where your friends are likely waiting on you."

"They're alive?" Peter said, vaulting half out of his seat.

**Reunion**

His heart pounded in his chest.

"Yes, Peter. They are alive. They are under my watch, though they do not know it. My men are keeping an eye on them for their safety. I would advise you to inform them they have no need to concern themselves with being found as long as they remain there. Not for the next few weeks."

"Weeks?" Peter asked.

He nodded. "There is to be a purge. I ask that you all ignore it. It can only go on so long."

"But we haven't found *anything* of use. I had to ditch the books I took. I don't think anyone got out with what we came for."

"You were there?"

Rashanna edged away from him in her chair. "I don't know anything, sir. I don't know this guy. I've talked to his girlfriend a handful of times, maybe, but I don't know her well either. If they're involved in something, I promise I have nothing to do with it."

"I'm aware." Lord Aren said to her.

One of the Thorns chuckled. "Folded rather quickly, didn't she?"

"Then..." she jabbed her thumbs in the direction of the door. "Can I go?"

He shook his head. "I'm afraid not."

"What do you want to know?" Peter said.

"Why do you not seem surprised by this?" Rashanna asked.

"Long story." He said.

"What were they looking for? We can start there."

"Grimoires." Peter said. There was little point in refusing to cooperate. Not with a reunion with Ariana, Lance and Ben contingent on his compliance. "I was having trouble learning how to use magic the way you do. Emma wasn't helping. I told Lance I didn't want to do it, but he made it sound like you ordered him to go on some kind of mission, and by the time we climbed out of the shadows, it was too late to turn back.

"Ben and Ariana followed us there. They know what's going on. Some of it, anyway."

"Do I get to know what's happening here?" Rashanna cut in. "Or are we still in 'I don't know enough to matter' territory?"

Chuckles from both of the Thorns.

"I like this one." One said to the other. "She's got guts."

"After the way she...really?" the other quirked his eyebrow. "Clearly, she just wants to go back to bed."

The first to speak snorted. "And leave her only friend all alone?"

"That depends largely on whether you would like to see your friend again." Lord Aren answered, ignoring them. "Ben is under my protection. If you comply here, you will fall under a similar protection, though you will still go about your duties in the palace as if nothing has happened."

"So...go back to life like nothing happened...or become your informant?" she clucked her tongue. "I expected torture."

"Quiet." Lord Aren said as the Thorns began to laugh again.

"I'm not making any uninformed decisions." She said. "You understand?"

"Look, you know enough at this point that they're not just going to let you go, whatever they say." Peter said, his gaze flicking pointedly to Lord Aren as he crossed his arms. He held eye contact. "It was Lance's idea to break into the library looking for whatever he thought might help me. There was this whole half baked idea of getting out of Shadovane too. He seemed to think there was a way to do it that wouldn't allow the army to follow us."

Lord Aren's lips firmed. "Did he say why?"

Peter shook his head. "Something that spirit said to him when she showed up that night you and Master Gregor brought us into...whatever you're doing."

Lord Aren gestured over his shoulder to the Thorns. "These two will take you to your friends."

"That's it?"

"For now, our goals appear to align. But in the future, include us in whatever plans you wish to execute. My men will be watching.

"In the meantime, I need the young woman to make her choice. I have no reason to fear *you'll* betray my trust. Not in haste, anyway."

Rashanna gritted her teeth. "That'll depend on you telling me what you're trying to get me involved in. If Peter's right, and I'm in too deep, I might as well know what I'm signing up for. I have long enjoyed the idea of living to see my next few birthdays."

"Rebellion." Peter answered. "They're disloyal to the queen. They hate her."

Her eyebrow shot up at that. "Really now? I'd never have guessed that was where this conversation was going."

One of the thorns guffawed.

The other laid a sober look against him. "Now is not the time."

"Oh, you're no fun." Said the first.

Peter dragged his palms across his cheeks, set a withering gaze on her. "Look, it's all pretty simple. Lance got involved with the furnace workers. They turned out to be rebel actors in the palace. He got me involved by accident. I don't know that he wants the same things they do, whatever Lord Aren says." He met the general's eye once more, a quick flash before settling on Rashanna. *Why aren't* you *explaining this to her?* "He was talking about some peacock lady when he took me to the library...it all sounds like nonsense."

"Peacock lady?" Lord Aren cut in.

# SPIRIT OF SHADOW

"Well, yeah. That's what he said. He saw a peacock, or maybe an old woman...it doesn't really matter. It was that spirit you were losing your minds over...I think. She put the idea about that way out in his head. That's why he had us looking for maps of the palace and stuff. And the grimoires to make it easier on me learning the kind of magic you do. I'm kind of a liability apparently."

"And they killed a Thorn as they were attempting to escape." He met the gaze of one of those behind him. "Not anyone loyal to the cause, mind. One of Lord Cree's informants. They removed an obstacle for us."

"I'm in." Rashanna said.

"That easy?" Peter asked.

"Is that a surprise?"

"Yes."

"How many times have you seen a servant beaten half to death over nothing?" she asked.

He was silent.

"You know Lord Elise has killed almost all of the ones he's been sent, right? Lady Tamalsen got what was coming to her when your friend took a cane to her backside. I was there. I saw it happen. It was terrifying, but...how many times can you remember not being able to sit down right for days because of her?

"We're just the help, guy. They don't like us and they never did. Personally, I was happy when I found out about Lord Bran. He was a monster. So yes, I will be happy to help in whatever way you need. As long as it doesn't put my life in danger."

Lord Aren cocked his head in the direction of the door. "Take them up."

The Thorns moved around the table. Rashanna and Peter climbed out of their chairs, and followed them into the dungeons.

**Reunion**

Lance vaulted to his feet as four figures rose out of the shadows. The Thorns emerging first set him on a razor edge, tempted him to call on the spirits and set them against them, but he stayed his hand as the white coats belonging to two servants emerged behind them.

"Peter?" he breathed.

Ariana's head jerked in the direction of those new arrivals. She launched out of her seat, crossed the classroom at a clip and embraced her boyfriend in a tight hug.

"Lance said you were...but I didn't believe—"

"It's okay. I'm here now." He said. "You don't have to worry about me anymore."

Tears brimmed in his eyes as a similar exchange happened next to him. Ben drew Rashanna away from the Thorns, and they descended into quiet conversation a little distance away from everyone else.

"Where's Lord Aren?" Lance asked.

"He cannot come to you right now." One of those Thorns said.

"He has them keeping watch over this place so no one finds you." Peter added.

Ariana drew away from him. "What's going on? Are they looking for us?"

"Yes." The Thorn said. "And it's best you remain here for the time being. The furnace workers will continue their training with you as soon as it becomes expedient to. We will see to it that you are clothed and fed, and a brazier is brought in so you may have heat."

"T-thank you." Lance said, for lack of anything else to say.

"Continue to work toward mastering control over your gift." The other Thorn said. "Learn as much as you can, but do not over extend yourself. Those grimoires you stole are good resources for making first contact with the spirits who can aid you, but there are always risks involved in courting them.”

“We should go.” The first Thorn said.

“Will we be able to walk out of here without you?” Rashanna asked, her gaze traveling from one to the other of them.

“Our men in the shadows will escort you back to the dungeons, where we will see to it that you are returned to your barracks. You will have one hour. This will be the norm from now on.” He answered.

“Your friends will fill you in on the relevant details in the meantime. It is better you hear it from them.” The second said.

They dropped into matte shadow, and left them the room.

Lance eased back against a desk, relief stealing over him with their departure. “What are they talking about?” His gaze settled on Peter.

“Lord Tarkenta and Lady Therien were murdered.” Peter said. “I think Sami did them in. Lord Aren mentioned something about the military conducting a purge in a few weeks. I’m guessing they’re going to try to draw you out of hiding somehow. He didn’t really go into detail.”

“Good.” Ben said of the death of his former mistress.

“Maybe. But the purge isn’t sitting right with me.” Peter grimaced. “He wants us to ignore it, but if they target other servants...”

“It would make sense.” Lance mumbled. “We’re all servants ourselves. I can’t think of a better way to pull us into the open.”

“Preying on our morals.” Rashanna growled. “And you wonder why I was so quick to join up.”

Her gaze fell on Peter.

He shrugged. “You also said you’d do it if it didn’t put your life in danger. From experience, it will.”

“If we’re as careless as we have been.” Lance said,

gripping the edge of the desk. "I think, for now, we just keep doing what we were doing. Learn to defend ourselves."

"And find a way out." Peter agreed. "What did you guys take away from the library? I had to ditch what I found."

"Figures." Ariana said.

"We got grimoires, but it sounds like they know that. Some maps of the palace and the city. I don't know how much use they'll be." Lance said. "Books about the Immortals and the Ten Kings. Those are probably useless."

"Not all of them." Ben said. "There's that one. The one with the spellbound pages."

Lance grimaced.

"Sounds interesting." Peter said.

"Can I take a look at it?" Rashanna asked, holding out her hand.

Ben crossed to the old teacher's desk and plucked a flimsy, leather bound book off its surface, which he brought to her.

She thumbed it open, read through it.

"This isn't well translated. Must have been done by someone who didn't know much of our language." She said.

"Can you make anything out of it?" Ben asked.

"Some. If I think it over long enough. When you say this is spellbound...?"

"Try to talk about what you read and it'll be like you're mute. Unless someone else has read the same words."

"So it works like that magic Lord Aren was using." She said. "Maybe one of those spirits can help."

"Should I call them?" Lance asked.

She shook her head. "Not now. Not unless you can find something in those grimoires that can help us read it without destroying it. Who knows what'll happen if you invite the wrong one."

"You might be right." He said.

"So what do we do in the meantime? We have most of an hour." Peter asked.

Ben shrugged. "I guess we catch up."

# Self Defense

Lance sparred with Peter in the middle of the classroom. Ariana watched from the sidelines with a grimoire bound in green leather open in front of her.  She drew up from her study of it occasionally to check on their progress. Both of them would have been useless in a real fight, with someone who had formal training under their belt, but it kept them busy, and focused on the tasks set before them.

The whole exercise seemed like a joke. Peter was shorter than Lance was, but he had quickly figured out how to use his height as an advantage. As he had discovered, Lance's knees were a weak point that he was finding difficult to defend, and most of these matches concluded on the ground, where Peter had a bigger advantage.

Lance's saving grace was that he was faster than Peter. When he did get going, his punches landed more often than not. Ben had taken to alternating with the losers of these skirmishes, but his fights with Lance were often unserious, with Peter serving as a judge of their fitness as they pulled

# SPIRIT OF SHADOW

their punches, and tapped out before their matches could get good.

Ben poured over that peculiar book called Compact, which was really little more than a pamphlet. The entire document could not have been much more than twenty pages. She hadn't touched it since the night Peter and Rashanna arrived with the Thorns, but it had become almost his sole fixation.

As heavy breaths gusted from both Lance and Peter, and they dropped onto the ground in a tangle of flailing limbs, she satisfied herself that this fight was over. It was just a matter of time until Lance tapped out and they extricated themselves from each other, readying for another round if Ben did not come up for air in time to relieve one of them.

They would all make terrible soldiers if they were conscripted into Shadovane's standing force, but then that was the point, wasn't it? It had become clear to her with the days passing on that every nuanced aspect of a servants' life was constructed in anticipation of this very outcome. They would all be dead now if not for the intervention of some unlikely allies. She was still having trouble believing this conspiracy rose so high, that a sitting councilman was in bed with this rebellion.

The servants had been raised to think every little detail, every incongruence, was the nobility looking out for their best interests; but from their lack of education to the canings in Lady Tamalsen's office, to the fact that the servants were not allowed to learn any magic beyond what was strictly necessary for their duties, it was clear they had been raised to be weak. If ever a moment came when the servants chose to rebel, they could be wiped away as if they had never been, and the aristocracy could replace them.

She thought bitterly of the library. Of the beating she had taken there. She would benefit from these sparring matches as much as any of them, and she had thought to involve

## Self Defense

herself more with them, but she did not believe Peter or Lance or Ben would take those fights seriously. They would be more likely to pull their punches, play nice with her, because she was a woman.

She studied the grimoires Ben had looted, and sometimes ventured over to the maps she had almost lost her life over. A way out would be necessary eventually. They could not hope to overthrow Shadovane's government, not least when the Emperor himself was in town, but she could learn to defend herself. Could learn to heal, too, and survive off the land. Those skills would be more necessary than any combat rites if they did escape, but to get there—to win free—would necessitate learning something of magic that could tip the scales in the battles on the horizon.

Lance broke out of the hold Peter had in him. He got his feet under him and their sparring entered unknown territory. Peter's fist sailed for Lance's chest, and he barely managed to dodge out of line, with the result that Peter's knuckles slammed past his shoulder.

*If I had known how to do what he can, I might have been able to stop that bastard Thorn. I could have defended myself.*

The incident-in-the-library had gone the way it did precisely because she couldn't—because none of them could. But what could they gain from using magic if they couldn't pick up the trick? They would be at the mercy of anyone with the ability to call on those spirits, as Lance had explained. She wanted to believe she could drag that power into her and face no repercussions, but if there was a better way, if there was any way to gain an advantage in the long term, she needed to master it. They all did.

"You need to pay better attention." Peter panted.

He twisted around Lance as Lance tried to land a punch, and put him in a headlock. Lance struggled to get out of it, but he was stronger than him. He dropped to his knees, taking Lance down with him.

"I mean...you do know why we're doing this, right?"

"Not really." Lance admitted. "This seems like a waste of time."

"You couldn't rely on magic under pressure. You got scared, and you lost control."

"Can you let me go?"

"Don't you fucking dare, Peter." Ariana said, emerging from behind the grimoire. "Show him how we do things!"

Lance shot her a scathing look.

"Do you feel helpless?" Peter asked.

"What kind of—"

"It's the kind of question you should've started asking the moment you realized you couldn't go back to the barracks." Peter said. "You almost died because you ran. You almost got everyone killed."

"I ran because I couldn't defend myself. If I had known a little more magic—"

"You still would've been useless. You need to learn to maneuver around your enemies. You need to learn to keep them in focus. You ran, and because you weren't looking at them, the Thorns had an opening. They took it, and Ben had to dig you out, but he didn't know what he was doing either.

"We need to learn how to maneuver without magic if we can't rely on it. Even if we can, we still need to be able to fight."

"I told you, I couldn't draw in the spirits because Ben and Ariana pissed them off. *You* should be focused on learning how to do it the right way so we don't have that problem again!"

"Dead is dead, however you get there." Peter released him. He backpedaled into a desk. It slid back an inch, unbalancing him. He nearly fell. "What if it was one of us? If we panic, that's bad enough, but if we can't get ourselves together, maybe it's a blow to the head next time. Maybe they light us on fire. Then what? I want to get out of here. I don't want to die trying."

The door slid open. Ariana shot out of her seat, spun to face it with the grimoire in one hand. Lance followed her gaze. If the intruder had been an enemy, he would have been dead. He was all out of steam, his body moving sluggishly and coated in greasy sweat. He needed a wash, and a break.

Rashanna poked her head in. "At least I know one of you is alert."

She opened the door, admitting Emma, who peered around the room with the same, cold expression she had set on Lance every time they crossed paths. Ariana relaxed on seeing them, and resumed her seat and her study of the grimoire.

"How are things on the outside?" Ben asked Rashanna.

"Same as usual. Lady Jain's shenanigans have been more tolerable lately."

"She's lightened up?" he said.

"Well, no, but knowing there are people in high places who hate her and the ground she walks on makes it easier."

"Why are you two all sweaty and looking ashamed?" Emma asked.

"We were sparring." Peter said.

"Ah." She nodded. "Well, as you've both stepped in the shit, I guess you have more time for defense lessons now. Which brings us to why I'm here. You still having trouble with the spirits?"

He set his jaw.

"That's a yes." She said to Rashanna. "Look, all of you need to figure this shit out. And now you have texts on the subject, there's really no excuse for procrastinating. Ariana, I always knew I liked you. I just hope you can whip these assholes into shape."

"Every day's a struggle, but I'm doing what I can." She flipped her hair.

# SPIRIT OF SHADOW

Emma took up a seat behind the teacher's desk, as she had done in the Headmaster's Office on their first foray onto this new frontier. "You might as well sit down."

Peter and Rashanna sat. Lance remained standing. His lungs were still on fire. He did not anticipate that prickling to go away by sitting down. Instead, he took to pacing the edge of the classroom.

"Okay." Emma said, watching him make his circuit.

"Sorry. Losing is a little tiring."

She snorted. "Last time we did this, you told me I drew in the wrong spirit. I decided I agree with you."

"That's a surprise." He said.

"But the only magic any of you know is shadow walking."

"That's not exactly true." Ariana's gaze fell on Ben.

"True enough. I couldn't do that again if I tried. It was just a spur of the moment—"

"You killed that Thorn somehow." She said.

"Moment of panic." He said dismissively. "I did what I had to."

"None of that has any bearing on what we're doing here, okay? Okay." Emma said. "What I'm going to do is call to the spirit of shadow. All of you already know it's nature. You just haven't learned its name. If you can hear it, and it answers, you should have no trouble shadow walking."

"And hiding yourself in the shadows." Lance added.

Emma raised an eyebrow. "It can do that?"

"*He* can, yes." He said.

"You learn something new every day." She rolled her eyes, tapped her knuckles against the desk. "Without further ado."

She called his name. A spider materialized on the desk just next to her hand, and spoke in that guttural tone for Lance and her to hear.

"Oh, by the way, Master Gregor wants you down in the furnaces for your shift. Said its been long enough you've been avoiding your responsibilities. Time to get to work."

"I can't really leave." Lance said.

"Of course you can. You just said Lothor can hide you." She said.

"But once I'm down there, how many of those guys do you trust."

She spread her hands. "All of them. We've been thorough about our vetting. Mistress Dina's the one with issues in that department. As you can plainly see."

"Mistress Dina's in on this?" Peter asked. "Why didn't she say anything?"

"Because she doesn't know you are." She said, as if it was the most obvious thing in the world. "But since you can leave this room at any time, maybe you should open up about it. Right now, you should focus though. You're not going to get around to hearing this spirit's voice if you're freaking out about something you really probably should've known already."

"How the fuck were we supposed to—"

"Older servant. Huge age gap between her and her sous chefs. And all of her other charges. There are signs." Emma smiled at Ariana, who growled something too low to hear. "Back to work, now."

Lothor's legs twitched as he crawled across the desk, and he collapsed once or twice as waves of pain washed over him.

Lance watched him mirroring his own circuit, and wondered what was troubling him.

*"Those younglings should be dead."* He mumbled. *"Dead and gone with the rest of them. The ones who use me so."*

"They're trying to learn, Lothor." Lance said. "They made their apologies, and they were sincere about them. They never had a chance to learn the right way, though. Who would have taught them?"

*"There are few in this palace that could."* Lothor grudgingly agreed. *"I do not have to like them."*

"I suppose not. But give them a chance."

"It really is creepy how you do that?" Emma said.

"What is?"

"That thousand yard stare you get on your face when you start talking to them. It's weird."

"You can't see them like I can."

"So what does it look like?"

"A spider. A big one."

She whipped her hands away from the desk. "Ew!"

Rashanna laughed. Peter's lips turned down in a theatrical grimace.

"Along came a spider." Ben mumbled. "The kingfisher's eye was trained on him, for two such creatures could not expect to get along for long, and they were not friends."

He chuckled.

*"Do not invite that creature here!"* Lothor snapped.

Ben stiffened. "What was that?"

"What was what?" Lance asked, growing excited.

"That. Just now." Ben said. "Someone was talking. They sounded angry."

Lothor paused in his transit. *"He hears what lay behind the screams."*

Ben repeated what Lothor said. "What does he mean?"

"Screams of pain. Heard as music to your ears when you attempt to shadow walk. Those are his." Emma explained.

*"Tell your tale, child."* He said. *"For it is an honest one."*

"What you mean the Kingfisher and the Spider? It's an old folktale. I don't know where I heard it."

*"From a mother who loved you. Who is dead now. The father far away but still hale."*

Melancholy stole over Ben's face. The others were all looking at him.

*"Bitter truths are not easy to hear."* Lothor said. *"Know my nature. Speak my name. Tell my tale, for it is truth."*

## Self Defense

"I don't know your name, but you're nature is shadow. I've been walking in it long enough. I suppose I *should* know."

*"It is Lothor."* He said. *"A wolf spider. Speak my tale for these others to hear. I would forgive you your indiscretions for hearing it from human lips one more time."*

"O-okay."

Lance gestured for him to do as the spirit asked. *Maybe they'll all figure it out if he can keep Lothor talking.*

"Okay." He cleared his throat. "This is kind of awkward. Um. *Okay.*"

"We're waiting." Rashanna intoned.

He glared at her.

"Along came a spider. A kingfisher hid among the bushes at a river's edge, and the river was murky. The kingfisher hid, because there were other animals in the jungle who might harm him. He had no love of the other birds in the sky. They were jealous of him because he could swim well, and caught fish on his beak whenever he dove into the river band. But there were creatures in the river who did not like him either, because though they liked the idea of an easy meal, and surely a bird in the bushes must be that, they couldn't catch him.

"Then one day, that spider showed up, and the kingfisher's eye was trained on him, for two such creatures could not expect to get along for long, and they were not friends. The kingfisher, content to hide in the bushes, now shared them with that lowly spider, and knew he was a better hand at hiding than him. He did not like to share his perch in the bushes, but the spider was a hunter like him, and spun great webs over the river, intent on catching bugs.

"One day, the kingfisher made to dive into the water, and came away without his prize. A crocodile had come along and snapped its jaws just short of him, and the fish he wanted was caught in its mouth. He shot from the water, fearful for his life, and became tangled in the spider's web. In his fight to be free, the spider took some of his power, and the kingfisher was snared. But the spider's web was broken with the kingfisher's flight, and they both went hungry. The spider hated the kingfisher for breaking his web, and though he toiled to fix it, he was starved, and could not make enough silk to mend all of the threads. So he climbed to the ground while the kingfisher took to its branch, and spun a web in the hollow of an old, dead tree. And though he couldn't catch the flies he liked best, he sated himself on the ants and the termites who lived in the log, and became stronger than the kingfisher because his meals came easy to him.

"But in his jealousy, the kingfisher told the ants and the termites of the spider's secret skills. The ants left the log to make a new home, and the termites thinned his threads with acid from their mouths. And the spider went hungry again, while the kingfisher hid in his bushes, and fished in the river, and was full."

He spread his hands with the conclusion.

Lothor chuckled. *"I do not work with darkness. He is cruel. But he got what was coming to him, for I told that crocodile of his weakness, and he could fish from that river no longer."*

Peter sank back against his desk. "That was fruitful."

"Can you hear him?"

"No, but Ben can. That's one more of us who can call on these things."

"Spirits, Peter." Emma said. "Show them respect. They won't help you if they dislike you."

"Then how is this better than dragging on them?"

"Shadovane's soldiers have more of a command on how to do that than we do, but earning the favor of these spirits means they might resist harder when they're called by other people who don't know them. That's where we have an advantage." She explained. "We might not know as many rites as them, but we can make it harder for them to use their magic.”

"We need every advantage we can get." Lance said. "If those grimoires can tell us how to call on other spirits, and maybe use their skills to our benefit, then the more of us who can do it right, the better."

"Finally showing some intelligence." Emma said.

He ignored her.

"Well, that should do for today." She glanced at Peter. "I'd say keep at it, but it looks like this might be a lost cause."

"Don't talk to him like that!" Ariana snapped.

"Or what?"

"Or we're going to have to fight. Isn't that obvious."

"You know, I like you. I really do. But don't start something you can't finish." She climbed out of her seat and left through the servant's entrance.

# A Quiet Celebration

A Thorn stood sentry as Rashanna entered the canteen. She avoided looking at him, but she felt his cold gaze on her. The hairs on the back of her neck stood on end, a static thrill pushing her heart to beat faster.

*This isn't right.*

The attack on Lady Therien and Lord Tarkenta had everyone in the palace on edge. The usual cascade of white noise from servants chattering over their dinner had reduced to a trickle—hushed words exchanged from one to another against the heightened surveillance under Lord Aren's men.

She wondered where Sami was hiding, why she had chosen to go rogue, if what had led her to her murder campaign was the same revelation that had led Ben, Lance and his friends to their choice. That had led her to choose a side in a conflict she had only just realized was being waged against the crown.

She joined the cue before the window where she would receive her tray from old lady Janice. A second Thorn sat at a table near the back of the room, his gaze roving over the crowd, giving away nothing.

She spotted Felicia where she sat near the middle of the hall, under the clock, as far away from either of the black-clad Thorns as she could get. Most of the other servants had situated themselves far away from the Thorns as well, a side effect of which was that they had formed a rather tight cluster with ample space at the fringes. It seemed even they, with their complete lack of involvement in the goings on of the day were not keen on being near the agents.

She could hardly blame them.

Though she knew they were of mixed loyalties, she could not help feeling the weight of their presence here.

Her tray in hand, she navigated the crowded rows and sat next to Felicia, who gave her a peck on the cheek.

"How was work?" Felicia asked.

"It was...it wasn't bad." Rashanna said distractedly. "They want me back this evening."

"Again." Felicia grumbled, nonplussed.

"I'm not happy about it." She said. "Lady Jain seems to think I don't have a life."

Felicia took the lie, though she favored Rashanna with a look of suspicion. She had been asking difficult questions for several days, since she had heard Rashanna was in the Teacher's Tower from one of her coworkers. An oversight Rashanna intended to correct in the future. It did not do to be seen entering that place by anyone who might turn snitch. Going forward, she would have to rely on the Thorns to take her there. *No more extra trips.*

She would tell Felicia the truth when she was ready, but she did not know when she would be. Felicia, so unlike her, was content with her life in the palace. To reveal all of the

# SPIRIT OF SHADOW

lies she had been told for what they were would destroy her. For the time being, her ignorance kept her stable, kept her from becoming a liability, and safeguarded her from being placed in danger should all of this turn bad.

*Judgment shield me, is it even moral to tell her?* A part of her wished she could say it outright and get it over with, that Felicia could be trusted not to go to the Thorns, or Lady Tamalsen, or some other person who would be equally as bad for them, and hand everything she knew over.

Ben flickered across her mind. *He would kill me.*

"As long as you're as miserable as I am." Felicia said dejectedly. "You could do a better job of acting like you are."

"The emperor isn't going to be here forever." Rashanna said in an attempt to placate her.

She scooped a spoonful of potatoes into her mouth. They were bland. With Ariana in hiding, Mistress Dina was working almost around the clock to compensate. Peter's limited contact with the Teacher's Tower was mostly restricted to nighttime adventures after everyone else was asleep or secure in their departments. He had been working double shifts almost every day since the library incident. Their extra labors, the increased demand from a noble caste now comprised of elites, soldiers, and clergy from two cities was made evident in the quality of the food, in the way Peter seemed worn out every time she saw him, and how Mistress Dina's voice could be heard almost twice as much as she bellowed at her workers behind the serving window.

"You're barely around anymore." Felicia complained. "And when you are, you barely talk."

"I'm sorry." Rashanna said. "Any idea why the Thorns are here?"

"None." Felicia replied. "They give me the creeps, though. It's like they think all of us are like those—"

"Those what?" Rashanna said too sharply.

Felicia set her jaw, and spoke in a low voice. "It doesn't matter. Ben is—"

"What?" Rashanna said and at the stubborn expression Felicia set on her added: "I want to know."

"Rashanna, he's one of them. He has to be." Felicia said. "If that Lance kid hadn't barged into his life, he would be sitting here with us wondering what's going on, but he's with them."

"You don't know that." Rashanna said, trying very hard to sound hurt by the accusation. "He could just as easily be a victim."

"If he is, he probably isn't alive anymore. I guess it makes a kind of sense. The Thorns and the Wraiths wouldn't exactly telegraph it if he died by their hands. He wasn't important." Felicia said matter-of-factly. She tucked into her food.

"I'm..." *I'm one of them.* She thought, offended by how easily her girlfriend pivoted to accepting Ben's death, the inconsequential nature of it in the grand scheme, even as she knew he was alive and safe.  She said instead: "I'm going. I need to be alone for a while."

"What did I say?" Felicia pleaded, but Rashanna was already on her feet, glaring at her. "Will I at least get to see you tonight?"

"We'll see how I feel." She stormed off. *If she could dismiss him that easily, what about me? Would she just* move on *if I died?*

She wasn't being fair, and she knew it. Felicia would be devastated if she died, whatever the nature of their relationship with each other. But she could not accept the woman's flippant attitude at the prospect of her closest friend's mortality, even if the entire line of attack was a poorly constructed lie.

As soon as she was safely away from the watchful Thorns, she pulled a piece of paper from her pocket and unfolded it. Instead of entering the stairs, she continued into the labyrinth of tunnels, taking the back way toward the kitchen.

She scanned the list written there in Ariana's chicken scratch. *I'll have to find a familiar face to take me up this time.*

*Flour, eggs...will Mistress Dina even part with some of this stuff?*

She shouldn't be handling this to begin with. If Ben had escaped without being seen and Peter was the one in hiding, this whole ordeal would be so much more convenient. And hadn't the Thorns said they would handle all the logistics of keeping everyone fed anyway?

She could hardly be expected to tote a sack full of foodstuffs up to the tower without being noticed. It would look suspicious to anyone who saw her. She would have preferred letting someone else take care of this errand, but she was the only one who could still move freely through the palace, and Ben wanted to do something special for Lance's birthday. He had always thought of her when her day came around. It was only right that she help him now he had found a boyfriend she approved of, even if it did make her life more complicated.

*He had better appreciate me after this.*

She entered the kitchens, and cut a line straight for Mistress Dina.


Knocks came at the door in series, according to what the rebel servants had agreed upon. It swung inward, admitting Rashanna, her arms laden with parcels for the occasion.

Lance was nineteen today, and though he would have preferred to handle his birth anniversary a different way, he intended to see to it that it was a good day for him. He had thought to put everyone in better spirits with a quiet celebration. Too much darkness had crept into their lives with their restriction to the uppermost levels of this tower.

## A Quiet Celebration

The Thorns watching from the shadows had been reluctant to let them leave, but Ariana had pushed them to allow it, if only to let Peter and Lance onto the roof where they could run laps around its perimeter, a test of endurance.

The Thorn who had gone with him had been amused by the prospect. He had known he would comply with them when he started offering suggestions for alternative training methods, exercises more in line with the military's standards. And that was for the better, wasn't it?

With guidance from a soldier, they might be better prepared to face others of their kind. If the Thorn could teach them some tactics or tricks to escape a compromising situation, all the better for their cause.

Ben set aside *The Compact* which he had been reading on and off since Lance said there was something worth knowing in it. He had yet to find a sign of what he was talking about, but he refused to give up. *Something will give eventually.*

He sat up, swung his legs over the edge of camp bed he'd been provided. Ariana was already at the door, met her in the doorway and helped her with her burden.

"Thanks." She said.

Rashanna handed Ben the heaviest parcels, and he took them to the brazier in the corner of the room, where Ariana had set up a makeshift kitchen, really little more than a bare patch of floor with an array of mixing bowls and tools scattered across it.  She set the rest down behind him.

Ariana started rummaging through its contents. She liberated a clutch of eggs, a glass jug full of milk, set them aside and dragged out more food stock from its depths.

"Did you run into any problems getting this stuff?" she asked.

"Mistress Dina was in a mood. I think she's happy you and Peter know the truth. But she's clearly overworked." She rolled her eyes. "She put up a little stink about it, but she parted with everything you asked for.

"She did tell me to let you know to beat those eggs until they're pale and foamy. Said you get impatient and then your cake doesn't rise."

"She can fuck off. I don't need to beat them that much if I'm using other liveners."

Rashanna snorted. "She said you would say that."

"She tell you to pass me any other bits of sagely wisdom?"

"Just that she expects you to answer for the dishwasher you trained in when she's done with this. Someone named Jalen. She thinks he's shit."

Ariana guffawed. She was already sifting flour into one of her bowls. "He *is* shit, but it's not my fault he can't figure out how to scrub a fucking pot. Peter's still down there, anyway. If she's got such a problem with Jalen, she can just stick *him* in there."

"You people are really weird, you know that?" she said.

"It's a kitchen, chick. Of course we are. We're a pack of degenerates, and we like it that way."

"The Thorns are everywhere, by the way. I was taking a risk coming here."

"Hopefully, they're not hangin' around the showers." Ben said. "I need one bad."

"You do kinda stink. All of you do." She chuckled at the look of indignation he set against her. "But I said what I meant. They're everywhere. I guess its better them than the Wraiths, but I can't tell who's who by looking at them, and its been creeping me out."

"At least we know some of them are on the right side."

"My how quickly you have taken to supporting the cause." Ariana mumbled.

He shrugged. "Twenty years, give or take, of bein' lied to will do that to you. I remember some pieces of my childhood. Wish I had more to go on, but what's there isn't all great. Most of it isn't.

## A Quiet Celebration

"I know my mother loved me. Enough to try to keep me safe. That's enough for me."

He approached the chalkboard, selected a slender piece of chalk and started sketching out an image, not really sure what he was drawing. A list of all the intelligence they had gathered from the Thorns, Peter, Rashanna and the furnace workers took up one side of the board. For all that was written there, they still knew next to nothing of the goings on in the palace. Lance's return to the furnaces had provided more insight than they could have hoped to gain otherwise. Regular contact with Master Gregor had proven a boon to them as they tried to work it all out, but they were still stuck on a way out.

Lance insisted there was some way out of this palace that would not allow the Wraiths to follow, which meant it was something that didn't rely on shadow walking. And if it was a powerful enough means to see them through, it must be something that could get the rest of the servants, and the rebels in the city, out with them. He just wished he had a clue of what it might be.

*No sense worrying over that now.*

He didn't want to think about any of it. He needed a break, a moment to just be. They had been throwing everything they had into answering this question, learning as much as they could of the magical arts. It had taken some time, but Ariana had broken through the barrier separating her from hearing those voices. Peter was still finding his way through. So was Rashanna, though he suspected she would become open to them before he did.

Whatever was keeping him back was rooted in trauma. It seemed that way to him. There was something in his past he couldn't get over, and every attempt they made to pull it out of him was met with resistance. Even Ariana had thus far proven unsuccessful at getting him to open up about it.

Just once, for a few hours, he wanted to distance himself

from what they had to do. Lance's birthday was as much about him as it was about giving the rest of them space to breathe.

He returned to the camp bed and sat down, observing his work. Rashanna embraced him in a half hug. "We're going to be fine."

"I know." He said.

A rough approximation of the snow white peacock he had seen on so many tapestries, in carvings and frescoes, and in books, throughout his life looked back at him. He thought to flesh out the seal with the other creatures there.

"Actually. Rashanna, can you draw the next one?"

"You want me to...what? Sketch out a fox?"

Whichever of the five you like best, I guess?" he spread his hands.

"Is this going to help you in some way?" She asked.

"Just seems like a thing to do." He admitted.

"Alright." She climbed to her feet. Approaching the chalkboard, she took up the stick he had left there, but instead of filling out the seal, she moved a little distance off and sketched out something else. An opaque mass in the shape of a cluster of small flowers, their stems interlaced and covered in tiny thorns.

She backed away.

"Not exactly what I was talking about, but good I guess." He said noncommittally.

"Reminds me of a dream I had once. The night of the emperor's arrival." She explained. "A lot of people who looked like me were dancing in a circle, celebrating my brother getting marked with this. I'm not the best artist, but it looked something like it anyway. I think it was seen as a good choice. It was a tattoo, and a lot of them seemed to have them.

"The details are a little hazy, but I think it was something to do with magic."

"Can you two do me a favor?" Ariana asked.

"What do you need?" Ben replied.

"Start the brazier up." She said. "Don't let it get too hot. We're gonna need it for this."

They liberated a basket comprised of metal bands from a corner where a series of burlap sacks and kitchen wares rested and hauled it into the center aisle. The weight of the basket strained Ben's muscles, and he was glad when he was free of it. Rashanna crossed to the windows, and cracked one open as Ben used a fire starter and kindling which he buried int the coals to coax fire out of them.

"Have you ever done anything like this before?" Rashanna asked.

"Not for a servant." Ariana said. "I've done cakes for nobles before. They like them more elaborate than this, but they barely eat them."

"I wonder why." Ben mumbled.

"They barely eat anything in public." Rashanna said.

Ariana turned up her nose. "It's part of the culture to waste perfectly good food apparently. Pisses me right off."

"What's the first thing you're going to do when we get out of here?" Rashanna asked, trying to keep things light.

Been squeezed her hand, thankful they did not have to dwell in the dark tangle of complexities surrounding their relationship with the nobility and the military.

"I don't know." Ariana said. "But speaking of dreams, I had one that same night. My grandfather and my father were arguing over where to send me. I think we were fleeing from some conflict." She said. "If we get out of here, I'll probably find somewhere to work and settle down in some shit hole or another until I can afford something better. Maybe in Haru. It seems like that's where I'm from."

"You know we're already violating about half of Shadovane's laws. We could steal some gold on our way out."

# SPIRIT OF SHADOW

Rashanna suggested.

Ariana guffawed. "That would definitely get us killed. The locks on those vaults are enchanted, right? We'd be walking into a death trap?"

"What would you do?" Ben asked Rashanna.

"I thought about going to Juakali. Maybe someone there remembers me." She answered. "If they don't, I can still learn about my culture."

Ben smiled. "I like that idea."

"I might go with you." Ariana said. "An adventure sounds like a great plan after this."

"So what would you do?" Rashanna asked him.

"I would watch the sunrise." Ben answered. "I don't know where we would end up, so there's not much point thinkin' about specifics, but the sun is the same everywhere, so it's somethin' I can hold onto."

"That's stupid." Rashanna said.

"I like it." Ariana protested. She was beating the eggs now, the sound of the whisk against the bowl a hypnotic rhythm. "There's something poetic about it. And it's not expecting too much."

"Where would you be looking at that sunrise from, if you had the choice?" Rashanna asked.

"Well...." Ben thought on it for a moment. "I think I was born in the Empire, so going home is out of the question. Or if I wasn't, the place I was born doesn't exist anymore. At least...it's probably not the same. I'd probably go to Del Zaros, in Gourum."

"It doesn't get much safer than that." Ariana said. She finished mixing her ingredients and poured the resultant batter into a cast bronze pan. She took that over to the brazier, where the last tongues of flame had gone and left embers behind to burn. "There's a lot in that book Lance got on the Immortals about it. They have a giant wall that has never fallen, and these soldiers called the Ironclad that sound like they're about as good as the Bloodless or the Enlightened. And their king is like our queen. I guess he's some kind of Immortal.

"The book called them The Children. They have these pendants that let them access the memories of the people who held them before. There's a whole elaborate ritual in Gourum for selecting a child who can bond with theirs, but the one here chooses its host completely at random."

"A pendant?" Ben smacked his forehead. He hustled over to a stack of books on the desk. "Maybe that's what he was talking about."

"Who?"

"Lance! He said there was something in that flimsy piece of...anyway, I read something about those pendants in there. Let me just..." he riffled through the pages, searching for what he needed.

He poured over one page near the middle of the document, an otherwise innocuous enough piece that hid its own insights in the language its writer had chosen. He ran his finger across the page, where were laid out various exemptions to travel between territories defined earlier in the treaty, for that was what it seemed to be, and before the specific actors representative of those territories were defined.

"Here." He said, landing on the information he needed. "Take a look at this."

He brought the book over to them, set it on the floor for them to read.

"I'd just tell you what it says, but...you know." He shrugged.

They put their heads together, Rashanna climbing down from her seat to get a closer look.

"This could mean a lot of things."

"It's like Ariana said. The Children have to be the Shadow

Queen and the Earth Child."

He read the section to himself as they poured over it.


*[1.1.13.1.1.] All visitation to the lands controlled by the Blood will be restricted with exception to The Children, as defined in this compact, who in possessing a fragment of godliness and being bound to it will have free access to pass beyond the Gates, those relics created by the Architects for relevant purpose of travel before their extermination.*

*[1.1.13.1.2.] They will remain in those lands not more than the time necessary to move from one gate to the next, and thus pass out of them, collectively referred to for purpose of this compact as Daranel or the Pure World, into the lands whose rulers they seek for diplomatic purposes. They may conduct diplomatic relations with the leaders of the Blooded Tribes as long as they do no harm while in their lands and do not seek to subjugate them by any means violent or otherwise. They may not seek to lock the gates or remove the restriction on travel through them, whether or not they have awoken to this power.*

*[1.1.13.1.3.] The locations of the gates remaining fixed, they will reside at the seat of government or religious ceremony in each of the territories party to this agreement, with no attempt to destroy or move them permissible without violating the terms of this compact and thus rendering the entire document void.*


"It's all right there." He said. "The Children possessing a fragment of godliness...that has to refer to those pendants."

"It could." Rashanna said reluctantly, a grimace painted across her lips.

Ariana was as hesitant to jump on board with his proposal. "Even if these gates can be opened with the queen's pendant, it doesn't really help us unless we can force her to open it for us."

## A Quiet Celebration

"And *we* would be violating this agreement if she did." Rashanna said. "The whole thing would be nullified if she let us step through that gate. She'd even be able to follow us herself once we made it through."

"You're seeing the forest for the trees." He said, glaring at both of them. "We don't necessarily need her to open the gate. We just need her to remove whatever barrier is blocking anyone else from going through."

"If she has that power. What is she doesn't?" Ariana protested.

"I don't know. But this is better than us having nothing to go on. And it makes sense of what Lance was saying about ways of traveling that Wraiths can't follow. This is it. Right here. We just need to figure out how to find it. Then we can use it."

"You think we should bring this to Lord Aren?" Rashanna asked, regarding Ariana with a harassed look on her face.

"It couldn't hurt." She said.

"I wish Lance was here." He said. "He'd be on my side."

"No one said we weren't. You just need to temper your expectations." Rashanna said.

"Let's just leave this alone for now. We can come back to it tomorrow. Tonight should be about Lance." Ariana said, making it plain this conversation was over.

They should've been here by now." Ben said, looking at a cuckoo clock they had salvaged from another classroom, which said the time at which Peter was meant to return with Lance had elapsed half an hour ago.

Several more minutes went by with no change.

The cake was finished. The brazier, a mass of glowing embers, provided ample warmth to combat the chill suffusing the classroom from the cracked window. Everything was in place, but the man of the hour was late, and he was beginning to worry.

# SPIRIT OF SHADOW

He saw his concern reflected in Ariana's face. Why are they not here yet? He would not let himself think they had been found. They had come too far to be captured now.

"We should check on them." Ariana suggested.

"We don't know where they are?" Rashanna protested. "They might have just had some...obstacles getting back here."

"You're not convinced of that." Ben intoned defensively.

"I'm hopeful." Rashanna replied.

"Let's just—"

A knock came at the door, the code they had agreed on.

"Quick, get in position!" Ben breathed.

He snatched up the cake, held it behind his back and joined Ariana and Rashanna as Peter slid the door open. He entered first, followed by Lance.

"Happy birthday!" They all shouted.

Lance clapped his hands to his mouth, his face gone lilac pink as he looked around at them.

"You did this for me?" he said.

Ben approached him, setting the cake aside as he traveled the length of the room, and laid a kiss on his cheek. "We thought we'd pull somethin' together for you."

Ariana took the cake off to a nearby desk and cut into it, plated up slices for all of them. As she did, Peter produced a clay jug like the one he provided had for their game of stones. He liberated some cups from the pile of kitchen wares and poured them each a draft of Mirrhvalian wine.

He set about handing the refreshments around.

"You guys really didn't have to do this." Lance said.

"Oh shut up and have some cake." Ariana said, pushing a plate at him.

He took a bite. "How did you—"

"Rashanna brought us the ingredients. Ariana handled the rest. I didn't want to fuck it up." Ben said.

## A Quiet Celebration

"It's good." He said around a mouthful, gesturing with his fork in Ariana's direction.

Ariana snorted. She dug into her own slice, washed it down with the wine.

"Might as well make your wish now." Peter said.

His skin was starched with a salt crust from his recent exertion. It seemed the Thorn had pushed them both hard, as Lance was in a similar state, his hair still oily and lank with sweat.

Lance screwed up his face. "I suppose I wish for—"

"Don't tell us or it won't come true." Peter warned.

"That's a stupid rule." Lance said.

"Doesn't matter. You can't break it." He said.

"Fine." Lance chuckled. He thought on what he should wish for. *A clean escape maybe? That no one else has to get hurt?* But he had a better idea, something he wanted as much as he wanted to get away from the palace, and so he made his wish. *To see Sami again.* "Done."

Peter held up his cup. "Cheers!"

The others mashed their cups together.

They drank, ate and made merry. For one night, Ben had his wish, and they chattered away into the early hours of the morning without thought or care for what they must do in the days to come.

They finally called it a night when a Thorn arrived out of shadow to take Peter and Rashanna away, leaving a hollow where they had been, as they were back in their compromising positions, and out of sight of the rest of their friends.

With them gone and the drink strong in him, Ben laced Lance's hands into his. He leaned in and kissed him. Lance, less inebriated than him but not by very much, took him to the cot and tucked him in, careful to leave one of his feet firmly on the floor.

"I—" he started, slurring slightly.

# SPIRIT OF SHADOW

Lance kissed him, cutting him off before he could say more.

"Go to sleep." He said.

He climbed onto the camp bed behind him, and Ben let sleep wash over him. His dreams were a confused tangle of hopeful scenes that night, of what life might be after Shadovane. The dreams, a taste of freedom, premonitions of an autonomous life...maybe even a happy one.

# Echoes from the Past

Lance dropped onto his back foot and swung his fist at Peter.

Peter slapped it away with his forearm. The missed connection strained the tendons in Lance's armpit, put him off balance.

Peter closed the distance, went for a jab.

Lance hauled himself to the side and Peter stumbled forward. Since Lance had started taking these sparring matches seriously, and with guidance from an often bored complement of Thorns, they had both improved. He knew he wasn't prepared for what was coming, and he intended to work himself to death if it meant being ready when the time came that he needed these skills.

They fought shirtless, their fists wrapped in strips of cloth. Both were covered in a thick layer of sweat now. Ben was in similar shape, though he played a different game.

# SPIRIT OF SHADOW

Ariana appeared out of the shadows near the curtains behind the desk. He spun to face her in perfect time for her to dive under the desk. Her head peaked out of his shadow. She smiled mischievously at Lance, tugged Ben's pants leg and vanished again.

Lothor seemed to enjoy these games. Since Ariana had picked up the trick to hearing his voice, he had been far more vocal than he ever was before. It seemed he enjoyed the idea that so many in one place might know him. The furnace workers seldom called on him, for his power was not of much use to them in their work.

The spider watched on from the edge of the desk, and though he did not offer comment, neither did he twitch and squirm as often as he usually did.

When he did speak, it was to provide guidance to the two as they explored the contours of his power.

The Thorns had not liked this game at first, but had come to accept the ritual as a necessary part of their education. Sometimes, when they bothered to surface from the shadows, Lance noted them listening to the spirit, and thought they must be gaining wisdom from his words. Tricks they may not have known.

"Dammit. You're too good at this, Ariana." Ben said.

Their game was called Shadow Tag. Ariana's job for the moment was to navigate around the classroom without being caught or seen. Ben was to try to spot and then capture her. When he succeeded or gave up, they would switch places.

*"There is a way to catch her."* Lothor intoned, distracting Lance long enough that Peter was able to put him in a hold and drag him onto the ground. *"There is the concept of Silencing. I would think those books you so often pour over would have mentioned it."*

"They might. But I haven't gotten that far into them." Ben said, his gaze traveling from shadow to shadow, waiting for

Ariana to resurface. "What is it?"

*"A binding. Once caught in the snare, your kind cannot hear us. It is a way to interfere with the connection. Made easier when the offender cannot hear us speak."*

"That sounds like something we should know." Lance said, his voice strained for Peter had him in a headlock.

"Yes." Lothor said.

"Care to enlighten us?" Ben asked.

*"Spirits and mortals...we are not so different. We were born to share in a symbiotic relationship, in mutualism. You call on us, but have you not wondered why we come? It is because we can hear you. Not your voices, but your souls."*

Peter released him. "What's going on?"

"Lothor...sorry, the spirit of shadow." Ben said. "He says he can teach us how to prevent other people from using magic."

"That would be incredibly useful." Peter said. There was an edge of envy in his voice. He was the only one in this room who had yet to hear Lothor speak with his own ears. It was understandable he would be somewhat irritated by that. Emma's efforts to teach him had been fruitless, and no amount of sitting in contemplation of the relative quiet in this room, or any of the other methods he had attempted, had helped either.

*"Mortal souls exude a frequency. A series of notes which denote your character. Everything that you are contained in a melody. It is the same with us. However, to wage conflict with those frequencies...it makes them harder to hear. The one who succeeds in this act of domination cries out louder to our ears. The other...we cannot hear him.*

*"To make this thing work, one must simply alter their own frequency such that it nullifies the other, cancels it out. But to do so, you must first hear yourself. Know yourself. Then you might compel the thread of another's music to silence."*

Lance dropped his fists. "That's enough for now. I'm

exhausted. And this sounds better anyway."

"Same." Panting, Peter climbing to his feet.

Lance liberated a towel from a pile of linens next to the burlap sacks that contained the bulk of their food. He rubbed himself down with it. It would be hours before it was safe to shower, and he yearned for one like he seldom had before the incident-in-the-library. There was something about not being able to access the showers when he wanted to that made him desire them that much more.

He glanced past Ben at the chalkboard. All of their problems had been summed up in the list of plans written there. They were treading water, and he knew it, but the others were not ready to admit it yet. Every day saw new plans added, old ones crossed off. Two remained to express their intent, and neither was particularly good. They were more aspirations than actionable strategies.

*Free the servants. Escape.*

There was no escape without the Shadow Queen's pendant. A brief but pointed conversation had begun on a hopeful note and then died when reality hit home. She was never apart from that thing. Her chambers were guarded by Bloodless, who stationed themselves just outside her door. The shadows would also be watched as Wraiths and unfriendly Thorns found stations there, and there was no assurance Lord Aren could give that they might have a long enough window to infiltrate, take what they needed, and get out.

Even if they could trust him to help him, what would he do if they were caught?

Using it would prove a challenge even if they did obtain it, as none of them knew how it worked. And by Ben's own admission, it was likely bound to her soul in some way, able to answer only to her.

They might lure her into a position that could benefit

them, but how would they do it? The best means of getting her where they wanted to was exposing themselves, and they were not strong enough to contend with her or her soldiers.

And the children? Those Lance had seen on a misguided journey down a staircase he should have left alone? There were more than just those somewhere. There must be. He recalled a place in which he was taught things like simple math and how to read when he was a boy, which looked nothing like the chamber he had stumbled onto. Getting to them would require figuring out where they were kept, and even then there would be guards there, just as there were at the bottom of that staircase.

Obstacles on obstacles barred their path. He only wished he knew how to overcome them. But this new revelation...it was something they could all learn to manifest. Something that might help them greatly when time came they could no longer content themselves with hiding in plain sight.

Time was not on their side. The jaws of the military drew closer together around them with every day that passed. They were as careful as they could be, but one slip up would have them all facing immolation sooner than later. He was growing tired of the old argument.

*If we wait until the emperor leaves, our chances will be better.*

They might think that, but they were wrong. When the emperor left, the last distraction keeping their queen occupied would be gone, and the full might of the military would be behind the search effort for them. All but Lord Aren's loyalists. The purge would not end with them. When their interrogations were done, the military would drag the general himself from his seat and see him executed, and then Master Gregor and his charges, and all the others they could root out based on the knowledge contained between the people in this room. *And Rashanna. If they find out she's on our side, they'll kill her too.*

# SPIRIT OF SHADOW

They needed whatever advantage they could get. If the military knew about this Silencing, they needed to learn it too. And if they could use it more strongly than them, all the better. There was potential in this new method for keeping them contained, if and when they came against them. Advantage in knowing something they didn't, and extrapolating on that in mimicking their arts. *All* of their arts. Whatever they could learn in the time they had left.

"Does it work more or less the same way?" Lance asked. "Do we just listen until we find it?"

*"In so many words."* Lothor grumbled. *"There are those who may help, but they are dangerous. Meddling with ways you do not understand can lead to...complications."*

"But that way is faster?" Ariana asked.

*"It is."* Lothor answered. *"It is nonetheless not without its risks. And I do not love those who would help you. It is not an easy thing without them, either."*

"Can you bring them here. These helpers?" she asked.

"Ariana!" Lance hissed. "Did you not just hear him. He said they were dangerous. It might be better for us just to let this go. Figure it out the old fashioned way."

She hit him with a withering look, her defenses on her. "Do we really have that kind of time?"

He didn't respond. *No. No, we don't. They're looking for us. Lord Aren can only do so much.*

She nodded, satisfied she had her way. "Can you bring them here now?"

"If they will come."

"Then please, do so."

"Are you sure this is a good idea?" Ben asked. But she had that look about her. The one that said she would wrestle a bear before she gave up on the idea, dared anyone to stop her.

"Do it." She said.

*"As you wish."* Lothor responded.

"I wish I knew what he was saying." Peter mumbled. "I don't like any of this, but the not knowing is making it that much creepier."

Lothor blinked. He was joined, in the next instant, by two creatures. One was the size of a small dog, with a bushy tail and a wide, shaggy face. The other manifested as a kind of bird, though for its neutral shape and incessant fidgeting, he could not identify what kind. He was not at all sure either of these animals were native to these lands. He had certainly never seen them on the palace grounds.

*"Identify them if you choose. Learn their names if you must. They do not need you to know them to do their work."*

"I would prefer to know them." Lance said. "I think we would all trust them more if we did."

*"He is blocked by his pain."* The dog-like creature said. *"He must be unveiled."*

*"They have tried, but he is stubborn."* Lothor responded dismissively. *"It may be a lost cause."*

Ariana winced.

"What?" Peter asked, confusion stealing over him.

"It's nothing." She said. "Nothing important."

"That looked pretty important." He said.

*"If I can touch him."* The creature pressed.

*"I am not your master."* Lothor said. *"Merely the messenger."*

The creature hopped off the desk, crossed the room to where Peter lounged. It climbed across him—evidently unfelt, as he did not respond to the sudden press of its weight against him—and wrapped strangely human hands around his head. It pressed its face against his, and was still.

"Is this the danger you spoke of?"

*"Indeed. And without her name, you cannot hope to stop her."*

"Fuck." Ariana clapped her hands to her mouth.

Ben's gaze shifted from one to the other of them. His

anxiety echoed theirs.

A tense moment passed, and Peter gasped. "What the...."

*"What keeps you back, when you should so easily spring forth into our hold."* The spirit whispered. *"What threatens to shatter you so."*

*"If we but spread the pain..."* the bird intoned.

*"You would break them."* Lothor grumbled. *"Tread carefully. They are only human."*

The bird bowed its head. A high pitched call escaped its throat, and echoes reverberated back to it from several directions at once.

Lance's head snapped back as he was struck by an intangible force, the blow feeling like a thunderclap inside his head. He collapsed against the desk, thrust out his arm to keep him from falling.

"What in—"

Around him, his friends were struck by the same force, and struggled to stay upright. The force bared down on his head and shoulders, pulsed within his soul, and a live wire pumped static up and down his spine.

He was dragged under, into a world foreign to him, stood with all of those others in a city far removed from Shadovane, whose every dwelling was a tower molded of igneous rock to resemble a coral tube, their windows outfitted with something like glass, which warped the reflections of the few people behind them.

The streets descended along the slope of a bowl, and it was unbearably hot. Mirages rippled over black pathways awash with lighter sand and gravel, and stairs and ramps connected one ring to the next on their way deeper into the reach. A red glow like sunset loomed at the edges of the city, blocked out the stars in a black sky which was interrupted by scudding clouds and smoke trails here and there, signs of life and sweeping rains that would not touch this land.

"Where are we?" he whispered.

He searched the faces of his friends for signs they might know, found just his confusion reflected back at him.

*"I told you they were dangerous."* Lothor's voice echoed in his ears, quiet but insistent. *"The spirits do not value the same things as you."*

"But they're helping us?" Ariana said, her gaze set on Peter.

He was leaning against one of those towers, hidden in its shadow where a narrow crossroad broke against this thoroughfare. People, mostly kitunes, ambled across this and the adjoining lanes, climbed down staircases intent on other places. No few tourists were among them; and they reflected the diversity of empire. Stout croni marched diligently along, pulling trenchers of ore on carts behind them, and merenern sipped steadily at waterskins as they made for whatever shelter they could find. The dry heat could not be kind to them, so used to living near water as they were, yet they came to attend to whatever business demanded their presence here.

A boy stood just behind Peter, and he was of a kind Lance had never seen before. He bore some resemblance to a kitune, but his eyes were too wide and his skin a shade of gray, mottled in places where strange lines formed a crisscrossing pattern that reminded him of fish scales. Thicker, more sinuous lines traced the contours of his slender neck, and a mop of shaggy, dark hair rode the dome of his head between his ears. He hadn't seen a wash in some time, and his clothes were soiled with road dust and ash.

Peter kept him back, away from the others, and the look on his face was animal fear, as if he did not recognize any of them.

"What's going on?" Ariana demanded. "What is this place?"

*"A place in time, enshrined in memories once stolen and*

*now returned."* The dog-like spirit whispered. *"A place far away, where this man was born. Where he became who he once was, and lost his way."*

"Fuck." She hissed.

"We should never have asked for their help." Ben said. "We'd have been better off doing things the old fashioned way."

"Don't be too hasty." Lance said. "If it gets Peter past his block, we're better off."

"I feel dirty being here." Ben said, looking around at their surroundings. "This is his private life. We shouldn't know anythin' about it."

"Does it help any of us to keep it all in." Lance insisted. "We all had those dreams the night the Emperor arrived, didn't we? There are more pieces you two are missing. I'm not so sure I remember everything, either."

"But *he* clearly does." Ben said.

"I agree with Lance." Ariana said. "Let's just do what we can. Look, he's moving!"

They followed him down a staircase, and were met with a new sight that sent a thrill traveling up Lance's spine. Great salamanders, as big as horses, pawed their way over a ramp. A procession of them clambered up from the heart of the bowl. The largest of them were the color of blood pulled from a vein, and their glistening hides were speckled with darker patches. The heads on all of those beasts were wide and flat, but those red ones were meatier, their bodies well muscled and bulky. They were accompanied by a scattering of others, some of them albinos, white as dead fish and bearing milky eyes with a blueish tint at their edges, the powdery tint mirrored in stripes along their flanks and banding crooked forelimbs. The rest were wickedly dark, their skin and eyes like crude oil, black and glossy, and flames guttered along their spines not unlike a mane.

Many of those bore riders clad in woolen cloaks, their hoods drawn up and their ears left exposed through hoses in the fabric. Those cloaks were embellished with dye, forming a script that read like sheet music and traveled from their crowns down their backs.

Peter steered clear of them as the boy in his wake goggled at the beasts, pulled him along and away down an adjoining corridor.

They pursued with Ariana taking the lead, keeping pace with him.

"What are those things?" Lance whispered to Ben as they followed.

"I don't know. But judging by the way those people carry themselves, they're soldiers. Probably this city's cavalry."

"Cavalry?"

"Horse warriors. Shadovane doesn't use them."

A vagrant seated in the shadow of a nearby building rattled a can, singing in somber tones. His voice was not pretty, and broke now and again as he tried to keep the tune. They passed him by as a human woman passed a few coins into his cup, and prayed over him.

Peter ducked into an alley, then nudged a tarp in the crook behind a dwelling aside. He passed through.

The boy dawdled outside for a few minutes while animated talk passed between others inside, and then Peter snatched him by the shoulder and dragged him in.

"This feels wrong." Ariana said as she pulled the flap open.

Inside, several other boys as disheveled as the one Peter had been dragging along with him were arrayed in a patch which should be a dumping ground for the inhabitants of that building. He was seated on a ratty old rug with another boy who was perhaps twelve years in age. A few younger boys, all of them kitunes, were arranged around the space, and all but one looked as if they were ready for a fight.

A woman sat across from the older boy. She was human,

# SPIRIT OF SHADOW

and wore a black tunic and loose-legged trousers. Her pale skin marked her as one from some northern reach. Her eyes were dark and held a wisdom beyond her years which he suspected was rooted in some trauma in her past, and her hair was arranged in loose buns at the sides of her head.

She did not smile as she met the grim-faced leader of this ragtag crew, did not extend any condolences or warm invitations to those children gathered around her. Peter grit his teeth as her fingers twined around the drawstring of a burlap sack, and she tossed it to the leader, who did not touch it.

"Wha's in it?" he asked, eying it like a serpent.

"Food mostly. Some coin to get you through. Your friend needs treatment for those cuts. There's not much I can do for that, but the money will help."

"Magical healing leaves traces." The leader grumbled. He still had not reached for the parcel. "He's better off healing the natural way."

"He may beg to differ." She glanced in the direction of a pallid boy with auburn hair, who shared much resemblance with the others. His conical ears ended in red tufts of hair and his nose was wide and somewhat smashed looking. He was skinnier than most of the others, and cuts across his legs which were crusted over with old blood indicated he had been involved in some kind of violence in the recent past.

She was right to think he would benefit from healing, and a brief flash of hope crossing his face suggested she was right to think he would take it if he was allowed to.

"How d'we know yer not some poacher?" he asked.

"You don't." She said. "But I didn't expect it to be easy earning your trust, either. I haven't been at this long, but I have had my successes. Two so far have come under my protection. They're about your age. A little older. They will be your sisters if you choose to come with me."

"Means leavin' Ash Island." Another boy mumbled. "On't know if I want ta do that."

Peter nodded in agreement.

"Ash Island is no place for an orphan." She said. "There are poachers and worse everywhere. You've done a good job keeping each other safe so far, but I doubt very much you've been this fortunate without a few setbacks. Maybe a close call or two with those bastards."

The leader's grimace said all that was needed.

"If I could find you this easily, what about someone who doesn't have good intentions?"

"We'll move ta a new hideout. We do 'at anyway, often 's not."

"Wa' happens if we go wit' ya?" the leader asked.

She grimaced. "If you come with me, you'll be set up in a house in Aranor. It's nothing special. I wouldn't even call it nice. But it's shelter. You'll have food and clean clothes, access to a wash basin. I'll even teach you magic. The real stuff. The kind you could use to knock me off. I can start doing that now, if you'd like."

"You'd give us a weapon to use against you?" that other boy, the injured one, said. A look of uncomprehending curiosity stole over him, as if he could not quite believe what he was hearing.

"Of course." She said. "I'll be here for another week. I won't force you to do anything you don't want to. If you don't want to meet with me, that's fine. But you know where I'll be."

She stood, made for the tent flap.

"That's it?" the leader asked.

"That's it. You've got until I leave to make your decision. There's enough money in that sack to buy you a room in a cheap hostel if you choose. They'll have baths there."

"Those are dangerous."

"Then you might find it accommodating to choose the one

# SPIRIT OF SHADOW

I'm staying in." She said, lifting the flap. "The little one knows where to find me."

She winked at the boy Peter had come here with, and left.

A few moments silence were broken swiftly by the leader of the group. "You were followin' 'er?" he snapped. "Could've got yerself killed! Or snatched! Wa' would ya 'ave done then?"

"I'm sorry, Roach." The little one sobbed. "I didn't mean to—"

"Well, it's as she said. He knows where she's staying." The injured boy said. "Maybe we'd be safe there until she leaves."

"You 'on't want ta go with her, do ya?" Roach demanded. "She's dangerous. Ya can see it."

"She might not be so dangerous to us. Maybe she's dangerous in another way, but what's in that bag might prove something else." The injured boy argued.

"Don, please." Roach pinched the bridge of his nose. "Everyone's dangerous who pretends otherwise. 'Ey all say the same things. Make promises 'ey know 'ey 'on't keep ta lure ya in so 'ey can sell ya off to whoever wants to buy ya."

"Not everyone is evil." Don, the injured boy, said.

"I don't want to go with her." Peter said. "We're okay here."

"What's in the sack, Roach?" Don tipped his chin toward the bag. "If you won't—"

"Okay!" Roach made a warding gesture as Don lunged for it. He pulled the drawstring loose and dumped its contents onto the patch of earth between them.

Fresh fruit, dried meats, crusty loaves of bread all rolled onto the ground, and following them, a fat sack that rattled like hard coin when it struck the dirt.

"That's one promise she kept."

"You can't be serious. It's a bribe! She wants us ta trust 'er so she can make 'er job easier when time comes to spirit us away! She even said she was gonna do it!"

"She said she'd take care of us. She's done that. And she didn't play nice with you like the other one did. That tells you something."

"Wha's it tell me?"

"She's not all sweet smiles and flowery words is what it tells you. She's about business. And her business...maybe it's helping people. Maybe she's like those monks up from the Free Lands who take on kids in their monasteries."

"They 'on't do 'at without a price." Roach groused.

"Where's she staying, Night?" Don demanded.

"City's edge." The boy Peter had taken here said. "By the bridge."

"What are we waiting for then?" Don asked the others, lifting his hands in an imploring gesture. "Worst case, we get the hell out of there before she sees us. It's a place to stay."

"We sleep 'is one off." Roach said. "Make a decision tomorrow."

"But—" another boy complained, but Roach cut him off.

"Tomorrow. We 'an decide tomorrow. In 'a meantime, she gave us food. We might 's well eat it."

The strange illusion collapsed, and in its wake, they all stood together in the old classroom, each of them where they had been before they were funneled into that other place. Lance gripped the edge of the desk with white knuckles, his legs feeling like water as he pieced together what he had just seen and what it meant. Ariana sank onto the floor. Her gaze was fixed on Peter, sympathy etched into the lines of her face. Ben pushed off his own support and started pacing.

"This is what you've been dealing with?"

"You might see why I don't want to talk about it. Remembering it once is bad enough without dwelling in it."

"But I didn't see any—"

"That woman shows up in the last memory I have before I was taken. The next thing I remember is being here, in a dark place with a dirt floor.”

"The cells where they keep us when they're trying to break us." Lance said. "I've been there. It's just as cruel as you remember."

"We'll put a pin in that for now." Ben said, meeting his eye.

"What I don't understand is how this is supposed to help me overcome it. Hear those voices you all do." Peter said.

*"Pain shields him from truth."* The dog-like spirit said. *"Rip it away, and he may hear, for the first time, that which he so desperately does not want to."*

*"In sharing this pain, you may help alleviate him of this block. To know yourself, and then know him, you might hear in him the inconsistency and purge it."* The bird added.

*"Our task is done."* The dog-like spirit said. *"It is up to you now."*

They both faded away, leaving Lothor the only witness to what might come.

# Binding Souls

riana poured over one among the maps she had stolen. The rest were bundled together in a corner of the room. Most of those were maps of the city, but a few were of other levels of the palace. She had thus far failed to come across anything of use, but she would not give up hope.

Lance stood across the teacher's desk from her, examining the layout of the servant's tunnels and the dungeons, that sprawling maze in a subterranean level of the palace which extended far beyond what he had ever anticipated. The dungeons were not precisely under the palace. They might have known that had they thought things over in more detail. The servants tunnels and the chambers housing those elements that kept water and heat and fresh linens flowing to the upper levels provided access to almost every part of the palace, from its towers to its center most reaches, but the dungeons did not expand back into the military complex either. It would have made sense, them being positioned there, but then the military complex was newer than the

# SPIRIT OF SHADOW

palace itself, and the dungeons were a necessary evil in containing those who would see the crown undermined.

They extended, by every appearance, into the cliffs. Underneath the city's first turn and then broadly under hundreds of spans of stone where there could be no possibility of escape. There was but one entrance they might take on foot, and that led first past the interrogation chambers where Rashanna and Peter had been detained briefly before arriving in this classroom for the first time. Together with Ben, they studied their magic with Emma, though she singled Ben out for more intensive forms, as neither Rashanna nor Peter had awakened to the voices of the spirits yet.

Rashanna meditated in a corner, screwing up her face now and again as she traced paths through the chaos of sounds she had only just begun to hear. She faltered frequently, opening her eyes, taking a breath and then driving down into the chaos again.

Peter lay on Ariana's camp bed, his hands laced across his belly, and performed the same ritual. Ever seeking what he could not find, and becoming increasingly frustrated as Emma lobbed jabs at him about his mediocrity.

"What do you think this is?" Ariana pointed to a large, vacant expanse at the far edge of the dungeons, past the majority of the cell-lined avenues that populated most of it. The area was not entirely fleshed out, but bucked up against the edge of the map where it fell into dissolution.

"Probably just a cave." He said. "Or one of the cliffs."

She shook her head. "The edge of the cliffs is marked here." Her finger traveled across the page, followed a sinuous, dotted line that cut across the dungeons to denote something on top of them. The boundaries of the palace were similarly marked.

"Then I'd go with my first guess." He said. "Just a cave.

There's one here, too."

He pointed to another open chamber somewhat north of the one she fixated on.

"I see why you would think that, but look closer. There's a door there." She said. "Two of them. That looks like some kind of chamber. Maybe like the antechamber outside the Grand Hall."

"You think there's something to it?"

"If I was trying to hide something in plain sight, I'd put it somewhere people weren't likely to go looking for it. A cave at the end of the dungeons would be perfect."

"It's so big though. You'd think someone would notice it."

"The military uses security clearances. Maybe this is under the highest level. It could also be behind an enchanted door."

"Which means we wouldn't be able to get through it." He said.

"We could take a look at it."

He shrugged. "Sounds like a bad idea. If we get caught, we'll probably be killed. I doubt they would even stop to interrogate us over something this important."

"The dungeons are under Lord Aren's control."

"We'll never see it if we get him involved."

"So you want to give the Thorns the slip?"

"What are you two talking about over there?" Emma demanded.

"Nothing." Ariana said. "Just maps and shit."

"Well you look way too pleased with yourselves. Knock it off."

"Don't talk to her like that." Peter said.

"Get back to your work, darling." Emma said. "I know it's hard, but you're doing great."

He flicked her off.

"Is that any way to—"

"If you had a sincere bone in your body...."

Ariana met Lance's gaze. "We need to see it. Actually get

our sights on it. If we can't do that, then what's the point in any of this."

"What you're talking about is dangerous." He said low enough that she alone would hear. "We get down there and then what? We can't trust all the Thorns, and if they're patrolling that area, we'd be targets."

"Maybe if we disguise ourselves." She said. "You can hide us with that spirit. The same way you did in the library."

"How did that turn out?" he groused.

She winced.

"Sorry. I just don't think this is a good idea." He said.

"We can leave Peter and Rashanna out of it. They can't do magic like we can. And we can clue in the furnace workers. Take Emma and Duardo with us."

"That's an even worse idea. We'd be putting a target on the furnace workers' backs."

"I see your point." She said. "So we go. Just the three of us. Steal some uniforms from the laundry."

"Peter isn't going to let you out of his sight. Rashanna probably won't be too happy being left out of this either."

"They're a liability."

"If we do this, we'll have to disguise ourselves as Thorns and keep as much distance between us and them as possible. We'll also need an exit strategy if things go south."

"Spirits to call on. Maybe those ones who Lothor called."

"You want to bring them back?"

"I think if we can learn how to use their abilities, it would give us a massive advantage. Especially that one you said looks like a dog."

"Then call for them. Ask them about their natures." He said.

"Okay."

"I didn't really mean—"

"Too late now." She called to Lothor, and he appeared atop

the map.

"Can you bring back that spirit from before?" she asked. "When they showed us Peter's memories."

*"To what end?"* he asked.

"I want to learn its name."

He bowed, splaying his forelimbs. *"If she does not like you...."*

"The bird would be helpful, too." Lance said.

Again, the spider bowed. *"As you wish."*

The dog-like creature and the bird materialized atop the map, both looking somewhat harassed. It seemed they did not want to be here for some reason, but he could not think for why. They had come easily the last time.

*"You call us?"* their gazes fell on Lance.

"In so many words."

"What are you two doing?" Emma demanded. "I didn't tell you to summon any spirits."

"Learning at our own pace, you piece of fuck." Ariana said.

Emma reeled back. She climbed half out of her seat, her fists bunched into tight balls, fury etched into her face.

Ariana sized her up. "Don't start something you can't finish."

"I can finish it." Emma shot back.

"You attack her, and you have me to deal with." Rashanna said. "We're all on the same side here. Leave it alone."

Emma spared a glare for her, but returned to her seat.

"Besides, I thought we liked each other."

"Sometimes." Emma agreed.

"We want to know your names and natures." Ariana explained to the spirits. "I think you can help us."

The bird tittered a laugh. *"So be it. But my companion will not come to you so easily. First prove your worth to her, then she might come."*

"Prove our worth?" Lance said under his breath.

*"The boy is still blocked."* The dog-like spirit said. *"I will

# SPIRIT OF SHADOW

*not cooperate if he cannot hear. The same is true of the girl who tries so hard but hears nothing."*

"So be it." He said, and ventured away from the table to where Peter was laying. "But how do I do this? You haven't been clear on that matter."

*"Know yourself. Then you may know him. More than just silencing can be achieved for the bond forged between mortals."* She said. *"I will go now."*

She disappeared, leaving just the bird to accompany them.

"Your nature?" Ariana asked.

*"One man thought I was a stranger. He searched, for he was sure he was not alone, but call as he might, he was met only with a mocking cry. In the end, he found himself, a mirror in the water to reflect on."*

"Odd way to reference an echo." She mumbled. "I thought that would be much harder."

The bird alighted on her shoulder, unseen and unfelt by her, and its power expressed itself through her, bending her voice as she announced to Lance she had figured out the trick, and causing it to reverberate throughout the room.

"What is your name?" she asked the spirit.

*"It is Bitri."* She said.

"Bitri, thank you, but I think you ought to go for now. I'll call on you later. Zente." She said.

"That was fast." He said.

"The riddle wasn't particularly difficult this time." She replied.

Lothor chuckled. *"May I take my leave?"*

"You need to ask." She asked.

*"A courtesy for a friend of the shadow."* He said. *"You amuse me. Do not forget it."*

"Zente, Lothor." She said, and the spider disappeared.

Lance sat at Peter's bedside, listened for the sounds of the spirits, not their voices but those essences that guided the cruder form of magic used by so many in this palace. Within that chaos, there must be a thread. There had been that business in their first lesson with Emma, that bit about dragging spirits in with the mage's power which she had been adamant was the wrong way to do things.

*There's something there, isn't there?"* He contemplated the sounds spiraling around him, and pulled away from them. In their wake, he was left in a deep pocket of silence, wherein even the sounds in his surroundings were muted. He lingered in that place for a long time, wondering at how it was maintained, what allowed him to suppress the sounds of people talking, of the wind whistling against the classroom's windows and pummeling the stones the tower was made of.

"It's not natural, is it?" he mumbled. "And if it isn't...."

He focused on himself. His heartbeat. The echoing pulse in his temples. He listened to the sounds of his body, driving deeper and deeper as his ears picked up nuances he might never have identified had he not entered this trance. Trickling as of stomach acid churning, as of blood filtering through his veins, the drumbeat of his heart, the vibrating of nerves as they passed messages throughout him all came together, were bound into a rhythm. And something else behind them gave them life, something he couldn't quite place. An electrified sound, it blended those other noises together, made something more of them. Biological processes became a melody, and that melody was joined by another, which guttered again and again to life just beyond his reach, but could not quite sustain itself.

He reached for it, and Peter's breath caught as the melody just found within him twined with that fluttering music, creating a harmony, and a third chain which was derived from the two, which highlighted the nuances between them.

His aura, for that must be what this was, spread over Peter's, wove into holes to fill patches of silence, rests that ought not be there, and filled them with something else.

Something that was entirely him.

He opened his eyes, saw the look of mixed horror and anguish on Peter's face as he held him steady, and then drew away.

"That was strange." Peter said. "It felt so...so invasive."

"Well, it was a start. I don't know what to do now, though."

"I'd rather you never did that again." Peter said. "It felt like you were touching my soul."

"I think I was." Lance said. "And I'm going to have to keep doing it if we're going to fix what's going on with you."

Peter held his gaze for a long moment. He sank back onto the bed, closed his eyes. "I guess there's no other way. Is there?"

# Silencing

They sat in a circle on the classroom floor. The spirits were absent, and though Peter and Rashanna were present, the Thorns were well within shadow, watching from a distance. Quiet hung heavy over their heads, but melodies played in their ears, and those belonged to no spirit. Lance had been the first to reach into the space between them, extending the rhythm of his soul to whoever would accept it. His explanation of what he had done to enmesh himself with Peter had not taken long to be accepted by the others. Absent this new training in the use of magic, Ariana, Peter and Ben had all been taught the trick when first they encountered magic, when they were learning to shadow walk. That they had not been taught to interlock their own rhythms with each other, to hear other melodies of the soul, could only be a strategic move on the part of their betters to prevent them from being able to resist should they seek to rail against the established hierarchy.

Again, as he sat in silence, Lance contemplated how intricate the palace's designs for them had been—how much of what they were taught, where they were allowed to go, how they ended up in their roles, was carefully structured to prevent them from mounting *any* resistance. There was so much nuance in those designs, and all of it organized around a quiet kind of oppression. If they were led to believe each act taken on by their betters was for their benefit, then they may never question whether the whims of those ghouls were just. Even to the extent that there were those who awoke to the truth, how many lived long after discovering it? They could not all have ended up in the furnaces or the kitchens, or what few other departments were helmed by people who knew the truth. There must also be those who descended the staircase, or went hunting in the library, as he had; who were slain when they were found in places they should not be. If Shadovane's elites had thought for how they must be trained, what messages need be drilled into their heads, what they ought to forget, then he could not believe they hadn't thought over how to dispose of their failures. There had been a few who seemed to disappear without a trace  throughout his short life, and he had believed each time they had trespassed on something they shouldn't have.

*It'll be the same with the other servants out there. They probably think we're vicious monsters. That we deserve whatever we're going to get when they find us.*

He felt the tug of another rhythm entwining with his, felt the peculiar sliding sensation echoing through his body, as a melody wove into his and formed a harmonious bond. A gasp from Ben told him who had initiated it. Another shortly followed from Ariana, as she joined with them.

Such intimate contact felt obscene, almost sickening, to him. It was like a warm hand slipping across his spine, a foreign body riding the contours of the bones beneath sheets of muscle and skin, playing cords of nervous tissue like some kind of instrument. His soul felt as if it was being held in suspense half in and half out of his body, as if some excess was being unfolded and drawn taut, as it drew out the slack in the others that touched it.

He sat with his palms resting on folded knees, and opened his eyes to see them looking at him, at each other, with wonder. Though he did not try to fight the sensation off, there was ambient resistance in those bonds, and the harmonies they formed grew in volume, the notes coming on more swiftly as shared power pooled where the three strands formed their web.

A grimoire lay open in the crook between Ben's legs, and he turned his attention to the page. "It says here that in order to silence someone, you need to adjust your rhythm to complement theirs."

"Does that mean to match it?" Ariana asked. "I don't know if I can."

He shook his head. "The language isn't as clear as I'd like, but I think it makes more sense to fill the gaps like Lance did with Peter."

"I guess we'll have to play around with it." Lance said. "Figure out what works and how."

"This would be so much easier if we had a real teacher." Rashanna groused. "I can hear myself, but I can't hear any of you."

"Let go of judgment." Ben said. "You'll get there."

"Besides, that's as much as you need to pull in melodies." Ariana said.

"But you shouldn't." Lance argued. "If you can hear that much, maybe you can hear their voices. You should try."

Rashanna nodded. "Okay."

"It is a little ironic, don't you think?" Peter said. "Asking for a real teacher when we have Thorns watching us all the time. They could show us how to do all of this."

"How much involvement do you think they want with us?" Lance asked.

He shrugged. "I just think it's worth asking them. They were willing to help us learn how to fight."

"The furnace workers are covering that." Lance countered.

"Emma?" he snorted. "She's just a servant. How much can she know."

"Master Gregor trusts her." He said.

"Would you two stop." Ariana cut in.

Ben nodded in agreement. "We're not goin' to figure this out by arguin'."

"I'm just saying—"

"Honey bear, just drop it." Ariana said. "We have more important shit to worry about."

"Rashanna, go ahead. Try it." Ben said, changing the subject.

She leaned back, closed her eyes. Her lips turned down in a slight grimace, and her brow wrinkled with a renewed strain.

*This is progress.* Lance thought to himself as he sought to adjust his rhythm—or perhaps it would be better to think of it as a frequency—without losing contact with the other two.

"I hear...music. It sounds like a bunch of people playing on top of each other. No singing. Just...sounds." Rashanna said.

"That's good. Just keep focusing on them. You'll hear their voices eventually." He said.

"How long did it take you to figure it out?" she asked.

"Figure what out? That I wasn't going crazy?" he chuckled, but there was no warmth in it. "I saw a spider in my window. Night after night. It was just there. At first, I thought the servants who were supposed to be cleaning my barracks had just been doing a bad job, but I kept hearing whispers in the night when I was trying to sleep. Eventually, I decided to talk back.

"I didn't know what I was hearing was related to magic at all at first. I guess the way I came into it wasn't normal, though. But I'm not really normal, am I?"

"No one is." Rashanna said, meeting his eye briefly before descending into meditative silence again.

"Most people can only hear them." He shrugged. "That's my understanding, anyway. I guess I had an advantage because I could see him."

"None of that's going to help us now." Ariana grumbled. "Not with this anyway."

Peter watched them as they worked their forms. His expression was unreadable, but Lance suspected he was upset about all of it. The Thorns did present a potential for better mentorship, but they would report whatever they taught them to Lord Aren, and he didn't want them to know everything about what they were doing just yet. He didn't think that was what was bothering Peter anyway.

*Everyone is making progress, and he's still stuck. It must be frustrating.*

"What about the other thing." Peter asked. "That gate."

"We don't know if there's anything there. It's just a theory at this point." Lance said.

"We should still check it out." He insisted.

"We'd be too vulnerable." Ben protested. "Besides, if we tell the Thorns, they can look into it themselves. They already have clearance to be in the dungeons."

"Can we really trust them?" Lance said. "I'd feel better about it if we didn't involve them—"

"Why?" Peter cut in.

"Because we can't trust Lord Aren." Lance said.

"He's been keeping secrets for you even though he doesn't have to. He set the Thorns to watch out for anyone who could threaten you three." Peter argued.

"He's doing all of that because we're useful to him. What happens when we're not?" Lance said.

"I agree with Lance." Ariana said.

"Great." Peter groused, spreading his glare for both of

them.

"It's not personal, babe. But think about it. If Lord Aren feels like he needs to turn on us to save his own skin, what can we do about it? He didn't get his seat by playing nice."

"He's been working with the rebels." Lance added. "The ones in the city. That's where he came from. It only makes sense he kept his contacts out there. But I doubt the dungeons are packed with foreigners, so he must have thrown some of those rebels to the wolves. Maybe it was when someone else on the council figured out what they were planning, but at the end of the day, he chose to keep his cover and fight another day.

"If someone finds us, we'll be on the chopping block, too. He'll keep his cover, and we'll probably be executed or made to disappear."

"He said he doesn't kill people who don't want to work for him." Peter protested, a dark flush was stealing over his face.

Rashanna snorted. "You believe him?"

"You don't?" he asked.

"Nope." She said. "A smart person doesn't trust anyone she doesn't know well. I agreed to join up because I don't like the nobility or the queen. They're all monsters. But that doesn't mean I think he isn't just as bad."

"Kind of paranoid..." he mumbled.

"All I'm saying is we should make sure *we* know where the thing is before we start thinking about how they fit into everything. That way we have something to go on that he can't just take away from us."

"What we're talking about could get us killed." Peter said.

Lance adjusted his rhythm, tried to match Ben's cadence. He was faced with resistance almost immediately, each note piling on top of something that was already there, amplifying those sounds so that he could barely hear Ariana's contribution to this harmony.

Ben winced. He clutched his temples. "Stop. Stop! That hurts."

"Sorry." Lance eased off, allowing his rhythm to return to its baseline. "Is that better?"

"Yes."

"Are any of you even listening?" Peter snapped.

"Of course we are." Ben said. "To be honest with you, I think we should tell the furnace workers, at least."

"Master Gregor will just tell Lord Aren what's going on." Rashanna pointed out.

"So we just keep it to ourselves, and go on another suicide mission because you said so?" Peter growled. He climbed to his feet, using the desk behind him for support. "I'm taking a walk."

He crossed the room, opened the door and closed it softly behind him. Lance loosed the breath he had been holding. He had been expecting him to slam it.

"Matching rhythms isn't the answer, then." Ben mumbled.

Lance eyed Ariana, his own frustration etched into the lines of his face. "You still think we should take him with us?"

"He's not going to stay if I'm going." She said.

"Am I allowed to go on this mission?" Rashanna asked.

"*You* aren't goin' anywhere." Ben said. "If Peter loses access to the kitchens, so be it. There's not much there that we can't get another way, and Mistress Dina'll know why he's not back without anyone needin' to explain it to her. But you're up in the Office of Operations. The information you can give us is too valuable."

Lance nodded. "Exactly."

"Besides. You haven't been around for the sparring lessons. You'd be useless in a fight." Ariana said. "No offense."

"None taken." Rashanna mumbled.

Lance felt his rhythm shifting, the thread shifting around his, the notes pitching high or low to oppose his. The frequencies canceled each other out, and he was left with just the mundane sounds of people talking, the ambient lowing of the wind, the brazier crackling behind them as it heated their evening meal.

"I think you just Silenced me." He said.

"Good." Ben beamed at him.

"What did you do?" Ariana asked.

"It's hard to explain. I listened for the individual notes. That was the first step. Then I adjusted what was coming from me so that I was hitting matchin' them with their opposites."

"It sounds like they canceled each other out." Lance said.

"Maybe to you. To me, the whole thing sounds much louder. There's a lot of resistance. I don't think I cold hold onto this very long."

"Interesting." Ariana mumbled.

Ben retreated, drew his frequency away from Lance's. He cut off the contact between them.

"Try it with Ariana. We need to be sure it works."

"You weren't enough?" she said.

"It was an experiment. I think we'd all feel more comfortable with some kind of verification." He explained.

"Make sure its repeatable." Rashanna mumbled.

Lance reached out, emulated the tactic Ben had used. He listened to the individual notes in the melody extending from Ariana, listened as the refrain repeated until he was sure he had memorized them in the order they occurred. He adjusted his melody.

"Sky Lord's mercy, that's a lot of resistance. It's like wrestling with a snake." He groused.

He forced his counter melody onto her, bound the two together by the sheer force of his will.

She winced. "Well it works."

Lance let go of the rite, withdrew contact. With the bond

broken, he felt more comfortable in his skin than he had since they started this exercise.

*I'm never going to get used to that feeling.*

Ariana moved over to the brazier to finish with the evening meal. Ben joined her.

Peter returned to the classroom as Ariana was spooning stew into bowls for all of them to eat. He more shambled than walked across the intervening space, and slumped into a chair near the stove.

"Sorry about earlier." He said, avoiding everyone's eyes. "You're right. We should handle this ourselves."

"You sure?" Lance asked.

He nodded glumly. "It's for the best."

# The Gate

coordinated knock on the classroom door saw Ben moving across the classroom to check it. Rashanna stood with Peter in the doorway, and both held sacks filled with supplies which the Thorns behind them contented themselves to let them carry. The Thorns dropped into their shadows without comment as they entered, and Ben closed the door behind them.

Peter's burden hit the floor with a heavy thud. Rashanna set hers down on a nearby desk more delicately.

"Lothor." Lance mumbled.

The spider materialized next to his hand, on the camp bed he sat on. The sheets had been folded and tucked at their corners, and the bedspread was neatly placed and free of wrinkles. It was the only of the three placed here that was made up, but he needed some routine to take the edge off, and tidying up had become a means of passing the time when he had exhausted his stamina trying to amass more skill in magic.

He had picked up a few words in that peculiar language

Lothor and the other spirits spoke. Commands were written in one of the grimoires Ben had stolen for them, and the spirits themselves were keen to teach him enough to work their arts. Lothor, in particular, seemed happy to teach. Even as he spent most of his time writhing in pain, it was as if having something else to focus on, something that might be seen as positive, helped to abate the pressure placed on him by so many using his power without his consent.

"Delanto seyan ojahs." He said. *Shut their eyes.*

Lothor bowed, and a flowering of cold rippled through Lance's body, bled from his feet into the floor where his shadow touched.

"I see you picked up a new trick." Rashanna said, hitting him with a dose of side eye.

"They shouldn't be able to see us, but we should hurry before they catch wise." He said.

"It wasn't easy smuggling those uniforms out of the laundry." She said. "Mistress Rosaline didn't like it."

"At least she knows what's going on." Ben mumbled.

"Does she?" She pulled several servant's uniforms out of the bag, began unbuttoning the coats while Peter rutted around in his sack, pushing aside vegetables before dragging a sack of flour free. He reached into it, came away with a smaller sack and an arm caked with fine powder, brushed himself off and then tipped its contents onto a table.

He shrugged. "She knows what she needs to know.

"Modeling clay." He said as he pulled a chunk of white clay free. "Just like you asked for, babe."

A mischievous grin alighted on Ariana's lips. "Is that for me?"

Rashanna pulled black, woolen shirts out of of the coats, and matching slacks out of those pants. Peter reached into his bag and came away with black, leather boots while Ariana took the modeling clay out of its bag, ripped a chunk off and started working it into shape.

"Did you manage to get any makeup?" she asked.

"No." He said. "Too risky. The noblewomen are the only ones with easy access to it, and those storerooms were too close to the military complex tunnel for us to get into them safely. I guess cosmetics are some kind of critical asset or something."

"They're expensive." Rashanna said. "All those powders and grease paints...I've seen the ledgers. None of them would be caught dead at these parties without *something* to hide behind."

"That explains why they keep them secured." He said.

Ben started organizing the uniforms Rashanna had so cleverly hidden by size. He took up the boots and peeked inside of them, looking for the numbers chalked into their insoles.

"Who's a size seven?" he asked.

"That's me." Ariana said. He eyed her up and down, and passed her a bundle of clothing together with the shoes.

"Size eleven?"

"Me." Lance said.

He passed a bundle to him as well.

"That leaves this one for me." He said to himself. "And...this is yours."

He held out a final parcel to Peter, who was already pulling his boots onto his feet.

Lance pressed his back against the chair he sat in. Its vertical bars pushed back awkwardly around his spine.

"I still think you should sit this one out." He said.

"I'll be okay." Peter replied. "Besides, I'm not leaving Ariana alone."

"I can handle myself." She groused as she struggled into her shirt. "God this thing is tight. Are you sure you got the right size?"

"They're all like that." Rashanna said impatiently.

"Are you ready?" Lance panned over them.

Ben tied his boot. "No, but we should go before we all lose our nerve."

Ariana twisted to show them her work, a sleek, tapered ear extended to a point behind her head. It dropped off immediately.

"Looks like that plan is a bust." Rashanna intoned.

"We can make it work." Ariana protested.

"We'll have to go without them." Lance said. "Without the makeup, we'll draw attention anyway. None of you are all that pallid."

"Fair enough. We'll just have to move quickly and keep our distance if we come across any Thorns." She said, deflating.

"If we get out of here, if we really get out of Shadovane, how are you gonna get us home?" Peter asked.

Impending silence filled the room, a sickle blade hanging over their heads.

"I don't know." Lance admitted. "But if we can escape, we'll have plenty of time to figure it out. If the queen's pendant can take us away, and the Wraiths can't follow us, then there's no reason to think we can't figure out the rest from there."

He sighed. "I thought you'd say something like that."

*"Woohoo. Woohoo."* The door in the cuckoo clock flipped down, admitting a little, startled looking bird and it's scaffold.

Lance glanced at it, noting the time. It was earlier than he had suspected. The long wait for Peter and Rashanna had made the time building up to this moment feel like it was dragging by. He wanted to be done with this errand, to feel in some way safe again. In this moment, he could strum chords on  every nerve in his body; the tension was so high.

"We should go." Ariana said. She was the last to finish dressing.

"Sor eya aiel a'surit, shar'Lothor." Lance breathed.

# SPIRIT OF SHADOW

*"You are not ready for that."* Lothor grumbled.

"Please." He said. "We'll be quick."

"Run with my blood, then. But if you die, you will only have yourself to blame." He said. "They will be more aggressive, the voices of the Dark Heart."

"I will accept the risk." Lance said.

"Do we get a say in this?" Ariana asked.

He rolled his eyes. "Not if you don't want to be seen."

"What exactly did you ask him to do, anyway." Ben said.

"I asked him to open a deeper path." He replied. "Like the Wraiths do when they don't want you to see them."

"A different layer of shadow?" Ben furrowed his brow.

Lance's shadow deepened. In a show of courage, Peter went through first. Ariana and Ben plunged in after him, leaving Lance to take up the rear, and close the way deeper behind him.

A sweat-slick palm wrapped around Lance's forearm and he followed where it led. "Ariana called on Shana already. We'll just follow her." Ben whispered into the stillness.

*"Who trespasses against us shall be blooded."* An unattached voice intoned harshly. *"Dragged over the hull and—"*

It cut off abruptly. Ben's grip on Lance's forearm firmed.

"It's going to be a fight keeping them under control." He said as they moved forward.

"The way is longer, too." Ariana called. "The angle of the lead lines is so much more acute. I can't even see where they've connected."

"Getting back will be difficult, then." Lance mumbled.

"If we get there at all." Ben said. "We might be better off asking Lothor to pull us into a more manageable place."

"We'd be seen then. The dungeons will be crawling with Thorns, and probably Wraiths, too. Who knows how much trust the Council of Liam has left for Lord Aren."

They traveled in silence, following Ariana's voice as they struck down others. Peter positioned himself between them as they marched onward and the whispers picked up intensity, coming more and more frequently as they tried to hold their guard.

"I can't push them back." He whispered. "I can hear them mumbling at the edge of my...." He trailed off as another disembodied voice boiled out of the shadows, and a deeper chill pressed against Lance's soul.

"I'd almost believe they have bodies this deep." Ben said.

"If they did, they'd have killed us all by now." Lance replied.

"Could you please not talk like that. We're not even in the dungeons yet and it already feels like this was a bad plan." Ariana called.

"Well that's interesting." Peter grumbled. "We can always turn back, if you don't want to go through with this."

"I didn't say that." She snapped. "And we have enough on our plate without you being passive aggressive about it."

"Save the arguing for when we're out of this place." Lance cut in. He could almost feel them glaring at each other. "How much further."

"Not sure." Ariana replied stiffly. "Not far, though."

Silence descended once again. They continued, and then halted abruptly. Lance walked into Ariana's back, almost toppled them both over. He felt the tension in her shoulder as she reached for something.

"I think this is the place." She whispered.

A sound like cloth tearing. The shadows parted, revealing yet more shadow.

"That's odd."

"We're deeper inside than usual. Maybe we just need to do it again."

"Maybe."

# SPIRIT OF SHADOW

They all took hold of her as she touched the portal. They rose into an abyssal plane, and Lance reached into the ether then. Another tearing sound, and dim light spilled into shadow. The edges of a poured stone corridor, a wide avenue lined with barred cells, resolved out of the gloom, and he touched the image.

They climbed, and emerged in the world beyond.

"That was creepy." Ben said.

"I feel exhausted already." Peter agreed.

"It's got to be harder when you're still stumbling around in the dark." Ben dry washed his hands against his shirt. He looked nervous standing there with his feet cocked outward and his shoulders slumped.

"Figuratively and literally." Lance added.

"Where are we?" Peter asked.

Lance looked around. The pool of shadows they stood in expanded for some fifty feet in either direction. Glow bulbs glittered in the distance, each trapped inside an aural cloud that preceded an abrupt shift into true darkness.

He could just see a poured stone slab in the far corner beyond one cell's bars. A fist-sized hole was cut into the wall just above it. Being so low on the wall, the air it let in would have created a draft at the back of the prisoner, forcing him to deal with a constant chill or sleep on the floor. It was cold down here, and damp, and there were no blankets on that slab. There was no straw on the stone floor either.

*It must be torture sleeping here.* He thought. *That's probably the point.*

"We'll have to be careful from here out." Ben whispered.

As if to punctuate his warning, an elf clad in form-fitting black reliefs—the collar of his shirt hugging his neck beneath his chin—crossed the hall at an intersection under the light of a distant glow bulb. The harsh light it exuded blocked the crossing path from sight, making it appear the Thorn had

# The Gate

walked directly through a wall.

For several seconds after the Thorn vanished, no one moved.

Lord Aren arrived in the dungeons early. He had been summoned here by the queen's order, and she had been less than forthcoming about the reason. He thought, perhaps, this was to be the moment in which she revealed some knowledge of the conspiracy against her, and his place in it, and stuffed those thoughts down. He had been careful. All these years spent playing his part in the grand scheme, solidifying his place of trust under her and on her council of generals, could not have come unraveled so easily. Not least due to the activities of a handful of servants.

He could understand if she believed the ineffectiveness of his Thorns was related to a streak of incompetence on his part, but she would have to extend that judgment to include the Wraiths, and Lord Giram—still acting as their commanding officer—had not been summoned.

A complement of his men was incoming, and among them would inevitably be those who knew nothing of his schemes, the rebellious acts he was party to. They would pose a complication for him if tidings soured before this visit was over.

He thought, too, perhaps it was Aldeirel's sudden disappearance that had triggered this visit, but then he had escaped before. It was no secret to the Council of Liam there were rebel agents secreted away within the military, and they had made no move to mollify her when she had come to this understanding after the old man's first escape under her rule. She had been furious then, and he suspected her anger was directly related to the eventual appointment of Lord Elise to his position. He did not believe they had been entangled then.

Their relationship had grown into what it was later, when she realized she had found in him a monster of equal depravity to herself.

Perhaps it was heightened scrutiny from the Emperor that drove her to make an assessment of his dungeons, their security. It would make a kind of sense.

The emperor's visit might be seen by the nobility as some supreme honor, but he suspected it was anything but that. Ten years it had been since his last visit, and in that time he had largely turned a blind eye to affairs in Shadovane. He did not need to come in person with the Light Well in his possession, an artifact ancient beyond reckoning, it provided him all the insight he needed. He could see, plainly enough, in its waters, all that transpired across the Sun Empire, see further into other lands. With that kind of surveillance at his disposal, there was little need for him to do more than send an occasional messenger under guard to their city.

No, he had come as a warning. Seeing this latest incarnate of his one great love rising too high for his comfort, he had come to remind her that she was, in the grand scheme, both inconsequential to him and replaceable. A military was of little consequence in foreign affairs during peacetime, and they had been at peace for thousands of years. No longer was there war between the Immortals and the Ten Kings. The Legion of the Sky was a relic of a largely forgotten past, and what threats remained to the emperor were domestic.

A rebellion in the borderlands could be met with a strategic blow to its leadership. With no one charismatic enough to lead in his stead, the would be usurpers would fade back into dissolution, vow to fight another day.

His arrival here had been timely, plotted explicitly to remove some influence from his concubine, and return a measure of fear and respect to the true throne of empire, where it belonged.

He marched toward the interrogation cells, where he intended to await her, and nearly stumbled as his gaze fell on a girl. Her servant's uniform was covered in old blood and her eyes shown an electrified blue. He had not seen her since inviting those Watchers to use her, wondered what they wanted. Why they had chosen this moment, at the worst of times, to reveal their surrogate to him.

"What do you want?" he asked. "And be quick about it. I'm expecting company of a kind that could destabilize what you've built."

"An interesting characterization of our activities." Sami spread her hands. "We will require our bodies soon. They are hidden here, are they not?"

"They are in a cell in the oldest part of this reach." Lord Aren agreed. "My men have seen to it you were fed and kept hydrated. I can do nothing for any atrophy that may have occurred."

"No need to worry about that." She said. "We require them to be moved. Somewhere more easily escaped than behind cadmium lined bars."

"I can arrange to have the door left open."

She clucked her tongue. "No, I'm afraid that will not do. They will need to be moved discretely to a chamber near the largest of this palace's ball rooms."

"You know of the Council of Liam's plot, then."

"We have looked into the minds of some servants with knowledge of these events."

"That was risky."

She nodded. "Sometimes risk is necessary. The nobility now fears for their lives. They do not understand our motives as well as your peers, and that serves our interests. Yours and mine.

"But move them. We will make our final move in this vessel there, and then release our hold on her."

"I will have loyal men stationed nearby so that they can assist her in escaping."

"That is for the best."

"Now, please move along. I cannot be seen in your presence lest I be required to slay you."

She bowed. "Your friends in the Teacher's Tower...they are here also."

He cussed under his breath. "Their guards?"

"Oblivious. It seems they have figured out a few tricks since you last saw them."

"The complications never cease." He mumbled as they departed down a corridor and away, deeper into the dungeons.

A few moments passed. He contemplated sitting in the nearest interrogation room, but did not have time to make a decision before his guests arrived.

Queen Meredith glided into the corridor with the emperor himself looming over her shoulder.

*What in the name of....*

"We require your assistance, Lord Aren." She said before he could find enough sense to prostrate himself. He dropped onto the floor and pressed his forehead to the ground. "Your excellence."

"Waste no time on formalities." The emperor chided. "Inform your Thorns they are to secure all avenues within these dungeons, ensure no active cell is left unguarded. All of those you have captured are to be under the direct watch of your men. As well, double security in the twenty-second corridor where it adjoins the twenty-fifth."

"The very edge of these dungeons." Lord Aren whispered. He climbed to his feet, bronze-shod boots scraping against poured stone. "Do you require escort."

"We will go it alone." The emperor said. "See to it that no one approaches us."

He bowed. "It will be done."

They passed him by, and he marched to the dungeon entrance to pass orders to the men stationed there, both captains in his ranks.

Lance gestured in the opposite direction.
Ben shook his head.
"Why?" Lance asked.
"A hunch." Ben replied. "The air's weird."
Ariana glanced in the direction the Thorn had come from.
"I saw a staircase on the map." She said.
Peter sucked his thumb.
Lance raised an eyebrow at him. *What kind of absurd....*
He pulled his wet thumb out of his mouth and held it above his head.
"What the fuck are you doing?" Ariana growled, echoing Lance's thoughts.
"Testing the air." Peter said. "The draft is going that way." He pointed in the direction where the Thorn had gone. "We should go that way, too. Your staircase might be over there."
"Fine." Ariana said. "Let's just go before we get caught."
"We can still go back." Peter intoned.
"Fuck off." Ariana hissed. "We're doing this."
They hurried on, passing the intersection. Darkness filled adjacent corridors much like the one they traveled. In the distance, Lance saw the glint of other glow bulbs as they breezed into another shadow strewn length of hall.
Just before the next intersection, Peter tested the air again. He led them down a side hall.
"Hey." The whisper came from inside a cell. Lance spun on his heels. Peter skidded to a stop. "Help me get out of here."
Ben caught a handful of Lance's shirt and pushed him forward.
"Fine. Fuck you, too." The prisoner shouted.
Lance was the first to start running. The others pelted after him.
They cleared three more crossings before Peter finally passed Lance. He stretched out his arms, blocking the rest of

them, slowed and then halted.

Lance collided with his back. His nose squished painfully against his lip. They fell over in a tangle of limbs.

"Shh." Peter said.

Ben tested the air as he had seen Peter do. He gestured down another corridor, but Ariana shook her head. She pointed to a wooden door whose face was painted black to blend in with the shadows that contained it. A tile bearing a black triangle was situated next to it at level with the knob.

"You think?" Ben asked.

"Why is it not guarded?" Lance wondered aloud.

He sat up, rubbing his nose. Peter helped him get on his feet.

"Sorry." Peter said. "We were being pretty loud. I was paranoid."

"It's okay." Lance replied in an effort to mollify him. "I panicked when that guy—"

"Is now really the time?" Ben cut in.

He approached the door. Lance, Ariana and Peter took watches of the adjoining halls.

Ben twisted the brass knob. He jerked it open.

A torch-lit staircase descended along a spiral track on the other side. The torches burned a conspicuous shade of violet. He urged the rest of them to get through, and closed the door softly when everyone was safe on the other side.

They hurried down the stairs. None of them were convinced of their safety, even being away from the dungeon halls. The staircase bottomed out against another door. It was identical to the first, with the same black triangle riding a tile next to it.

Lance reached for the knob. The other three piled in to one side.

He whispered the name of the spirit of shadow, thinking to test for defenses against a hasty exit if he could. He was met with a wall of silence.

"I can't make the shadows respond." He said "They won't cooperate. I can't open mine."

"Me either." Ben said.

"Let me try the other way." Peter said.

"That'll just piss him off." Lance protested.

"Do you see a better option?" He insisted.

Lance scowled at him. "Fine."

Peter looked to his shadow, his teeth grit together as he attempted a rite he had no business trying.

"No luck?" Ben asked.

He shook his head.

"Would you guys shut up already?" Ariana snapped.

Silence descended.

Ben was smiling for whatever reason. Ariana looked nervous, and Peter's eyes were so wide Lance would have thought he'd been drugged. He'd never seen his friend so fearful. Then again, Peter had been distant from the rest of them in the Royal Library. He could just as well have been this spooked then.

Lance cracked the door open and peered through the slit. Ben, Ariana and Peter piled in around him.

Through the crack, he could see what appeared to be a cave. The ceiling was high and domed. Stalactites marched away from a massive, glowing crystal that drove the shadows out of the room, and a mesmerizing arch stood out in stark relief at its heart.

The arch was a twisted, marble mass that spun from origin to end like the stream of water following a large fish as it broke a lake's surface, frozen in time before it could fall and rejoin the current. Violent, sky blue veins broke up its surface. Like gnarled roots or lightning, they ran through the stone, broken and uneven, raking at its bones. Within that arch was housed an aurora. It rippled and flowed like cloth, and radiated light in all of the colors and their hues—from vibrant greens to virulent reds, from ocean blue to sun yellow, every color present, shifting and vibrant.

He had never seen anything like it. It was beautiful, awe-inspiring in the way it seemed to bend the laws of nature to its will.

Someone whistled. A smack cut the sound short. Lance received a nudge, and looked around to find Ariana peeling her hand away from Peter's mouth. Ben pointed earnestly back through the door.

Lance returned his attention there. The emperor stood before the veil. As he watched, a harmony shattered the quiet, a sound like many voices screaming, and underneath it, symphonic harmonies played with an elegance to make a man weep. Green light passed through the veil, a capsule that preceded the arrival of a figure clad in a scarlet-slashed dress—the skirts black and flowing, the bodice tight across her breasts. The light faded when she was beyond the gate.

While the kitune woman eyed the emperor, by every appearance sizing him up, another green capsule emerged from the veil. This one contained the Shadow Queen. Her gown was lavender embellished with warm, golden-white pearls.

"Time to go." Ariana whispered.

Lance held up a hand to stop her.

"Who is *she?*" Peter mumbled

"Good of you to come." The emperor said, but his welcome lacked warmth.

"My extreme displeasure, Light of Ignorance." The kitune woman's words had a stabbing quality, like knife thrusts.

"Were it that another of your order was chosen for matters of diplomacy, we would all be better served." The emperor said.

"I would sooner it was the Watcher bitch, myself." Queen Meredith added. "Much as she fills my mouth with bile."

"While this is truly pleasant, I am sure you did not summon me here to insult my allies." The kitune woman said.

"No, I certainly did not." The emperor agreed. "We signed an accord."

"I signed no such thing." The kitune woman said.

"As a surrogate for King Ferenze and his steward, you are bound by its terms like the rest of us. Seek to violate those terms, and you will be replaced."

"Like all of your concubines." The woman looked pointedly in Queen Meredith's direction. "This one's better than the last one you sent, I'll give you that. She's a fair bit smarter, but then you've never liked that in a woman, have you?

"Prefer them *meek* and subservient, yes?"

"You flatter me." Queen Meredith touched her heart, but there was nothing in her eyes to suggest she felt anything other than contempt.

"Time to go." Peter whispered.

"Okay, just...." Lance slid the door a hair closer to closed. He paused when the woman spoke again.

"You are quite as vain as your new name suggests if you think Lord Zouis would so easily rid himself of such a powerful weapon. That he would risk Arganon's loyalty, more so."

Ice ran through Lance's veins. Those were the names of two of the Ten Kings. He thought he knew who she was, too. A very dangerous woman, an enemy. *Why is she here?*

"Time to go." Peter repeated.

He eased the door the rest of the way closed.

"What did she just say?" Ben asked. "I didn't quite—"

"Later." Lance insisted. "Now, we go."

He moved away from the door.

Ariana was already three steps up the staircase. They ran for higher reaches.

Meredith's attention was fixed on Llayne's back. Not a

queen in truth, nor a power akin to those relics of the past—
The Immortals and the Generals Elite of the Legion of the
Sky, all turned kings and queens of their own territories—she
had come into some power to extend her life and the reach of
her hand since the capture and incarceration of her
predecessor. Llayne was not a queen, no, but she enjoyed the
kind of influence a queen did in her land of Demeli, had risen
from the ashes of Lun and fled to join their enemies, carrying
everything she knew of the Sun Empire's dealings, their
secrets, all of those critical assets they possessed in the time
of Queen Anastasia.

More than most of those rulers, she was a danger
specifically tailored to counter the Sun Empire, should open
war ever break out. And though Meredith hated her, she
found in her also a rare respect, humility, and inspiration.
Llayne had done what no one else in the history of this
sprawling empire had; what queens of Shadovane past had
failed to do despite their best efforts. She had undermined the
throne, had stolen off with all of her power, and suffered no
consequence for any of it.

Llayne bored into Conan's eyes, daring him to inflict what
harm he so clearly wanted to on her. There was no fear in her
gaze. Her pose was stable, her shoulders square. If she had
learned lessons in the wake of her betrayal, they had been
different, emboldening her to confidence in the face of this
creature. She did not have to act in secret, plot and scheme in
the shadows, amass weapons that might be used to claw her
former ruler down the few pegs necessary to make him equal
to her. In her mind, he was already beneath her, dirt on her
shoe.

"We seek only what we have always sought, Light of
Ignorance." She said softly. "The movements of that gang you
have thus far failed to keep contained have become an
alarming reminder of what happened under their previous

leader. We are concerned they may violate our border at Gorozoan, and threaten our military activities in that region at a time of immense volatility which King Baris has need to meet with subtlety.

"Should they mount an attack on our border, we will consider them to be acting on your behalf, and respond accordingly."

"They are not acting on our orders, and you know that." Conan said, matching her tone. "They will nonetheless be dealt with. If that is the only reason you sought this meeting, we could have handled this via messengers."

"No, this is a matter of pretense." She said. "I suspect you understand that quite well. Rather it has come to our attention you possess persons of interest to us which we would like to see assumed into our control. People we thought you had exterminated in the wake of the incident at Lazul."

"You wish to have my citizens extradited? What do I get in return?"

She clucked her tongue. "Access to a vital bit of intelligence. A useful agent in Darkridge has recently come across something we believe you will find of interest, as it pertains directly to you, and your Shadow of Lies."

He stepped forward. She was a wall in his path, unmoving.

"Send word to your master, then." He said. "If he wishes to negotiate in good faith, he will convene with my concubine in person. I would have it that she heard his words from his own mouth."

Meredith stiffened on reflex. She tried to cover it by shifting closer to Llayne. "If that is all."

"The conspirators are the usual suspects, of course. The site of the disturbance is to be Aranor, in your borderlands. You know what lay under the city." She said. "Consider our proposal, but know your time is limited. Not a matter of patience." She shook her head. "Though I would disagree with him in this, King Zouis believes we have ample time to wait;

however, there is no telling when these Crossmen will act. And when they do..." she spread her hands. "Do not squander our generosity."

"Who is it you want us to release into your custody?" Meredith asked, earning her a hard look from Conan.

"Know your place, woman." He spat.

"It is a fair question." Llayne said, a sly expression on her face as she turned to set her gaze on the Shadow Queen. "Of course, you cannot expect us to show our hand having gained nothing from you. I will arrange an audience between your queen and King Zouis.

"Now, I would like to leave."

"You do not command me?" Meredith hissed.

"My mistake. Though it appears your master does not either. Not near as well as he believes." At the look of suspicion that passed from Conan to Meredith, she cackled. "So easily led. Arganon would be so pleased."

"Go back to your home then. I have nothing more to say to you." Conan growled.

Llayne turned toward the gate. "Come, woman. The decor in this place has me wanting for home. Your taste is...well, you are certainly not your predecessor."

Meredith whispered a curse for her as she positioned herself before the arch. She raised her hands, drew on a power not bound to the spirits, which was her right to wield as the Mother of Night Incarnate. The stone in her pendant, that fragment of Celesti's soul made physical, pulsed with harsh, green light, as she spread her arms as if to embrace that ethereal curtain. The threads of enchanted cadmium, those lightning-like veins, emanated white light, their color deepening almost to black as she performed the work of opening the way. Llayne did not wait for her, but stepped through the arch.

She spared a last look over her shoulder at Conan,

registering the anger there. *He'll be insensate by the time I return. I'll tread lightly for the time being.*

She passed through the arch behind the Steward of Demeli, and into another world.


At the top of the stairs, Lance wrenched the door open and flung himself into the dungeon hall. He ran into something soft and woolen. His gaze traveled up the snug shirt to the glaring face of a shadow elf. Worse, a Thorn.

He disengaged.

"Fuck." Ariana whimpered.

Lance opened his mouth to call on a spirit, thinking to summon fire to burn him. The Thorn clapped his hand over his mouth.

He cast around.  The Thorn was not alone. He was one of several in the crossing. Still more were incoming.

"Be still. We have little time. They will expect me to attack you if you resist."

He removed his hand, but Lance was not the only one who had thought to resist. Already, heat was swirling around Ben, casting mirages into the air as three foxes sat in a line next to him, watching intently as what might have been a containable situation unraveled.

"BEN NO!" Lance shouted.

He threw the rite in motion. Fire blasted away from him, a wave that caught several of the Thorns as it passed, sparing the one who held Lance as the Thorn drew water out of cold air to stave it off.

Steam hissed from the site of impact.

Screams punched the air.

Ariana, Ben and Peter scrambled to their feet.

Blood flew as those others closed in on the scene. The musty odor of iron tainted the air.

"*Bitri!*" Ariana shouted.

Her voice echoed away from her, came back up the hall as

# SPIRIT OF SHADOW

a bird in silhouette materialized over her shoulder.

Pain ripped through Lance's guts as he struggled to get past the oncoming Thorns. He collapsed, bashing his jaw on the poured stone floor.  He looked up to see claws like smoke and shadow dressing the hands of the Thorn closest to him as he thrust down for the killing blow. Song in the voices of several spirits accompanied the Thorn's rite. With them, a guttural, pained growl he associated with a friendly spider.

Ben was there in the next moment, lashing out with blue flame as several others shielded their ears, their eyes squeezed shut against the carrying sound from the Spirit of Echoes.

Figures boiled out of the walls to meet them, reflections of those Thorns attempting to kill them. What protection they may have had from Lord Aren's men was cast off as they turned on the reflections, attempting to save their cover by aiding in those others' disposal.

Wraiths streamed out of shadow as Ben called to Lothor.

Lance felt his gut. It was sticky, tender. There were too many ridges there.

Hands dragged at him in both directions. Ben cast fire against another figure.

"I can't hold out much longer!" Ariana hollered.

The hands on Lance's ankles released their grips as the pork odor of smoldering flesh and the musk of burned wool filled his nostrils.

Hands under his arms. Dragging him back. Harsh cold against his back and then....

Shadows played with his eyesight. He was blind.

"It's gonna be okay." Peter whispered. "I got you. We're gonna be fine."

He dropped Lance, shouting. Heat washed over Lance's face, followed by the sounds of a scuffle, a scream and something heavy dropping.

Peter's hands were on him again. Ben was calling to Lothor again. They plunged through a rent in shadow. Deeper.

He was being dragged, Peter babbling incoherently as he pulled him along behind Ben and Ariana.

Shouts rang out in the distance, and he was not sure if they belonged to the Dark Heart or Shadovane's forces.

A hole shredded the darkness. Light spilled in, revealing the contours of a classroom.

The quieter light of candle flame pushed back the gloom as he lay gasping against solid ground, the mundane sights of the world outside a welcome relief after their flight through shadow.

"Did they...see us?" He croaked.

"I don't know." Peter said.

Pages flipped too fast and the sound of heavy breathing replaced Peter's voice.

"This is deep." Ariana said. Her voice quivered.

"What happened? Why is he...?" Rashanna demanded.

"Never mind that now." Ben said. "He's going to die if we don't do somethin'."

His voice echoed oddly back to him.

"Zente, Bitri. The danger isn't here." Ariana said, her voice shaking.

Pain bloomed in his stomach. Lacking the strength to cry out, he hissed.

"Where is it?" Ben shouted. "There has to be something."

Thorns boiled out of the shadows in the walls.

Ben opened his mouth, cold terror rippling through him without rational thought to guide it.

"Stop!"

A thread of music rippled across the room, and whatever Ben had been about to do disintegrated behind a wall of silence.

"Are you—"

"Lord Aren's, yes. Now step back. He needs healing."

"What you did was reckless and stupid." His companion said. "You could all have been killed. To plot this out while the Queen and the Emperor were present...."

"We...we didn't. It wasn't intentional." Ariana whispered. "We didn't know they were...."

"They know you were there." He snapped. "They will lean on the Council of Liam more now than they have before. Lord Aren will not be able to keep you safe here."

"We...we didn't know if...if we...."

"Out with it girl!" the first snapped.

She shook her head.

"They still don't trust us." The other said.

Hands on Lance's midriff, pressing down against the wound. Pain like he had never felt, fire clashing with his insides, gnashing teeth biting into organ meat. Then cold, the shock that came with it.

More hands met his torso. Light pulsed. His insides writhed. Something rocky sloughed away from is skin. His vision cleared. Ice and heat warred for control of his body.

The feeling faded, leaving him alone for one, blissful moment, floating on a quiet sea. *Adrift.*

He looked around himself as his vision cleared.

The Thorns had retreated, leaving space to be filled by his friends.

Ben and Ariana were covered in blood. Peter stood next to him with one hand on his chest, the other laced together with Ben's, his face hidden in the crook of his shoulder. He peered out, saw that Lance was okay, that he had by some miracle of luck been healed.

Rashanna leaned against a desk, candle light illuminating her round face, touching on hooded eyes as she clutched her chest.

"Did they see us?" Lance asked.

"Yes, they did!" the angrier thorn snapped again. "Be grateful we were able to subdue them while you ran off. That trick won't get you far a second time."

"It was foolish to go it alone." The other said. "What you did could have put everything in jeopardy."

"What in the Sky Lord's name could you have been after down there, anyway?" The first thorn gestured wildly, his face contorted in a rictus of rage.

"Calm down. They had a near brush with death. Anger will not help them now."

He fixed his glare on his peer. "If it keeps them from doing something that reckless again, it's justified. Would you treat another soldier any differently?"

"These are not soldiers. Much as they would like to pretend otherwise. Now, what is it you were seeking down there."

"Answers." Lance gasped. "A gate. Proof it worked."

"We got both." Ben mumbled.

"This gate...what is it intended to do?"

Ben, Ariana and Peter were silent. They exchanged nervous glances. The Thorns took note.

The more reasonable of the two sighed. The other began to pace.

"After all we've done for you, you still don't trust us." The reasonable one said. "Spending our days looking after your hidey hole so that you don't get caught by the wrong people. Putting our lives at risk to keep you safe. Even healing your friend of the injury—"

"—A foolish, reckless, asinine—"

"—he landed himself with for his shortsightedness. Is none of it enough."

"Tell me something." Lance said. "If you were in my shoes, would you trust your leader?"

The one stopped pacing.

The other glared at him. "Of course."

"That's foolish." He said. "It's not *you* I don't trust. It's *him*. They don't trust him either.

"We're new to this, but what seems clear is that he didn't get his position without making sacrifices. How many people has he killed, imprisoned and betrayed to keep his role in all of this a secret? You can't blame us for thinking he'd throw us to the wolves if we got between him and whatever it is he wants."

"He wants a free Shadovane, kid." The incensed Thorn growled. "It's what we all want. You and that girl have been making it damned difficult to get there lately."

"They've figured out a lot we never anticipated we'd find."

"And yet half the palace is hellbent on hunting them down. They suspect they have allies in the city and the palace. How much damage do they have to do before it robs us of our ability to move effectively."

"So you don't trust us, either." Lance said.

"Of course not!" they snapped.

"You see my point, then." He sat upright. "Thank you for healing me. And you should tell Lord Aren I appreciate everything he's done for us. But if you want to know what we know, we need some kind of assurance that he's not going to let us all die if he feels his own status is being threatened. We've already sacrificed almost everything we had for a cause we barely understand. What has he given up."

The Thorns exchanged a look. Neither of them brought a challenge to him right off. Then one of them, the angrier one, lifted his shirt. The other reached out to stop him, but he shook him off.

He raised his shirt up to the collarbones, exposing a pale chest and stomach. Across one peck was a brand in the style the Wraiths carried, with a portrait at the heart of the knot of script.

"That is my brother." He said. "The lone way a commoner can enter the Wraith Core is by killing a close relative in combat. A brother, or a father, or a cousin. To prove our loyalty to the crown. The practice started generations ago. Queen Tania stopped enforcing it for a time, later in her life. When Queen Meredith brought it back, it felt so much like a betrayal. She was from the slums like any of us. She should have known better."

"She's a psychopath." The other whispered.

"He has one just like this. Most of us do. Those of us who joined the cause. You know, you're not the only ones who've lost people. I didn't want to kill him, but he forced me to. He was dying anyway. There's never enough out there to eat. No one has the strength left to heal." His words came out thick now. He rolled his shirt back over the tattoos. "So maybe the next time you want to behave like a bunch of asshole kids, you'll think twice about it. We're not your enemies."

"We found a document in the library." Lance said, earning him cautious looks from the rest of them. "Can you...Ben, can you get it for me."

"We can't—"

"Time for games is over. If they want a show of trust, they can have it. We've taken as much as we can from it anyway. Now get it. Please." He said.

He rushed to a desk where their books and scrolls were stacked, and took *The Compact* from the top of one. He brought it to him.

"Take this to Lord Aren. I don't know how the spellbinding on it works, but maybe he can use it."

"What...what is it?"

"A treaty. Nothing in it makes much sense. Kind of undermines what we were told of the lay of the lands." He explained. "But there are things in there we were able to verify tonight. The gates it mentions exist. The queen's pendant can open them. If this is correct, they're all in strategic locations, near centers of government. But there are rules for how they can be used, and the pendant is the key.

"I think...I think we need to steal it if we're going to get out of here."

"Our plans don't include escaping." The Thorn who took it said, looking to his counterpart.

"They do now." Lance said.

"For a child to—"

"Quiet." The Thorn held up a hand. He kept his attention on Lance. Helped him move closer to the teacher's desk, to lean against it. "Now, if I may be candid."

Lance nodded.

"Master Gregor, Mistress Dina, Mistress Rosaline, and Master Jalen have all been working with us for some time. Since Queen Meredith rose to power and enslaved them."

"Who is Master Jalen."

"Master over the Gardeners." The other Thorn said. "They're the ones who were smart enough not to resist. The rest from their generation are dead."

"Leaving your handling to a handful of nobles. That's not important right now. Most of you servants are former orphans who were sold to us by poachers. Some of you are political prisoners. I can understand why you would want to escape, but for the rest of us...this is our city. This is our home. Whatever may have come to pass here to make it into what it is today, we can fix it. Queen Tania was not so bad. If the next incarnate is another like her, we may fair better."

"That *slum lord* was our best hope before." The other said. "Look how she turned out."

"We weren't in open rebellion then."

"If you still think..." Lance gasped. The healing done, some residual pain was still ambient in the region where the injury had been. Breathing was difficult with the area around his ribs still stiff. "...you can change anything about this city while the Emperor is in control, you are more foolish than any servant. He will never loosen his grip on this place. It's too important to him."

"How would you know—"

He took the book from Ben and flopped it into the Thorn's lap. "This explains a lot more than just how to get away from here. It doesn't leave a lot of room for hope, but it *is* instructive. We want to escape, and get everyone else who still has some good in them out of here with us. It can be done...with that pendant. If we can steal it."

"We can't use it without her." Rashanna pointed out. "Someone has to be able to use it."

"I think I can." He said. "If I can get my hands on it."

"How certain are you?" The Thorn asked, picking up the book and tucking it into his waistband.

"Not certain at all, but I'm clearly unique. If I can see the spirits, there's something going on with me that isn't normal. And in all of those books we took, the only one that mentions anything like this lays it at the hands of a king in the Free Lands who has lived as long as any of the Immortals. Maybe longer. He must use the same power as them, and if we're alike...maybe...maybe I can, too."

"That would set an alarming precedent, kid." The other Thorn said, but his anger was giving way to curiosity as he eyed the book secured against his counterpart's back.

"We'll take what you've told us back to Lord Aren. Don't make any moves until we have a *clear* strategy, okay." He intoned. "We can't afford you blowing up our whole operation right now. Not with the Emperor still here."

"If we don't move soon we may not have a chance again." Lance said.

The Thorns panned over the others, who all wore different masks. They were clearly discomforted by the idea of putting themselves in the line of fire while Mirrhvale's forces were present, but he believed Ariana saw his logic. He shared it with the rest of them.

"Emperor Conan and Queen Meredith have a tense relationship, don't they? He might be the best distraction we have. When he's gone, she'll have nothing to focus on except finding and killing us. So, if we're in some way important to your plots, it's better to move before he leaves."

The Thorns locked eyes.

"We knew we were going to have to make a move of some kind before then, anyway." The one who had been eying the book said.

"To keep them secure." The other argued. "We'll leave it to Lord Aren. We shouldn't give these kids false hope that he'll go along with their ideas."

"I take your point."

The Thorn checked the book in his back pocket. He called on Lothor, and they plunged into their shadows.

# Reflections On The Past

Lord Aren studied the book laid open on top of his desk. Just having a copy of this text could see him executed. Not knowing who the copy belonged to, which of the original documents it was tied to, posed its own complications. He knew what this text was, had seen a copy just once in his lifetime, and had not been close enough to read it.

It had been while on a surveillance operation in the Thirteenth Ward that he first encountered it. Two men, both now infamous, had been pouring over the text, discussing its contents such that though he saw their lips moving, he could not make out most of the words they spoke. They had been all smiles as they poured over the details therein, speaking at the same time of ancient beings who were revered in some cultures as deities. The Five Saints, the Ten Kings, the Immortals...a few others.

He reached for the book, hesitated.

# SPIRIT OF SHADOW

Contained in these pages was the truth of a long dead era. Here were references to events that transpired thousands of years in the past, which had laid the template for the workings of their modern world. There was no single document more consequential in the world than this text.

He leaned back in his chair, shot a glance at the shepherd's hook hung over his head. *Was it one of hers who translated it? Could that be why she sought to separate the Ring of Fire from the Empire?*

His gaze drifted back to the text. The cover was worn, the lettering mostly scrubbed away so that but one word remained to call to what it was. *Compact. The Compact of Morania...accords guaranteeing peace between the Ten Kings, the Ancient Ones and the Immortals, ending the bloodiest war our kind has seen, and guaranteeing the erasure of a deeper history as it did.*

He laced his fingers together in his lap. The cabinet he kept filled his periphery, and an itch formed in his chest, where the brand he'd received when he became a Wraith was tattooed into his flesh.

He climbed from his seat, rounded on the cabinet and drew its doors open. He pulled down on a bar supporting several hangers with uniforms for various occasions hanging from it, and a hidden door in the back popped open.

He pushed aside the raiment and slid the door aside, unbuttoned his tunic and let it drop behind him.

A mirror looked back at him, a letter pinned to the wood next to it, and beneath that, a compass. In the mirror, two faces passed their judgment. His own, and his brother's framed by vows to serve the Shadow Queen and the Sun Empire. Vows that meant nothing to him.

The letter was written in his brother's handwriting, and the battered old compass, its needle tightened so that it pointed due east and would not move, had belonged to him, too.

*There is a land out there where we can be free. One day, you'll see it. Let my sacrifice guide you to the land and the king who will shelter us.*

*If it is here, brother, we must fight for it. We cannot surrender. We can never give up. You will have to fight for it with everything you have, but do not place all of your hopes in this place. It is home, but if home cannot be a place of safety, it is best you look elsewhere. Do not leave our people behind. Do not seek to betray my legacy. We have given everything to this cause.*

*Let my death mean something, and do not feel guilty that it is your hand which delivers it. We have known for sometime that I will not survive to see our paradise. Mother has kept me comfortable, but I must go the way father did. I am the founding stone on a path to a brighter future. Remember it. And if you see it one day, lay me to rest.*

*I have faith that you will.*

He slid the door gingerly shut, steeling himself as tears threatened to spill from his eyes, and returned with the compass to his desk.

He seated himself, ran his thumb over its face as he flipped the cover of that ancient treaty open, and began to read.

It did not take long to get through the document. It was no lengthy thing. It spelled out terms for the division of lands, who would claim authority where, which zones were to be neutral and who had latitude to handle matters of diplomacy. It was straightforward, written for practicality. The language was not flowery or complicated, though the translation had been done rather poorly. It had been no scholar who drafted this thing.

Nonetheless, hidden truths peered out through plain text, mounting a case that not all was as it seemed.

*A land of spirits. Pillars. A plane that has nothing and*

*everything to do with either. Why would the Immortals give such a boon to the Ten Kings if they had won this war? Why would either party bother with a treaty if their victory over the other side was at all decisive. This reads less like a treaty than a constitution.*

He closed the document, flipped it over so that the eroded name was visible to him.

His brother's words rippled through his mind, an echo of what the Thorns told him of those children's wants.

*Let my sacrifice guide you to the land and the king...who will shelter us. It is best you look elsewhere...survive to see our paradise. If it is not here....*

"What would you do in my place?" he mumbled, flipping the compass over in his hands, feeling the fine chain slide against his wrist. "Would you fight, knowing even her death might not fix what is broken? Or would you flee in hope that you might find a better place?

"If the opportunity presented itself to bring everyone out, even if it was slim, would you take it?"


Sami emerged from shadow in the armory. Lord Halan was fussing over a suit of armor which belonged to a common maul, pulling out a dent in the breastplate with a tool designed for the purpose. He worked a crank in the device as he stabilized the piece of armor with his palm.

Several armorers, seeing her, stopped what they were doing. She saw, from her vantage, the fear in their gazes.

"Please not him." She whimpered. "He's not one of them. He can't be."

"We are not here to kill him." The Jua Watcher said. "He is nonetheless important to us."

"Then...you're not going to hurt him?"

Through her vantage, she saw the Master of the Armory turn around, square himself in the face of the insurgent, of her. A song bloomed from him, threatening violence, and was snuffed out under Silencing pressure from the Watchers acting through her.

His eyes flashed blue. His head snapped up, and he collapsed.

Lord Halan clawed at the floor tiles, attempting to right himself. Pressure bared down on his back, keeping him still. He looked around at his charges as one by one their eyes flashed and they collapsed.

Tears leaked from the eyes of some. Harsh whimpers and gasps issued from each of those affected by Sami's alien power. A tangle of disjointed memories swirled through his mind as his once friend forced him to witness all she returned to them.

Scenes of violence, of fire and blood, of dealings with poachers, of children being seized from their parents, their parents being put to death, stormed through him.

He stopped resisting, fixed wide eyes on Sami, those cold, lightning blue eyes so incongruous in a face ill suited to them.

"You're..." he breathed. "You're not you."

"No, she is merely serving as a vessel for us." She said. "If you are among the good in this palace, reflect on the truth, and pick a side."

More memories pushed the others aside, spelling out how they had come into his care, how each and every one of these servants was tortured, raised to believe a complex series of lies, and then forced to forget their former lives. How those people who had been attacked and slain by her hand were complicit in the conspiracy.

Her unnatural gift retracted from him, leaving him to linger in this miserable state. To linger with the dark truths that made this whole system possible implanted in his mind's eye.

"You have allies." She said. "Go to them."

# SPIRIT OF SHADOW

A last flickering, a scattering of faces, and it was done. He breathed in slow, and exhaled.

"The time will be on us soon. Pick a side." She retreated into the hall, and amid startled shouts from the guards stationed there, ran away.

# A Plan

Lance toiled before a furnace with a team of Burners. No new initiate nor any stage labored over the small mountain of coal in his periphery. Instead, Emma had taken up the duty herself, feeling a need for a change from her usual duties or being ordered there by Master Gregor. He was not sure which. Did not feel comfortable asking, either.

The roar of the flames greeted him each time a worker opened the grate in the furnace he had been assigned to. He was already coated in thick sweat and the night was not close to over, needed a break soon or the headache would come on. He called to Phia, and blasted raw heat into the grate, coaxing the coals inside to life and amplifying the effect of the flames so that a harsh glow radiated back to paint his face with echoes of a fox's power.

Above and at his right, a portly figure emerged from behind a series of pipes along the catwalk. Duardo mounted the stairs, hurried down them and across the pit. He closed on him, slowed to a halt at his side.

"Tag in." He said. "You're needed in the office."

Lance noted his nervousness. "Is something wrong?"

"Ta be honest, I 'on't know." He shook off the anxiety. "'S neither here nor 'ere. Master Gregor wants ya. Ya gonna ignore 'im?"

"No, I don't think I will." Lance said. "I'll be back soon, okay."

He patted Duardo on the shoulder, and left under the hawkish gaze of Emma, who had stopped shoveling and was descending the mound. More coal spilled from the pipe as she planted her shovel in the base, and accepted a towel from another worker to wipe her face clean.

He climbed the stairs, made for the door to Master Gregor's office. Through the window, he saw Lord Aren seated across from the Master of the Furnaces.

*Shit.*

He pushed the door open, and walked in without comment. He closed it behind him, and took the seat Master Gregor gestured to.

"What's this about?" he asked, casting his gaze to include both of them.

An itch was building between his shoulder blades.

"Let's start with the most pressing issue, shall we?" Lord Aren asked, his attention on Master Gregor. "The Council of Liam has decided to smoke you out of your hiding place by sacrificing servants in your place. They will be rounded up the night before the Emperor leaves. A ball will be held to see him off, leaving most of the nobility in one place while the servants are brought to the Grand Hall."

"Wait—"

"Names will be called. Servants from this and other departments will be named conspirators acting on the interest of the rebels, and they will be immolated. The trial will go on until you reveal yourselves among them, and *you* will do that."

"They're not a part of this." Lance said coldly. "I want to get them out, don't get me wrong, but your people are responsible for ensuring their safety. We're just kids."

"Most of them aren't." Lord Aren agreed. "But the framed conspirators will be selected from among the armorers, furnace workers, cooks and couriers. Corresponding with the departments you chose. There is nothing I can do about that without exposing everything we've built. Some of those will likely be friendly to our cause.

"I have a plan to counter their strategy. We will use your reveal as a distraction while the other pieces fall into place. It is important that you do not die while these proceedings are taking place. Your friends will have a role in this as well."

Lance averted his gaze, found a neutral place outside the window to focus on. "I'm sorry. This is all just a little abrupt."

"I read the document you passed to my men." Lord Aren went on.

"First I'm hearin' 'bout any document." Master Gregor mumbled.

"That is probably for the best." Lord Aren dipped his head in acknowledgment.

"The relevant departments are being informed of our plans by my men. They will be charged with smuggling supplies into the dungeons, to be brought to the place you identified. My Thorns and other allies will protect them, but they will be met with significant resistance. There is the matter of the Emperor and his forces to consider as well. We do not know how they will respond once we reveal ourselves.

"That is where the furnace workers come in. You have been teaching them combat magic. With probably exception to the boilers, the other friendly department heads have done no such thing. They have been far more cautious about their affairs, and we cannot rely on them to mount the kind of resistance you are capable of. You will provide support from strategic locations while the rebels in the city push in from the outside.

"My Thorns will open the palace gates to them, but once they have arrived, it will be chaos."

He turned his gaze on Lance, who reluctantly met his eye. "Your friends will not be up to the challenge of taking on seasoned soldiers. I want them pulling the children out of their cells. There are more in another location." He pulled a piece of parchment out of his coat pocket and passed it to him. "Ensure they find and seize those children, too."

"We can't escape without the queen's pendant." Lance said. "There's only a sliver of hope even if we do have it. I don't know how to work it."

"But you believe you *can* work it." He said. "And as long as the queen does not have it, we will be at an advantage. Her command of immortal power is tied to it. In its absence, she will be greatly weakened. We may even be able to kill her."

"And if ya do?" Master Gregor asked. "What then? Do ya stage a coup? Emperor Conan 's still gonna be 'ere."

"I have arranged with someone else to handle him. Or, I suppose it would be better to say they have made arrangements with me they believe to be to our mutual benefit."

"Who's 'at? 'Nother cabal o' secret agents?"

"Not quite."

"Friend, I 'preciate yer confidence in us, but my guys 'on't need to be in 'a line o' fire without certain assurances. So ya want my cooperation, yer gonna 'ave ta tell me wha's goin' on here. Who 'ese people are?"

Lord Aren grimaced. "In truth, the queen has done something that could jeopardize our collective stability. It's only coincidence I stumbled onto her secret.

"She has been collecting Watchers. It's how she prevented

the servants from remembering their past lives. How she kept them in line. Without Lady Therien, she no longer has a means of keeping them under control, and they have escaped anyway.

"Their bodies are already positioned at locations they designated for their use. They need only come into contact with a servant called Sami. Then, they will be able to provide support against the Emperor, wherever he materializes."

Lance bit back the urge to holler at Lord Aren, maybe even to launch himself at the old general. He kept his features smooth, gave no outward sign he was angered by this simple utterance, yet inside he was boiling.

*He expects us to trust him...but he's responsible for everything that she's been through! He let them possess her! Use her to murder people! She could have been cut down and he'd never have thought about her again, and he wants me to believe he won't do the same thing to us?*

Master Gregor sniffed. "Thought o' everything 'in't ya."

"I am a general on the council for a reason, Master Gregor." He said.

"How am I going to get the stone?" Lance asked.

"*You* will not concern yourself with that. To steal it would place you in immense danger, and you are not ready for the challenge she poses even in her weaker state. She was a formidable fighter before she ascended to the throne, and she continues to be that."

"So...."

"I will handle stealing it myself." He explained. "When she is vulnerable."

*You go ahead and think that.*

"She has no reason to believe I'm anything other than a loyal soldier." He said. "Besides, I do not intend to fight her."

*Of course you don't.*

He nodded, but privately he had other ideas. Without the involvement of his friends, this plan of the general's would

# SPIRIT OF SHADOW

not be possible. It was because they had ignored his directives that they had the knowledge they did, that they had seen the gate, that they had made such progress as they had.

He had been absent from most of their affairs, had quickly become a non-issue in the grand scheme as he sought increasingly to maintain his cover. And there was not a doubt in Lance's mind that if this whole scheme failed to take off, his friends would become disposable quickly, even if *he* didn't.

Lord Aren might seek to save him from death, but it would be because of *what*, and not *who*, he was. It would be a bid to salvage a viable weapon for his use. He would not act out of any sense of compassion.

*He can try to steal it, but it'll end up being me who does. I'll just have to time it well.*

He decided to keep this act of defiance to himself. He wouldn't tell his friends, either. They would only try to convince him not to do it. The Emperor would be leaving in a matter of days, which meant they had precious little time to make good on their plans.

"You're trying to get everyone out?" Lord Aren asked.

"That would be the best scenario." Lance nodded.

"Then we are aligned in our intent." He said, smiling. "I'll leave the Thorns watching over you at your disposal. They will ensure you are protected until the time comes for you to reveal yourself."

*I'll have to give them the slip. Aughere and Lothor can help with that.*

"I will pass the stone to you when we reconvene at the gate. You will have as much time as I can buy to figure out how to use it."

"Understood." Lance said.

"Then I had best take my leave." He climbed out of his seat. "Lothor?"

## A Plan

The spider materialized on the desk surface as his shadow deepened to an abyssal shade. He tipped back on his heels, and plunged into it.

Master Gregor eyed him slyly. "Yer not gonna stick to 'is plan are ya? I 'an see it in yer eyes."

"Are you going to try to talk me down?" he asked.

Master Gregor snorted. "If ya still 'on't see reason ta trust 'im 'ere's nothin' I 'an do ta convince ya otherwise. But ya should think before ya act, a'right?"

"Are you going to tell him?"

"Get back ta work an' leave grown folks business ta grown folks." Master Gregor said.

He clapped him on the ass on his way by.

# A TASTE OF FREEDOM

# Party Crasher

Lance lay awake in his bed. A soft glow from the embers still burning in the brazier hugged the chalkboard, and as Ben lay asleep with his arms wrapped around him, he examined the various pieces of information written there— what he could make out from his vantage.

He had not warmed to the idea that Lord Aren would be able to remove the queen's pendant from her successfully. For all that he was master over the palace's spies, had fooled them all into believing the carefully constructed image of a man loyal to the crown, his long tenure in the military had only seen a worsening of conditions in the palace and the city beyond.

He had not missed the truth of that.

Lord Aren had served under two queens that he knew of. His best efforts had left him either blind or complicit to the sudden emergence of an underclass of servants woefully unaware of the violence they had endured in childhood, who accepted their tormentors as their saviors. He might have a complicated network of informants and agents scattered across the city and these halls, but what had he really accomplished with them? The people outside starved, by his own admission; and constant surveillance left their best efforts to organize a rebellion in constant jeopardy as their leaders were taken into custody, likely with the lord's own approval. The gluttony of the city's lords and ladies left them all weaker, and though he might sympathize with their condition, he had not suffered like any of them. Had not known the bleak reality they faced every day personally.

How could he really comprehend the urgency with which they must feel a need to act from his place of relative safety? He need only maintain the mask to enjoy the comfort so many of his peers were denied, and perhaps it was that measure of comfort that had kept him content to move in the shadows for so long.

*He can't succeed.* He thought to himself.

The queen's pendant was as far out of their reach now as it had been when first the truth was revealed to him. Little new information had been added to that list since their ill conceived adventure into the dungeons, but they had what they needed. Every servant knew where Queen Meredith slept. All of them knew what kind of security was employed there, at least enough to know they ought to tread lightly when they were assigned to clean her chambers. There may be features in place they knew nothing about, certainly, and the Council of Liam may have had a hand in constructing some of those barriers, but they couldn't know everything. Their queen was a cautious person, had been able to maneuver in a palace hierarchy, which was often hostile against her, effectively for all this time. She might believe herself above it all, but she could not be foolish enough to believe there were not those in her city, within her palace walls, who would rather see her dead. She did not strike him as the kind to trust anyone.

He snuggled himself closer to Ben, feeling his warmth

radiating against his back as his arms tightened around him. His presence was little comfort, but it did drive back the chill. There was safety in his arms, for a time, but he sensed danger on the horizon, and knew he would be vulnerable when the time came to act. It was almost on him now.

When the emperor left, the palace could breathe again. The greatest threat to the schemes of those who held disdain for him could resume, and the queen could focus her attention on rooting out whatever was left of the rebellion against her without him to distract her. There would be nothing left to bar her from doing exactly as she pleased, and she would. Her cruelest impulses would come to bare. They would all be dead within a week.

*I have to do this. I can't let them get hurt, and we can't afford to fail.*

He would hide himself in plain sight, cover his tracks, take a way into her chambers that wasn't as well guarded as the obvious routes. He wouldn't have any need for pretense—not like Lord Aren. He could do this.

*He'll just have to forgive me when its over.*

If he was going to do this, it would have to be tonight. The next night would see the trap sprung and all of them in their places, but she would not know her pendant had been stolen until then anyway. Right now, with the witching hour on the horizon, she was probably asleep. She was at her most vulnerable in this moment.

*If I wait, I won't have this chance again.*

He lifted Ben's arm and slid out from under it.

Ben stirred as he sat up. He stroked his hair, kissed his forehead.

"Can't sleep. I'm going to take a walk." He whispered.

Ben nodded, his eyes still closed. "Don't take too long." He yawned, and drew the covers up under his chin.

Lance climbed off the camp bed. He tiptoed across the

classroom to the series of sacks resting against the wall. He selected the lone empty one, and crossed to the desk where their various books lay in two stacks. One by one, he slid them into the sack, carefully laid them in the bottom so as not to make too much noise.

Lord Aren still possessed the Compact, but he had nearly memorized it. It wouldn't do them much good once this was all over anyway.

He carried the sack off, set it next to a desk, and then set about carefully moving the other sacks, full of food and clothing and linens into that spot to join it.

If something went wrong, he wanted his friends to spare as little time as possible getting out of here. The Thorns could help them get away, relocate them to a safer place. Of course, he'd be dead by then. If he did not succeed here, the Shadow Queen herself might take his life. If he got away from her chambers, one of the Bloodless stationed outside her front door, or a Wraith in the shadows, would do him in. He had no illusions about his ability to escape if she raised the alarms.

When it was done, he took a knife from where it lay on a student's desk, and slipped it into his pocket. He pulled a shirt on, and looked everything over. Ariana and Peter slept soundly atop a second cot in the darkest corner of the room. Ben's face had vanished into their coverlet.

Rashanna was the only one who could still move freely throughout the palace, and he hoped she had the sense to play along as if she knew nothing.

He crossed back to the chalkboard, picked up a strip of burlap they had been using as an eraser, and scrubbed away the bulk of what was written there. Weeks of planning, useful rites painstakingly notated, rumors and gossip and the like fell into obscurity behind a cloud of dust, leaving behind a ghost of what had been.

He picked up a length of chalk, and wrote his final message to them. He would not be coming back here before the trial the following day. He had not told them about Lord Aren's scheme. Now, he wrote out the details they needed to know.

He fidgeted with the chalk for a moment as he took all of it in. *I should have told them sooner, but it's done now.*

He touched the chalk to the board underneath the instructions he had left for them, and scribbled out a final message for Ben, fighting back tears as he thought it all over. *I'll come back to you, don't worry. I'll come back.*

"I may never see you again." He whispered. "But at least, if I don't, you know. At least you have a chance.

"Lothor." He whispered. "Sor eya aiel a'surit." *Open the deeper passage.*

He tipped back on his heels as the spirit answered, and plunged into his shadow.


Sami drifted along the shadowed corridors of the palace to the muted music of laughter and banter come from some distance off. The Watchers were in control. They seemed to know where they were going, where they would find their final target. She let them lead, while she played the passenger in her own body. She had not seen a wash in so long she had lost the ability to smell her own putrefaction, the rank odor emanating from her, and was glad she could not feel the layers of dirt and grease rimed into her skin.

She drew a halt at the edge of an intersection. The voices were louder here. Doors came open and banged shut amid drunken laughter and the pops and whines of party favors.

*The harvest festival must be tonight.* She thought. *But how do they plan on getting Lady Jain out of this?*

"We are born wit' many gifts, child."

An kitune woman stood with her. They watched the world together through her eyes as if through an open window.

## Party Crasher

She looked to her, and the world outside lost for a fraction of a second; then back to the scene.

She was peering around the corner now. She tugged at the length of rope coiled around her shoulder. There was a gag somewhere in her pockets, too—a chunk of blue, cotton cloth she had torn free of a sheet earlier in the day.

The crowd around the corner was alive with joy. Noblemen and women bantered and giggled over crystal chalices filled with wine. They wore veils and masks to cover their faces, and there were Mirrhvalians among them. This gathering was smaller than she had expected. From the sounds issuing from this room, she would have thought she was entering onto a ball, not a scattering of drunkards enjoying each other near the entrance to someone's private chambers. There would undoubtedly be more revelers inside, but how many could fit in so small a space? She wondered who's party it was, and why they had chosen this night, of all nights, to celebrate.

"There is to be a ball tomorrow." The Watcher said. "A last night to celebrate the reign of your emperor before he leaves. But there are those who will have convened behind the guise of camaraderie and entertainment, when in truth their purpose here is to make powerful connections they might otherwise have no time to.

"They are here to secure bonds with each other."

Some of those nobles swooned and teetered on unsteady feet, or puffed at fat cigars, blowing the smoke in the faces of those they conversed with.

The door of a chamber a hundred or so feet from where she hid banged open, admitting a drunken Lady Tamalsen leaning heavily on her husband's arm. Through the open doors, the silhouettes of dancers painted the floor as stronger light from the chamber suffused the corridor, and she heard the sounds of a lively tune played by a chamber band.

"The time is now." The kitune woman said.

# SPIRIT OF SHADOW

Her body sprang into the hall and took off at a sprint. Wind blasted from both of her hands, slamming bodies into either wall amid the gasps of onlookers.

"Rebel!" a nobleman shouted.

She whipped him off the ground by the force of her rite, and sent him to crash against a stone table. A vase walked off its surface and shattered over his head.

The doors into the chamber blew off their hinges. She bolted through.

The dancing stopped. The music sputtered out.

She stood in the heart of a sitting room which had been gutted of most of its furniture, eyes hunting through the crowd for a melted wax figure.

Her gaze latched onto Lady Jain. The lady's face was a mass of jowls and wrinkles, with two, beady jewels of purest onyx peering out around a drooping, hooked nose, and a plump bulb of chin fat hovered like a gonad over a neck like a flag on a day with no wind.

Judgment had been fair to her. More still, now the Watchers had found her.

The silence and the stillness broke. They used Sami's body, summoned the wind and blew all of those around the old hag away.

Suddenly, everyone was running for the door, screaming for help, ramming each other out of the way as a knot of ten or more of them clogged the only exit.

It fit their character well to put themselves first, to jeopardize their safety in favor of saving their own skins. They might have killed her if they worked together, but fear drove them down irrational avenues, away from reason.

Lady Jain backpedaled. Her neck waddled, her chin a-quiver, eyes wide and fearful. She dodged left, ran toward the door and smacked into a wall of solid air three steps into her flight.

**Party Crasher**

The Watchers manipulated her into a corner with ease. They trussed her up like a hog in the middle of the chamber floor, using Sami's hands. They shoved the gag in her mouth and strapped it into place as she cried for anyone to help her. With her bound, Sami shoved her into the shadows.

All of those cowards she had summoned here for her entertainment had fled. None of them had even tried to help her.

# The Queen's Chambers

ance reached out to the shadows, darkness and the muted susurrations of the Dark Heart his only company, and pulled at what felt like oiled cloth. Light pierced the darkness, revealing a hall, its tiled walls washed in silver and gray, and a window through which the moon glimmered in a sea of stars.

He touched the portal, and rose into the world.

The hall was empty for the moment, but there would be patrols sweeping through soon enough. If he did not act decisively, he would encounter them before he was able to secure passage to the queen's chambers one floor below.

*Going by the usual paths would be a death mission.*

He looked around. The front door was not an option. The shadows in that area would be watched, too. Even delving into that deeper place wouldn't be much help. The Wraiths would probably be there, too, waiting for intruders.

### The Queen's Chambers

His gaze hung on the window. Crossing bars broke the frost rimed glass into sections, obscuring a world cloaked in snow and ice. He approached it, unbound the latch, pulled it open. A bone chilling draft filtered through it, and clumps of snow dressed the ledge outside. He sat on the sill, swung his legs out. The snow bit into his ankles as he scraped it away to the sides in search of firmer stone on which to find his footing.

The chill burned his cheeks and fingertips. *We should've stolen coats.*

One would have come in handy for this, but it was only the nobility and the soldiers who left the palace. They were the only ones who needed such heavy raiment, and such things were not as easy to come by in the laundry.

*I could have taken a blanket, at least.*

He used the windowsill to stabilize himself as he twisted around, planting his feet as firmly as he could on the bare ledge, and pulled the window shut when he was stable.

He looked down the wall, then. The bricks didn't provide much in the way of hand holds, but they would have to do. He wedged his bare fingers into the grout lines, slid his lead foot to the side. Snow cascaded from the ledge.

He winced as it tumbled earthward, and wet and cold slid into his shoe.

He dragged his hind foot forward, then picked up his step, setting it down carefully atop the snow this time. He adjusted his grip, continued to march like that as his fingers numbed and the cold stiffened his muscles, until he was near the center of the windowless wall.

*What now?*

His fingers traveled across fat bricks. He widened his stance, placing his weight on his thumbs as he twisted at the knees. He descended into an odd sort of crouch, his heart pounding in his chest as some of his former stability was lost. Then, sitting on his knee four stories above the ground with a

# SPIRIT OF SHADOW

foot of ledge separating him from a skull-cracking fall, he let go of the wall with his trailing hand.

"Don't look down." He whispered, his heart hammering against his ribs. "Don't look down, don't look down."

He planted his hand beneath the snow, released his grip on the bricks, and used the stone ledge for support as he swung his legs, ever so carefully, out into open air.

He let out a slow breath, relief flooding in to ease the tension. He pulled the knife from his pocket.

*Now for the hard part.* He set the hilt between his teeth and bit down.

He crossed his arms between his legs, took a firm grip on the ledge, and slid off.

For a moment, he was certain he had miscalculated. He clamped down harder on the knife, his feet dangling in free air, his fingers numb and stiff. Seconds took on the shade of ages, and he was falling. The arc of his life formed in the back of his mind, ready to march across the intervening space as life slipped away into death.

His feet landed on something hard. He saw the window before him. Frost masked what lay beyond, but the details of that room didn't matter. It was dark in there. The queen was not inside,  or she was sleeping. Either scenario worked to his advantage.

He adjusted his feet for better purchase, grasped the windowsill with one hand and removed the knife from between his teeth with the other. He hunched over, slid the knife into the space between window and frame, and worked it across until he found the latch. It gave after a few tense moments of wobbling the blade around, and he pulled it open.

"Aughere? If you can hear me, now would be the time."

*"Isn't this a sight?"* The weasel swam through the air a short way from his shoulder. He glanced at him. *"What might you be up to?"*

## The Queen's Chambers

"Can you hide me?"

*"Oh, I suppose."* The weasel pawed its cheek, performed a back flip as a sly chuckle escaped its throat.

Smoke washed over him, rippled across the ledge, a thin vapor.

He snuck through the open window, and closed it softly behind him.

Muffled grunts and slow creaking came to him from behind a closed door. A woman's hoarse cry gave him pause to consider whether the emperor had paid Queen Meredith a late night visit.

He recalled the reception ceremony, the friction between them as the emperor's gaze fell on the queen's pendant. Her frustration as she climbed out of her throne and allowed him to take his place there. *Could that have been an act?*

He looked around. He had never been in her apartments before. Had never been assigned duties there.

The chambers were lavish. Snapdragons, now well and dead, peaked out from a vase atop an ebony hutch which was accented with gold leaf in intricate patterns. A hearth occupied much of the wall nearest him. A band of worked gold crossed under its granite head, displaying foxes hunting a rabbit, watchful ravens flying in their wake. A mirror— whose gilt frame had been worked to resemble vines, and leaves, and flowers—hung over it, and two, plush, high-backed chairs sat atop a batik carpet that, by itself, was worth more in gold than Lance had ever seen in one place, even at his stage in the Palace Treasury.

Everything from the doors to the wall hangings was fine made and designed to draw the eye, yet with so much opulence, no one thing could hold a viewer's attention for long. There would be too much for a visitor to talk about in these chambers, too many artifacts and fineries to draw out conversation. He suspected her visitors were nonetheless quiet while they were here, that what conversation these pieces might inspire was to be had after they had left, with peers who would see every statement about the decor as a braggadocios sleight.

She's never had to struggle for anything, has she? It seemed wrong that anyone should live like this, more so when considered against the state of the commonry.

A louder cry punched the air. An exhausted gasp chased after it. The rhythmic creaking stopped, and a quiet broken occasionally by a man's whimpers settled in.

Lance found a chaise against the wall by the window. He dropped onto his belly, and shimmied under it, not trusting Aughere's camouflage to be enough.

The queen and her suitor cooed to each other beyond the closed door. Boots tapped against floor tiles. The door vaulted open, and the suitor's hand thrust out to catch it before it could bang against the wall. A willowy figure was framed in the door beyond the suitor, her back pressed against the wall, a sheet cupped to her breasts.

The man's black hair was in disarray, a detail that shattered the illusion she had been visited upon by the emperor. He held his shirt in one hand, worked the fly of his pants closed with the other. He bound the buckle on his belt as the queen watched him.

*Who is he?*

"Are you sure you don't have another one in you?" the queen asked.

"You are insatiable, woman." He said. "Perhaps later. Now, I need rest."

She crossed the intervening distance, drew him to her by his chin, and pressed a passionate kissed against his lips. He took her by her hair, plunged his tongue into her mouth, and they held there far longer than was necessary.

He released his grip on her, stepped back. She leaned forward, and he entertained her desires for a moment longer before stepping away again, leaving her to gaze upon him as he slid his shirt over his torso.

"We'll continue this later?" she asked.

"When I have caught my breath." He turned around, and Lance saw his face.

He suppressed the urge to gasp, but then perhaps he should have expected this. Should have recognized the man's voice, at least.

*Lord Elise?* She did favor him in a way she did not his counterparts on the Council. He had seen the way she looked at him at the reception, how he had seemed to be more than just a professional curiosity to her.

"You are my favorite part about this assignment." He said. "The way you humble me...I..."

"Hush." She said. "Go to your post. I will call on you when I am ready."

"If I am not?"

She batted her eyelashes like a girl half her age and with none of her power. "Then you will find the strength to take me, and do it properly."

He made a sound low in his throat, a lustful growl, and then left the doorway, passed through the sitting room and into a hall choked with darkness.

She followed in his wake, her hands pawing his flanks, teasing the hem of his trousers, sliding over the pleats across his legs.

*Now or never!* When their backs were turned, Lance negotiated his way out from under the chaise.

He crept across the room, through the door, got his footing and began his search.

It was not hard to find the pendant. The queen, in her carelessness, had left it laying atop a nightstand in plain view of the door.

The surface of the stand was petrified wood, and glittered like stone in an array of vibrant colors. The bed it lay next to was a large, plush thing. The top sheet was gone but the coal black bedspread remained, bunched to one side. A canopy of violet lace obscured whatever damage the linens had taken, but the odor of sex, sweet and sickly, pork-like, hung on the air.

He could take the pendant now, but he hesitated. To take it when she was wakeful would be to alert her to that it was gone well before his allies and friends were prepared to move against her. Instead, he climbed into the space beneath the sturdy side table, and waited.

A door clicked shut, and soft pattering echoed to him from the hall. She returned to her chambers, slid into her bed and pulled a canopy on the side facing her window closed. He waited still longer, until the sound of her breathing steadied, and he could convince himself she slept.

She had made the mistake of leaving the door to her chambers open, and perhaps this was part of some game to entice Lord Elise back into her bed. Perhaps it was that she had some agreement with him, that he could wake her for his use when he was prepared. He could conceive of how these two, both monsters in their way, would come around to games of this nature, but the open door left him with ample advantage. He would not need to make much sound as he exited.

He climbed out from his hiding place, scooped up the pendant, placed it around his neck, and passed out of the room.

When he was clear of the bed chamber, he eased the door almost all the way shut, leaving it cracked just slightly as to give the impression Lord Elise may have come back. To leave the invitation open to him if that had been her intent.

*He'll come back, won't he?* He wasn't at all certain, but thought it more likely than not given the nature of their conversation. When he had grown bored of maintaining his guard, his mind might wander back to her, which suited Lance just fine. The distraction he provided might just keep her attention away from that pendant a bit longer.

He unlatched the window he had come by, and slid it open.

# Dawn on the Day of Reckoning

Meredith awoke to morning light streaming through her window, the curtain on her canopy bed blocking out the offending rays of the sun. She rolled to the edge of the bed, reached through and felt around the night stand there for what she knew must be just within reach.

She had allowed Lord Elise to take it from her, to set it aside and make them closer to equals, to give the man a chance in a game of matching wills for her own entertainment. There had been no stakes in the games they played with each other in their earliest encounters, and she had tired of the old charade quickly. These forays into more dangerous enclaves had become more frequent as they came to know each other, had invited a renewed sense of excitement into her that she could not remember feeling since she was a girl barely into her twenties.

Without the stone, she was vulnerable. She could only tolerate the longing ache of being away from it, even just a few feet from the source of her power, for so long, and now she needed it. But her fingers failed to close on it, even to nudge the chain.

*Did he move it out of my reach?*

She reached further, as far as she could without pushing the curtain aside, and still she could not find it.

Her heart was beginning to beat harder in her chest, a nervous thrill was stealing over her. *It's there. It must be there. If he moved it. If he took it....*

But he knew the rules. Knew that their relationship must end, together with his life, if he violated her so. He wouldn't risk it, would he? Mad as he was, he understood the limits of their relationship, and he was still too entertained by her to risk her wrath. She was still too entertained by him to believe he would throw away his own life over something so meaningless.

She pushed back the curtain, squinted in the harsher light come through her window. A light dulled by shadows cast by the palace wall, her bedchamber being situated on the western side of the palace as it was. Beyond that window was the blocky obstruction of the military complex, its eastern face painted in harsh light, bringing out white shades in the gray stone it was made of, and beyond that was canyon wall blocking all obvious routes for an assault on her palace from the rear.

She groped for the pendant as her eyes adjusted, looked over the surface of that table, a relic from Queen Mariah's time, and found her pendant missing.

She climbed hurriedly out of the bed. *Did I place it somewhere else?*

She dropped onto all fours, peered under the bed and found nothing. She moved through the room and checked over

# SPIRIT OF SHADOW

the other furnishings, a walk in closet almost as large as the bedchamber where her various gowns were housed, poured through jewelry boxes, passed into the sitting chamber and then the basin, hunted through every drawer and across every table surface, rummaged through cushions on chaises and couches she was only half convinced they had used in the course of last night's various sessions.

"Where is it?" desperation edged into her voice as she ripped the cushion from a chair before the hearth. She approached the mantle, swept her arms across it, flinging everything to the ground as rage mounted to push back anxiety. "WHERE IS IT!"

The door to her chambers boomed open. Lord Elise stood in the hall with another Bloodless.

"What's wrong, m'lady?" the Bloodless asked, eyes wide and searching.

Lord Elise approached her.

"Did you take it?" she demanded, rounding on him.

"Take what?" he asked.

"MY PENDANT!" she raved, her bangs flying unbecomingly into her face. "CELESTI'S SOUL!"

He backed up a step. "I haven't. You set it on the nightstand."

"IT ISN'T THERE! IT ISN'T ANYWHERE!"

He nodded. There was no fear in the gaze he set on her, but she registered a measure of concern she had never seen in him before.

"I will order a search."

"NO!" she snapped. She sighed heavily, tensed her fingers. "No."

"Then what would you have me do?"

"Find Lord Aren. Bring him to me. You two will handle this discretely, do you understand. It cannot become public knowledge that I am without it. My enemies will see me as vulnerable.

"Sky Lord's cursed mercy. The Emperor will too." She buried her head in her hands.

He approached her then, wrapped her in a loose embrace. She tried to shake him off, and he tightened his grip on her. "You needn't worry, woman. There is to be a purge of the servants this night. We will draw those rebels out, and take back what is rightfully yours when we do."

"Do you think...do you think *they* took it?" she asked. "Are my defenses so weak that a mere *servant* could steal off with my greatest weapon in the night?"

"No, not any servant. But there is that one the Watchers ride." He whispered. "We will find her, but I do not believe it is in our best interests to involve Lord Aren."

"Why not?"

"Because he is compromised." He said. She felt his sneer against her neck. "He is not trustworthy."

"You question my judgment?" she growled, at last shoving him away. "You will never—"

"It is not your judgment I question. It is his." Lord Elise cut in. "He has had a month to find them. In that month, he has overseen three murders, a flogging and an abduction, a building rebellion among the servants, and the loss of the city vermin's most cherished leader. He is incompetent."

"Then bring Lord Giram into it." She seethed. "Just find my damned pendant."

"I will do that." He said. "Fear nothing. I will see to it that it is done."


The low whistle of the cuckoo clock heralded the arrival of morning. Daylight streamed through the breaks between curtains in the classroom, a thin bar slashing across Ben's face, bringing him around to wakefulness. He stretched his arms and yawned. The last night's rest had been fitful, broken at times when the weight of what today meant washed over him, but he had found a period of uninterrupted sleep in the waning hours, and though he would have liked that period of bliss to last a bit longer, as his eyes adjusted to the dimness and his vision cleared, he knew there would be no return to slumber for some hours.

He rolled over in the camp bed, intent on drawing Lance to him, waking him up gently if he wasn't already alert, and found him absent.

*Did he come back to bed?*

A half remembered bit of conversation came to him. Soft rummaging after it. Lance had been fussing over something as he chased after sleep, had said he was taking a walk, hadn't he? But where would he have gone? Where *could* he go with the Thorns watching the shadows. They would not have let him pass under their noses a second time. Not after the dungeons. *Not after he was wounded.*

He sat upright, panned over the room. Ariana was just climbing out of bed, and Peter was seated behind a desk not far from where they had taken to sleeping. He was staring at the chalkboard, his knuckles balling rhythmically as he squeezed the planar edge of its writing surface.

Ben rubbed the grit out of his eyes, and followed his gaze.

The collected bits of information—most of it come from Rashanna or Emma over the last weeks—had been wiped away, and Lance's clean script crept across the ghost echoes of what had been there before.

"Whassat?" he said thickly as a yawn gusted from him. He leaned his elbows on his knees, and read.

*Lord Aren and Master Gregor plan to get us out of here tonight, but I don't agree with everything they want to do. So I'm stealing Queen Meredith's pendant tonight. If I am not back by morning, don't assume I'm dead. Whether or not I succeed, it will be too dangerous to come back here.*

## Dawn on the Day of Reckoning

*Go along with the plan Lord Aren came up with. Go to the staircase. Ben knows which one. Go down there and free the children, and take them to the gate in the dungeons. I marked another place on the map that you need to go to before you get to the gate. Lord Aren said there are more kids there that need to be freed. Make sure they all get to the gate before you do anything else. The Masters of some of the other departments will be heading there with supplies for the journey. The furnace workers, Lord Aren's men and the rebels in the city are all involved.*

*Don't do anything stupid. Don't try to be a hero. They're going to gather the servants in the Grand Hall tonight and stage executions. I'm going to present myself there to stop it. I think Sami will show up there eventually, too.*

He lingered at the bottom of the message, traveled to the top and read it over again.

"Free the children." Peter mumbled.

Ariana was reading the text now, too.

"Mistress Dina and Mistress Rosaline...I'm sure he means they're the ones bringing supplies." He went on.

"We can't just leave Lance to himself." Ben said, his voice cracking.

"The fucking idiot! You'd think he'd trust Lord Aren by now." Ariana grumbled. "He's going to get us all killed."

"It's quiet." Peter pointed out. "If they caught him, I bet they would have people searching every inch of the palace for us. The Thorns would have said something."

"So you think he's still out there?" Ben turned his gaze on him, but Peter kept his focus on the chalkboard.

"Maybe." He said.


When a knock came at the door to Lord Aren's apartments, he contemplated fleeing into the shadows. He had, as yet, done nothing to expose himself, but those kids were on his mind. Whatever their successes thus far, they had been reckless fools in every one of their exploits. With all that was to be done today, he was on edge, anxious in a way he rarely was; and he had momentarily believed his cover was blown.

He splashed water from a basin on his face, wiped it clean of what traces of shaving cream striped his cheeks with a hand towel, and slid into a tunic he had intended for after his morning's wash. A tangled snarl of white hair hung down his back, but there was no time to set it right. Not without foreknowledge of who awaited him outside.

A second, more earnest knock. *Not one of my subordinates, then.*

He hurried out of the wash room, crossed through a sitting room whose decor would be most politely described as utilitarian. There were no wall hangings in the expanse, and a single carpet dressed the stone floor in front of a cold hearth—the gilded banding along the mantle a relic from when the military complex was constructed—which was the most ornate of its furnishings. Cold light streamed through the breaks in velvet curtains, and a scattering of chairs, couches and end tables were all wreathed in shadow, providing ample opportunity to escape should it be needed.

Down a short hall, he went, and opened the front door onto a brighter lit hall, where Lord Giram was standing.

"Get dressed and report to the dungeons. Gather your Thorns. Whatever our queen has to say about it, I will not have the search conducted without all of our best involved."

"Search?"

"It seems someone stole Celesti's Soul." He growled. "Lord Elise reported to me with demands that I sick the Wraiths on whoever did it. He further explained that you are not to be a part of these affairs. He seems to believe he has a shot at my seat if he can keep that fickle cunt happy, but *she* doesn't command our forces. I do."

Lord Aren raised an eyebrow. "You know better than to

say that aloud."

"It's true, isn't it?" he said. "It's been that way since Anastasia's time. Those women can point wherever they like and say attack, but they don't understand the first thing about mounting a successful strike, be it at home or abroad. As long as I remain in my seat, our forces will do as I say.

"Frankly, I'm getting sick of Lord Elise wielding his influence as if it makes us equals. Not least, when he fucked his way onto our council."

He glared over Lord Aren's shoulder, rubbed wide hands together. "Well get to it. I want them found before nightfall."

"The servants. Right." Lord Aren breathed. "They'll be behind this."

"Any idea why?"

Lord Aren grimaced. "One, but it's far fetched."

Lord Giram snorted. "Far fetched would be a pack of rebel servants breaching the dungeons and fucking off to who only knows where without a damned trace. Far fetched would be them killing off a sitting general single handedly while he's got his cock in a nobleman's wife.

"I'm ready to accept what seems far fetched as fact, friend. We've gone well past the times when I thought those children were docile simpletons."

"They might believe they can use Celesti's Soul to escape." Lord Aren said. "But given the stone only resonates with the soul of a woman, and then only to one woman until the moment of her death, they will have effectively backed themselves into a corner just having it."

Lord Giram patted his shoulder. "Good. Hubris has been the downfall of far more cunning bastards before. Let us hope it is again."

"The executions—"

"Will proceed according to the original plan. Everything is already in place. If we find the thief, we might just use *him* as bait to draw the others out of hiding. Spare ourselves having

# SPIRIT OF SHADOW

to go through the trouble of replacing a dozen or so servants when it's all over.

"But go get dressed. I've kept you here too long already. The Wraiths are already being mobilized. I want the Thorns to join them within the hour."

He backed up a step, and marched away down the hall.

Lord Aren closed the door behind him. He called on Lothor to open his shadow, and plunged through as soon as the door was well shut. What he needed was not here, but in his office. Everything he needed would be there.

*Curse that boy for a fool.* He thought to himself as he traveled, half-dressed and disheveled, through that world beyond sight. *What did he believe he would accomplish....*

# The Plan Revised

Lord Aren emerged from shadow in the Teacher's Tower, in a room in which three servants were already well within the process of putting themselves together ahead of what they must believe would be a fight. It was not lost on him that they had chosen the stolen military uniforms they had been wearing, according to reports, when they were found inside the dungeons.

They had been lucky his men found them first, then. He was lucky now, to have found them all in one piece and still unexposed.

He panned over the room. A chalkboard in the back was home to a long message which Ben was reading from a few feet off as he pulled a clinging, wool shirt over his torso.

He scanned it, flinched at the separate message at the bottom the boy was fixated on.

# SPIRIT OF SHADOW

*If I have to die tonight, know that these weeks have been some of the best of my life. You have been good to me. I only wish I could have prevented you from getting wrapped up in all of this.*

*Please, stay alive, Ben. I love you.*

Ariana was the first to see him as he marched to stand with the courier he had gone to such great lengths to see placed in his care, who had almost immediately thrown his gift and his protection to the wolves in favor of the very boy who wrote this last message to him.

He recalled the last time there had been a significant clash between Shadovane's armies and another of the Sun Empire's Wards, when the Jua uprising in the south had taken place. There had been many soldiers in that day who, not knowing if they would survive those conflicts, believing they might die in battle, had fallen into whirlwind romances. Who espoused declarations of undying love for each other when they had not been together long enough to know each other's favorite color.

This gave him the same impression. These two could not have been together for more than a few weeks, and yet this fatalism, this constant uncertainty, had galvanized their relationship, had given them license, it seemed, to defend a fleeting possibility from whatever might come their way.

"What are you doing here?" Ariana asked, taking a step toward him.

He held up his hand for her silence, clasped it onto Ben's shoulder. Mail plating shielded the back of his hand, and a leather strap crossed the palm of a thick glove underneath it. He wore a full suit of armor, his hair spilling unfettered over a backplate made to look as if smoke had been trapped in the metal. His pauldrons were in the shape of raven's heads, and violet silk interrupted the feathering around the beak and eyes where it had been wound around them. Silk sashes in violet and black were wrapped around his midriff, and wickedly curved hooks situated behind his hips held his shepherd's hook staff in place, the snowflake pendant dangling from its crooked end.

He felt the power of the man to whom that staff belonged flowing through him from a distant past, burning pride and bravery into him and burying his insecurities. One day, he would go to the Ring of Fire, and he would find the remnants of the resistance there who still held onto the old way, but that day was not now. Now, he needed to focus on escape, and with the critical piece in the scheme he had put together missing, he needed to adjust his plans.

"Are you willing to die for him, lad?" he whispered into Ben's ear.

Ben flinched. He turned slowly, looked into the general's face. "I don't...I guess."

"I need you to be sure. Show some conviction. If you feel for him what he does for you, that is the kind of thing you must be willing to die for. Now, are you willing to die for him?"

"Y-yes. Yes, sir."

"Then I need you to take care of the kids. Once they are freed from the dungeons, these two will be needed elsewhere." He gestured curtly to Ariana and Peter, both of whom were staring at him now. "You will take them to the gate, and hold it down until help arrives, do you understand. I will be there as soon as I can be, but with Lance AWOL, our entire situation will be messier than I would have liked."

"Where do you want us?" Peter asked, and to his credit there was not an ounce of fear in his voice.

"I want *you* to go to the Kitchens, and do so immediately. I want you to tell Mistress Dina our timeline has been moved up, and she will need to organize her charges around getting as much food as possible to the dungeons." He turned his attention to Ariana. "*You* will go to Mistress Rosaline and pass orders to her on my behalf. Linens, anything that can be repurposed for bandages, soaps suitable for use in washing, and clothing...all of it need to be brought to the gate chamber."

"First the children." Ben said shakily. "Then we go our separate ways."

"I will come as soon as I am able. But I have been here too long. I must meet with my Thorns." He pushed off Ben's shoulder, and marched away. "Do be warned, all of you. Be as discrete as you can in your movements. Do not invite any conflict. Do not be seen. The Wraiths are already in pursuit of you. I can only do so much to slow them down."

"Understood." Peter said, all of the soldier.

Lord Aren tipped forward, fell through his open shadow, and away.

# To End a Child's Suffering

riana emerged to her eyes in the shadow of an age-worn table. The dungeon room was a close space. A set of chairs arranged around the table were both occupied by Wraiths, and the edge of a water trough was just visible from her vantage. She twisted around, noted the two pairs of eyes looking back at her from positions at either end a wall of dark glass, through which she could make out nothing.

The Thorns who had accompanied them on Lord Aren's orders rose out of the shadows as, seeing no benefit to revealing herself yet, she slid back into the world below.

"Two Wraiths at the table. The Thorns will deal with those." She whispered.

"There's another one at the entrance." Ben whispered back.

# SPIRIT OF SHADOW

Behind them came Peter's heavy breathing. Ben had descended into an uneasy silence. She suspected the corpses scattered about their feet, the ones the Thorns had taken out before they arrived here, were making the work of keeping the Dark Heart in check more difficult, requiring more of his focus to maintain the pocket of quiet around them. Lothor's domain seemed to feed on death and grow stronger. At least, the Dark Heart had been emboldened by their proximity to death in the past.

"So what? We leave the guards to them and then run away with the kids?" Peter asked.

"Pretty much." She said. "You should probably leave it to us."

"Why?"

"You know why."

"I can still—"

"Not without pissing off the spirits, you can't." She growled.

A warm, soft hand found her wrist. Ben spoke. "Now isn't the time. Peter can shadow walk. If he can't do anything else, he can still be useful for that. The spirit of shadow might not like it, but sometimes we have to take the risk, Ariana. Let him walk with us."

"Thank you." Peter said. "Now can we get on with it?"

"The cells are over here." A hole shredded through darkness revealed Ben in low light.

A wall carved over with bloody tallies, too many to count, was revealed through the portal. In places, so many of the scratches overlapped that the gray of the blocks those walls were made of was gone, leaving patches of white behind to remember it by. In yet other places, the grout had been chipped away, leaving holes between the blocks where past occupants had attempted to escape. At least one of those bricks was loose, had been dragged so that it sat at angle with the rest, one side protruding and the other pushed back.

A Wraith would have noticed that. *Would he care? None of these kids can do magic. How much trouble would they be if they escaped?*

The Force of Wills crooned at her. She pushed it away. If not the recent deaths inside this abyssal plane, then the memories she tried so hard to force down gave them strength. Memories of living in filth, having been allowed just a shift to keep her warm and that ripped where she had taken scraps of cloth to clean herself. The walls scratched over with those tallies, some of them her own doing as she tried desperately to keep track of time. Her fingers ached. Her nails were a frayed mess. Her hair was a dirty tangle snarled together so badly just to run her fingers through it hurt her head, and her scalp itched. Oh, how it itched.

Echoes of those aches and pains, the incessant itching, the greasy feel of her skin lingered on her as she observed that wall. As she stepped around the scattered debris at her feet, shuffling and shifting course when her foot struck a corpse. She positioned herself under the next cell, Shara's tracers aligning with a point above her, and ripped a portal open.

Soft light danced across her upturned face and shoulders. Peter had taken position along the expanse, too, and was now bathed in a low light of his own making, where his own portal stood open and waiting.

"Ready?" she asked.

She did not wait for their answer, but touched the portal and shot through.

"Traitors!" the yell that came from the Wraith was muffled by the glass wall, but it was earnest, full of hate.

Something banged against the wall. She cried out in surprise as a rubbery sound followed it, exposed skin sliding against the glass there.

Cracks spidered away from the site of impact, and something wet pummeled the glass. With the emergence of the cracks, the enchantment on what had, from the outside, looked almost like a mirror, what from this side looked like another stone wall, was broken, and the profile of the Wraith was revealed in stark relief, sitting against the ground. Behind him, one of the Thorns stood over the dying man, his hands and forearms dressed in a black, pulsating substance that looked almost like oil smoke, but held its shape as wicked, beastly claws. The Thorn's expression was impassive as he dragged his shrouded forefinger across the Wraith's throat, and killed him.

She turned away from the scene of violence, and laid eyes on the child who was this cell's lone occupant. He was a boy not older than four years. His face was hidden behind a shaggy mop of hair, and for the darkness she could not make out its color. He hugged his knees to his chest, wrapped his arms around them, refused to look for fear of what he might see. She had seen him before, an echo of him in her memory, a girl in her minds eye who could only have been her, who buried her head in her shift to avoid seeing. To avoid seeing, as each day a tray clattered against sandy earth, a cup of water rattling against the metal sheet where her day's stale bread awaited her.

She grit her teeth as another, more difficult memory wove its way through the greater chaos storming through her, all of those petty traumas laid bare for her to see. She knelt before the boy as a woman once knelt before her. She reached for him as the woman had reached for her. She dug behind arms gone tight against her hands and lifted his head free, trying on a smile she hoped was a comfort to him, and feeling like a monster because that woman had done the same.

She knelt before the boy, whose name and origin she did not know but who looked Giida, not unlike Ben in his way, and whose wide eyed gaze was full of fear and wonder. And though it pained her, she repeated the words so long ago given to her, and knew they had been hollow then, but they would not be now.

"It's okay now," she said softly. "I'm going to take you away from here. You're safe with me."

She reached for his hands, took them in hers, noted how small and delicate they were as a lump built in her throat. She took him in hand, helped him onto his feet, and then lifted him into her arms.

"*Lothor*. It's time." She said. "Open the way for me, please."

"*As you wish.*" He said. As she stroked the boy's hair, drew his bangs out of his face, she descended into that world of shadow, and hoped her words for him were not lies.


Peter stepped over a pile of broken glass. He sat on his haunches, touched a little girl's shoulder. The blast that had taken down the wall had come from the outside, and both Thorns stood in plain view there around the table. One Wraith lay half in and half out of a nearby cell, and the other was sprawled out, a battered doll, in the intervening space between the table and the wall.

One of those Thorns was clutching his side, where a damp patch was swiftly growing against the knit fabric there. The girl raised her head from between her knees as Ariana emerged from shadow near the table, and set the boy she had liberated on top of it, where he sat against its edge.

"It's going to be okay." He told the girl as she fixed him with a wide eyed gaze.

There was no trust in the look she set on him. She had been broken down, but not so far she could not salvage some of the defenses that had allowed her to survive this long on her own. She was not so far gone as to see him as a hero. Not like he had Queen Meredith, when she came for him.

"We're not in the clear yet, and you're going to see things you don't want to." He continued. "I can't promise it'll be easy, but I'm here." His voice took on a watery edge. "I can't bring your family back, but I can get you out of here. If you'll let me."

The little girl stared at him for a long time. Under the shock, she could be thinking anything. This was not the queen's lies and empty promises. It was not an act meant to secure the girl's compliance, to make her love him like the parents she had lost.

He looked to Ariana, saw what lingered in her gaze. For all that this moment had brought all of the darkness festering in silence within them to bear, the look she set upon him was love.

Just that.

Just love.

The little girl nodded almost imperceptibly.

"Can I carry you?" he asked. "There's broken glass. I don't want you to cut your feet."

She held out her arms. He hauled her off the ground. She wrapped her legs around his sides, and he carried her out of the cell.

Ben came up the hall with one child in his arm, and another following hand in hand with a third.

He situated them around the table with Ariana's charge. Peter set the little girl down with them. They returned to the cells and the hall, both returning with more children.

There were just six in total. They wore blank expressions. Their faces were dirty, their knees and feet scabbed and crusted with grime. What little in the way of clothing they had was filthy—dingy yellow where it should be white; gray and brown where it had been blue, pink, red or yellow; splotched and worn and, in some cases like the girl's, tattered. Among them were a merenern whose scales were pale gray—him not being old enough to have developed the vibrant coloring he would one day, hopefully, come into—and

## To End a Child's Suffering

two kitunes. The rest were human. One was dark-skinned and coconut-headed, a Jua girl. The other two were pallid with thin lips and soft, straight hair—imperial borderlanders likely as not.

The Jua girl clung to Ben. The kitunes leaned against each other. They were both hazel eyed and had the same, long nose. They must be brothers.

Tears ran across Ariana's cheeks. Peter's eyes watered, on the point of shedding tears of his own. He sniffled softly.

Ariana sat on the bench with the children, unsure how to treat them. Did she hug them? Tell them it was going to be okay? She resigned herself simply to be in their presence.

The boy looked into her face. He reached out and grasped her arm with his tiny hand. She smiled, wiped the tears from her eyes.

"This is where we part ways, isn't it?" she said.

Ben nodded. "I'll take the kids to the arch." He panned over the two Thorns. "You're coming with me."

"It will be far less safe for your friends if we do."

"They know how to handle themselves. And they'll be among friends. Where we're going will be dangerous."

The Thorns exchanged a look.

"I take your point." One of them said. "We should go to the nursery first. Then you may split up."

Ben shook his head. "No. No, we need to hurry. The faster we can get everyone in place the better. The furnace workers will be getting into position soon, and I want to be..." he straightened his back, balled up his fists, said his piece with conviction. "I want to be in the Grand Hall when Lance gets there."

"So be it." The other Thorn said, earning him a reproachful look from the first. "We will stand guard in your stead."

Ben turned to Ariana and Peter. "Don't die out there."

# SPIRIT OF SHADOW

"We won't." Peter promised.

"We'll be back before you know it." Ariana added.

She ambled over to where Peter stood, kissed him goodbye. In the next moment, she slid into shadow, and was gone. Peter was short behind her.

"Let's get these kids to safety." Ben said, looking from one Thorn to the other.

They nodded, and converged on the children. He was surprised to see they treated them with gentle care, gave them space to build up the courage to take their hands, to follow them into shadow. He helped them with the charges he had liberated, and brought them to the waiting portal one of those Thorns had opened, which the other had already dropped into, to receive each child as they dropped into the dark.

With the last of them through, he stepped into shadow, and called on Shana to guide them to that place in the dungeons, the nursery Lord Aren had spoken of.

# Betrayal at the Hand of a Lover

L ine up! Out of bed!"

Rashanna's eyes snapped open at the call. A Bloodless stood at the end of her barracks. He was flanked by two Mauls.

*Shit*. She thought. *They're starting early.*

She twisted around under her coverlet. Felicia was still asleep. The woman would sleep through an invasion if she was left to it, and that wasn't far from what Rashanna suspected was about to happen.

It never factored into her calculations that the Council of Liam would see fit to send a fully fledged Bloodless to escort the servants to their killing field. The purge they intended to conduct shouldn't be happening this quickly, but this couldn't be anything else. She wondered how Lord Aren factored into this. If he was making his move even now. A deep wave of nausea twisted her guts at the same time, for if the Bloodless had been called to escort the servants to the sham trials and executions she had been expecting for some weeks now, then someone must have done something reckless. Someone must have been exposed.

And that meant she was compromised, too.

She shook Felicia.

Felicia stirred, stretched her arms.

"What time is it?" she grumbled.

"Form a line!" the Bloodless shouted.

"What's going on?"

"We need to go." Rashanna whispered. "Whatever they have planned for us isn't good."

Felicia sat up. She pulled the drawer beneath the bunk open.

"You don't think those rebels have something to do with it, do you? I still can't believe Ben joined them. That Lance kid really messed with his head." She said as she pulled out a pair of pants and handed them to Rashanna. She pulled another pair free for herself.

"Leave your belongings!" the Bloodless commanded. "Take nothing that is not absolutely necessary!"

She snorted. "He says that like we have jewelry or something."

A cue had formed in front of the soldiers. It snaked halfway down the barracks and was still expanding.

Rashanna cursed herself for not telling Felicia what she had been up to before now. It was too late to amend her mistake.

"Listen to me." She said. "They're not our friends. They are going to kill us if we go with them—"

"I don't see why." Felicia cut in. "Unless they think we're a part of it. It's not like we can do anything about it anyway. They're blocking the only exit."

"There's another way."

"You don't know how to shadow walk."

Rashanna hesitated. She may not be as skilled as the others. Exempting Peter, anyway. But she could do enough. She could take them away from here if she was careful.

## Betrayal at the Hand of a Lover

*Calm down. Think rationally.* She shook herself. *They'll take us somewhere where they have better control over us. There's still time. If we can just break away from them when their guard is down, I can get us to a safe distance and then...*

And then what? If she tried to go back to the Teacher's Tower, she would be leading the Wraiths straight to her friends there. She would only expose them then, and they would all be killed for her efforts to warn them.

*The dungeons. If they're moving, Lord Aren's probably making something happen anyway. And the gate is down there. If I can get us to it, we'll be safe. They can't shadow walk in that place, and there's only one entrance. I bet he's already got Thorns there watching it.*

*For now, just...just play along. Act natural.*

Felicia met her eye, and her expression changed. Skepticism became mixed concern and fear. She jerked away from Rashanna. The distance between them was a no man's land, and the whole expanse was about to be razed.

"You *have* been acting weird lately." She said. "I thought maybe...the absences. You're one of them, aren't you?"

"No, Felicia. Please don't do this. I'm not! I swear!" she pleaded.

Her thoughts traveled to her friends in the Teacher's Tower. *They don't know this is happening. How could they?*

Tears slid over her cheeks, salty and bitter. "Please don't do this. I love you, Felicia. Please, just listen—"

Epiphany stole over Felicia, and Rashanna watched as, in real time, her hopes of saving this woman died. Watched as the feelings of love and of trust she shared with her shriveled up and became something ugly and mean. "Oh my god. I can't believe I was so blind. You've been in on it this whole time." Her eyes narrowed, her posture stiffening. She retreated a step.

"Just listen to me, please!" Rashanna was on her knees now. "They're not our friends. They're going to kill you if they—"

She snatched at Felicia's hands. Felicia yanked them back, looked on her with feral disgust. "All this time I thought you were cheating on me. I should have broken up with you over it, but I had *convinced myself* something else was going on. I thought I was just being paranoid.

"But this is *so much worse*." Her voice was tight, constricted and raspy. "I wanted so badly to trust you, and the whole time you were working with *them!*"

She backed away another step.

"Don't do this, Felicia!"

*Time's up.* The thought gripped her like icy talons driven into her brain. Creek water dumped into her spinal column, spread across every nerve in her body as she made amends with what would happen next, accepted that nothing she did or said would change the outcome. *Fight or die. Fight...or die. Fight...or...die.*

"I love you." She whispered.

Felicia turned toward the Bloodless. She cupped her hands around her mouth. "Rebel in the barracks! Rebel right here!"

The Bloodless rushed in her direction. Rashanna dragged at the silence behind sound, fell into the storm of singing voices beyond the veil and shouted the name of the spirit she needed. The only name she knew.

"LOTHOR!"

She lunged forward, her shadow deepening beneath her, plunged into it head first.

In darkness, amid shouting from disembodied voices only some of which belonged to corporeal entities, she ran. She slammed into a solid figure, spun round him as a melody whispered through her as if from a great distance, and pelted off again. Footsteps chased after her. Voices raised in anger shouted all of her insecurities back at her, and her best efforts to shove them away failed, leaving her exposed to the raw wrath of the Dark Heart as she careened through a world of shadow, not thinking for where she was going.

*Get away. Just get away.* There was safety in the dungeons. She needed to get there and fast. She reached above her, snatched at a barrier with the feel of oiled linen. Light rent the shadows. She did not think for what was on the other side, only for the escape it offered.

She touched it, and shot through.

# Mistress Dina

Being so close to the Grand Hall made Peter nervous. In the antechamber to the Kitchens, he was met with the echoes of a recent past which felt years behind him. The servants toiling away at an array of passed hors d'oeuvres to be sent to a ball held for their captors, the flash and sizzle of cuts of meat hitting hot pans, the gurgle of the fryers chewing on whatever it was they were preparing today—pave, herbs for a panko or a dirte or some other textural accompaniment, prosciutto, or if Mistress Dina was feeling cheeky, croquettes. He could hear her barking orders and insults at her staff somewhere beyond the entrance, and knew then the Wraiths had not come to her just yet, that they were preoccupied, perhaps, with the servants in their tower, with drawing out the multitudes within the barracks there. This would be their last stop, as not to disrupt that party for the nobility, the send off they were to have for the Mirrhvalians before their departure.

*Judgment, hold them back long enough.* He prayed. *And let this all go smoothly for us.*

## Mistress Dina

It would only take one soldier coming down at the wrong time to ruin everything.

"Chef is going to...." He shook himself, tensed and released his fingers, and stepped through.

As the eyes of the cooks settled on him, silence descended like a wave. Shouted jokes and cuss words, pots clattering against cooktops, even the hiss of steam punching out of pans were forgotten as their gazes fell on him. Hands stopped moving. The slapping of knives on cutting boards, the clink of tweezers against polished plates, petered out.  A last few clicks as a cook at the garde manger station, a rookie, finished with his plating and set his tweezers aside, and then he was at center stage, the spotlight on him, a discomforting chill sweeping through him as he panned over them in search of his former master.

A pot of pasta boiled over.

"Shit." The cook who had been handling it pulled it hurriedly off the heat as foam hit the flat top, hissed and chortled.

"What's the hold up?" Mistress Dina snapped. "If I don't have a brisket in front of me in five seconds, I'll beat you all over the head with a fry pan, hear me?"

Peter saw her before she saw him. He drew up short.

Mistress Dina finally found him. Her eyes flashed emerald green. She took up a heavy chef knife and slammed it, point first, into a cutting board, missing another cook's hand by inches.

"You have a lot of nerve showing up here after what you've done." She growled. "Betrayed my trust, didn't you? How much blood is on your hands, now?"

"Drop the act, chef. The time has come." He said forcefully, with a confidence he did not feel. He could not remember a time when he stood up to this woman. There had been many times he had a reason to. Her temper was irascible, but it was not the done thing in a kitchen to talk back to your superior. Just as the commis did not raise their voices at him, he would not do so to this woman either.

Her eyebrows shot up, and for a moment he thought she might take that knife to him. Her knuckles were white against its handle. But what he initially took for anger quickly evaporated. As her grip on the knife eased, her brow descending to its usual place, she looked, if anything, relieved.

A sob punched the air, watery and thick. It came from another cook.

"Quiet, Kent." Mistress Dina barked.

She let go of the knife. It stayed resolutely upright. She stalked toward him, her jaw set. Her eyes darkened to veridian.

"I wish I could have left under better circumstances," Peter explained as she closed the distance. "And you can cuss me out over it when this is all over, but right now...right now we need to gather as much food as we can. We need to get it to the dungeons. Lord Aren's orders. We're getting out of here."

"You were my favorite subordinate, you know. I always thought Ariana had bigger balls than you, but you had a way with these idiots she didn't. Knew how to talk *to* people instead of just *at them*. There's a place for both, and knowing when to use the one over the other...it makes all the difference."

She panned over the others, many of whom flinched under that hard-eyed gaze. "I haven't been entirely honest with you." She eased up against a prep counter. He could not remember a time when she looked so vulnerable, when she seemed so...was delicate the right word? *No, never that.* "Much as I wish this one would have seen fit to trust me, he has nonetheless stumbled across the truth. All of you have been lied to your lives long by the people who have positioned themselves as your family. The department heads, the nobility...there's a special place in the Pits for Lady Tamalsen especially. They have *all* been lying to you.

"You have families on the outside. In far flung places the world over. Many of you came from as far away as Haru or Soldran. Some may have even been sold into some filthy poacher's custody and then hawked like a common amulet to a Wraith under Lord Tarkenta's direct control. I believe many of you have nightmares about the pasts and the families you left behind. I've heard from many a servant over my tenure as Mistress of the Kitchens the same stories, bearing the same themes from I can't even tell you how many mouths. Those dreams are your real lives. I don't know how they made you forget, but they did something to each and every one of you to sell you on a narrative that is simply a pack of lies."

She turned to Peter then. "I've been waiting twenty years for this day. I came here under Queen Tania. Life wasn't exactly great then, but it was better than this. Came here with Master Gregor. He's my cousin, you know. Country bumpkin that he is, he's always been bolder than me. It fits that he'd have raised a small army when I was too cowardly to tell even my most trusted people the truth."

"Chef, I—"

"No, don't. Words won't make it better. I can only say I'm proud you got this far, but how sure are you we can get out of here?"

He grimaced.

"I thought so."

"The plan is solid, but there's a big question in the middle of it that could make us or break us, and the person we need went missing last night."

"Isn't that convenient."

"Well, missing isn't the right word. He's just reckless and stupid, and made a—"

"We're wasting time." She cut in. Her gaze flicked to the

nearest cook. "You're taking helm. Take the dinner crew to the store rooms. Start with staple goods. Heavy starches, grains, meat, as much salt as you can carry. Then worry about produce. Make sure you don't forget the vinegars and yeasts. We'll need them to preserve what we have. If we have time for a second run, we'll worry about spices and flavorings then."

"But...you...you're going along with...with this?" he stammered. "He's a rebel. They killed—"

She reached out and backhanded him across the mouth. Singled out the next in line.

"You're taking helm now, Pat. Have someone bind him up while you're going about the other affairs." She raised her voice for the rest of them to hear. "If you have a problem with my orders, or with your sous chef's actions, you can have what Barry here is having. Otherwise, start gathering hardware. Start with the largest cook pots and fill them up with as many tongs, spoons and what have you as you can. I want them here!" she stabbed a thick finger at the ground. "Ready to be taken to the dungeons in the next ten minutes. The sooner we're out of this hole, the better. Understood!"

"Yes, chef!" came a chorus of voices. In the next moment, everyone was scattering. Half the crew was filtering into the hall through the antechamber he had left behind and the other half was pulling down pots and utensils and flatware. A few had gone off into the dish pit to start stacking earthenware and cheesecloth into crates for easier transport.

"Ten minutes isn't a lot of time." Peter said.

"Trust your subordinates, Peter." She responded coolly. "It will be enough. Now how do you intend to get us out of here?"

"There's a gate in the dungeons." He explained. A room they won't be able to shadow walk into. The entrance is narrow. A spiral staircase bucking up against a door. If we can get to that room, we'll be able to hold off whoever comes for us. Hopefully long enough that Lance can get back with Queen Meredith's pendant."

She looked at him then as if she had never seen him before.

"He stole her...." She breathed. "How in the name of Amorahiya did he manage that?"

He shrugged. "Don't know. Wasn't there. But they'd have dragged him out in front of everyone to be executed if they caught him."

"I take your point."

"This gate. We don't know where it goes. We barely have an idea how to use it."

"But you're sure you *can* use it."

"If Lance can activate the queen's pendant, it'll open. We've seen it work once already."

"It'll have to do, then, won't it?"

"If it doesn't work—"

"Then it was nice knowing you. And I'll see you in Amorahiya."

# A Path Carved Through Darkness

Ariana emerged in the palace laundry to the chortle and swish of clothing and linens being pushed with long oars through boiling water. The laundry was a peaceful place at this hour, and though the servants here labored over those massive tilt kettles, or blasted warm air currents at hanging lines laden with sodden raiment, or used their rites to propel spinners to extract water and soap foam from their burdens, there was a sense as of this reach of the palace being isolated from the melodrama so often unfolding just above them.

The work could not be kind to their bodies, but she did not see anyone scowling as she passed them, and none paid much mind to her as she marched between those monstrosities in metal on her way to meet with this department's mistress.

She found Mistress Rosaline precisely where she had

expected. She was seated behind her desk atop the poured stone platform at the rear of the laundry, a series of shelves sprawling away from her which housed the various uniforms of the Mauls, the Wraiths, the Thorns, and the servants. Further removed and locked away would be the effects of the nobility which needed to be returned to their chambers by the couriers who were assigned here for the day.

She suspected it was the common occurrence of those couriers rising out of the shadows to take up a burden for one noble or another that allowed them to ignore her so summarily as she passed them. If they had known who she was, someone among them would have sounded an alarm. She assumed they would anyway. It would only be right.

"Fancy seeing you here." Mistress Rosaline said inflectionlessly. If she was surprised at a rebel servant coming within spitting distance of her, she did not show it. She almost seemed to have expected her to arrive here.

"Did Lord Aren tell you I was coming?" she asked.

"No, but you learn to read between the lines with him. He left a note." She searched the neat piles of paperwork on her desk, mostly orders from the other departments or the military for deliveries of fresh linens, and towels, and other accouterments they might need for their day to day operations. She selected one of those orders, and plucked it from the pile. "Right here."

She passed it to her.

"This is just an order for uniforms."

"And some other things." Mistress Rosaline held out her hand, and Ariana passed it back to her.

"Lord Aren is pretty good at spelling, but you wouldn't know it looking at this. You wouldn't be wrong for thinking he had a shit scribe scratch this message out for him. He does make use of them." She explained. "But see here. How the "w" in towels gets a little long and then it looks like he tried to scratch it out. Or there, armbands is missing the "r'. Put all of the typos together and you get "Teamas eya baahela."

"What the fuck does that mean?" Ariana asked.

"They will come the fun." She said. "Kind of ambiguous until you realize there's a missing word there. The name of a spirit *you* don't know."

"But you do?"

"You're not surprised I know about the spirits?"

"You know about Lord Aren." Ariana said flatly. "We're wasting time. He wants you to get as many changes of clothes as you can, and whatever we can use for bandages after this is over. I can take you to the drop off point."

"Straight to business." Mistress Rosaline said sardonically. "I suppose humoring an old lady is out of the question." She shrugged one shoulder. "Well...I suppose that's fine. What's the plan, anyway?"

Ariana explained the plot in broad strokes. She was growing impatient, and it showed in her tone of voice as she rushed to the finish, leaving plenty open for further questioning and making clear at the same time she had no intention of entertaining a lengthy conversation about any of it.

"Time is of the essence." She said, clapping her hands together. "Peter is already talking to Mistress Dina about all of this and the Wraiths are inbound."

"Well then we better hurry."

"That's what I've been—"

Mistress Rosaline climbed out of her seat. She approached a bronze rail at the edge of the poured stone block and shouted for all of her charges to hear, her voice strangely amplified though Ariana had not seen her call on a spirit to facilitate it.

"Stop what you're doing. Time's up!" she shouted. "Gather whatever hasn't already been packed up and get ready to roll. We're leaving!"

She turned around then, faced Ariana and grinned. "Happy?"

The servants behind her were climbing down from their platforms, abandoning oars, moving away from spinners and approaching drying lines to yank down what was settled against them. They drew carts already crammed with uniforms and bedsheets and towels and all manner of other items from hiding places behind the kettles and spinners and the rest, and lined them up along the widest channel, in plain view of Mistress Rosaline's desk.

Animated chatter accompanied their actions as they prepared for the departure, earning Ariana's surprise. She had not expected they would know anything about the rebellion brewing in the palace, let alone that it might mean something to them.

"You told them?"

"Everything, yeah." Mistress Rosaline reclined against the rail. She was chuckling now. "You really thought Master Gregor was the *only* one who had a reason to let his people in on the secret? The nobles never come down here. No one's checking on us. The same goes for the boilers. We're our own little world here, so you can go ahead and wipe that look of surprise off your face. It shouldn't be any big shock that my servants are ready for this.

"Now, can we get moving? I don't want to be here when those soldiers arrive. We can pick off the new guys fine, but the veterans won't give us much chance."

"You're not afraid the Wraiths are watching?"

"I'd be more afraid if I hadn't picked them off myself."

Ariana hissed through her teeth.

Mistress Rosaline chortled. She pulled something out of her shirt, a pendant inset with a piece of what looked like sapphire. "You wouldn't believe where I had to hide this to smuggle it in."

"What is it?"

"Bit of enchanting work an old acquaintance made in exchange for some Myranh gemstones something like twenty five years back. He ended up contracting with the Hoga family instead. There's a bit of a rivalry there. But he was nice enough to let me keep this, and a couple other things. I couldn't take those with me, but this...well, it's small and unassuming isn't it? Easy to stash where no one would think to look."

Ariana rolled her eyes. "If you're not going to tell me what it does, at least keep it close in case we need it."

"That reminds me." She shuffled off, leaving Ariana to catch up with her as she descended from the block onto the main avenue where the servants were all awaiting her now. She approached a duct inset into the floor behind a spinner and dipped the pendant into it; and held it there for a few seconds while it pulsed with vibrant, blue light.

She retracted it, wiped it against the hem of her shirt, and placed it around her neck where it belonged.

"Ready to go?" she asked.

"I was ready a while ago."

"Then let's get to it."

"Lothor, open my shadow." Ariana said.

"Oh how droll." Mistress Rosaline chided. "Let's try it this way. Lothor ab Aran, oldbo cha'an porto!"

A guttural chuckle pronounced Lothor's arrival, and as it washed over Ariana and the rest who could hear him, the shadows darkened along the avenue, extended from the flanks of wide carts and from the feet of those servants. Ariana's shadow was caught in the twist and flung far forward, adjoining to Mistress Rosaline's as it became bloated and distorted before her, and then linking to all of those others as they bled together into an ocean of darkness.

"How the fuck did you—"

"I've been practicing magic a lot longer than you have,

hun. It comes with the territory."

The carts descended first, then the servants gathered around them. Ariana felt her feet sliding into shadow beneath her, looked down to see she had descended to her knees. Mistress Rosaline was short behind her, and as they dropped into shadow, the first soldiers arrived at the entrance to the laundry. She saw them, saw fire flung from their hands, shadow tracers soaring across the walls, under tilt kettles, extending their reach as they sought the head of department and Ariana both.

And missed.

The shadows collapsed into dissolution, and they were gone from the world above, in a world which lacked sight.

The first Wraiths dropped into the shadows as she called on Shara to guide them away. Screams and dull roars from the rear as fighting broke out there. The clangor of weapons meeting weapons. She could not tell if those belonged to the servants or if the Wraiths fought amongst themselves, but she could not believe it was the latter. Their ranks could not have been compromised the way the Thorns were, could not be under such direct influence from Lord Aren, who had nothing to do with them.

A gargled scream. Something heavy dropped against Ariana's shin. She stepped away from the twitching corpse.

"Get moving!" a man's voice almost at her ear. "We'll cover you."

"Who are—"

"I SAID GET MOVING!"

She was running. Mistress Rosaline's voice behind her called the charge for her servants. Cart wheels squealed into motion. The iron ring of knives bashing against each other, the screams and pummeling feet, shouts echoing back and forth as the Dark Heart came to play with all of those gathered here.

She ran on as yet more skirmishes broke out before and

around her, was forced off course twice as the tracers narrowed, the angle between them growing more obtuse the closer she got to her destination.

She ripped at the darkness above her when the angle abruptly shifted, and light spilled into the shadow, revealing smoke, carnage, Mistress Rosaline panting and clutching her knees, the servants still at a distance but closing in fast.

"Can you do that thing again?" she asked.

"Doesn't work that way, hun. You're just gonna have to hold open the portal until everyone's out."

"I don't know if I—"

The first cart arrived. The servants who had run it this far gripped onto its sides and touched the portal Ariana had opened. They shot through with their quarry.

The next cart arrived, and the servants repeated the action. More and more arrived and shot through, and she was not at all certain they were met with safety on the other side, but whatever lay there must be better than this. Must be better than the storm of voices echoing in her ears, threatening to drag her under as Thorns and Wraiths fought blind and in shadow against each other, as dying men fell to soak the shadowed floor with their blood and feed the voices growing ever stronger as the Dark Heart took its pound of flesh.

And behind all of that chaos, she heard Lothor's voice, a constant refrain.

"I will kill you all. I will kill you. Every one of you who used me. Every one of you who caused me pain. I will kill you all."

She heard the mirth in his voice, the absolution. There was no guilt in the spirit for what transpired, no intention to pull the Dark Heart back, to reign it in. He was enjoying this, and his joy made her feel nauseous. That he would revel in all of this death.

## A Path Carved Through Darkness

Mistress Rosaline cupped her face in her hands, looked into her eyes. She realized she had not been paying attention to her surroundings, that at some point she had simply checked out.

"Lead them to the gate. I'll keep the portal open. You need to go." She said. "You're at your limit. You need to go."

She guided Ariana's hand to the portal, forced her to touch it as, with her other hand, she clawed at the ether.

Ariana shot through, into a dungeon hall choked with push carts and disheveled servants, to lead them to the last place they might find safety.

# The Nursery

en followed the Thorns out of the shadows, into a poured stone tunnel he had been down a hundred times. The cold, impassive light of glow bulbs illuminated every crack in the walls, darkened every water stain against the gritty, worn floor.

The sound of a great many marching feet echoed from somewhere in the distance. The low hum of murmuring voices, fraught with anticipation, drifted along the passages with it.

*It's startin'.* Ben thought, dreading the outcome if they didn't finish with this task in good time. Even if they did, people were going to die. Some of those were going to be servants.

The Thorns took up positions to either side of the door, kept watch from their knees for anyone who came too close.

He ran his fingers across the black triangle glazed into the tile near the door's knob. "This is it?"

"That's it. Now get a move on."

The children they had liberated from the dungeons were

## The Nursery

arrayed around him. He hesitated.

These children did not know anything of what lay beyond this door. They had never been inside this place, but he had. Though his memories of it were untrustworthy things, he had been here, had lived in this confined corner of the palace for the queen only knew how long before they finally let him loose on the palace halls.

He did not want to enter this place. Wanted these children to witness whatever breakdown he might have even less. It would be better to enter alone, but to do so would leave them in danger's path.

"Watch the kids." He said to them. "I don't know what's waiting for me in there. I don't want them to see—"

"We get it. Now get moving." The other Thorn cut in. "We don't have all night."

He nodded. It was all he could do. He took the doorknob in his hand, twisted it. He was surprised to find it gave easily, that the door opened without any resistance. He left it open as he stepped down the central hall, and looked into bay windows at the rooms all dark and empty, the women cleaning up the messes their charges left behind with damp towels, or putting toys away in wide trenchers situated along walls which were covered in scribbled drawings. Most of those depicted haunting scenes from these children's half remembered pasts.

*Please hurry, Lance. Everything is riding on you.* He thought to himself. If there was a way to make all of this stop, it lay in the power of that stone. If they could leave this palace, they could be free. Those kids could have a better life then. *Not just them. All of us. Every one of us could have a better life if we could just get away from here.*

The poured stone and glow bulbs of the outside hall yielded to a scale replica of the palace halls above them. Glowing, white tile dressed the floors and walls, reflecting the pooled light from mirrored lamps scattered down the central hall's length. To either side were rooms filled with the trappings of a nursery. One room was home to a long rug and a number of chests that Ben knew, though he wasn't sure how, were filled with toy wagons and dolls. Another was the canteen in miniature. In a third were little desks situated in rows before a chalkboard, not unlike the classroom he had camped in with the others for the last month. A final room contained a replica in miniature of the barracks, and each of those beds was occupied by a child clad in white reliefs, like he was.

A flash of memory scuttled across his mind in which he fought over a toy carriage with a strawberry-blonde boy. The other boy was red faced behind a smattering of light freckles, scream-crying in the way that only the very young found dignified.

Ben flinched at the memory, left the sleeping children behind.

A lone, curtained window inside the barracks caught his eye. It emitted a soft, silver glow like moonlight, though there could be nothing but poured stone behind it.

Suspecting something nefarious, he called on Lothor, and was met with silence. The rite he had so often used for shadow walking fell apart. Even when he tried to use force to draw Lothor in, he was met with the same silence, the same unraveling of what ought to open a portal where he desired. There were other melodies within the cosmic orchestra, that chaotic tangle of sounds, and he heard those quite clearly. But Lothor's voice could not drive through the chaos, would not come to his ears with any clarity.

These were the rooms that had caused Sami to go on a murderous rampage. Perhaps it had been those very images crossing the walls that compelled her to venture down her path. Maybe in seeing the way those children were housed, how they were made to believe their enslavers were their saviors, she had come to identify with the Watchers, and let them take command of her. She might have even seen them as a necessary—

His breath caught.

At the end of the hall, along the far wall of the chamber it let out on, were arranged a series of shackles. The chains connected the wrist cuffs to the ankles, leaving little room for maneuverability. It would have been almost impossible to sit comfortably given such scant little slack in the binds. It would have been torture to be stuck in whatever position they would allow. Enough to sit in a way, but never to lay down. Never to rest their heads or find a comfortable position in which to sleep.

The shackles were empty, but he suspected they had once contained the bodies of the Watchers riding Sami, who had taken her over in their pursuit of vengeance, or perhaps justice for all the wrongs Lady Therien and the others had committed in the years since the rise of Queen Meredith.

Anger welled up inside him. *There's no bottom to these people!*

"Lance? Is that you?" It was a voice he recognized.

"No. No, it's Ben. Are you—"

Sami emerged from around the corner. She looked a mess. Her hair was a matted ruin barely clinging to its strawberry blond coloring, and her clothes were covered in dirt and blood. She smiled at him nonetheless.

"Don't mind this." She gestured to herself. "I'm okay. They didn't give me time to put myself back together before they...well..." she turned toward the break in the wall, to look at something he couldn't see.

"Why are you *here*? Of all places." He asked.

"I figured someone would come for the kids before long." She said. "I was right, wasn't I? You might as well come out now, Maera."

"Who is—" but before he could get his question out, a tall

woman emerged in the gap. She was a kitune, her hair running down her back as a dense curtain. Her eyes shone the most peculiar shade of blue, and upon seeing him, they ebbed to a more natural umber.

"He's a friend." Sami said to her.

The woman regarded him with a gentle gaze. He did not get the impression she was unintentionally cruel, nor that she had much love for violence. But he saw in her, too, an internal strength of the kind that was hard to fake. A self assuredness that whatever she set out to do must be right, lest she cease to be able to look herself in the mirror, and believe she was just.

"What *happened* to you?" He asked, the words returning to him.

"A lot of things I don't want to talk about. I'm free now. That's what's important." She said.

"Lance was worried."

"Hopefully, he can get unworried by the time this is over." She giggled. "This is all thanks to him, isn't it?"

Ben nodded.

"Then I'll have to work a 'thank you' in while I'm laying into him for being such an idiot."

"He stole the pendant." Maera said. "We saw him on our way here. It was a brief encounter. He is your lover, is he not?"

"How did you...no, you're one of the Watchers, aren't you?"

She nodded curtly. "He is alive. His errand was a success. But he will go to the Grand Hall before the executions begin. We will be needed there, too."

"Can you fight?" He asked Sami.

"You're not leaving me behind after everything I've been through, if that's what you're asking."

"O-okay. It'll be dangerous, though."

## The Nursery

"That's why Maera is coming with us."

"I have two Thorns with me. They're going to guard the kids."

"Lord Aren's men." Maera explained to Sami. They will be trustworthy."

"Will you read them anyway?" Sami asked.

"I will do that. For your peace of mind."

"Thank you."

"Let's get going, then. We'll get the kids out of bed and bring them to the gate. We can go back to the Grand Hall once they're safe."

Maera nodded. He took Sami's hand in his, felt the well developed callouses against his palm and knew they had not been there before she had disappeared.

*How much hell have you been through.* He wondered.

They roused the children. It was no easy feat getting them all out of bed. The women in the rooms fussed about their cleaning as if they could not see them, and he wondered if that was the Watcher's doing. If she had brainwashed them somehow, or if they had simply given up hope of keeping intruders out with the death of Lady Therien.

"Why leave them alive?" he asked, observing them.

"Evil takes on many forms. For them it was complacence. They view this as a job and nothing more. Something to pass the time. That one..." she tipped her chin in the direction of a portly woman in her middle years. "...was never able to have children of her own. She is not the only one who is barren. She took up a role in this place so that she could raise a family of her own, and settled into the humdrum of it all as the children progressively matriculated into your ranks. By the time you came along, she had convinced herself she could protect you from Lady Therien's worst impulses, if she only stood between the woman and you.

"She may have deluded herself into believing some part of this was right, that she may even be justified in her actions.

She does not view herself as evil, certainly. Do you see fit to kill her? Or would you reserve judgment for the psychopath who she served."

"I see your point." He said, helping a boy out of an undersized bunk and guiding him into the hall. He was among the last to have been taken out of the beds, the rest formed orderly lines at Sami's direction, and he suspected they did so more out of fear for what the crazed looking savage might do to them than any sense of kinship, or safety.

With the last of the dozens of children there drawn into the hall, Ben took up a position at the back of the cue, and Maera joined Sami at the front.

Her eyes flickered lightning blue, and their gazes mirrored hers. Wordlessly, they sprang into motion.

*That's terrifying.* He thought to himself. The ease with which she compelled them to do as she wanted did not sit right with him, but he did not comment. It would be better if they met as little resistance from them as possible until they were well within the shadow of that arch, where they could be protected.

The Thorns joined him as he emerged from the chambers, and one leaned into his ear.

"Who are they?"

"Sami is the roughed up lookin' one."

"She's the one Lord Aren threw to the Watchers." The other Wraith explained at the queer look from the one who had spoken.

"The other is one of the Watchers. Her name is Maera. They are friends."

Maera looked over her shoulder. Her eyes flashed blue a final time, and then subsided into umber. "You three can shadow walk. Take us down or shut their eyes."

"We will shut their eyes." The Thorn who had asked after her said.

## The Nursery

He spoke the command for Lothor as the other moved to join the two women at the front of the cue. He took the lead.

"Is it safer to go this way?"

"The dungeons are our stronghold." The Thorn explained. "We know the layout better than the Wraiths or the Mauls. But there will be fighting in the shadows there before long. It will come over ground eventually, but that will happen later. When those loyal to the crown realize they cannot stop us without leaving the safety of familiar ground."

"So we stick to the halls." The other added. "For now."

"You would do best to do the same on your way to the Grand Hall." The first explained. "Blend in with the servants there."

"Okay. I'll take your advice." Ben said. "If Lance shows up before me, tell him not to look for me. No one can get out of here without him, so if he tries to resist, you tell him I can handle myself. Even if you don't believe it."

The Thorn smirked. "I'll do what I can."


Gooseflesh crawled across Rashanna's skin. A static surge of fear rushed down her spine like cold water. Everywhere she looked she saw structures that advantaged Master Gregor and his crew. If this errand turned to violence, it would be to the detriment of the military. They would come to regret the oversight of allowing an entire faction of servants command over fire and air, whether they knew it or not.

She had never been into this reach of the palace, but upon learning that her friends were not hulled up in the Teacher's Tower, the most obvious place to look for them, in her mind, was here. The furnaces stank of grease and coal, hot metal and unwashed bodies. She understood, then, why Lady Tamalsen warned so many away from them.

"You know better than that." She whispered to herself as she navigated the wide channel between furnaces on her way to find Master Gregor. *She hates kitunes. The mess is just an excuse.*

She found herself squaring off against Emma, who appeared from around a bend in the path. The furnace crews continued about their work. None seemed in much of a hurry to get away. *Do they know what's going on right now?*

Emma approached. She wore her customary scowl.

Given the circumstances, Rashanna chose to ignore it. She idled, waited for Emma to come within range to hear her when she spoke, which was much closer than she would have liked given how loud those furnaces were.

"What happened?" She shouted. "Why are you here?"

"They're gathering all the servants now! Lance and the others are gone! I almost got—"

"Come with me! We'll tell Master Gregor!"

She followed her through the furnaces and up the wrought bronze staircase onto the catwalk above where Master Gregor's office was situated.

Seeing them passing, Duardo exchanged a few words with the crew he'd been working with, and jogged over to join them.

"Wha's goin' on?" he asked as they climbed the last few steps. He was panting, covered in sweat from his hairline to his boots.

"They're moving." Rashanna said. "Soldiers came to my barracks to round everyone up."

They emerged in Master Gregor's office, where he was reclining against his chair, his boots crossed over the edge of his desk.

"They're moving, Gregor." Emma said, echoing Rashanna's words. "The soldiers. I'd bet—"

"Cool it, missy." Master Gregor cut in. "Plan's changed. We're not needed jus' yet."

"You knew about this?" Rashanna breathed.

## The Nursery

He kicked his legs over the desk and planted his feet firmly on the ground, leaned forward to address them properly.

"Look, I 'on't claim ta like it, but it is what it is. Lance, that idiot boy, moved early. I knew he would. Wish he didn't, but ya can't stop soemone's got 'ere mind made up, so I let it go.

"He's got the pendant. 'M sure of it. He's got it an' 'at's why 'ere movin'. Best we 'an do now is get in position an' wait."

"Wha's 'at mean?" Duardo asked.

"Means you ought tha supreme honor o' goin' to 'em boilers an' lettin' 'em know its game on." He said to Duardo. "You jus' meet up wit' us in 'em rooms cross from 'at Grand Hall. We'll be 'ere."

Duardo saluted. "Yessir."

He departed from the office without further comment.

"You go on down 'ere tell 'em ta stop what 'ere doin'. "S ain't a drill, got it. We're leavin'."

"Leaving." Emma breathed. "But we—"

"Plan's already set. Half o' it's in motion 's we speak." He said. "Do it right and we might jus' get a taste of freedom 'fore we die. So get to it."

She grumbled something under her breath. The only word Rashanna caught as she brushed past her on her way out was 'idiot'.

"Lovely 'un 'at girl is. Couldn't ask fer better." He chuckled. "You'd bes' get goin' too."

"Where?"

"Well, I'd guess based on 'at look on yer face, you ought someone you want to protect. So, absent anywhere else obvious, I'd say ya go get 'em."

She nodded shakily. "They'll be in the Grand Hall."

"Then maybe you link up wit' us once ya got 'em. We'll be waitin' in 'a wings."

# SPIRIT OF SHADOW

"T-thank you, Master Greg—"

"Jus' Gregor'll do."

"Thank you, Gregor."

She walked out of the office, down the stairs, and then out of the furnaces. She didn't trust taking to the shadows with the Wraiths after her, but took a roundabout way back to the servant's entrance to the Grand Hall. If the soldiers were coming for those burners and breezers, they would arrive by the shortest path. That left the longer way back the more obvious choice should she wish to avoid unwanted eyes.

# A Conspirator's Resolve

en emerged with Sami and the Watcher, Maera, to the sound of marching feet. A glance around the corner revealed a double file of servants moving toward a larger cluster, who passed through the massive, open doors into the Grand Hall. Bloodless stood sentry along the outside track of the hall, moonlight from the windows throwing them into shadow.

"They're expecting us." He whispered.

"They 'on't know what to expect." The woman said. "Never confronted this kind of enemy."

"A Watcher?" Sami asked, looking to her now.

Her expression was unreadable, her eyes dark for the moment.

"An enemy whom they cannot put a face to." She said. "They may have some idea of what you look like, but they 'on't know how many of you have turned on 'em, nor what we're capable of, nor where exactly we're hidden."

"Did you pick that up with your power?" Ben asked.

"'S intuition." She shrugged. "Time to go."

She pushed him onward. They joined the file of servants.

"That's—" one of the servants whispered.

The woman's eyes flashed lightning blue. The servant cut off abruptly.

"What did you—" Ben started.

"I told him all he needed to know, and the others for good measure."

"You really are somethin' else."

They marched with the file. Each time they passed a Bloodless, her eyes flashed. None of them seemed to notice Ben and Sami as they passed with her.

"Can they see us?" Ben asked, growing suspicious.

"Of course they can." Sami said. "They just don't know it."

"I don't get it." Ben said.

"You don't have to." Sami smiled warmly. "I get it for you. I've seen how it works, remember."

"You've seen the effect. Not the cause." The woman reminded her.

Sami shuddered. "Don't remind me."

"For what it's worth, I *am* sorry we put you through that. We had no choice in the matter. It was business."

"It will take some time." Sami acknowledged her with a light squeeze of her wrist. "But I don't hate you. I guess that's a start."

"Remind me never to piss you off." Ben said under his breath as the Watcher's eyes flickered blue again, cutting off another attempt by a servant to give alarm.

"You needn't worry." She replied.

Her eyes flashed blue and held to that hue as they passed by four of the Bloodless inside the entrance to the Grand Hall.

They followed the crowd of servants, and joined the hundreds of others already gathered there.

They wove between servants—some as young as twelve years old and others well into their middle years.

"'S with Meredith alone they were taken." The woman said, answering his question without need for him to ask. Her eyes flickered and strobed as she panned over the crowd.

"First were men and women taken to make a statement. Mostly, they were family of rivals stepped out of bounds. They switched to kids, still mostly taking 'em from families who had offended the queen or some noble or other. Your lover's father was one of the most notorious of 'em."

"You know who Lance's father is?" Ben whispered.

She nodded. "Yours, too. Both o' yours."

"Who is he?"

"Man by the name of Henry, from Ozos. Ya never met him. Your mother was Lazuli. She's dead now, but she got you out 'fore the city fell. Gave you a token to show to the one person who might save ya, and he saw fit to hide ya in the borderlands. You were taken when 'a police there realized who ya were."

"How?"

"Recognized yer last name. I can only see so much given it comes from yer point o' view, but seems to me they thought they could get a ransom out o' him. Problem is you were more valuable as a bargaining chip to Mirrhvale 'an a borderland court. Might come in handy, knowing yer family name. One day."

Ben nodded slowly. "Maybe."

"'S Abiia. You ever find yerself in Ozos, give 'em at name. Might just save yer life."

"O-okay." He said. A complicated mix of feelings welled up inside him, but he didn't have the bandwidth to process them. Not when in the next moments, he may see the deaths of friends, of loved ones, at the hands of Shadovane's soldiers.

# SPIRIT OF SHADOW

Fear and the anticipation of violence were much more immediate concerns. Who he was, or who he might have been, was a thing to digest when the dust had settled.

But he needed a distraction. Something to take the edge off. And so he kept the conversation flowing.

"What about Sami?" he asked.

"I don't think I want to know." She said.

"Nonsense." Ben said. "It's better if you do. That way you have somethin' good to remember when you think of them."

She hesitated. "Fine. Tell me."

The woman grinned. "You were born in Trom. You'd have grown up riding horses across the plains 'round 'ere had you been allowed to stay, but like so many others 'round yer age, you landed here because yer father pissed someone off.

"Yer father's name was Timothy Mathus. He served the leader of an organization called The Cross, and was cut down by his predecessor. When you awakened to the truth, I think it was this memory that came to you. The Spirit of Dreams was not kind on the night of the emperor's arrival."

"Do all of us have connections like these?" Ben asked.

Her grin went away, was replaced by a stony expression. "We did what we had to do." She said with conviction. "Some o' you had obvious connections 'at might benefit us in the end, if ya could be made ta remember what happened ta ya. We decided it was best to lock up some o' yer memories in safe places, where ya could still access 'em but 'ey wouldn't look too suspicious."

"Like dreams." Ben said.

"Like dreams." She agreed. "Some few o' you seem to have drawn close together. There were others, mind. Not all directly related to each other. Peter, fer instance, only ever had a couple run ins with the Cross. Was just happenstance wit' 'im. But you two...both o' yer fathers served Markus Whiteheart at a time, and when Hugo came to call, he killed the disloyal ones over it. Maybe it has somethin' 'a do wit' why you became fast friends, I won't claim to know. But I do know 's good ya found each other, or none of this could have happened."

As Maera spoke to them of their distant pasts, Ben found the reason for this gathering. Beyond the rows of heads and shoulders, past the last skylight, a stage had been erected. The stage was constructed of unvarnished wood planks, a stone disk at its heart. Human silhouettes were scorched into the stone, leaving permanent imprints behind as a living history, a story of scandal and treachery for the ages. Handprints gripped the beveled rim. Portraits blended together like the remnants of some horrifying chimera, its last bid for escape immortalized.

Lord Cree stood to one side of the circle. He rested on his sheathed sword, its point wedged in the seam of two boards. He wore his full suit of armor—bronze plate cast to look as though smoke had been forged into it, violet and black sashes wrapped around his waist, the Raven and Thorns sigil embroidered into them in thread of silver.

A Thorn mounted the short flight of steps leading up to the executioner's platform. He exchanged some words with Lord Cree, who dismissed him, then pushed off his sword and tucked it into the violet sash around his waist.

*He knows we're here.* Ben thought.

He thought of the Bloodless in the hall. The likeliest probability was that there were Wraiths watching from the shadows, searching for the leaders of this rebellion, for *him.*

He did not know how the Watchers' power worked, but he suspected it did not transcend dimensions. The Shadow World was its own place, with its own rules. As long as the Wraiths hid within it, they were most likely safe.

Lord Cree cleared his throat. The rough sound echoed through the chamber, crystal clear to Ben's ears.

"You are wondering, I am sure, why you are here." He

said.

Ben looked to Sami, then to Maera. Her eyes sustained that eerie glow now. She stood board straight and unnaturally still, and he wondered if she was still within her body, or if she had gone to possess another, as she had done with Sami.

"One of you has stolen something from your queen. She feels she has been betrayed. Has she not been good to you, she wonders? Has she not treated you like her own children? She is deeply hurt by this transgression against her, and has every reason to believe the thief among you is not working alone.

"Fortunately, she has eyes in many places. They watch from the shadows, and from those shadows, they see all. There are those men and women learned in the craft of interrogation among us, too, whom would do anything for her, if only to make her happy."

The woman relaxed. Her eyes lost their glow, returning to their more ordinary umber.

"It is done." She said. "Now we wait."

"Wait for what?" Ben asked.

"To the rebels among you," Lord Cree continued. "We know your names. We have seen your faces. For your sake and for the sake of your fellows, I will ask this once that you turn yourselves in. Face judgment, or face execution. Mercy will be given to those who come forward, but should we see fit to expose you, you will be granted only death...by *fire*." He gestured airily to the stone disk, earning a collective flinch back from the servants gathered before him.

"They're bluffing." Sami said.

"How do you know? They might not know what *you* look like, but they definitely saw *us* in the dungeons." He said.

"Are you gonna turn yourself in, then?" she asked.

"Of course not. We've come too far to turn back now." He said.

## A Conspirator's Resolve

"Lance really found something special in you." She favored him with a look that made him uncomfortable, like some anomaly observed through a microscope. "When we finish this, I'll make sure to let him know I approve."

Ben chuckled. "You never take anythin' seriously, do you?"

"Oh, I do." She said. "But if you'd been through what I have, you'd want a little joy in your life, too."


Rashanna navigated the narrow channels between servants, using the taller of them as markers while she nudged the shorter out of her path. Alesha was somewhere among them. With the stage set for the escape, she could breathe a little easier.

*If I find her here, it'll all be okay again. She'll be here or by the arch.*

She couldn't allow herself to linger on the alternatives. That one or both of them might die her. That this entire plan might fail and all of them meet violent ends. If she considered how severely the odds of success were stacked against them, she might find herself stuck on the hard truth that they were outmoded and out matched—that, at the end of the day, they were all just screaming into the void and hoping for a miracle.

This plan was full of holes. Its reliance on a pack of young adults with their days as scullery maids barely behind them was perhaps the most glaring of the problems with it. That one of them might actually have lifted the queen's most valuable possession off her in the night was an appallingly glorious moment for their side, but it could all end there—with everything that came after a failure of the greatest magnitude. Even her being here, knowing Alesha may well seek to hand her over to the soldiery as she had done before, was a sign of ill tidings to come, and she was not oblivious to it. She was aware this entire scheme of hers, this desperate

# SPIRIT OF SHADOW

attempt to save her on again off again girlfriend was a fool's errand, and she was an idiot for attempting it. But she could not leave her behind. However volatile their relationship, however much the girl annoyed her, she loved her.

If the Sky Lord knew mercy, she would find the girl she had fallen in love with, and defend her to the bitter end.

She hunted through faces familiar and unfamiliar as she drove further into the crowd. Alesha was nowhere among them.

Servants were still arriving through the great doors at the back of the chamber. She dared not get too close to them. The rebel position was a delicate one, and would be until it was well and over. She did not want to be the reason it failed.

*Come to me, Alesha.* She prayed. *Before I lose you for good.*

# Uninvited Guests

The forward gate was a monstrous set of stone doors rising to a height of fifty feet. At its foot was a frieze depicting ravens hunting for grubs among brambles. At its crest, a second frieze depicted ravens in flight. Etchings of vines and roses climbed the surface of the doors, the thorns along the stems exaggerated in length and breadth to look like daggers.

It was a magnificent structure. Enchanters, engineers and sculptors had worked tirelessly to create it. The care they had taken showed in the ripples and bumps along the vines, the soft, rounded petals of the flowers, and the feather-work on each bird.

Lord Aren bypassed it, headed instead toward the gatehouse—a room to the left of the gates whose door lay open. Soft light spilled from the gatehouse door, and the chatter of the guards inside trickled out with it.

"Place your damned bid, Sansiel!" one of them said. "I'm running out of patience."

"You act as though you had any to begin with." Another quipped.

Lord Aren approached, pushed the door further inward and stepped past the threshold.

As soon as they saw him, the guards scrambled out of their seats. They took rigid stances, saluted him.

He made a show of looking around the room. Atop a heavy, oak table were several piles of playing cards, a clay jug and four matching cups, and a corncob pipe still smoking faintly from its bore.

He plucked a silver coin out of a small pile in the middle of the table, flicked it into the air and caught it. He tossed it back onto the pile, and picked up the clay jug instead, sniffed its contents.

"Drinking at a time like this." He said conversationally. "And gambling?"

The guards stood up straighter. One examined his state of dress. It was uncommon to see an officer wearing full plate armor when the circumstances so clearly did not demand it. An unasked question lingered in the space between them. *Has something happened?*

Perhaps he thought he had missed an order from his commanding officer. Lord Aren intended to exploit his confusion.

"Can you not hear the urchins outside?" he asked. "They are *insufferable.*"

No sound penetrated the great, stone doors, but the guards strained to hear something. Authority was a funny thing. It could inspire those without it to believe the wildest conspiracies, lead them to do things they otherwise would not. Though they could not possibly have heard any such commotion, they deluded themselves into thinking they heard *something*. All because Lord Aren, whose rank was so far out of their reach, claimed he had.

Were they deaf? Had the drink taken too much of the edge off, left them less able to do their job? He could almost hear the gears spinning inside their heads, the little wheels squealing as they tried hard to reconcile the stillness and the silence with the claims of their ranking officer.

Lord Aren whipped the jug at the ground. It shattered; the wine it contained splattered a chair, the leg plates of his armor, the guards reliefs. He picked up a cup, chucked it as well, his expression unreadable.

"I may be willing to forgive this indiscretion." *Crash!* "If you perform your one and only duty." *Crash!* "And open the gates." He tossed the last cup, up and down, watching their eyes follow it as it climbed and fell, climbed and fell. "A company of Mauls is inbound as we speak." He lied. "How mad do you think they will be if they must wait for the gates to open. And the nobles, forced to hear the savages whine and bitch about their condition for a little longer than was absolutely necessary. I am sure they will be forgiving."

"Sir." One guard said timidly.

Lord Aren tossed that last cup a little higher.

The guard winced.

*"Well?"* He caught the cup, tossed it once more. "Get to it."

He withdrew his hand. *Crash.* The cup shattered.

The guards marched into the entrance hall. They positioned themselves two to a door and touched fingertips to their surfaces, summoned a complicated rite that, even coming faintly to Lord Aren as it did, was like a pale impression of life, stilted and dry but lively. Behind that music, he could hear the spirits screaming.

*I'm sorry.* He thought. *But I could not have opened this gate on my own. Even with your blessing, it is beyond me.*

The roses and thorns glowed in vibrant, electrified shades

# SPIRIT OF SHADOW

of crimson and sap green. A series of hollow bangs rippled within the surrounding walls. The *clack-clack* of gears engaging each other chased the bangs away. The doors scraped open, traveled outward over a broad, stone landing outside.

Across a grassy yard from there, a wrought bronze fence separated the palace from a horde of commoners. They waved torches, threw glass bottles and chunks of stone over the gate and fence. The debris shattered well short of the doors. They roared curses against the throne and the nobility—inexorable, indefatigable, incensed.

Lord Aren turned to the guards, who had lined themselves up in plain view of the commoners outside. They saluted him like the studious soldiers they were, as if this was all according to normal procedure. He gripped the hilt of the sword at his hip, whipped it out and triggered the enchantment in his right gauntlet at the same time. He carried the sword across their necks so swiftly and viciously the blade blurred. Four heads toppled. Four bodies followed.

He sheathed his sword, turned toward the fence. Sharp pain crawled through his wrist as he slid the sword back into its sheath. He unlimbered his staff, and aimed it at the lock on the door. A blast of white light flashed from its tip. Ice crept over the mechanism, across the chains. They shattered in several places at once.

A man near the front of the horde pushed the gate inward. A loud cheer rippled through the commonry. They charged across the gap, into the palace. Thousands poured through the open gates, converged on Lord Aren. He spun and ran with them.

"Lead the way, Silas!" one of them shouted.

"FOR SHADOVANE!" he roared.

He lead them into the palace, toward the Grand Hall for the final clash.

## Uninvited Guests

***

Lord Cree sighed. "No takers, it seems. Then we must commence with the executions."

He gestured to the Thorn he had previously dismissed. The Thorn approached, handed off a roll of paper. He unfurled it as the Thorn took his position next to a torch whose staff was of blackened metal.

"Among you is a girl whom stands accused of aiding the thief in his efforts. An armorer." He said.

Ben's insides squirmed. His gaze flicked to Sami, then to the floor. If a Wraith came too close, he intended to kill him. *No one is going to die if I can help it.*

"Laura," Lord Cree said. "Judged on the basis of evidence gathered by our Thorn fact finders to be guilty of treason."

"So, this was their plan." Sami said.

Startled gasps precluded a break opening somewhere close to the front of the crowd. A girl with chestnut hair and dark brown eyes, a smattering of freckles across her nose and cheeks, was dragged onto the stage.

"Please." She pleaded. "I don't know anything! I'm not one of them!"

She fought against the Wraith holding her arms behind her. He pushed her toward the circle of stone.

*"You have to believe me!"* She shrieked.

"The time for repentance is over. Your claims fall on deaf ears." Lord Cree said. "You must be dealt with in accordance with the law. The punishment for the crime of treason is death by immolation, and you will face it with or without dignity."

"They're going to kill her. We have to do something." Ben said.

"Wait and listen." Maera intoned. "If we act now, we will put the whole plan in jeopardy."

"Begin." Lord Cree said.

# SPIRIT OF SHADOW

"We can't just stand by and let—"

"They are doing this with the hope they will draw *you* out of hiding. You will only give them what they want."

"But—"

"Quiet, Ben." Sami said. "I know it's hard, but she's right. Who is going to get them out if we get caught up in that?"

The Thorn pulled the torch free of its holster, marched toward the girl with it held in both hands.

A series of rattling bangs pulsed within the walls. Ben's attention snapped to the row of granite columns obscuring the servants' entrance to his left. Lord Cree's eyes darted in that direction as well.

A faint glow traveled down that wall, its source masked by the shadows. It approached the columns, passed beyond them behind the stage.

"Hold steady." Maera whispered. "We're almost there."

She followed the glow with her eyes as it broke from the columns.

"Go!" She said sharply. Fear reported on her features, sudden and fierce. "Make for the side entrance."

"Why?" Sami asked.

"'S too dangerous for ya here now." The woman said. "The situation has changed."

"But—"

"Go!" the woman snapped. "Both o' ya. 'S not safe here any longer."

"Lance said the emperor glows, didn't he?" Ben mumbled.

"No." Sami breathed. "Why here? Why now?"

Ben took her hand and led her away. The Watcher pushed past the servants in front of her, moved toward the stage.

The Thorn halted short of the stone circle, his torch held at the ready. He, too, looked toward the glow as it mounted the stage from the right side.

Lord Cree fell to his knees, bowed his head.

"The shadow preserve you." He said loud enough for all to hear.

The glow resolved into the figure of a man. He was taller than any elf Ben had ever seen, dressed in flowing robes of purest, snow white with gold trim at the cuffs and high collar. He wore a diadem of gold, broken and bowed like a beetle's horns at its crest, with sapphires and turquoise dripping from it. His eyes were white within white, with only a silver band to give the impression of an iris.

"This is bad." He whispered. "This is really bad."

"Rise, Lord Cree." The emperor commanded.

The general stood.

If Rashanna's suspicions proved accurate, there were already rebels immersed in the crowd. If they were here, at least some of the servants knew the truth, but which ones?

*Do we have a move to make? There must be some way to counter him.*

"The emperor himself has decided to preside over the executions." Lord Cree announced. "Will you not show him the respect he is owed."

No one moved. The rattling in the wall grew louder.

The emperor turned his attention to the Thorn, electing not to notice the servants' indiscretion.

*Does he know?* Rashanna wondered. *Why else would he be here?*

"Fire?" he took the torch from the Thorn, held it like a chalice as he examined it with contempt. "How crude." It turned to ash in his hand.

Rashanna froze, her heart palpitating fiercely as she watched. *We're going to die here.*

"Truth resides in the light." He said. "It is the light which purges sin."

"Truth indeed resides in the light." A woman's craggy

voice echoed him. "The truth that drives away ignorance.

"With me was the idea born to murder your families, to whisk you away to this hellscape, and steal your memories...."


"You know the plan?" Emma asked.

She spread her gaze across the three furnace workers before her.

Master Gregor had done well in drumming up a fighting force. Most of his workers were skilled with both fire and air rites. The official policy of the nobility was that the training of servants in magic be limited to one form with one purpose. If he had been caught, his indiscretion would have seen him executed. He had taken a dangerous risk, but that risk was about to pay off.

Duardo and Emma were the only furnace workers who could shadow walk with Lance absent. The three of them together were to captain the teams positioned in the rooms down the hall opposite the Grand Hall's holding chamber. A dozen furnace workers stood behind her. They were to serve as support for her when the fighting began.

The boilers and the gardeners would have taken up positions at other strategic points in the area. Some of them were scattered among the servants in the Grand Hall itself, but they would not be enough to combat the soldiers here. The department heads would need to work together if this was to work.

*Please let them be in position. Don't let them be found.* "Repeat it back to me." She said.

"When we start to hear a commotion—" A burner, Tim, said.

Emma cut him off. "At the first sign of commotion. Go on."

"At the first sign of a commotion, we begin. Open the

doors. Half of us give cover—"

"You weren't fucking paying attention." She growled. She turned her gaze on a breezer standing next to him, Sara, who she could have thrown across the room with little effort, so small was she. "Think you can do better?"

"The outside rooms provide cover. The inside rooms blow the wall." She said. "We cover the retreat, emphasizing the Bloodless as targets. Then the Wraiths. Then the Mauls."

"Why?"

"The Bloodless are the biggest threat to us. The Wraiths use ambush tactics. The Mauls are the easiest to see coming. Assuming they can't shadow walk. If they can...."

"We're fucked." She said. "Don't bring shame on me, now. If we're going down, you assholes better at least make them sweat."

"We'll do more than that." Tim said under his breath.

"Does everyone know what to do?"

"Yes." The furnace workers barked.

"Good. Now form a wedge. It's going to start soon.

She took her place behind a cedar door that led into the hallway. *These fuckers better be ready for blood. There's about to be a lot of it.*

# Blood & Faith

Rashanna's eyes snapped in the direction of the new speaker. The voice was familiar, and to her shock its source became evident in the interceding moments. *Lady Jain.* Between the heads of the servants, she saw the woman, floating on some mystical current in the moonlight shed by broad skylights in the ceiling. The angelic wings fanning over her shoulders were a supreme irony, as the woman herself was no better than a common beast.

The emperor watched her, cold fear in his eyes. Rashanna would not have believed he could fear anything, powerful as he was, but here was the proof. He looked on Lady Jain and was terrified.

"What you are is my invention." She said. "All that you are, I made. All that you could be, I stole. And all that you were, I destroyed. Hate me, for I am the reason your families perished. Hate me, for I am the reason you have all suffered. I am the nightmares that awaken you. I am your fears. I am all that you know."

"Truly tactless, that man."

Rashanna spun.

A shadow elf, far too emaciated to be of the nobility and too ragged besides, stood behind her. She reached out to the spirits, intent on defending herself against him, and then noticed his eyes. They were lightning blue, too vibrant to be natural.

"You have nothing to fear from me, girl. It is almost time, but you must leave."

"What's going on?"

"The old man of the savanna thought our best hope of converting so many servants at once was to use the Lady Jain to shock them awake. It would take too much time and energy to return a thousand people's memories when there are but twelve of us, though we have made a point to alert the important ones." The elf explained. "Now, if you'll excuse me. I do hope my old office treated you and your friends well, but if you'll excuse me, I have business with a certain ruler to attend to."

He breezed past her, moved between the other servants gracefully on his approach of the stage.

Lady Jain descended from the air, toward the stage and the stone dial. She alighted atop it, faced the emperor.

The emperor's fear turned to rage. He traced a line across her path. An explosion of white light wiped the stage away.

When it cleared, all that had been Lady Jain was gone.

"That foul woman!" The emperor seethed. "To hide Watchers from me in defiance of the law! She has never known true fury!"

He turned on the crowd.

The booms grew louder still.

"Now!" someone shouted.

She ran toward the source of the sound. Eight Watchers approached the stage, every eye glowing like lightning. They converged on the emperor, each dressed in an aura of dazzling, white light, dark wings like those of a crow fanning out from their shoulders.  They rose into the air like Seraphim from story and myth, soared about while the emperor lobbed projectiles of burning light at them.

"Now, I said!"

The wall around the servant's entrance caved. Columns crashed to the ground. A wave rushed across the path of the servants, blocking all but the lights from the Watchers' fight with the emperor from view.

"Aargh!" someone screamed.

Rashanna looked in that direction in time to see the water consume a Wraith. His skin turned red and blistered. Steam rose off the crest of the wave, and Rashanna knew the rebels had arrived.

A team of servants, boiler workers, maintained the wave of water, injecting it with heat while they manipulated it into a wall spanning from floor to ceiling.

A second blast chased down the first. Firelight poured into the Grand Hall from the tiled hall beyond. Shouts and screams rang out from that direction.

"This way!" *Emma?*

Red-orange flames clashed with violet fire beyond the blasted section of wall.

"Stage two!" Came another call. *Is that Ben?* "Couriers to the dungeons! Secure the retreat!"

Rashanna ran for the gap. She picked up Ben's call as she did. "Couriers to the dungeons!"

A number of others picked up the call and sent it back.

As she broke away from the Grand Hall, lightning streaked out behind her, where the stage had been. The emperor's glow winked out.

*Where did he go?* She wondered, panic rising in her like bile. There was no question he was still alive.

The wall of boiling water fell outward, toward the stage. Servants stampeded through the gap, into the hall outside.

One fell somewhere in front of her. She rammed her way through the frenzied crowd, threw a girl aside before she could trample over him, and helped him to his feet.

"This way!" Ben called.

"Boilers, retreat!" Came a voice she didn't recognize.

She broke out of the Grand Hall, into a chaos of another kind.

Burners clashed with Bloodless. Corpses lay everywhere with more belonging to servants than soldiers. Some of those were small children, their lives taken too early, their bodies burned and broken.

Emma fought with a Wraith up the hall from the blasted wall. A Bloodless threw violet fire at a pudgy kitune while his elder, Master Gregor, volleyed an impossible wave of flame at the assailant.

Calling the name of a spirit, her hands wreathed in fire, she launched herself at a Wraith, sent waves of heat and red flame at his chest, watched as he caught light. She ran toward Emma, laying about with her flames, dodging blasts of violet fire, leaping over lines and patches of suspicious darkness.

"Into the tunnels!" Ben shouted, but she could not see him. "Retreat!"

She took down another Wraith, narrowly avoiding a palm full of shadow as she slid out of his way.

Desperation made her brave. The thought of dying before she could see Alesha, Ben, Ariana—so many faces—drove her to fight harder, with a frenzied abandon she might come to wonder after later, when the dust had settled.

She scrambled to her feet and rushed on.

Emma caught sight of her and bellowed. "GET OUT OF HERE RASHANNA! GET TO THE GATE!"

A blast of air cast from Emma's hands knocked four wraiths off their feet. She followed her rite with raw flame.

Rashanna pivoted, made for the nearest stairwell and the promise of a greater safety in the tunnels.

# SPIRIT OF SHADOW

Ben threw everything he had at the combatants coming for him. He stood in the entrance to the stairwell.

"GET TO THE GATE!" He swore Emma had said Rashanna's name, could not leave without her.

Raw fire left his hand and struck a Wraith full in the chest. Around him, burners, breezers and boilers were closing in on the Bloodless among those soldiers. Thorns materialized out of shadows to lend their weight to the fighting. The Hall was in chaos, fast filling with smoke as the servants who could not fight, who had nothing to do with any of this and had only just learned the truth, streamed past him and into the tunnel, pushed each other aside to get down first.

He reached out and grabbed one by the back of the neck, slammed him into the wall as he tried to shove his way past two others. They made it through, and the momentary clot at the entrance was loosened.

"Hurry but don't panic you fucking assholes!" he shouted within inches of the boy's face. "You're not going to get there faster by jamming shit up!"

He let the boy go, turned in time to cast fire against an incoming Wraith and watched him topple to the ground.

Heat flew over his head. Violet light burned bright bars across his vision.

He hit the ground. Shadowy claws descended on him, and evaporated like smoke as the Wraith behind them fell still, half out of the shadows.

He scrambled to his feet. Dark lines ran across his path, missing his shadow by inches. Another corpse hit the ground beside him.

He looked for the source of the rite and found Master Gregor, his hand pressed to the ground, more lines streaming from his fingers.

A Bloodless bared down on him from behind. Flames caught the Bloodless in the chest.

Master Gregor and a cluster of furnace workers hurled a volley of flame at him.

The Bloodless turned and loosed a cloud of what looked like ash. It spread across the corridor.

Several bodies dropped.

A blast of wind flew from Master Gregor's hands, blowing the cloud away.

"Into the tunnels!" Emma roared. "Head for the dungeons!"

A second miasma caught the old kitune across the back, fell over his group. His eyes depressed into his skull, dried and shriveled. His skin paled. He fell over, a week's worth of rot already apparent on his corpse.

A blast of wind blew the ash back. Emma rushed over to him. Violet flame caught her up before she could reach him.

She screamed.

Ben ran.

A Wraith emerged out of the shadows. He bared down on Sami, newly materialized at the break in the wall, with smoky claws. Ben lashed out without thinking, a blast of air sailing from him to knock the soldier back.

A section of wall came down at Sami's left.

*We have to get out of here!*

Servants rushed out of the gap, ran for the nearest entrances into the sublevels.

Booms and flashes of light filled the corridor. The smell of burning flesh and hot metal hung on the air.

A Bloodless approached Sami from behind. Ben rushed in her direction.

Rashanna launched herself into action.

"No!" she screamed. "You can't have him!"

Ben lunged.

Fire blasted from Rashanna's open hand. It caught the

Wraith in the face. He ran, screaming, trying to put it out, and hit the ground.

"Are you okay?" She asked, but he was already climbing to his feet, already moving on Sami, pulling her up, getting her out of harm's way.

"We need to get out of here." He said for both of them to hear. "This is getting too crazy."

A spear of light soared across their path. Ben and Rashanna pulled Sami clear, but the spear went wide, caught a Bloodless in the chest plate, pierced through it.

A Watcher flying near the ceiling—blue eyes roving over the corridor, hunting for new targets—soared away toward a door blocked by servants struggling to make it through.

A blast rang out. The wall shattered, widening the opening.

Servants poured in.

And then Emperor Conan was there, at the end of the hall, and the Watchers were on him again.

"Find cover!" It was Rashanna who screamed this time.

She hurled herself through a doorway. Sami grabbed Ben and threw him at the blasted-out hole where the Grand Hall's holding chamber had been. She surged into the gap there screaming something about shadows.

"Lothor! Lothor help us!" Ben babbled.

His shadow darkened beneath him. He latched onto her, and pulled her through.


Dark fire rolled past the broke section of wall Lance hid behind. He was pinned down, alone except for a few servants who had ducked in for cover with her.

The fire lapped at the wall. It crashed and fell away.

He resisted the urge to look into the hall, pulled a girl back as she tried to.

"We're gonna die. We're gonna die." A dark-haired boy

breathed. He rocked back and forth, his knees cradled in his arms.

"That's the emperor out there." The girl who had tried to look whispered. "Why is he trying to kill us?"

"She'll wish she never took the throne when I'm finished with her!" the emperor raved.

White light took sight and sound away from him. It consumed all that existed, wiped away the darkness, took away the broken walls, the overturned pillars, the scorched floors, the corpses. Everything fell away.

It faded, leaving a crest of bright flame behind to dance atop the section of wall he hid behind. The boy's face was buried in his knees. The girl covered her eyes.

Lance crept past her. He peered into the hall.

The corpses, the soldiers, what servants had been in the path of that rite were gone. Only their shadows remained to tell their tale. The Watchers stood in a line with their backs to him. Their number had dwindled to six. The emperor was gone.

Lance tapped the girl's shoulder. "It's okay. You can look now. Just...not at the floor."

Renewed sounds of battle came from somewhere in the distance. Metal clashed against metal. Flames roared like lions and their light painted the far wall of the hall in shades of red and orange.

"No." he said. "Not yet."

He grabbed the boy by the arm, led him over to the girl and grabbed her as well. "We need to get away from here while its quiet. Reinforcements are coming."

"Why can't we stay here?" the girl asked.

"Do you want to die?" he growled.

She sobbed.

"I'm sorry." He said, regulating his tone. "We just...really need to get out of here. The army isn't on our side. It'll be bad if they find us."

# SPIRIT OF SHADOW

She let him help her up, and followed him.

Doors creaked open to either side of the hall. He saw Rashanna peer out of one. She pushed it wide, and another six servants filtered out of the room with her.

Her gaze fell on Lance, and she rushed over to him.

"Where is Ben? He was with Sami a second ago."

"He's not...not dead. They didn't get caught up in...he killed his own soldiers." Lance whispered.

He couldn't believe it. Those had been the emperor's allies, many of them among the most elite forces in the Empire, and it hadn't mattered to him.

"Fear not." One of the Watchers said, approaching from beyond the door of another of those rooms. "He is gone from this place, now. He will not return."

"We should get out of here." He said, his gaze falling over the Watchers, only taking in cursory details. "Before we get caught up in that."

He pointed in the direction of the glow. The screams and roars of fighting men were getting louder.

Rashanna nodded and joined him in helping the others along the hall into the servants' tunnels.

# The Dungeon Halls

Peter charged down the dungeon hall. Pipes burst overhead. Boiling water flowed unnaturally, called to shape by the boilers. Wraiths popped out of the shadows, launched attacks and vanished again, and the Mauls were fast closing in, worrying at the rear of the stampede of servants with swords and death rites.

"This way!" A courier somewhere ahead of him shouted.

He had no idea how they had come to be directing the retreat, but he was grateful for it. With them shepherding the hordes, he could fight freely, unbothered by the terrified innocents flowing past him.

He shoved a Maul into a barred cell and rammed the door shut. The Maul roared a string of cuss words, shook the bars. *Why is he not attacking?*

Peter ran away from him. He turned a corner, passed the

courier.

A Wraith emerged from the courier's shadow.

Peter pulled the servant away by the front of his shirt. He rammed a shadow-clad hand into the Wraith's chest and sent him back the way he had come.

"Watch yourself." He snapped, his eyes wide with adrenaline.

He shoved the courier back and released him, then ran off again.

The door he needed was in his sights now. A long line snaked away from it, moved at a sluggish pace. He saw some of the kitchen workers among them, those he had lost when the fighting spilled into dungeons, when they had been ambushed by the Wraiths on their way to meet with Ariana and Ben, the children and the laundry workers, and whoever else had made it back by then.

He pushed his way through.

"Hey, get in line!" someone snapped.

"Move, idiot." Peter shot back. "We don't have time for this."

"What are you doing?" Another said as Peter shoved past her.

He managed to get to the door with a little effort. It was painfully intact when he arrived.

"Clear out!" he shouted.

"Why?"

"Because I'm going to blow the fucking thing open. Now get back unless you want to get caught in the blast."

The servants retreated a few steps. He imitated the rite the Thorn had used to shatter the glass on the cells where the children were being kept—earth heavy, with elements of air and fire, birdsong and beastly roars—and put as much power into it as he dared. He may not have the advantage of knowing these spirits names, of hearing them like the others did, but he knew how to listen. They might not like it, but he didn't have time to play nice with a bunch of ghosts just now. They would have to endure this pain.

The rite screamed in his ears, threatened to blow his eardrums, and he thought he heard something deeper in them. Something he had missed before. He ignored it, the sound almost of talking, of weeping as he drew that power in.

The doorway blasted apart. Earth flew outward, dusty and fine. The servants in the immediate vicinity coughed and wheezed.

Peter lunged through the gap. He blew the second door at the bottom of the staircase in the same way, and entered the cavernous room beyond. The flow of servants marching into the space increased to fourfold what it was, and he counted his blessings for that.

Mistress Dina stood in front of him. She directed the newcomers to join large groups to either side of the room, an expression of shock still plastered onto her face. A Haru woman—tall and haughty—stood near a double file of carts overflowing with supplies. Her charges tended the injured, fashioned tourniquets out of strips of bed sheets and applied salves of the Sky Lord only knew what to burns and abrasions.

Lance was still not there, but near to the Haru woman, Mistress Rosaline of the Laundry, was a knot of some thirty children. The six he had freed with Ariana and Ben were among them.

Relief flooded him. *They're safe. It's all going according to plan now. I just need to wait for the others.*

He told himself they were all still alive, all on their way.

Ariana nudged her way through the crowd. He didn't see her until she was almost on top of him. She vaulted toward him, and wrapped him in a tight hug, showered him with kisses.

"Sky Lord's Mercy, Peter. I thought you were dead when

# SPIRIT OF SHADOW

Mistress Dina showed up without you. Are you hurt? Did you see anyone else?"

"I'm fine." He said, drawing her away from him so that he could get a better look at her. A bandage encircled her forearm, but she was otherwise unharmed. "What happened there?"

"I got burned during the fighting." She said. "It'll be okay. I'm just glad you're not dead."

"If you two have nothing better to do, you can help us defend the entrance." Mistress Dina said.

Mistress Rosaline spared a wink for him, and turned her attention back to the blown doorway. They went back to the work of directing the new arrivals to join the others around the gate.

"Who'd have thought something like *that* was here." Mistress Dina mumbled.

"That gate is our only way out." Ariana said. "We just need Lance to get here so we can open it."

"Did you see him on your way here?" Peter asked her.

She shook her head.

"Me neither."

"Let's hope he's close by."


Lord Aren laid about his enemies with his staff. Waves of ice and snow blasted away from him in every direction. He blocked gouts of flame with his kite shield, used every hidden advantage his armor gave him.

Walls shattered and crumbled around him. Doors were blasted off their hinges. Dark lines and patches appeared on the ground and were as swiftly wiped away.

Ragged commoners clashed with Mauls and Wraiths. The Bloodless had not arrived yet, and he held out hope they wouldn't. The commoners outnumbered the enemy but for how long? Three of them died for every one of the palace's soldiers.

He tried not to think of who might have fallen already—elders, childhood friends, allies in the cause, cousins, aunts.

Fire blew past him. He slung his shield over his arm, slapped a shadow-clad hand against a Maul's cheek, and then kicked a Wraith in the chin.

He laced his other arm into the shield straps and rammed himself deeper into the chaos. The Grand Hall was so close he could almost smell the blood and smoke of the battle that was fought there. A few more feet and they could regroup with the servants. Then they would have the advantage.

A gale of dark flame took a cluster of commoners. An ash cloud felled another dozen like stunted trees.

Lord Aren drew his sword and rammed it into a Maul's eye, withdrew it and slashed another soldier's neck, pushed in further.

"This way!" he shouted. *Just a little further.*

He sidestepped an incoming blade, took hold of the bearer by the wrist and pulled him in, baring his own sword at the poor fool's neck.

It slid in.

He pushed the Maul away and sheathed it.

*"LINE UP!"*

Lord Elise's voice was loud and full of rage. Lord Aren looked across the hall, past the intersection, and found himself looking at the general and a line comprised entirely of Bloodless.

He finished off another soldier, spun and called to the commoners. "Retreat! Find the Stairs. Retreat!"

"Hold steady!" Lord Elise commanded.

The common folk didn't seem to hear Lord Aren's calls. He needed to get them away from here but there were no good options for doing so.

Thinking quickly, he crafted a rite of earth. Low bass

# SPIRIT OF SHADOW

imitated the earth's vibrations. A tremor ran through the floor, and for a moment he thought he had not been strong enough.

Then, it collapsed.

Commoners and soldiers fell into the tunnels below. They screamed in pain and surprise as the floor gave way beneath them and carried them away.

Lord Aren dropped into the massive hole he had opened as the Bloodless prepared to follow.

"RETREAT DAMMIT!" he roared.

He lead the charge away, into the Servants' Tunnels.

# Alesha

Ben fell into the shadows. Heat washed over his shoulder. He ran, dragging Sami after him, listening for disturbances.

He ripped a hole in the shadows. Light spilled into the darkness. He was surrounded. At least eight Wraiths closed in on him, all with shadowy claws dressing their hands and forearms. He did as he had seen Lance do, called to Lothor and compelled him to take them deeper. They descended behind a second layer of shadow, and into the deep reaches where the Dark Heart was at its strongest.

He ran hard with Sami's hand in his. Those maddening voices chased after them, pressed pain into his temples, threatened to drag him down. He reached above him, yanked at the ether and rose. Yanked again, and emerged in the midst of a chaos like that he had left behind in the expanse outside the Grand Hall.

Shouts and screams filled this narrower, poured stone corridor. Several glow bulbs had been shattered. The walls were covered in soot, and corpses littered the ground.

A pipe burst overhead. Boiling water streamed by him, pummeled the breastplate of a Bloodless.

The Bloodless screamed and ran.

More pipes burst. Water rose from the floor, fell from the ceiling like rain.

He shielded Sami from the flows with blasts of air, dodged counterattacks from the soldiers as they pelted on.

Boilers shuffled in to block the soldiers in pursuit. They funneled the steaming flows into a wall before them and shoved, sending it flying through the rank and file of pursuers.

A boiler took him by the collar of his shirt. She shoved him onward. "Move."

He stared at her.

"Are you deaf?" the girl said. "Go!"

He shook himself.

Wraiths dropped into the corridor out of the shadows in the ceiling.

He launched himself into the fray, took one in the throat. The girl doused another in scalding water.

Fire swept across her path. She pulled water from the floor and blocked it. Steam rushed into the air.

Ben ducked under it, pulled the boiler and Sami down with him.

The girl directed the flow of water into another Wraith's face as more people streamed by behind them.

"This way!" he looked in the direction of the voice. A servant waved the others on, down a hall that joined onto the one where she fought. "Dungeons this way!"

He ducked under another flare. Pressed his hand to the ground, and pushed himself onto his feet. Black lines zigzagged across the corridor, and bodies crumpled.

Fresh roars came from behind. Firelight painted shadows against poured stone.

## Alesha

"Shit." He hissed. "REINFORCEMENTS INBOUND!"

The boiler's concentration broke. She looked down the hall. A Maul swung his sword for her throat.

Ben cut his arm off with a focused blast of air. He pulled Sami along behind him, left the soldier for dead.

The boiler clambered to her feet and pelted after them.

"Don't let your guard down." He growled. "Run. Now!"

"But—"

"They're coming!"

Mauls burst into the tunnel. With them were elves dressed in rags. More of the urchins flooded in from the opposite direction, cutting off the Mauls' retreat.

He watched as urchins threw fire and danced among the soldiers with shadowed claws.

"What the—"

The Mauls forced themselves into the corridor where he stood with the boilers.

He shoved the girl aside, hurled fire at a Maul bearing down with a hand full of shadow and a wicked sword.

The ground shook underfoot.

"For Shadovane!" someone shouted.

The call was echoed by others. Fire consumed the hall. The girl added her water rites to the chaos. Her fellows laid about the new force with their own rites with renewed vigor.

The Mauls fought desperately to regain control, but they were being overwhelmed from three sides.

"Don't give them any ground, damn it!" Someone commanded. "Keep them pinned, you hear me!"


Lance and Sami rushed through the tunnels toward their destination. They were close now. The crowd of servants was thickening, but the presence of soldiers was stronger here, too.

The fighting was frenzied. Whole sections of wall had been

destroyed. The bars of several cells lay scattered across the ground with numerous bodies, some of which still smoldered and smoked.

The sickly-sweet smell of death hung rancid on the air. Ash clouds drifted from the hands of Bloodless. Wraiths appeared and disappeared, taking servants and commoners with them into the shadows. Everywhere, people died.

Rashanna's mind was stretched to its breaking point. How was one to process so much carnage, so much death?

She let go of her grip on Lance and ran.

"Don't leave me here!" He shouted as he ran after her.

"Alesha!" She shouted. "I saw her. Alesha!"

A girl up ahead with hair the color of wet sand and squinty eyes halted in mid-step, turned to face her.

A Bloodless emerged in the crossroads she stood in.

"No!" Lance sprinted after her, lunged at the last moment and took her to the ground.

An ash cloud left the Bloodless's hand. It consumed Alesha.

She screamed.

She shoved him off of her, scrambled to her feet and ran for the girl she had chosen to love's corpse.

The Bloodless turned in her direction.

*I will not lose another friend!* Lance thought savagely.

He flung himself past Rashanna as the Bloodless reeled back to cast his rite a second time, lunged at the elite soldier's chest. They went down in a pile as he closed on her, desperately seeking to pull her out of harm's way.

Dark fire glowed in the Bloodless's hand. Lance pitched to the side, fire flowering against his palm and slammed his hand into the soldier's neck.

The Bloodless's eyes widened. He whispered something and the whisper was lost in the chaos of the battle raging around them.

He died.

## Alesha

Lance pushed himself onto all fours and crawled to Rashanna.

"We have to go."

"I can't just leave her here. She's—"

"You don't have a choice. We have to get out of here now."

"I love her. I can't just—"

"She's dead, Rashanna! That isn't her anymore. Now we need to get out of here."

He grabbed her under the arms and hauled her away. She resisted him.

A Maul bared down on them with a sword, and then Lord Aren was there.

He struck the Maul over the head with his staff. The Maul froze. He struck him once more and the soldier's body shattered, turned to powder.

Rashanna looked into Lord Aren's face.

"Go on, woman." Lord Aren commanded. "No sense wasting your life on the dead and the damned."

Lance pulled her away from Alesha.


Somewhere ahead of where Lord Aren fought a great blast of heat and a wave of dark fire, far larger than any he had seen before, consumed the hall. It cleared, revealing the figure of a woman dressed in a pink, sleeping gown.

"Queen Meredith." He breathed.

She marched down the intersection, waved her hand. Another blast of fire blew through the passage ahead, laying waste to whoever fought there. Friend or foe, it didn't matter. The queen's expression was murder, indiscriminate of allegiance or virtue.

"Get to the gate." Lord Aren said coldly, for the servants and commoners still around him to hear. "I'll do what I can to hold her off."

He ran for the queen, his staff at the ready for the conflict that would transpire there. As he ran, his resolve hardened

# SPIRIT OF SHADOW

until he wore it like a shield. If the boy did not find a way to take them away from here, he must be prepared to die. Here and now.

There was no turning back. There was no other means of escaping, and there would be no new path forward, which he might carve out of this chaos. This night, the queen would be deposed, the innocents she lorded over would escape, or he would die saving as many of them as he could from her and her forces.

He would sacrifice himself for the cause, as he had done. He would sacrifice himself, because it was the right thing to do. And whether or not the night's events resulted in them all being taken away from here, maybe, when the sun crept over the horizon once more, a new and fair queen would take the seat left open by the tyrant he knew. Maybe, he would get lucky. Maybe, he would take her down with him. And then his people could know peace.

# Celesti's Soul

Lance shoved his way past servants who themselves shoved their way toward the door into the cavernous room where the arch, their only means of escape, resided. More had arrived here ahead of him than he had anticipated.

Rashanna lagged behind him, shoving her way through as he shouted for the servants to make way. They didn't listen, but of course they wouldn't. They did not know he was their ticket to escape, that he had the queen's pendant on him. To them, he must be one greedy bastard among many, trying to get to safety at any cost.

"MOVE ASIDE!" he roared. "I'M NEEDED AT THE FRONT!"

"Who the fuck do you think you are!"

"He's the guy who's going to save you!" Rashanna snapped, elbowing a servant out of her way. Her tears had dried. She had been in a state of shock since Alesha's death, but at least she was holding steady. At least she still had this much fight left in her. "Now give him...some space!"

Someone had blown the door wide, providing more space

for servants to move into the gate chamber. He would thank whichever friend it was when he saw them. With the doors blown, there was no way they were not here already.

*Thank the Sky Lord and the Shadow of Judgment for that.* He prayed.

He shoved past the last few servants, ignored their protests as he entered the staircase. A few of them, seeing him for the first time, recoiled against the walls to let him pass. He reached behind him and pulled Rashanna through. Ben would be so happy to see her when they won free of these hordes of terrified people. And if her girlfriend was here, it would set her mind at ease all the more.

"Clear the way!" Came a voice he recognized as he negotiated his way down the stairs. *Ariana. Immortals be praised.* "If you fuckers want to get out of here, you'll let my friend through!"

A few more broke apart ahead of him, letting him by.

"Thank you!" he shouted to her.

He emerged from the staircase into the room with Rashanna short behind him. The crowds there already filled more than half of it. Soon, it would be packed to capacity. He needed to open the gate now, before that happened.

He nodded to Mistress Dina as he passed her.

"Thank you." He said.

She glowered at him, adjusted her expression to something a hair more pleasant when she realized who was speaking to her.

"Get on with it, boy. We're running low on time." She growled.

He noted Ariana standing to one side of the steady stream of servants entering the chamber.

"Thank the Sky Lord you survived. It's chaos out there!" he said to them. "Have you seen Ben or Sami?"

"They're not here yet." Ariana said. "Peter's by the arch."

She cocked her thumb over her shoulder.

"Oh." Lance moved in that direction, leaving Rashanna with her. He heard them talking as he left, expressing their worries to each other.

Peter sat with his back against the archway. He stood up when he caught sight of Lance, embraced him in a tight hug. The pendant felt cold against his chest in the presence of the arch and its technicolor veil.

"I knew you wouldn't let us down!" he said. "You could've given us a little warning though."

"It was now or never." Lance replied. "You guys would have stopped me if you knew what I was thinking of doing."

"You're right." Peter agreed. "And we would've been right to do it. Lord Aren was going to steal it tonight anyway."

"He wouldn't have been able to. The only reason I got it was because she wasn't wearing it. And she wasn't wearing it because she was fooling around with Lord Elise. If we had waited, there's no way he would have taken it off her. He would have had to take it from around her neck."

"You couldn't have…I guess it doesn't matter now." He said. "Just don't make us worry about you next time. We could've talked this through, at least."

Lance produced the pendant from within his shirt. He removed its chain from around his neck and held it in his palm.

"Did you figure out how to use it?" Peter asked.

"Not exactly." Lance admitted. "I heard some of the rite the queen used when she came out of the arch, but not all of it. And it didn't sound like she was calling on the spirits to make it work."

So, she must have been using some other kind of power. But that's why you're the one who has to do it, right? You can use it, too."

"Maybe the spirits—"

"The spirit of shadow isn't going to be any help here. He's

# SPIRIT OF SHADOW

blocked from entering, remember."

"There's another one who might be of help." He said, meeting Peter's gaze. "Aughere!"

*"You called?"* A weasel cast in silhouette, his eyes ghostly white orbs set in his boxy face, waded through the air above him. He could smell smoke faintly in the spirit's wake.

"I need help, okay. I need to figure out how to use this." He held up the pendant. "To open that." He gestured with it at the gate.

*"I see. But that isn't something you can accomplish relying on the power of samiyel. No, it is not the domain of the spirits the Children relied on, nor are their avatars restricted to using us."*

"Then you can't help me." Lance mumbled.

"If the spirits can't help, you're going to have to find another way, Lance. We don't have time for their games."

*"This one has little sense. Deaf to our voices, isn't he? But that is his own cross to bear."*

"He might be able to help in another way." Lance said. "I'll take whatever I can get."

"You worry about making it work, then." Peter said. "I'll watch for our friends."

"Deal." Lance agreed.

He turned the pendant over in his hand, focused on the silence behind the noises of servants stamping feet and murmuring voices, the distant bangs and booms of combat in the halls above, the rippling of strips of cloth being torn from bed sheets.

"Aughere, what is this other power? If it doesn't rely on you, then how does it work?"

*"It is oul, the namesake of the Oulae, who you call Immortals. It is part of us, but not. We are, all of us spirits, merely watered down expressions of its strength. But you've used it before, Lance. Once, when you were a small child. You*

*used it in front of your uncle, to send him home when he was no longer welcome company to you."*

"That's not helpful."

*"When the chosen few are young, dear boy, they often lash out with unexpected power when their feelings are hurt. Perhaps it is a matter of you feeling particularly vulnerable. I do not claim to know. Nonetheless, it is an expression of your very soul that allows such power to flow through you. You need only focus on it long enough. Then, perhaps, you might identify what brought it forth from you."*

"Can anyone do this?" he asked.

*"Your friends cannot help you, I'm afraid. There are but five in any era who come by it naturally. There are others like you, I am sure, but they are not here. Nor are they close. Nor do they know what it is they harbor inside."*

*This is going to be a problem, isn't it?* He flipped the pendant over in his palm, hoping some trick of the light would reveal to him its secrets. *Something's going to give.* He seated himself against the arch opposite the post Peter had taken up, which gave a clear view of the door. If not for the post, their backs would be to each other. As it were, he was met with the sight of numerous small children, all of them confused and scared, and in varying states of disarray. The worst of them were the youngest, and all of those were dressed in soiled smallclothes, calling back to a time not so long ago when he had been trapped in the bowels of this palace. He knew without sight for any other sign that they had come from that place. That his friends had liberated them from a hell of an uncommon kind, where cruelty began to look like salvation, and a person could be led to believe his captor was his savior. *Something will give.*

"Ben!" Peter said.

Lance looked over his shoulder. Ben emerged from the gap. Sami trailed behind him. They were covered in soot and blisters and blood. The white of their reliefs was entirely gone, replaced by gray and brown tones from all of the soil of the battles they had fought to arrive here.

"They're coming!" she shouted.

Ben wriggled free of the pack. He ran across the intervening space and took Lance in to his arms. Rashanna watched on, satisfied that he was alive perhaps, or that he had his little bit of relief. They must have talked before he broke away from the entrance.

Relief flooded Lance, but it was a temporary reprieve. Ben's embrace on him, the sight of Sami returned, her arm sliding in to break them up, to lay her own hug on him after so long spent apart and all the brutality that had come to him.

"What happened to—"

"There's no time for that right now." Sami said. "We can talk about it after we get out of here. The queen...she's coming, Lance. We need to hurry."

"I don't know if...I don't know how to use this thing. It doesn't rely on the kind of magic we know."

"Then we'll figure it out, okay." She said.

"We knew this was going to be a struggle." Peter added. "What did the spirit tell you."

"He said I'd used this power before. But I don't remember how I did it. He said I used it when my emotions were running high."

"Is he still around?" Ben asked.

"*Yes.*" Aughere said.

Lance nodded.

"Then tell him to help you do it."

"*That would almost certainly kill you.*"

"Aughere, we're all going to die if I don't do *something*. If it's between me dying and thousands of others—"

"He told you it would kill you?" Sami said in a tight voice.

"If it comes down to all of you dying because of something I did, or me dying to save you, I know which choice I'm making." He said, spreading his gaze to encompass all of them. "I couldn't live with myself if I let you all go."

"We don't have time—" Ben cut off, as Sami launched herself at Lance, held him tight. He thought she might never let go, the way she embraced him, and felt he understood better the limits of their friendship. That he was looking into a mirror of who he was with Rashanna at his side, who they were because of each other. That the friendship these two shared ran deep enough that they might sacrifice themselves to save the other.

Lance pushed her away, looked into her eyes. "I'm going to do this, okay."

"We'll see each other on the other side."

He nodded, but to Ben's eyes, his expression did not rise to the level of confidence he wanted from him. He stepped into the space between them, and planted a kiss on his lover's lips.

"We'll be waiting."

"Aughere. Please proceed."

*"You understand, I will have to deplete the mortal energy you use, to open the way for the immortal energy laying dormant within you. Draw on me to the fullest extent you can, and then keep drawing. Such effort would deafen a normal person, but you are not normal. And know that if you do not succeed, death will not embrace you. You will become like that boy near Butuyari in the south, who was killed when he was young and yet lives still as a ghost. He cannot pass on, you understand, but lives as a warning to people like you not to do as he did."*

"I am willing to accept the risk." He said.

He drew in Aughere's power, drew it in until pain formed behind his temples and a deep fatigue stole over his limbs. Drew in that power until he thought he would explode, until the song the spirit sang was so loud he could hear nothing else around him.

With so much power coursing through him, he felt as if his

body would give out, as if his soul would be rent to pieces. And still he drew it in, drew it in on the desperate hope that whatever secret power it unlocked would see them all out of this place safe.

Lord Aren squared off against his queen. Rage twisted her features, making her ugly to his eyes as she stood against him, her pink night robe flowing around her on unnatural currents as dark fire coalesced against one palm, and void black pressed against the skin of the other.

"Then the infestation goes to the top." She said through gritted teeth. "How many did you turn, Lord Aren? How many in my palace did you bring under your wing?"

"Not near enough, I confess." He said. "But we are past words, aren't we?"

She nodded, and lashed out with her flames. As a wall of fire lanced toward him, he slammed his staff into the floor. White ice shot from the ground, spread to cover the gap. It evaporated in seconds under the heat of those flames.

Tracers of dark energy spun toward him, a geometric array traveling in three dimensions, across every surface of the hall in defiance even of the cadmium lined bars of the cells there. He would not win free by trapping her in one of them, a revelation that required a recalibration of his tactics.

He launched himself forward, using ice under his metal shod boots to block those tracers from touching him. His staff came down, and she spun out of its path, her trailing hand threatening him with death as dark shadow came within inches of touching him, and he threw himself out of its path.

*I don't need to kill her. Just slow her down. Without that pendant, she's just an ordinary woman.*

But that was far from the truth. Queen Meredith was many things, but she was not the docile noblewoman she pretended to be. She was far more fearsome than her predecessor had ever been, more akin to the warmongering Queen Anastasia than any queen had been in recent memory.

And she was still capable of using that foreign power which defied the spirits so. A power that boggled the mind for its ability to defy rationality.

Even now, absent her pendant, she drew on it as if Celesti's Soul was with her, as if she had never been separated from it. He heard no melodies or harmonies issuing from her, no call and response from the spirits to guide her magic.

A mortal woman she might be, but ordinary was not a word one could use to describe her. She had awakened something, even if just a taste of it, and he was learning to deal with its consequences.

He struck the wall with his staff. It fixed itself in place as he activated the iron in his armor, that taboo substance that heightened its wielder's reflexes, his speed, stamina and strength, and poisoned the blood all the while it did, and drew his sword from its sheath.

The kite shield he cast aside, and took the sword up in both hands.

He came for her then, wild energy thrashing around him as the spirits came at his call, as he drew on powers of earth and fire and funneled them into that sword.

His opening swing went wide as the queen dodged out of its path. It struck the ground, and a violent explosion rang out from the site of impact.

She hissed, and blasted dark fire against him, a blistering wave to swallow the hall.

He tipped forward and into shadow, drawing on Lothor's power, and at the same time called Bitri and Aran, echo and space, to cover him.

Echoes interfered with the acoustics in the area immediately around them, casting a disorienting afterglow to give the appearance he remained in the physical world. He ripped at darkness and rose, his sword leading, into her shadow, saw the blackened palm descending to meet his forehead, and abandoned the pursuit.

*She's going to kill me if I keep this up.* He thought bitterly. *I'll just have to make my death mean something.*


The booms of the clashes overhead grew louder as the fighting grew closer to the arch. Servants flooded in now, fighting each other for entry. Mistress Dina's best efforts could not soothe them, and Lance was no closer than when he started to making the stone work.

A number of other servants watched him intently. By their expressions, they were growing impatient, and fearful because it was taking so long for any sign of change to come.

He drew on Aughere's power as dull auras rippled across his vision, as a deep lethargy stole over him. Soon, he would be driven into unconsciousness. There would be no choice in the matter. Completely depleted, he would simply slip away, and then he may never wake.

As the energy leaked away from him, a fitful fluttering of light echoed inside the pendant. It was faint, but he was not the only one who noticed.

"That was something." Sami said. "We're getting somewhere now."

"We don't have time for this." Lance groaned.

"Don't let your frustration get in the way." Peter said encouragingly. "You need a clear head right now."

"That's getting harder to find. I'm barely holding on as it is."

The booms had reached the stairs. The flood of servants thickened and accelerated. They overran Mistress Dina, fell into whatever space they could find. The room was almost to capacity and still Lance struggled.

Then, fire blasted from the staircase, dark and wild and vast. It consumed the staircase, the servants, left nothing but smoking corpses behind. Mistress Dina launched herself out of the way just in time to save herself, but at least twenty other servants were not so lucky.

The queen stepped on their bodies as she entered the room, and Lord Aren trailed in her wake. He held his staff in one hand and a sword in the other, swung both wildly in an effort to slow her down.

"I am tired of this incessant fly buzzing about my head." She snapped.

She reached behind her, made a gesture as if clutching something. His eyes bulged in their sockets, and he hit the ground hard.

Lance froze in place as soon as he saw her. Sami stumbled backward into the stone arch.

Peter pulled Ariana close to him. She gasped.

"Not this." She whispered. "Not now."

"You!" the queen bellowed, her eyes all for Lance, who held the pendant aloft in his hand.

Dark fire alighted atop her palm. She propelled her arm forward with force. The fire blasted across his path. He dove for cover.

She closed the distance between them, reached for him.

"Steal my pendant." She said. "After all I have done for you. After what I alone was willing to do for all of you.

"Was the food not enough? Did you not enjoy your petty duties? Was it not enough to give you a purpose in your pitiful lives?"

She grabbed him by the front of his shirt, pulled him to his feet. She panned over the crowd, and her gaze hung on the children.

"Ah. So this is what went wrong. You violated my most sacred rule, and now you feel entitled to a more peaceful existence." She snapped her fingers. One of the borderlander boys winked out, his silhouette painted on the floor in fresh soot. "You thought to leave? You can leave as that one did."

She let him go, pressed her fingers together again. Sami launched herself between them. She shoved the queen. The queen lost her balance, snarled as she landed on her back.

She snapped her fingers, her eyes all for Sami.

And Sami was gone.

Lance fixated on the space where she had been. Soot remained to mark her presence, giving him only the vague impression that she had died.

*What happened? Where did she go?* For several moments the truth betrayed him. In that time, the queen righted herself, snatched the pendant out of his hand.

Screams and sobs rippled through the crowds. Lance watched as the queen placed a little distance between them. His faculties caught up to him in small steps.

*She killed her.*

The queen observed her pendant, as if she was not convinced it was real. As if she could not quite believe what she held in her hand was Celesti's Soul and not a piece of costume jewelry.

*She killed her.*

She raised her hand to a level with Lance's chest.

*After everything, she....*

Snarling, he lunged at the her.

Behind Queen Meredith blue flame tore from Lord Aren's hip. He bellowed, reached behind him and cast a flimsy book from its place at his waist. The book's pages burned, the entire document turned to ash in mere moments.

Lance clawed at the Shadow Queen's hands, closed his around the pendant. They wrestled with each other, faces contorted into rictus masks of rage, tugging at the pendant's chain, emotions spiraling out of control.

The queen crafted a rite. The stone glowed faintly. What

## Celesti's Soul

remained of the book smoldered where Lord Aren had cast it.

He cried out, drew on Aughere's power not to shield him but to end this woman, not knowing what it might do but hoping the spirit had the power to invite death, to destroy and destroy, and destroy, until there was nothing left of that monstrous creature.

For one, mad moment, he thought he finally understood her. *Her nature is passion and shadow, the dark side of the heart.* A plague of rage soured his stomach, electrified his nerves, made his skin crawl. He lashed out at her with the rite and found silence, a most blissful sound after all of the rage and chaos storming through the palace halls. The fighting, the losses, everything building up to this point was made meaningless in that vacuous pocket where even the voices of the spirits were lost to him, and all that remained was raw energy, unbound, unchecked.

The stone glowed brilliant green. Light pulsed from it. Echoes of that light pulsed around the gathered servants.

His hand descended on the queen.

Fire blossomed against her palm as she rammed it into him.

Her expression turned from anger to shock as the light pulsed brighter, a song like victory or agony, vibrant and loud and carrying, filled Lance's ears, and it was like nothing he had ever heard before. Not the work of the spirits, but of another kind entirely. It echoed as it unfurled, washed over everything, drowned out all of the fear and anger and sorrow he felt, and consumed him as surely as a tempest wave consumed all that existed on the distant shore.  He drank it in, reveled in it as his hand crept ever nearer the queen.

Light blasted from the stone, consumed him. He flew away from her, away from the world he knew.

Darkness crawled in to replace the light. For an undefinable time—it could have been years or seconds, he didn't know—he drifted.

A shower of stars fell all around him, through the dark of a night's sky. The ground rose at him from far below. It advanced toward him, moving too fast.

He fell toward it.

They collided.

# After

igid grass pressed against his cheek. Cold earth dusted his hands. He opened his eyes. Amber grain rose up to a height of a few feet near the site of his landing. The pendant dangled from a red capped strand of amaranth.

He reached for it, took it in hand, pushed himself to his feet. Around him, others rose out of the grasses. A double file of carts occupied the space behind an arch that was twin of the one they had left behind, with blue veins of some metal coloring the marble frame and a veil that shined in every color rippling within.

Some of those who rose up were servants; others, commoners dressed in rags. Some were mostly unharmed while others were severely injured or wore bandages of torn cloth around their wounds.

He spotted Mistresses Dina and Rosaline, then Ariana and Peter, who held each other close. Ben emerged some way off with Rashanna, and he waded through the grasses toward them.

# SPIRIT OF SHADOW

The hour of the night was its darkest, preceding the dawn. Lance's friends converged on him. Sami was absent.

He looked around for her. *She must be hiding.*

They were with him now—Rashanna and Ben, Ariana and Peter—and Lord Aren was approaching with a scattering of others, Maera among them.

"We did it." Ben said.

Lance nodded. "I wish I knew where Sami was."

Ariana exchanged a look with Peter. Ben observed them, seemed to understand something in that look that went over Lance's head.

Peter patted Lance's shoulder. He wore a solemn expression. "She's not coming, Lance."

"She has to." Lance said hotly. "She wouldn't have stayed."

"Not by choice, no." Peter agreed. "She's dead."

Lance felt like he had been punched in the gut. He looked from face to face, trying to find the lie, but there was nothing there to be seen. No lie spoken into the stillness. Nothing save a slow building grief felt by all of them, his closest friends, for the loss they had suffered.

"She can't be." He whispered.

"You saw it yourself," Ariana said. "We witnessed it happen."

"Let's not talk about this right now." Lance said. He couldn't face it. "What do we do next?"

The others looked to each other. Rashanna looked to be on the point of breaking. Tears leaked over her cheeks, and she clutched her fists at her sides, her knuckles pale and bulging.

Ariana looked to the sky, where the first purples of dawn were pushing the black of night back. "We watch the sunrise."

She wrapped one arm around Lance. Ben embraced him from the other side, wrapped his free arm around Rashanna who rested her head on his chest. Peter held Ariana to him.

They stood in a line, watching the red and orange shades

## After

mingle with lavender in the predawn light, the sun crest the horizon in the east.

For a moment, everything was still. He could exist without thinking. They all could.

*There will be time for grieving later.* He told himself as the tears came on. At first, they came as a trickle, and then they came as a flood. He watched the sun cross over the horizon, crawl into the sky.

And he cried.

# SPIRIT OF SHADOW

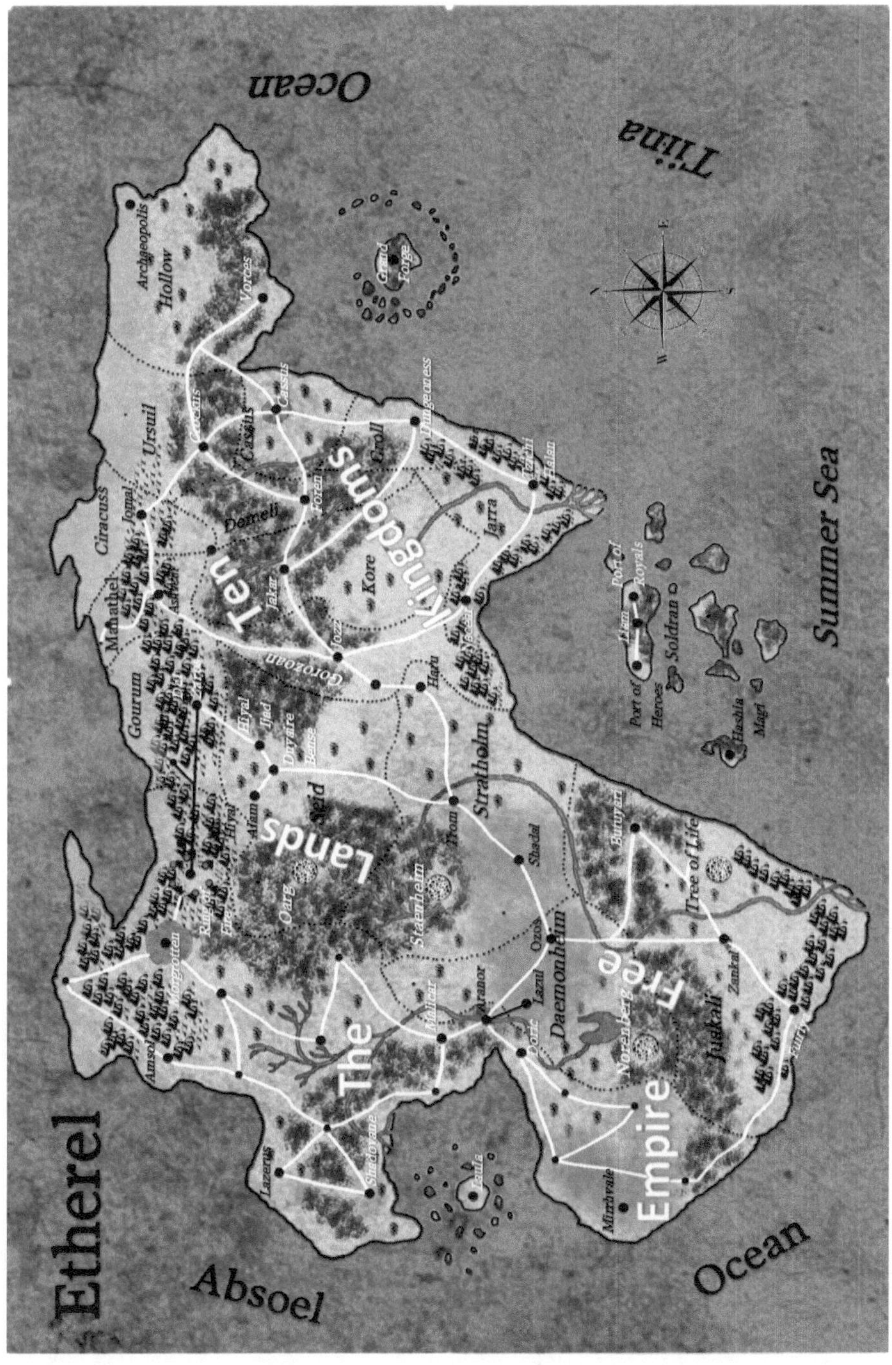

# Glossary

**Astral Plane:** A separate plane of existence believed by followers of the Faith of the Five Saints to be the location of the Sky Lord's prison.

**Bloodless:** An elite force of troops in the Shadovani army. They are known throughout the world for their extensive knowledge of death rites, and their seeming ability to be in multiple places at once.

**Breezer:** A servant trained in magic who specialize in summoning and dispelling currents of air, and who has chosen a path of service in the furnaces.

**Burner:** A servant trained in magic who specializes in summoning and dispelling flames, and who has chosen a path of service in the furnaces.

**Cosmic Orchestra:** A colloquial term for the melodies associated with magic. A summary term referring to the chaotic nature they take upon a first hearing, before specific melodies can be isolated and conducted into a rite.

**Council of Liam:** The second most powerful military organization in the Empire, and the most powerful military organization in Shadovane. The Council of Liam is comprised of the six highest ranking generals in Shadovane's standing force. Five of the members of the council helm the various branches of the military while the sixth (currently Lord Giram) is considered the leader of the council.

**Deafen:** To permanently remove the ability of a mage to hear the melodies that drive magic, thus removing his or her ability to perform magical rites.

**Death Magic:** A magical form concerned with ending life, as distinct from necromancy.

**Earth Child:** The ruler of the Free Land nation of Gourum, who is believed to be the reincarnation of the Father of Lands.

**The Sun Empire:** The largest territory in Etherel which is governed by the Immortal Light of Ignorance. The Empire covers the majority of the western third of the continent of Etherel. It is officially atheist.

**Enchanting:** The art of imbuing objects constructed of susceptible materials with magical energies. Materials so imbued take on a variety of effects. More complex effects can be achieved by using different materials in conjunction with each other. The art of enchanting is a semi-passive magical form in which certain conditions can be set on an object which allow those who either cannot normally use magic or do not wish to expend their own energy to use magical rites that may, in some cases, exceed their natural abilities.

**Enlightened:** An elite force of troops stationed in Mirrhvale. The most powerful military force in the Empire. They are known for their command of light-based rites and illusion casting, and their seeming ability to appear anywhere almost instantly.

**Faith of the Five Saints:** The most popular religion in Etherel. The Faith of the Five Saints concerns itself with the worship of the Immortals, the Sky Lord and five heroes of ancient times who are attributed with sealing the Sky Lord away.

**Father of Lands, Argor:** A figure believed by practitioners of the Faith of the Five Saints to be the son of the Sky Lord.

**Five Saints:** The heads of the five spiritual houses, believed to be the guiding forces of magic. Each represents one of the five elements, called a House. They are represented in artwork as a peacock, a wyvern, a fox with nine tails, a sea snake, and a falcon. These five figures are central to the Faith of the Five Saints. Practitioners of the faith believe these five spirits are intimately associated with the God Slayers.

**Free Lands:** The free territory between the Empire and the Ten Kingdoms. The Free Lands is comprised of four named territories, each of which is home to a number of city-states. Two nations also exist within the Free Lands. Those are Soldran and Gourum. Both nations are thought to be ruled by an Immortal: the Light of Honor in Gourum, and the Light of Truth in Soldran.

**Force of Wills:** A term given to the collective malevolent will of mortal kind which plagues the Shadow World. The Force of Wills is the manifestation of ill will in mortals, which swarms unprepared travelers through the Shadow World and may breed incurable madness into them. Prolonged exposure to the Force of Wills can be fatal. A mage can resist the Force of Wills by exerting his own will against it, but this resistance will only hold for so long before it becomes necessary to emerge from the Shadow World.

**Gardening:** A magical form focused on the propagation and manipulation of plant life. Practitioners of this kind of magic are known for their ability to extend the blooming and fruiting cycles of plants, to communicate with them through certain channels, and, in some cases, to weaponize them.

**Gift of the Blood:** Inborn magical abilities some people are born with. There are five gifts in total, respectively: of the Watcher, of the Whisperer, of the Shield, of the Seer, and of the Seem. These abilities may be trained up in those who possess them, but for those who do not, they cannot be learned.

**God Slayers:** Five heroes who are credited with being instrumental in the sealing of the Sky Lord. These five heroes are the subject of numerous stories and are central to the Faith of the Five Saints. They are Boreas, the Hero; Anastasia the Pirate Queen; Black Brother Sura; Pythos the Oracle; and Esmerelda the Hunter.

**Grimwok:** A kind of dark creature believed to have been created by Baris of the Ten Kings. They are half raven, half human hybrids who were created via a bastardized form of Gardening often referred to as Life Magic.

**Headhunter:** Cannibal associated with a number of tribes of Jarra, who worship and follow Omari the Crocodile, of the Ten Kings.

**Immortals:** Creations of the Sky Lord who are believed by followers of the Faith of the Five Saints to be the Sky Lord's weaknesses made flesh. They are thought to be teachers or guides to mortals, who are charged with keeping them on the good path.

**Ironclad:** An elite force of soldiers known for wearing armor of enchanted iron in battle, which is taboo. They are widely considered the strongest forces in Gourum, and are among the most feared military forces throughout Etherel, respected both by the Ten Kings and the Imperial leadership.

**Jinn Tamer:** A class of enchanters and soldiers who are known to use a kind of evil spirit called a Jinn in combat. The Jinn are contained inside golden vessels which the soldiers wear in plain sight wherever they go. They are Ozos's most elite troops.

**Kitune:** A race of mortals believed to be descended from foxes who are particularly gifted in the use of fire magic. Blindness is more common among kitunes than other races, which has gained them a reputation for being particularly strong fighters.

**Legion of the Sky:** The armies which followed the Sky Lord during the years before the Sealing.

**Light of Honor:** Also called the Earth Child. The Light of Honor is the reincarnation of the Father of Lands. He is the ruler of Gourum, and generally has the shortest lifespan of any of the Immortals, surviving, on average, for ten years from the moment of his elevation to rulership. The Light of Honor is blessed with the memories of all of his predecessors.

**Light of Ignorance, Conan:** The First Born of the Immortals, who was created of the Sky Lord's sense of ignorance. The Light of Ignorance rules the Empire, and has done since the day of its founding. He is considered by his peers to be petty and wrathful. Out of a sense of loathing for his given title, he has come up with a variety of other titles for himself including Light of Bliss, Dawn Lord, and Lord of the Morning. He is the spiritual leader and supreme ruler of the shadow elves, whom are the exclusive exception to the official atheist ideology within the borders of his territory.

**Light of Life, Felicity:** The Light of Life is the Immortal responsible for the molding of new life. With her handmaidens, she harvests the fruit of the Tree of Souls and molds new bodies around them. Her power is in giving life, and she is the wife of the Shadow of Death. She resides in the city of Morania, in the Astral Plane.

**Light of Truth, Azerith:** The Light of Truth is the embodiment of the Sky Lord's sense of Truth. He was expelled together with the Shadow of Lies as one concept cannot exist without the other. The Light of Truth is believed to be the ruler of Soldran at the Black Tower by some. It is also believed that he cannot lie, as lying causes him to age rapidly. Some believers think to lie is fatal to him.

**Maul:** Infantryman in the standing military force of Shadovane.

**Merenern:** A race of people thought to have descended from fish. They are capable of breathing underwater and on dry land. Racial mixing has resulted in the rise of a class of halflings who develop scales and pronounced gills only when they come in direct contact with water. For most merenerrn, these features are permanent. The merenern are particularly gifted with water magic and are known for their skills in healing. They hail from the strongholds of Morgrotten in the Empire and Morgrou in Gourum. Both cities are wholly contained under the surface of large lakes.

**Morania:** The city of the dead. Morania is located in the Astral Plane. It is home to the Light of Life and the Shadow of Death, their subjects and thousands of the recently deceased. It is here that the recently dead wait for their day of judgment. Morania is also the place where new life is shaped.

**Mortal:** A person doomed to die of natural causes or by way of serious injury or sickness. Mortals are distinguished from Immortals by their significantly shorter lives and lesser magical power. The term mortal is a blanket term which refers to all of the races of mortal kind, including kitunes, elves, merenern, humans and croni. The term is not generally extended to include dark creatures like Grimwok, who are also sentient.

**Mother of Night, Celesti:** A figure believed by practitioners of the

Faith of the Five Saints to be the daughter of the Sky Lord.

**Prophet:** Honor guard to the Emperor. Among the most elite soldiers in the Empire, who are chosen specifically by the Emperor to serve him.

**Shadow Elf:** A kind of elf characterized by their shorter, stockier build. Shadow elves primarily hail from the westernmost region of the Empire around Mirrhvale and Shadovane, and declare their loyalty to the Emperor and the Shadow Queen, accordingly with which city they live in.

**Shadow of Death, Ansa:** The embodiment of the concept of death. The Shadow of Death is the reaper of mortal souls, and resides alongside his wife in Morania. He is known to have nine subordinates, each of which represents a pathway into death and culls their stock from those who die by way of that path. In his capacity as the leader of these nine, he is called Death Lord, while they are referred to as Guardians of Death or Reapers.

**Shadow of Judgment, Seraphel:** The last born of the Immortals and their leader. The Shadow of Judgment rules the city of Amorahiya, in the Astral Plane. He is the judge of all sin, concerned with the balance of good and evil, and not the eradication of either. Seraphel is often depicted as a pallid, ten-year-old boy with black hair and eyes, with a shadow like a demon. He is widely respected and feared by practitioners of the Faith of the Five Saints, who see him as the gatekeeper to the afterlife. His subordinates are called Seraphim and Nepherim, and are believed to serve as his regents and judges, charged with both punishing those who lead sinful lives and guiding those who lead lives of virtue to the Arc of the Afterlife.

**Shadow of Lies, Rahkna:** The embodiment of the concept of a lie. He is considered the most deceitful of the Immortals, and rules Ash Island and the Ring of Fire. In many places throughout Etherel where worship of the Five Saints and the Immortals is common, effigies of him are burned ritually to ward off evil.

**Shadow of Morality, Cane:** Second born of the Immortals, he is the embodiment of the Sky Lord's sense of morality. Cane is the most widely worshipped of the Immortals. In paintings and friezes, he is often depicted standing in opposition to the Shadow of Judgment. He is often prayed to for protection against the dark side of judgment, and as a guide on the moral path. He is depicted with the head of a lion and the body of a man.

**Shadow of Passion:** The incarnate of the Mother of Night. This title is officially given to the possessor of a pendant housing a green stone which is closely associated with her.

**Shadow Queen:** The queen of Shadovane, who is considered to be the incarnate of the Mother of Night and is also referred to as Shadow of Passion. In her capacity as Shadow of Passion, she is considered to be equivalent in power to an Immortal. The Shadow Queen possesses all of the memories of her predecessors. She is traditionally the wife and lover of the Emperor.

**Shadow Walk:** To make use of a series of rites which permit access to the Shadow World.

**Shadow World:** A world that exists alongside the world of mortals which is comprised of all mortal shadows and the shadows cast by inanimate objects. It is closely linked to the inner darkness inherent in mortal kind. Because of this association, it is dangerous to remain in this realm for too long. An untrained mage who attempts to walk in this world may succumb to an incurable madness or die. The Shadow World is a world of imposed blindness. It is impossible to see within it, and so other senses must be trained up in order to navigate it. Traveling this way significantly reduces the amount of time it takes to cross vast distances. A distance of one mile can be covered in a matter of a few seconds by way of this travel method.

**Silence:** To temporarily block a mage from hearing the melodies that drive magic, rendering them incapable of performing magical rites.

**Sky Lord:** The one, true god of the world, who created the Immortals and was sealed by the God Slayers under the Tree of Souls in the Astral Plane. The Sky Lord is considered to be a great evil. The day of his return has been prophesied by many seers and oracles throughout history.

**Ten Kingdoms:** A series of allied kingdoms which cover the eastern third of Etherel. The Ten Kingdoms is characterized by a reverent worship of the Sky Lord. Each kingdom is ruled by one of the Ten Kings. Some rule openly while others rule in secret.

**Ten Kings:** The rulers of the Ten Kingdoms. The Ten Kings are widely thought to be immortal, with most of them having lived since the time of the Sealing. They are the most feared individuals throughout Etherel.

Each of their names is recorded in the histories, and each served as a general in the Legion of the Sky before the Sealing. They worship him zealously, and attribute their unnatural, long lives to a gift given by him. The Ten Kings have held a shaky truce with the Empire and the Immortals of the Free Lands for two millennia, and in all that time they have awaited the return of the Sky Lord.

**The Arc of the Afterlife:** A great arc in the Astral Plane believed to be the nexus between the tangible world and the afterlife (in the Faith of the Five Saints referred to as What Comes After).

**The Children:** A term which refers to the son and daughter of the Sky Lord, prior to their deaths and reincarnation as the Light of Honor and the Shadow of Passion. In this frame of reference, they are called Mother of Night and Father of Lands.

**The Cross:** An organized crime syndicate based in the Imperial Eleventh Ward which, fifteen years prior to current, were almost responsible for violating a treaty between the Ten Kingdoms and the Empire. In the modern era, they are a thorn in the side of the Empire with high profile connections in many of the city states within the Free Lands.

**The Pits:** Referring to the Pits of Amorahiya, where the sinful are punished for a period of time equivalent to the length of their life by the Nepherim. Often used as a curse.

**The Sealing:** The event in which the God Slayers and the Immortals drove The Sky Lord into a prison under the Tree of Souls, which they had constructed to keep him at bay. In the Faith of the Five Saints, this is seen as the day of salvation, in which the greatest evil in the world was thrown from his seat of power, and a new era of peace was ushered in.

**The Tree of Souls:** A tree in the Astral Plane which rests in the heart of a forest of trees of its like. The tree is depicted with a bone-white trunk and a canopy which resembles starlight. The forest which surrounds it is considered to be the source of the fruit of life, which the Light of Life uses in the crafting of mortal kind. The Tree of Souls is the prison under which the Sky Lord is believed to be trapped.

**Thorn:** An intelligence operative in Shadovane's military. Thorns are feared even by the nobility, as they answer only to their master on the Council of Liam and the Shadow Queen, and their investigations have been known to topple heads of great houses alongside commoners in the past.

**Watcher:** A person born with the Gift of the Watcher. Watchers possess the ability to project their consciousnesses into the minds of other, manipulate what exists there, and possess their hosts.

**Wraith:** A soldier of Shadovane specialized in navigating and manipulating the Shadow World.

x

**If you would like to support the author, consider leaving a rating and/or review on Amazon, Goodreads or wherever you like to talk about books.**

**Thank you for reading Spirit of Shadow. Chapters of the sequel, Broken Bonds, are currently available on Royal Road and Scribble Hub.**

# ALSO BY
# D. A. HOLLEY